STUDENT AMBASSADOR
THE MISSING DRAGON

Written by Ryan Estrada
Art by Axur Eneas

Lettering by Chas! Pangburn
Additional Colors by Amanda Lafrenais

strange and amazing

inquiry@ironcircus.com   www.ironcircus.com

Ryan Estrada - Writer
Axur Eneas - Artist
Chas! Panburn - Letterer
Amanda Lefrenais - Additional Colors

C. Spike Trotman - Publisher
Andrea Purcell - Editor
Matt Sheridan - Art Director & Cover Design
Beth Scorzato - Print Technician & Book Design
Abby Lehrke - Proofreader

Published by
Iron Circus Comics
329 West 18th Street, Suite 604
Chicago, IL 60616
ironcircus.com

First Edition: August 2020
ISBN: 978-1-945820-60-1

10 9 8 7 6 5 4 3 2 1

Printed in China

STUDENT AMBASSADOR: THE MISSING DRAGON

Publisher's Cataloging-In-Publication Data
(Prepared by The Donohue Group, Inc.)

Names: Estrada, Ryan, author. | Eneas, Axur, illustrator. | Pangburn, Chas!, letterer. | Lafrenais, Amanda, colorist.
Title: Student ambassador. The missing dragon / writer: Ryan Estrada ; artist: Axur Eneas ; lettering: Chas Pangburn ; additional coloring: Amanda Lafrenais.
Other Titles: Missing dragon
Description: First edition. | Chicago, IL : Iron Circus Comics, 2020. | Series: Student ambassador ; [1] | Interest age level: 008-012. | Summary: "A student ambassador is sent on a high-stakes diplomatic mission to a far away land, where he and a newly crowned boy king are thrust into a globe-trotting action-adventure mystery"–Provided by publisher.
Identifiers: ISBN 9781945820601
Subjects: LCSH: Ambassadors–Comic books, strips, etc. | Kings and rulers–Comic books, strips, etc. | Government missions–Comic books, strips, etc. | CYAC: Ambassadors–Fiction. | Kings, queens, rulers, etc.–Fiction. | Government missions–Fiction. | LCGFT: Graphic novels. | Action and adventure fiction. | Detective and mystery fiction.
Classification: LCC PZ7.7.E88 St 2020 | DDC 741.5973 [Fic]–dc23

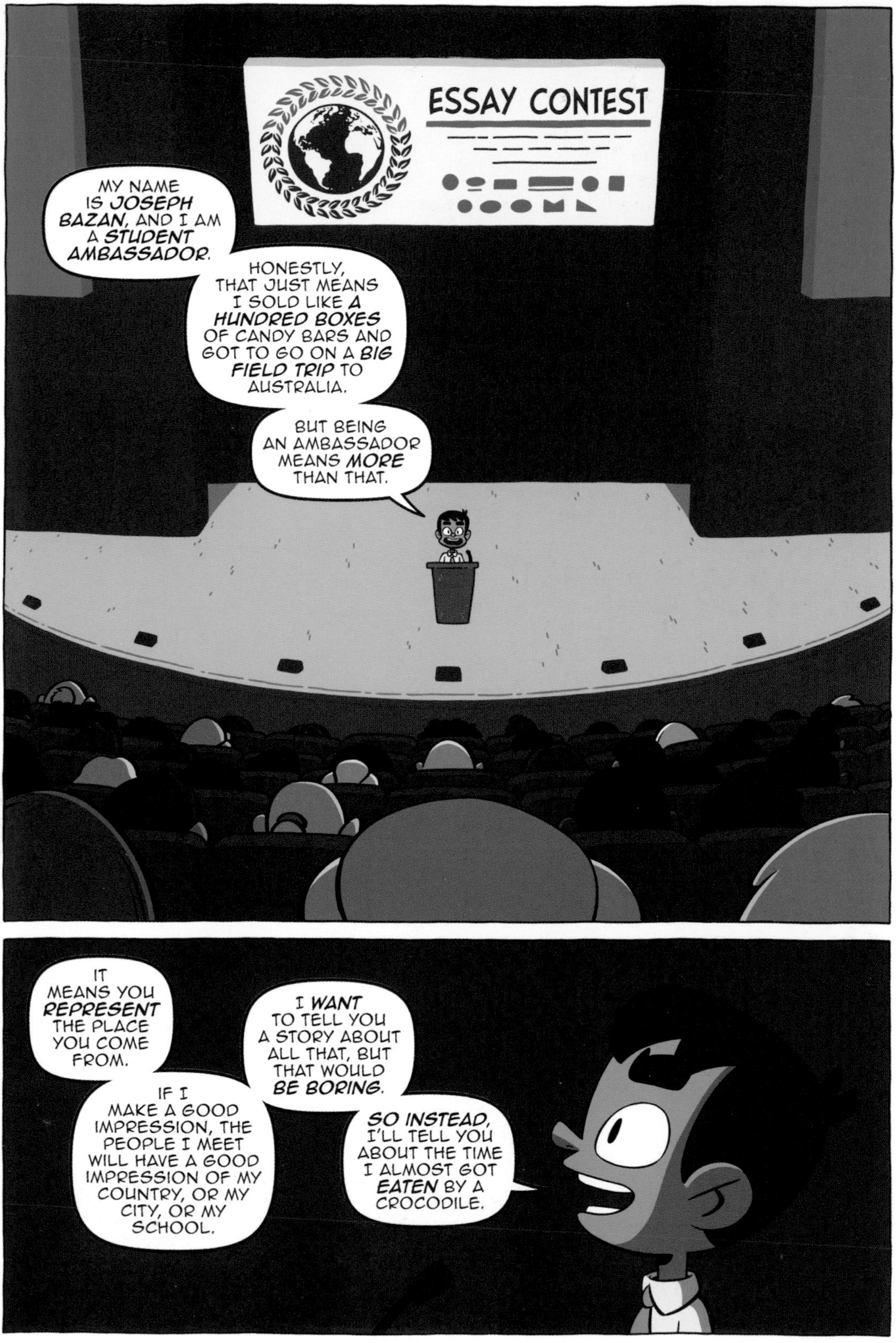
ESSAY CONTEST
MY NAME IS JOSEPH BAZAN, AND I AM A STUDENT AMBASSADOR.
HONESTLY, THAT JUST MEANS I SOLD LIKE A HUNDRED BOXES OF CANDY BARS AND GOT TO GO ON A BIG FIELD TRIP TO AUSTRALIA.
BUT BEING AN AMBASSADOR MEANS MORE THAN THAT.
IT MEANS YOU REPRESENT THE PLACE YOU COME FROM.
IF I MAKE A GOOD IMPRESSION, THE PEOPLE I MEET WILL HAVE A GOOD IMPRESSION OF MY COUNTRY, OR MY CITY, OR MY SCHOOL.
I WANT TO TELL YOU A STORY ABOUT ALL THAT, BUT THAT WOULD BE BORING.
SO INSTEAD, I'LL TELL YOU ABOUT THE TIME I ALMOST GOT EATEN BY A CROCODILE.

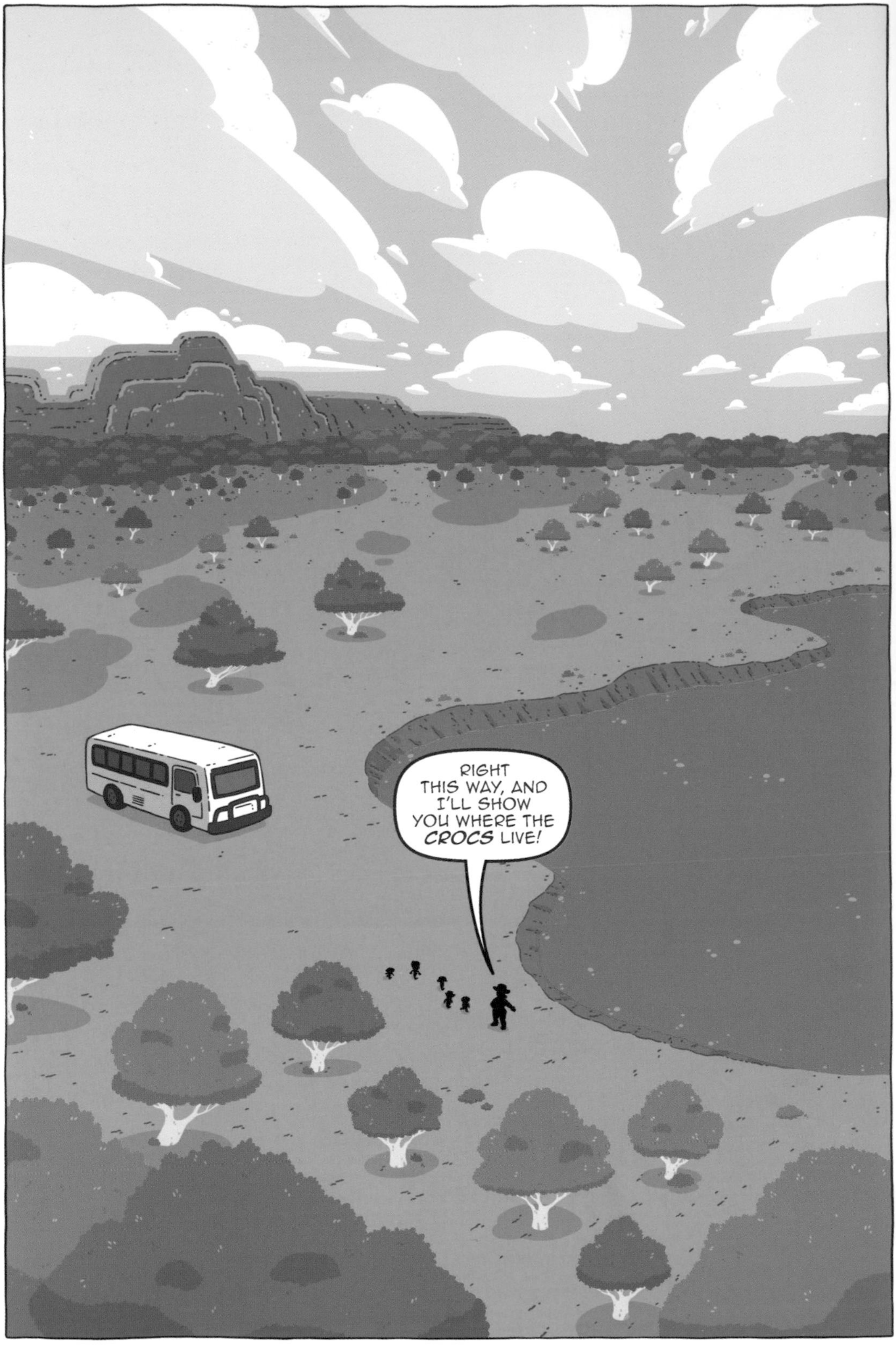
RIGHT THIS WAY, AND I'LL SHOW YOU WHERE THE *CROCS* LIVE!

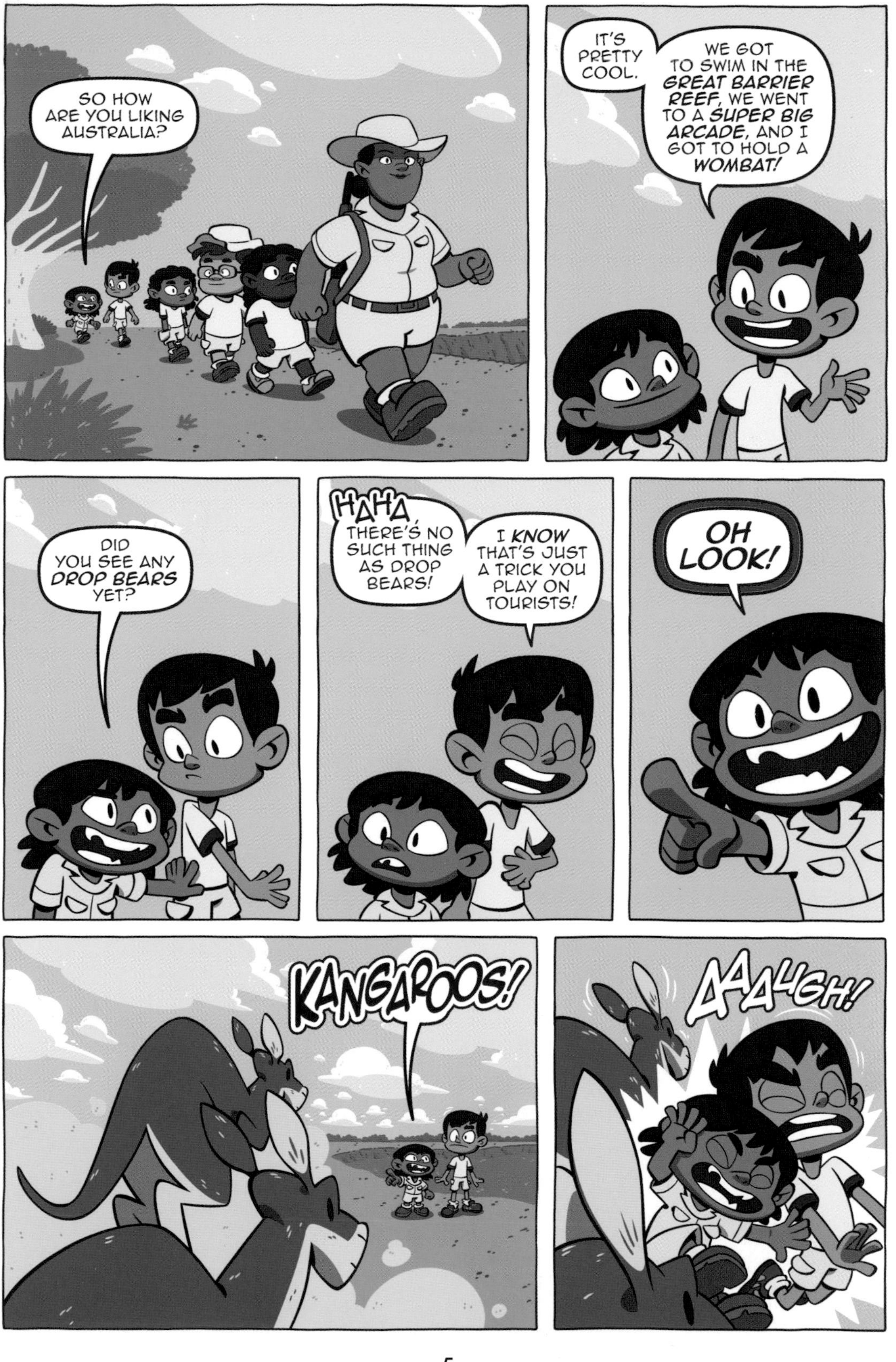

SO HOW ARE YOU LIKING AUSTRALIA?
IT'S PRETTY COOL.
WE GOT TO SWIM IN THE *GREAT BARRIER REEF*, WE WENT TO A *SUPER BIG ARCADE*, AND I GOT TO HOLD A *WOMBAT!*
DID YOU SEE ANY *DROP BEARS* YET?
HAHA, THERE'S NO SUCH THING AS DROP BEARS!
I *KNOW* THAT'S JUST A TRICK YOU PLAY ON TOURISTS!
OH LOOK!
KANGAROOS!
AAAAUGH!

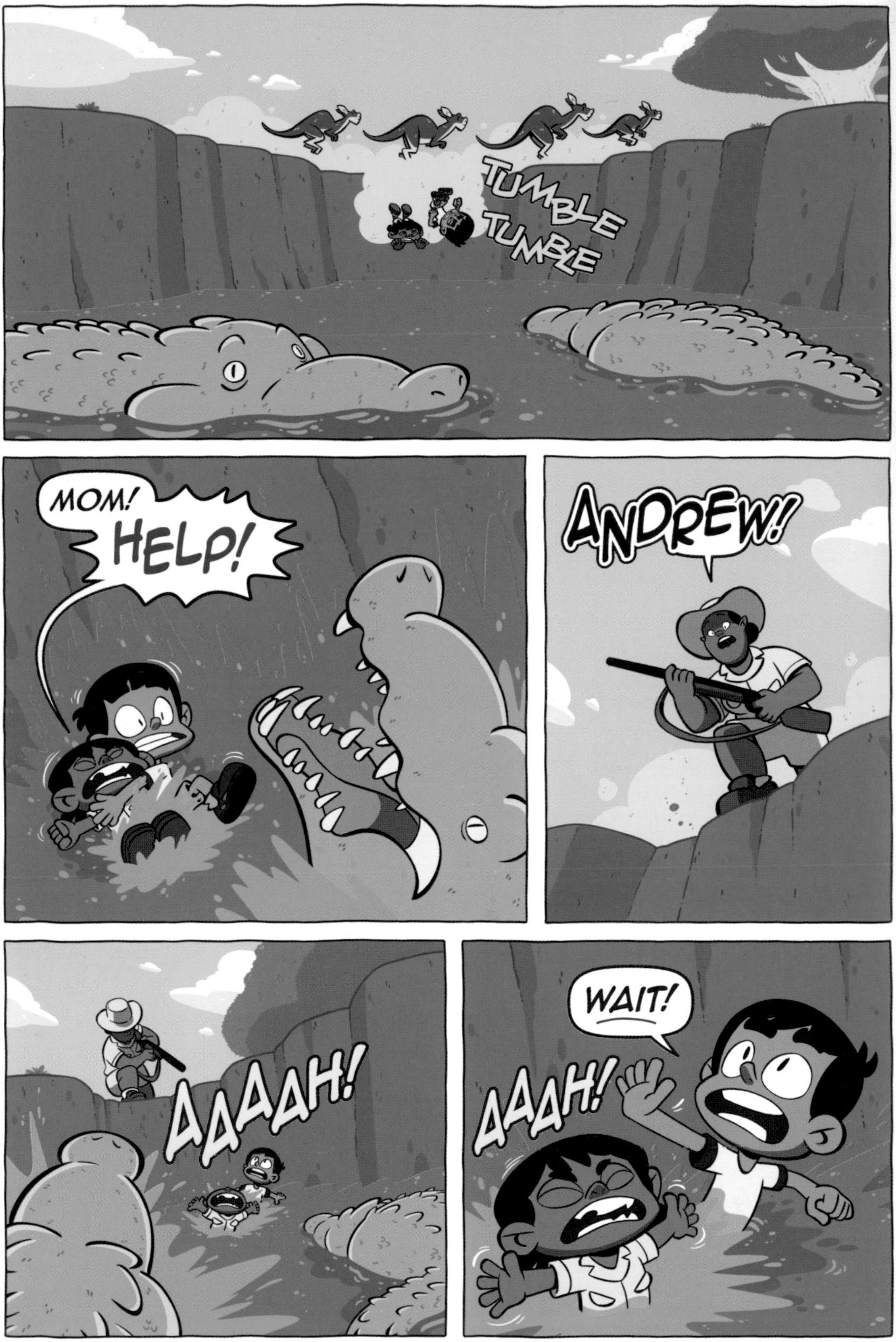
TUMBLE
TUMBLE
MOM! HELP!
ANDREW!
AAAAH!
WAIT!
AAAH!

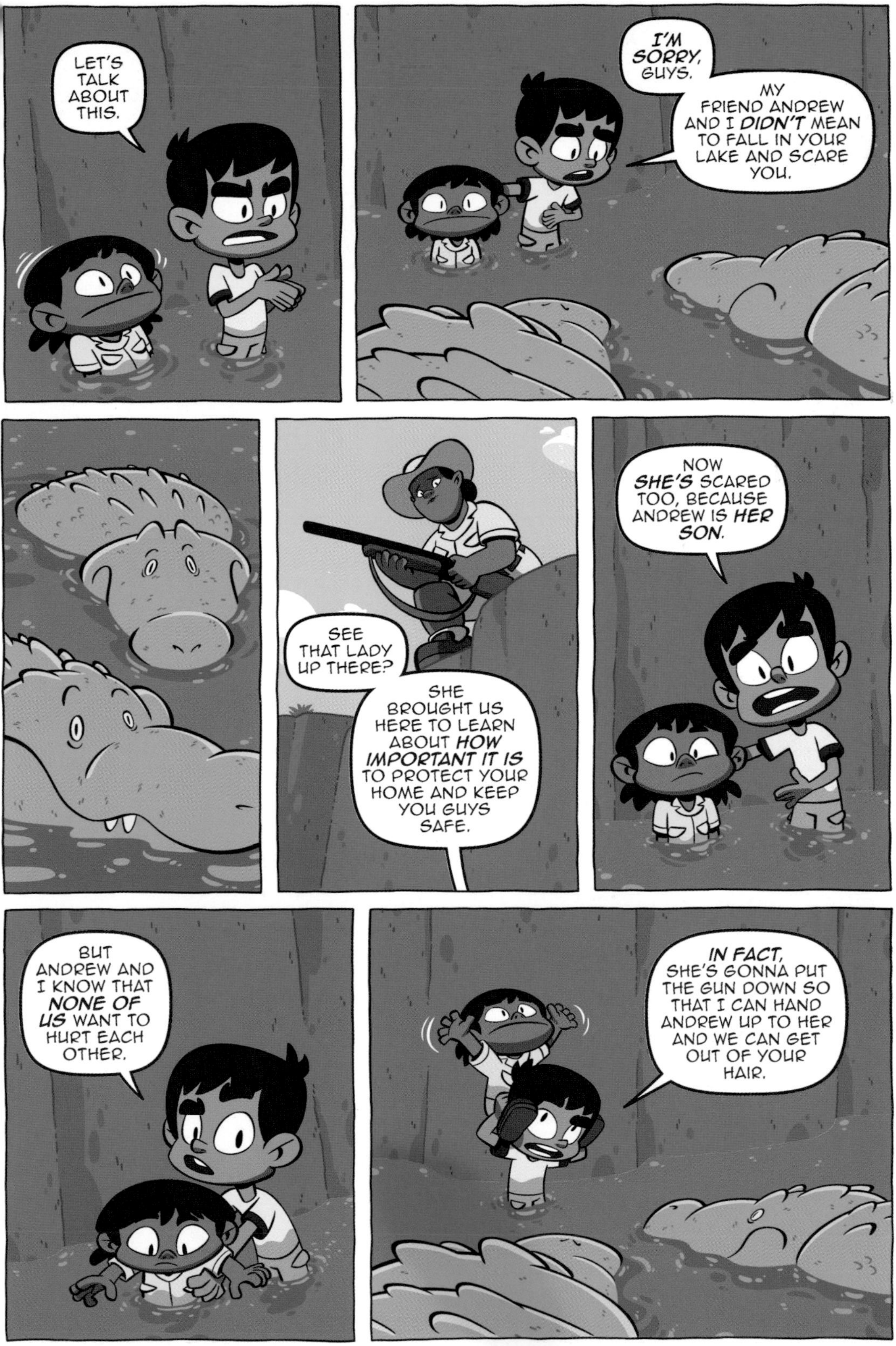
LET'S TALK ABOUT THIS.
I'M SORRY, GUYS.
MY FRIEND ANDREW AND I DIDN'T MEAN TO FALL IN YOUR LAKE AND SCARE YOU.
SEE THAT LADY UP THERE?
SHE BROUGHT US HERE TO LEARN ABOUT HOW IMPORTANT IT IS TO PROTECT YOUR HOME AND KEEP YOU GUYS SAFE.
NOW SHE'S SCARED TOO, BECAUSE ANDREW IS HER SON.
BUT ANDREW AND I KNOW THAT NONE OF US WANT TO HURT EACH OTHER.
IN FACT, SHE'S GONNA PUT THE GUN DOWN SO THAT I CAN HAND ANDREW UP TO HER AND WE CAN GET OUT OF YOUR HAIR.

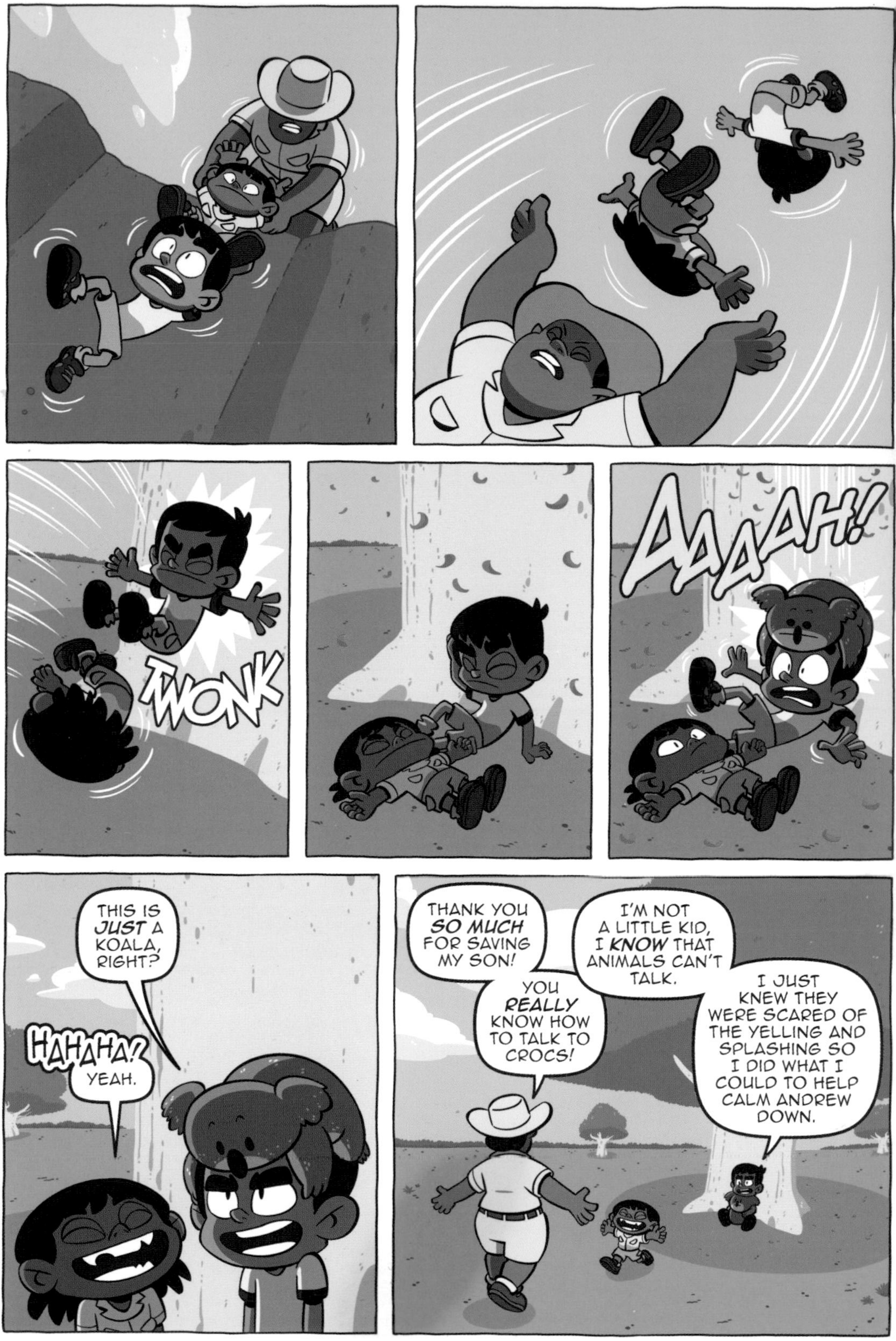
TWONK
AAAAH!
THIS IS JUST A KOALA, RIGHT?
HAHAHA!
YEAH.
THANK YOU SO MUCH FOR SAVING MY SON!
YOU REALLY KNOW HOW TO TALK TO CROCS!
I'M NOT A LITTLE KID, I KNOW THAT ANIMALS CAN'T TALK.
I JUST KNEW THEY WERE SCARED OF THE YELLING AND SPLASHING SO I DID WHAT I COULD TO HELP CALM ANDREW DOWN.

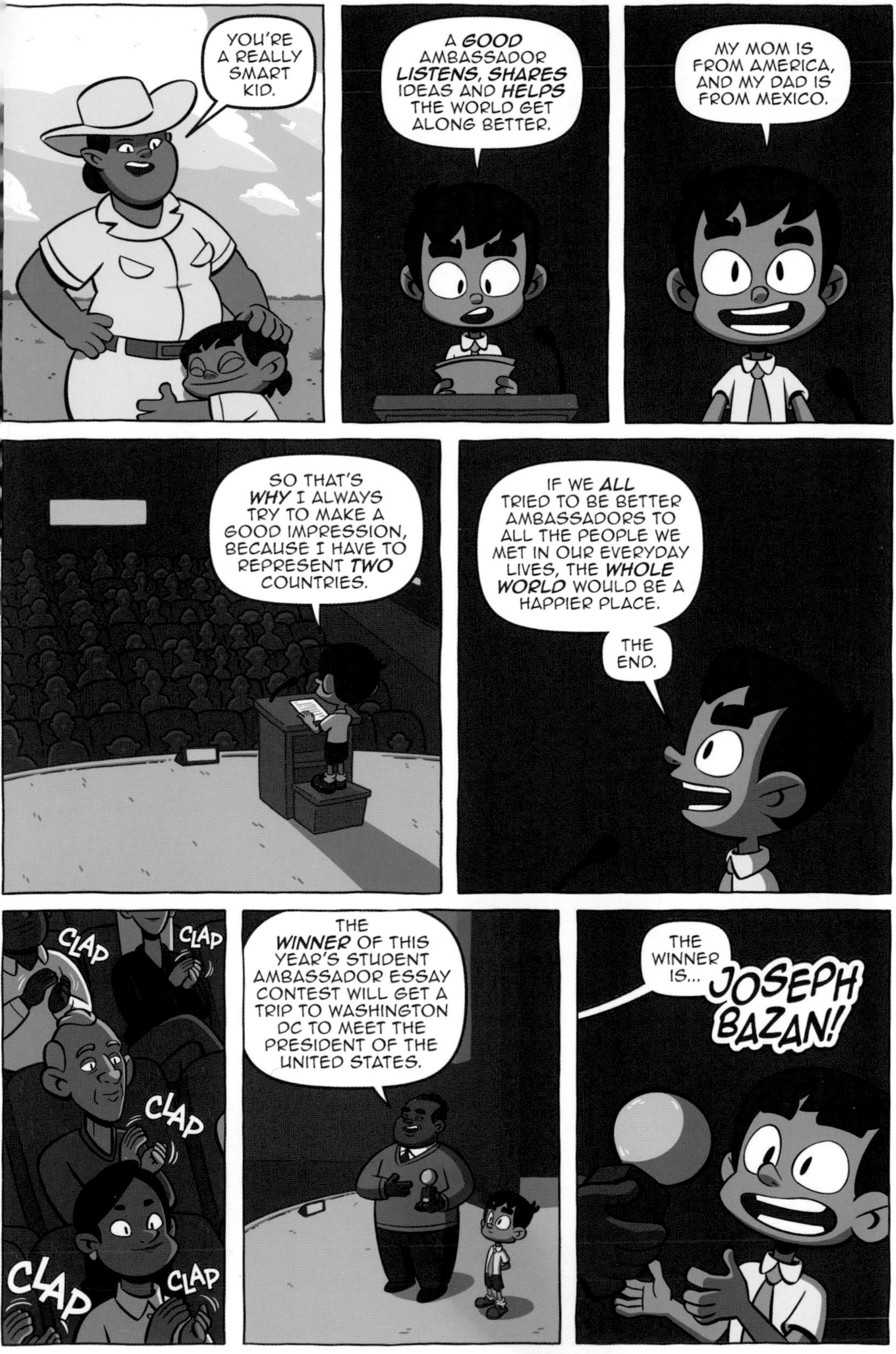
YOU'RE A REALLY SMART KID.
A GOOD AMBASSADOR LISTENS, SHARES IDEAS AND HELPS THE WORLD GET ALONG BETTER.
MY MOM IS FROM AMERICA, AND MY DAD IS FROM MEXICO.
SO THAT'S WHY I ALWAYS TRY TO MAKE A GOOD IMPRESSION, BECAUSE I HAVE TO REPRESENT TWO COUNTRIES.
IF WE ALL TRIED TO BE BETTER AMBASSADORS TO ALL THE PEOPLE WE MET IN OUR EVERYDAY LIVES, THE WHOLE WORLD WOULD BE A HAPPIER PLACE.
THE END.
CLAP
CLAP
CLAP
CLAP
CLAP
THE WINNER OF THIS YEAR'S STUDENT AMBASSADOR ESSAY CONTEST WILL GET A TRIP TO WASHINGTON DC TO MEET THE PRESIDENT OF THE UNITED STATES.
THE WINNER IS...
JOSEPH BAZAN!

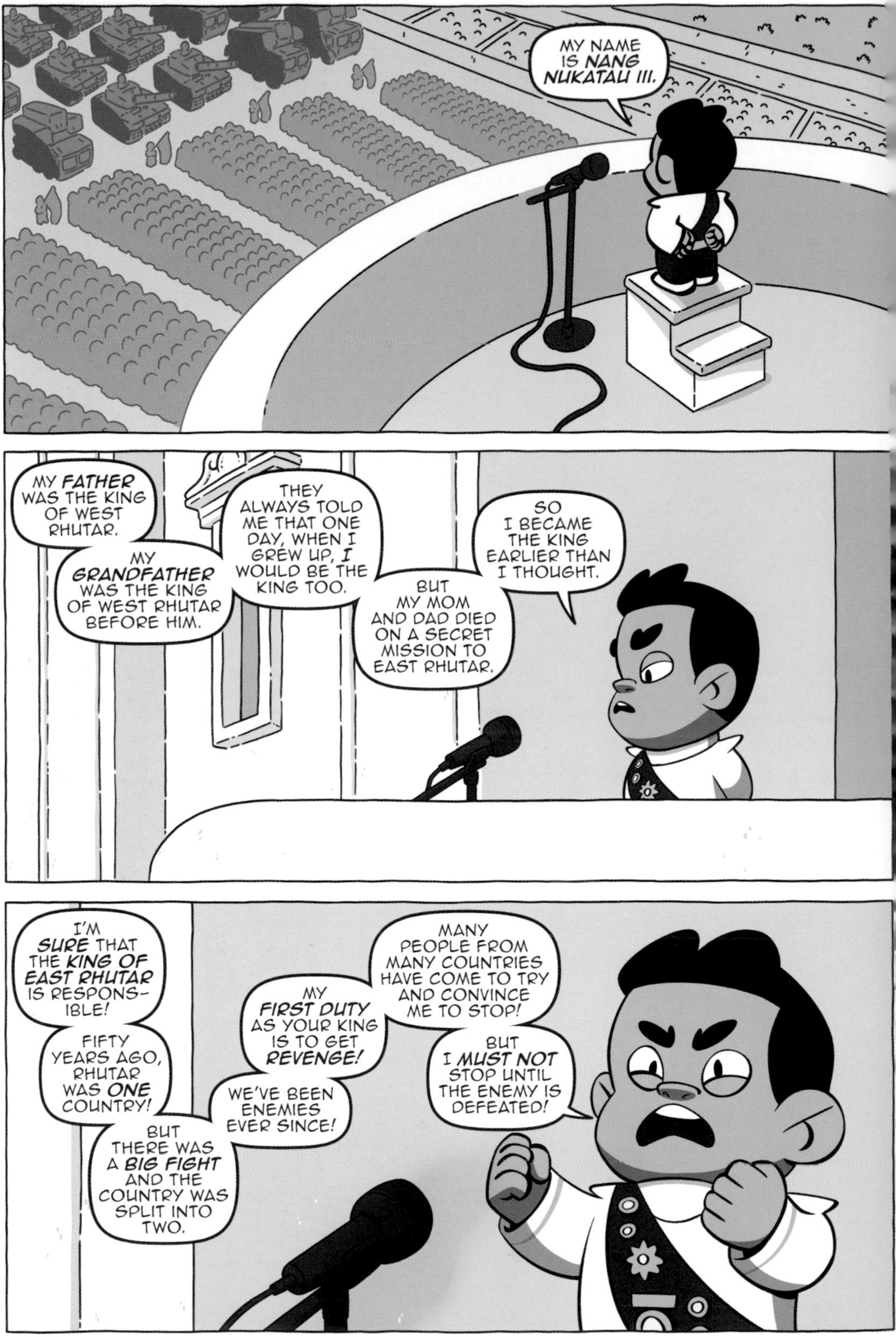
MY NAME IS **NANG NUKATAU III.**
MY **FATHER** WAS THE KING OF WEST RHUTAR.
MY **GRANDFATHER** WAS THE KING OF WEST RHUTAR BEFORE HIM.
THEY ALWAYS TOLD ME THAT ONE DAY, WHEN I GREW UP, ***I*** WOULD BE THE KING TOO.
BUT MY MOM AND DAD DIED ON A SECRET MISSION TO EAST RHUTAR.
SO I BECAME THE KING EARLIER THAN I THOUGHT.
I'M ***SURE*** THAT THE ***KING OF EAST RHUTAR*** IS RESPONS-IBLE!
FIFTY YEARS AGO, RHUTAR WAS ***ONE*** COUNTRY!
BUT THERE WAS A ***BIG FIGHT*** AND THE COUNTRY WAS SPLIT INTO TWO.
WE'VE BEEN ENEMIES EVER SINCE!
MY ***FIRST DUTY*** AS YOUR KING IS TO GET ***REVENGE!***
MANY PEOPLE FROM MANY COUNTRIES HAVE COME TO TRY AND CONVINCE ME TO STOP!
BUT I ***MUST NOT*** STOP UNTIL THE ENEMY IS DEFEATED!

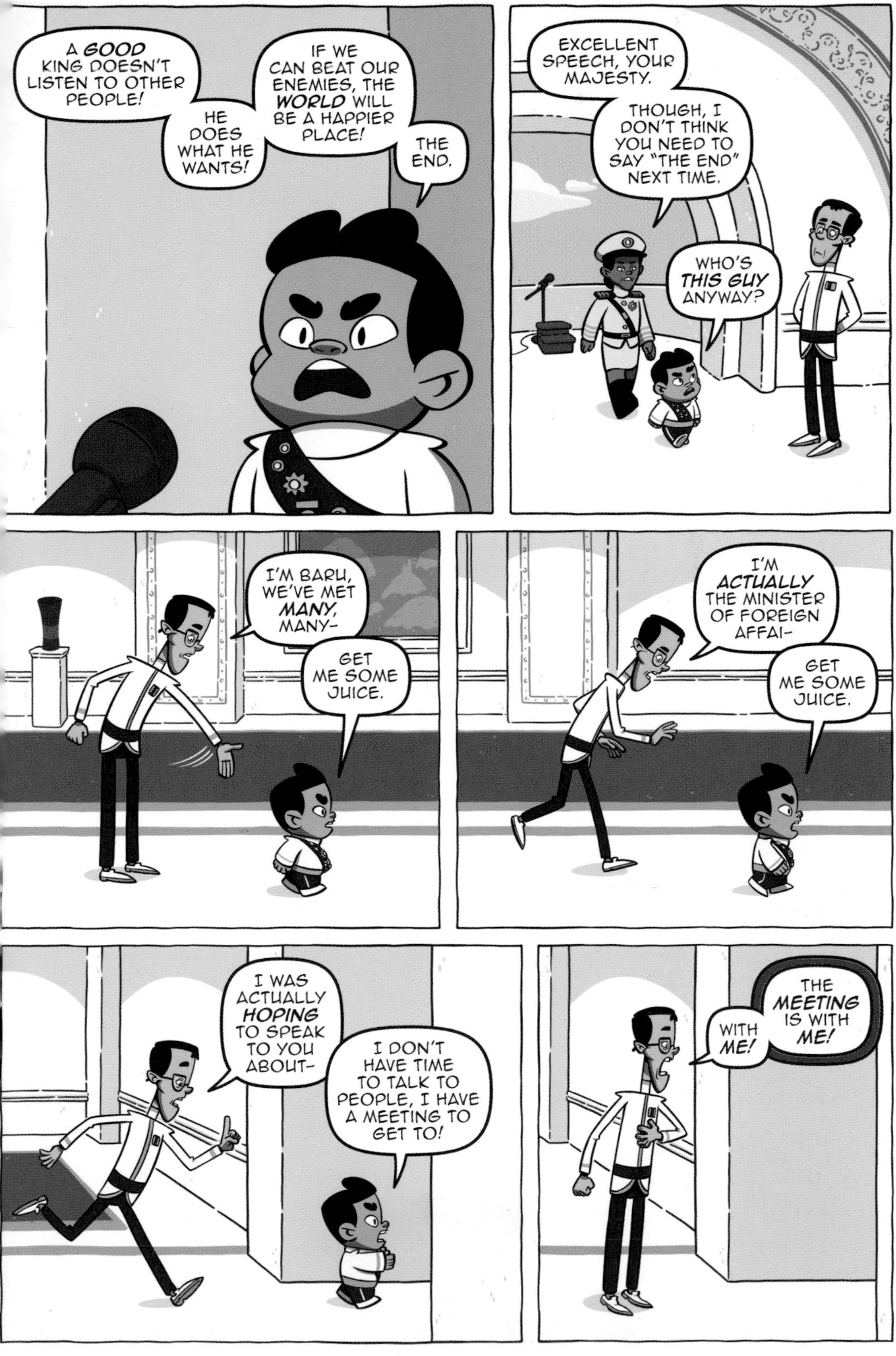
A GOOD KING DOESN'T LISTEN TO OTHER PEOPLE!
HE DOES WHAT HE WANTS!
IF WE CAN BEAT OUR ENEMIES, THE WORLD WILL BE A HAPPIER PLACE!
THE END.
EXCELLENT SPEECH, YOUR MAJESTY.
THOUGH, I DON'T THINK YOU NEED TO SAY "THE END" NEXT TIME.
WHO'S THIS GUY ANYWAY?
I'M BARU, WE'VE MET MANY, MANY-
GET ME SOME JUICE.
I'M ACTUALLY THE MINISTER OF FOREIGN AFFAI-
GET ME SOME JUICE.
I WAS ACTUALLY HOPING TO SPEAK TO YOU ABOUT-
I DON'T HAVE TIME TO TALK TO PEOPLE, I HAVE A MEETING TO GET TO!
WITH ME!
THE MEETING IS WITH ME!

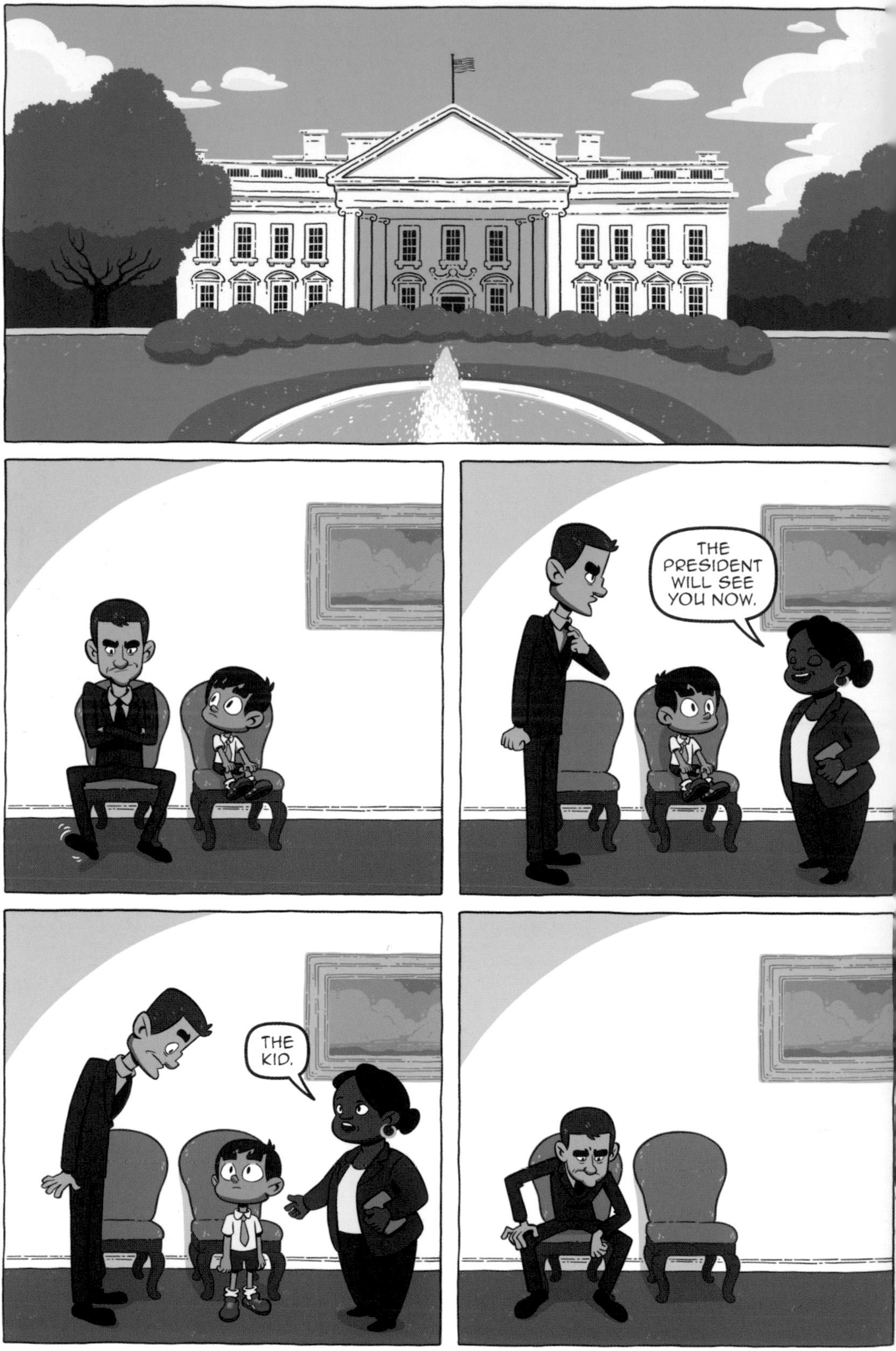
THE PRESIDENT WILL SEE YOU NOW.
THE KID.

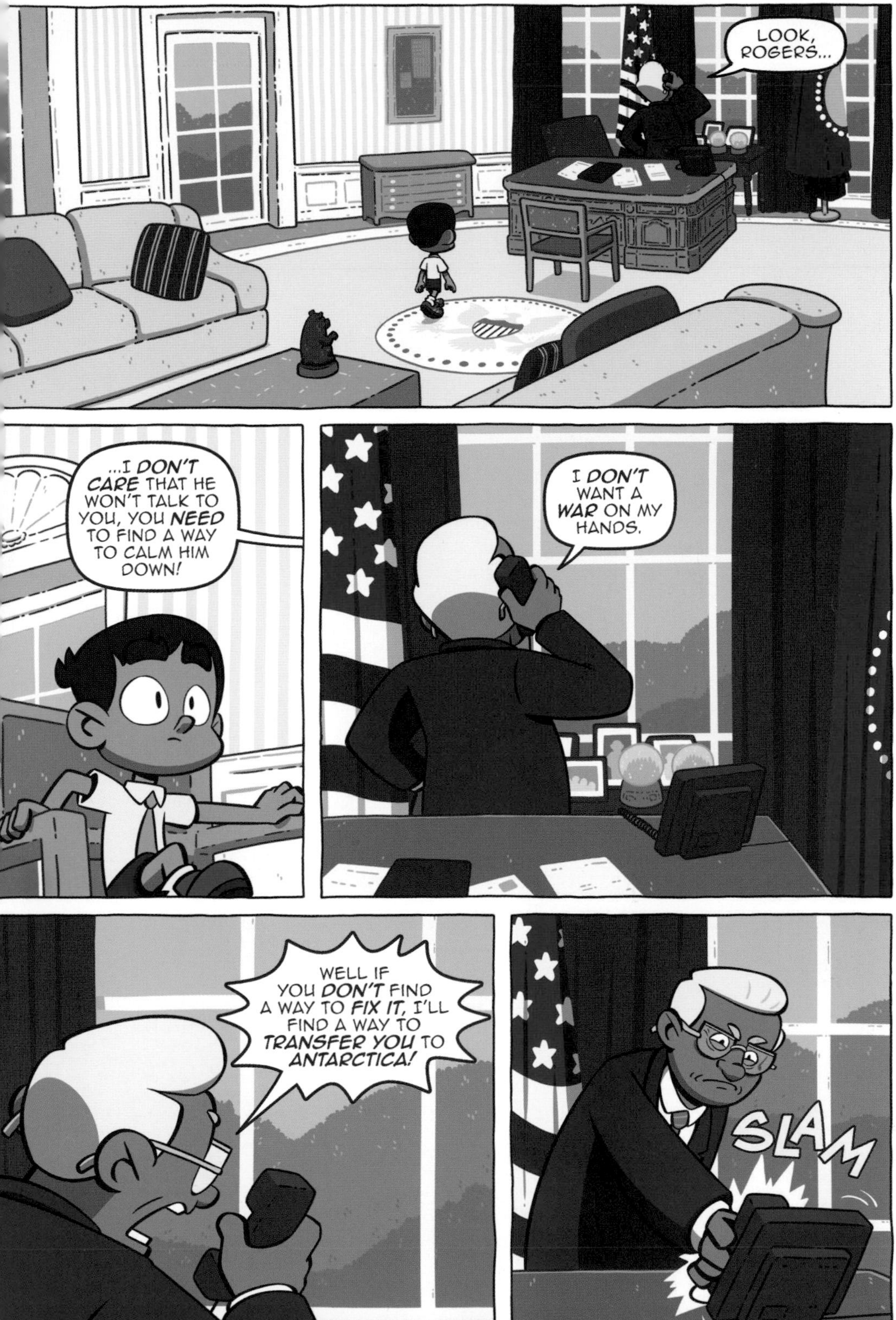
LOOK, ROGERS...
...I DON'T CARE THAT HE WON'T TALK TO YOU, YOU NEED TO FIND A WAY TO CALM HIM DOWN!
I DON'T WANT A WAR ON MY HANDS.
WELL IF YOU DON'T FIND A WAY TO FIX IT, I'LL FIND A WAY TO TRANSFER YOU TO ANTARCTICA!
SLAM

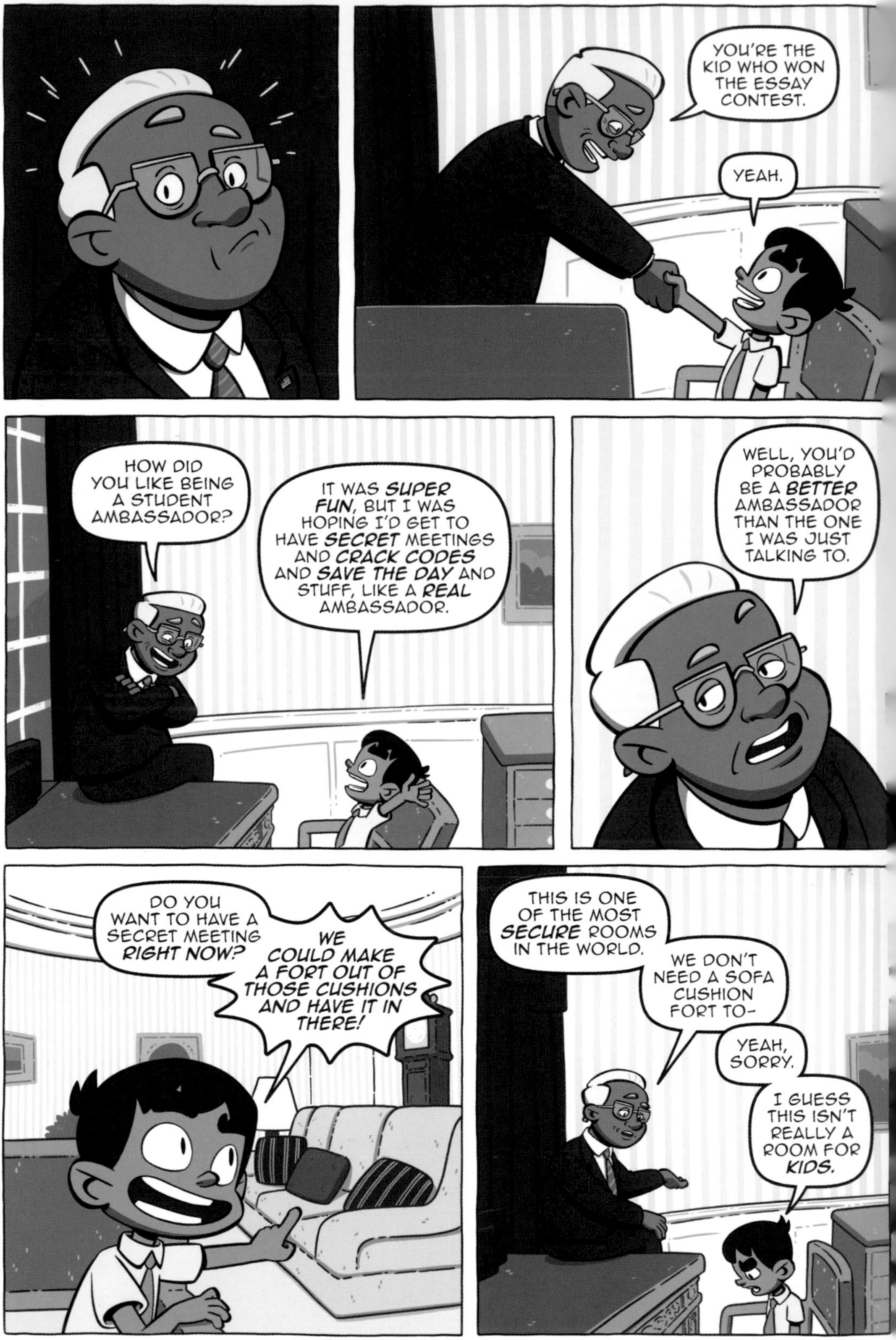
YOU'RE THE KID WHO WON THE ESSAY CONTEST.
YEAH.
HOW DID YOU LIKE BEING A STUDENT AMBASSADOR?
IT WAS *SUPER FUN*, BUT I WAS HOPING I'D GET TO HAVE *SECRET* MEETINGS AND *CRACK CODES* AND *SAVE THE DAY* AND STUFF, LIKE A *REAL* AMBASSADOR.
WELL, YOU'D PROBABLY BE A *BETTER* AMBASSADOR THAN THE ONE I WAS JUST TALKING TO.
DO YOU WANT TO HAVE A SECRET MEETING *RIGHT NOW?*
WE COULD MAKE A FORT OUT OF THOSE CUSHIONS AND HAVE IT IN THERE!
THIS IS ONE OF THE MOST *SECURE* ROOMS IN THE WORLD.
WE DON'T NEED A SOFA CUSHION FORT TO-
YEAH, SORRY.
I GUESS THIS ISN'T REALLY A ROOM FOR *KIDS.*

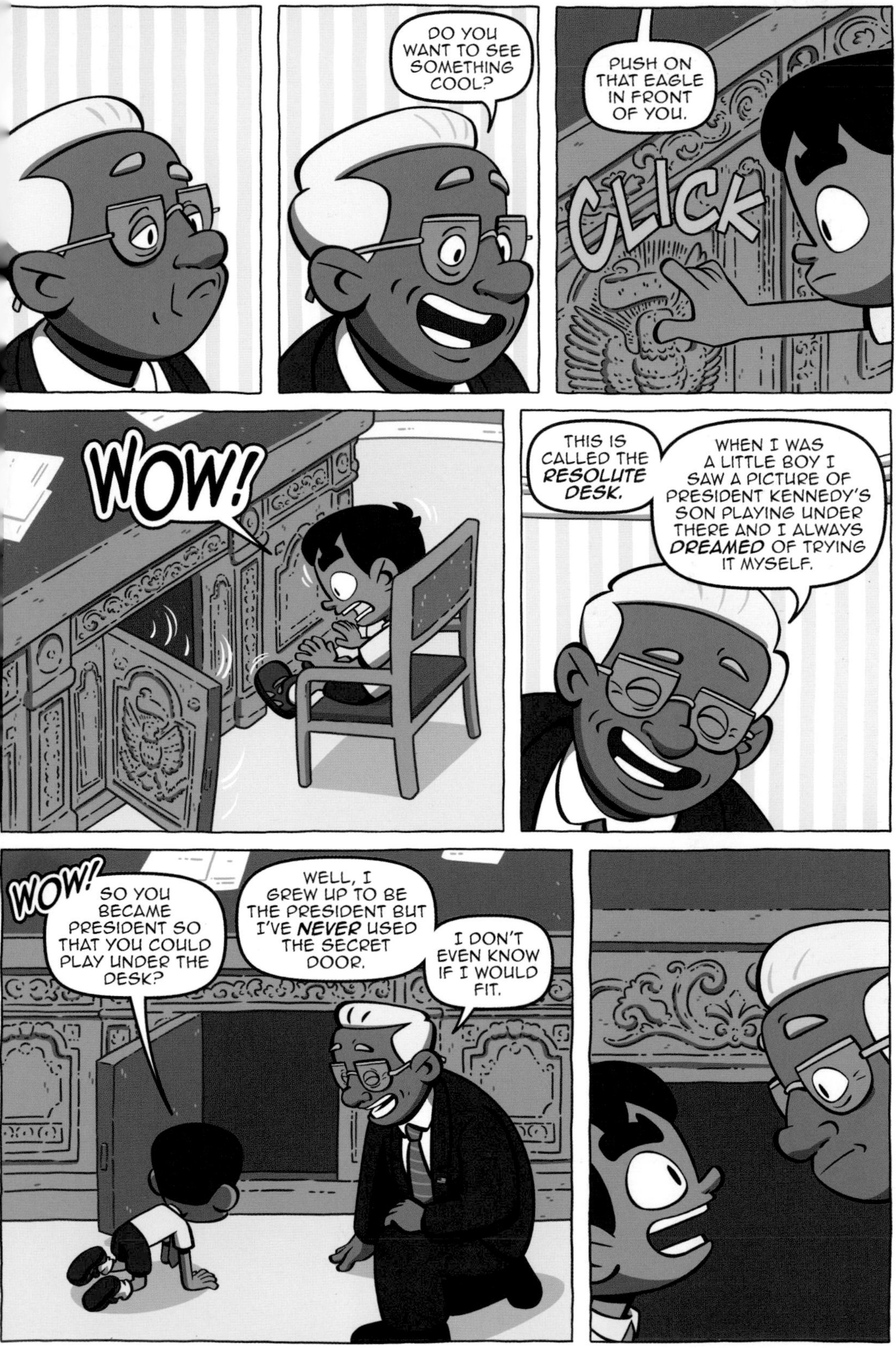
DO YOU WANT TO SEE SOMETHING COOL?
PUSH ON THAT EAGLE IN FRONT OF YOU.
CLICK
WOW!
THIS IS CALLED THE ***RESOLUTE DESK.***
WHEN I WAS A LITTLE BOY I SAW A PICTURE OF PRESIDENT KENNEDY'S SON PLAYING UNDER THERE AND I ALWAYS ***DREAMED*** OF TRYING IT MYSELF.
WOW!
SO YOU BECAME PRESIDENT SO THAT YOU COULD PLAY UNDER THE DESK?
WELL, I GREW UP TO BE THE PRESIDENT BUT I'VE ***NEVER*** USED THE SECRET DOOR.
I DON'T EVEN KNOW IF I WOULD FIT.

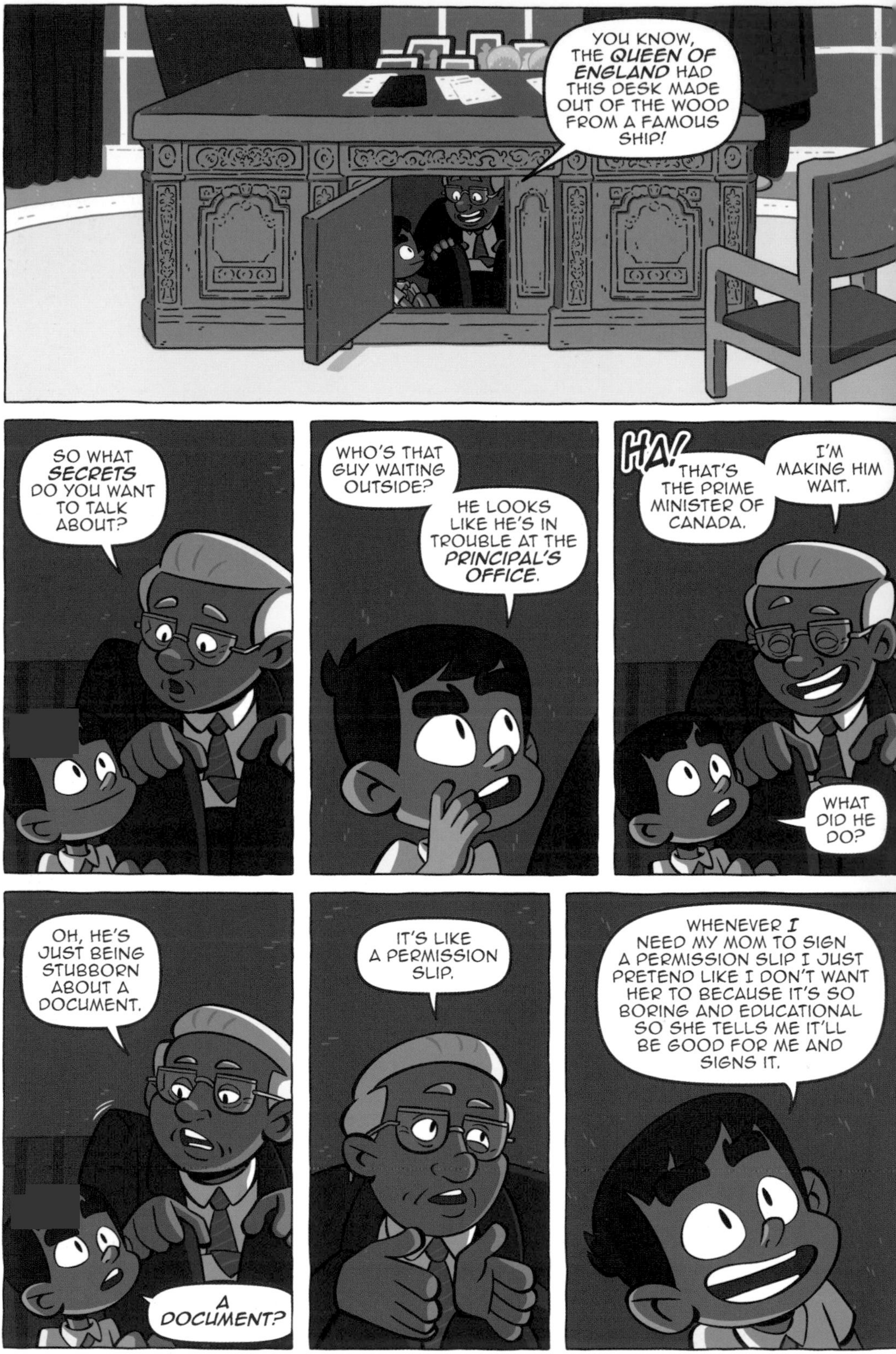
YOU KNOW, THE **QUEEN OF ENGLAND** HAD THIS DESK MADE OUT OF THE WOOD FROM A FAMOUS SHIP!
SO WHAT **SECRETS** DO YOU WANT TO TALK ABOUT?
[redacted]
WHO'S THAT GUY WAITING OUTSIDE?
HE LOOKS LIKE HE'S IN TROUBLE AT THE ***PRINCIPAL'S OFFICE***.
HA!
THAT'S THE PRIME MINISTER OF CANADA.
I'M MAKING HIM WAIT.
WHAT DID HE DO?
OH, HE'S JUST BEING STUBBORN ABOUT A DOCUMENT.
[redacted]
A *DOCUMENT?*
IT'S LIKE A PERMISSION SLIP.
WHENEVER *I* NEED MY MOM TO SIGN A PERMISSION SLIP I JUST PRETEND LIKE I DON'T WANT HER TO BECAUSE IT'S SO BORING AND EDUCATIONAL SO SHE TELLS ME IT'LL BE GOOD FOR ME AND SIGNS IT.

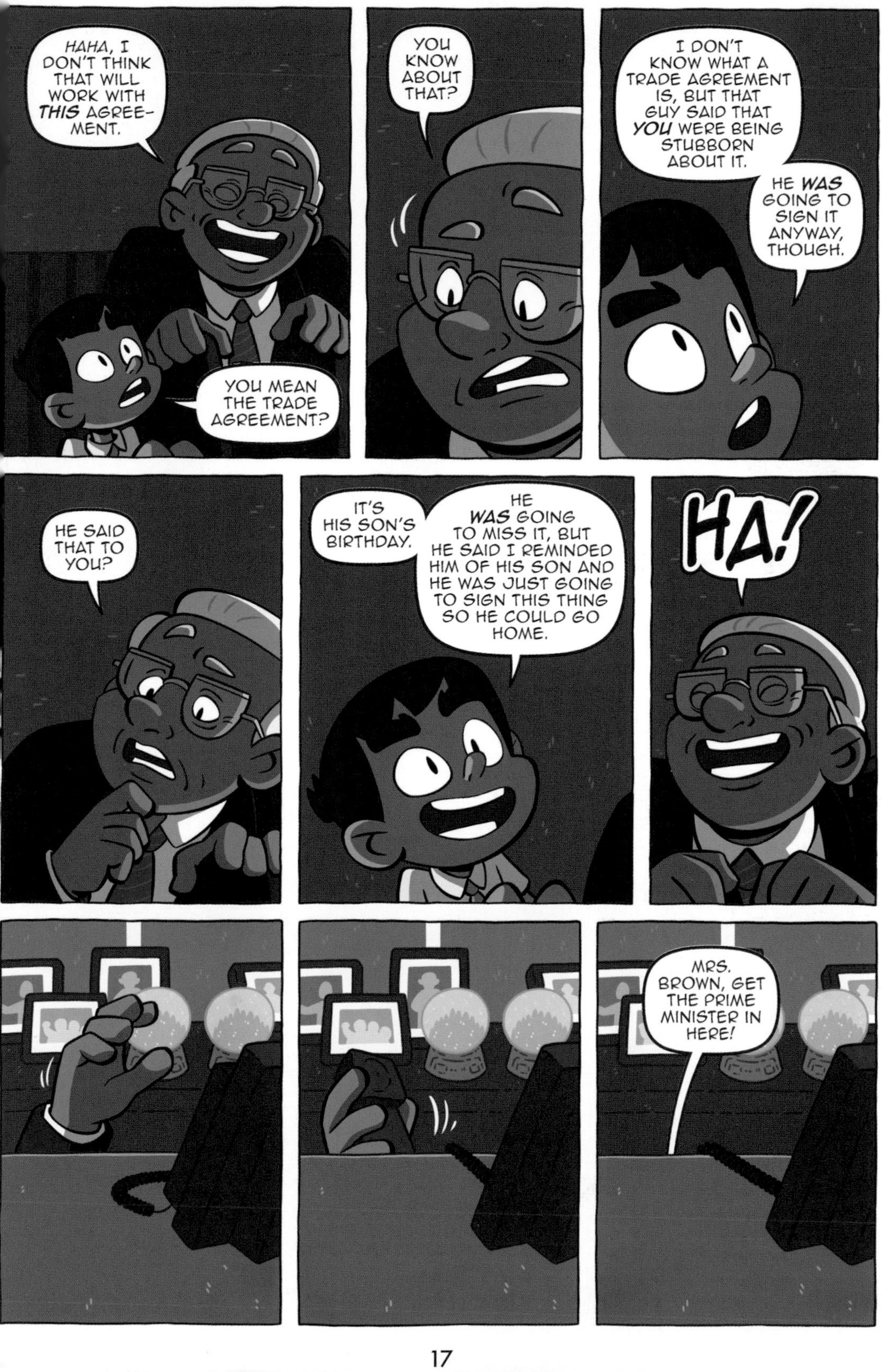
HAHA, I DON'T THINK THAT WILL WORK WITH THIS AGREE-MENT.
YOU MEAN THE TRADE AGREEMENT?
YOU KNOW ABOUT THAT?
I DON'T KNOW WHAT A TRADE AGREEMENT IS, BUT THAT GUY SAID THAT YOU WERE BEING STUBBORN ABOUT IT.
HE WAS GOING TO SIGN IT ANYWAY, THOUGH.
HE SAID THAT TO YOU?
IT'S HIS SON'S BIRTHDAY.
HE WAS GOING TO MISS IT, BUT HE SAID I REMINDED HIM OF HIS SON AND HE WAS JUST GOING TO SIGN THIS THING SO HE COULD GO HOME.
HA!
MRS. BROWN, GET THE PRIME MINISTER IN HERE!

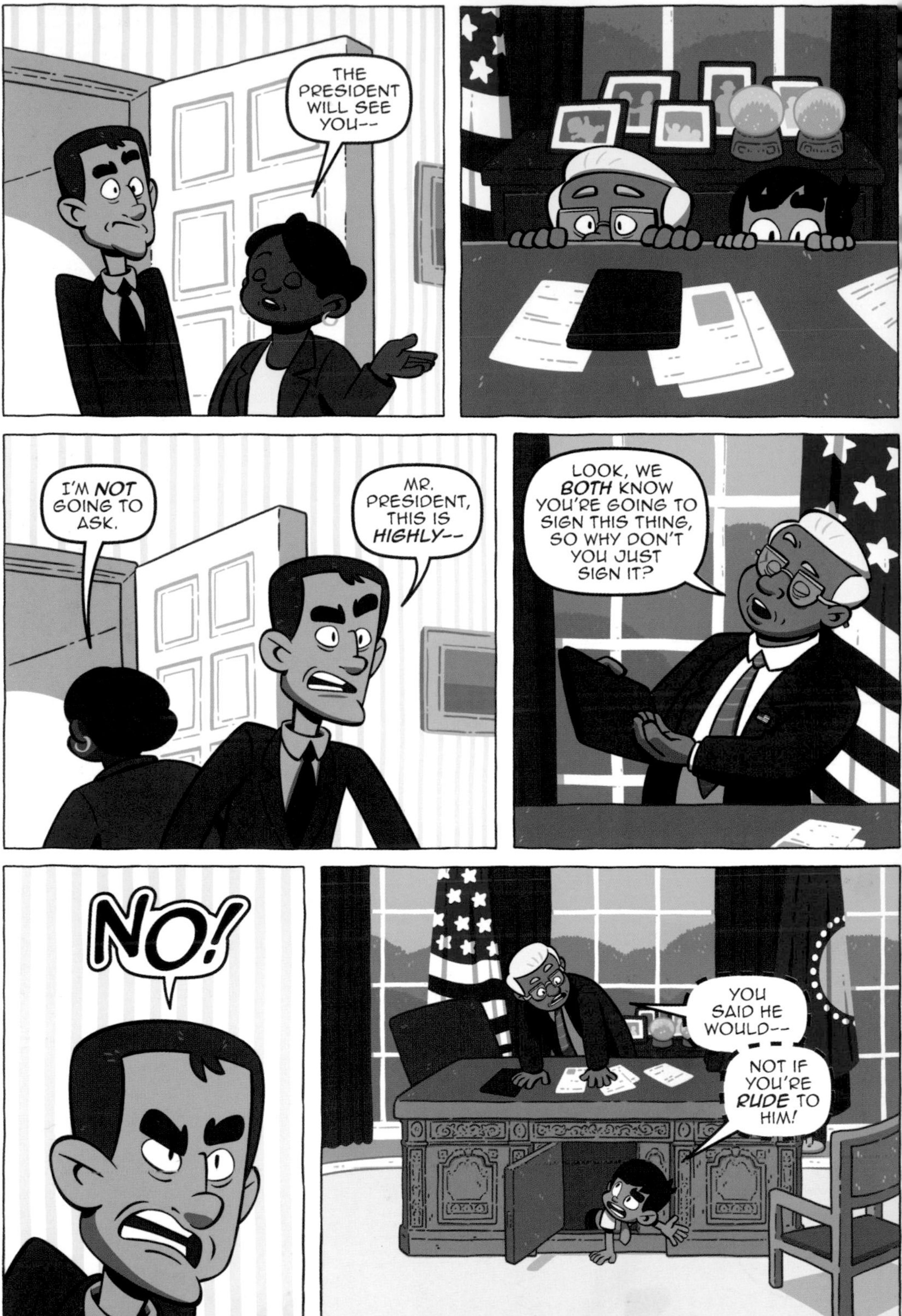
THE PRESIDENT WILL SEE YOU--
I'M *NOT* GOING TO ASK.
MR. PRESIDENT, THIS IS *HIGHLY*--
LOOK, WE *BOTH* KNOW YOU'RE GOING TO SIGN THIS THING, SO WHY DON'T YOU JUST SIGN IT?
NO!
YOU SAID HE WOULD--
NOT IF YOU'RE *RUDE* TO HIM!

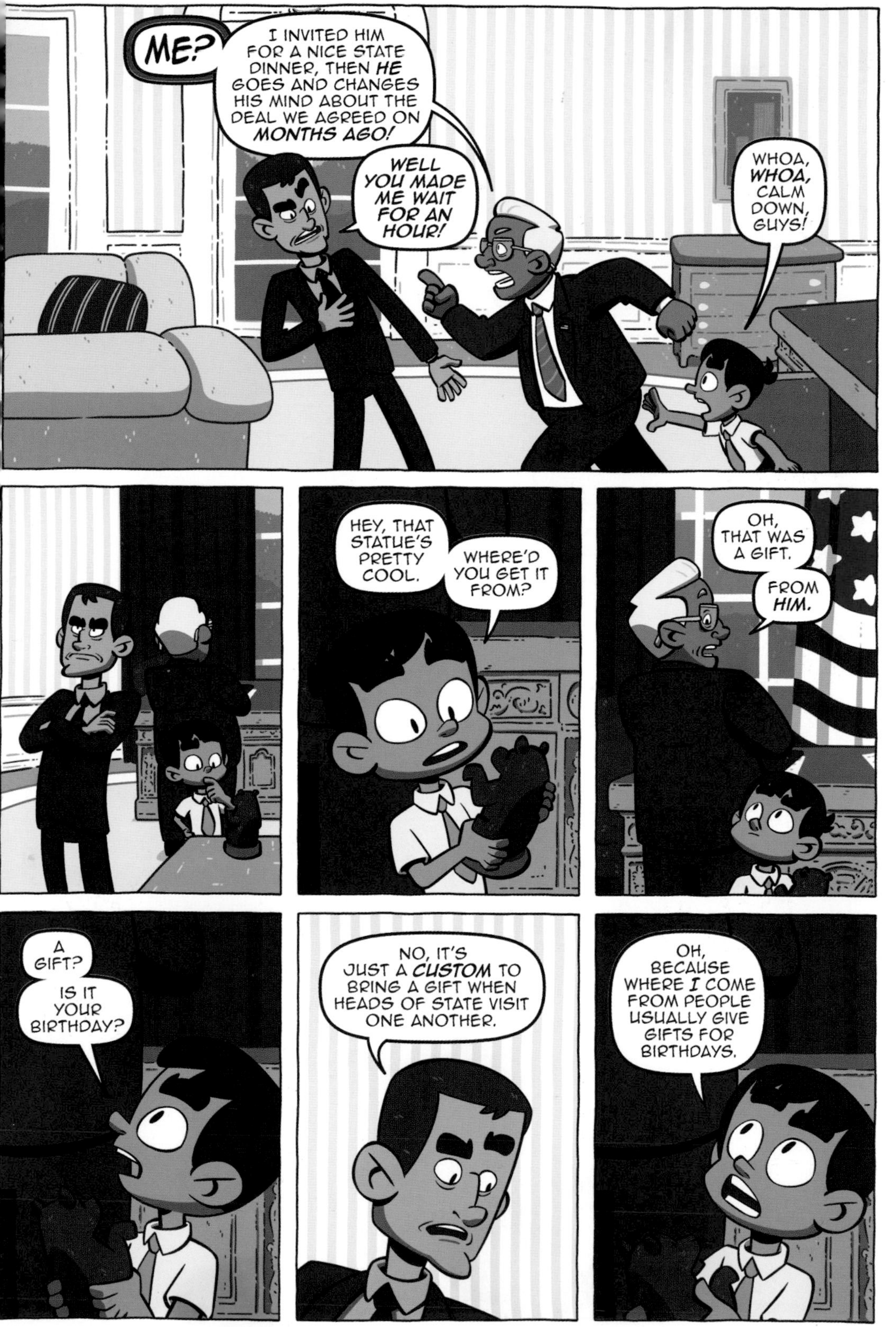
ME?
I INVITED HIM FOR A NICE STATE DINNER, THEN HE GOES AND CHANGES HIS MIND ABOUT THE DEAL WE AGREED ON MONTHS AGO!
WELL YOU MADE ME WAIT FOR AN HOUR!
WHOA, WHOA, CALM DOWN, GUYS!
HEY, THAT STATUE'S PRETTY COOL.
WHERE'D YOU GET IT FROM?
OH, THAT WAS A GIFT.
FROM HIM.
A GIFT?
IS IT YOUR BIRTHDAY?
NO, IT'S JUST A CUSTOM TO BRING A GIFT WHEN HEADS OF STATE VISIT ONE ANOTHER.
OH, BECAUSE WHERE I COME FROM PEOPLE USUALLY GIVE GIFTS FOR BIRTHDAYS.

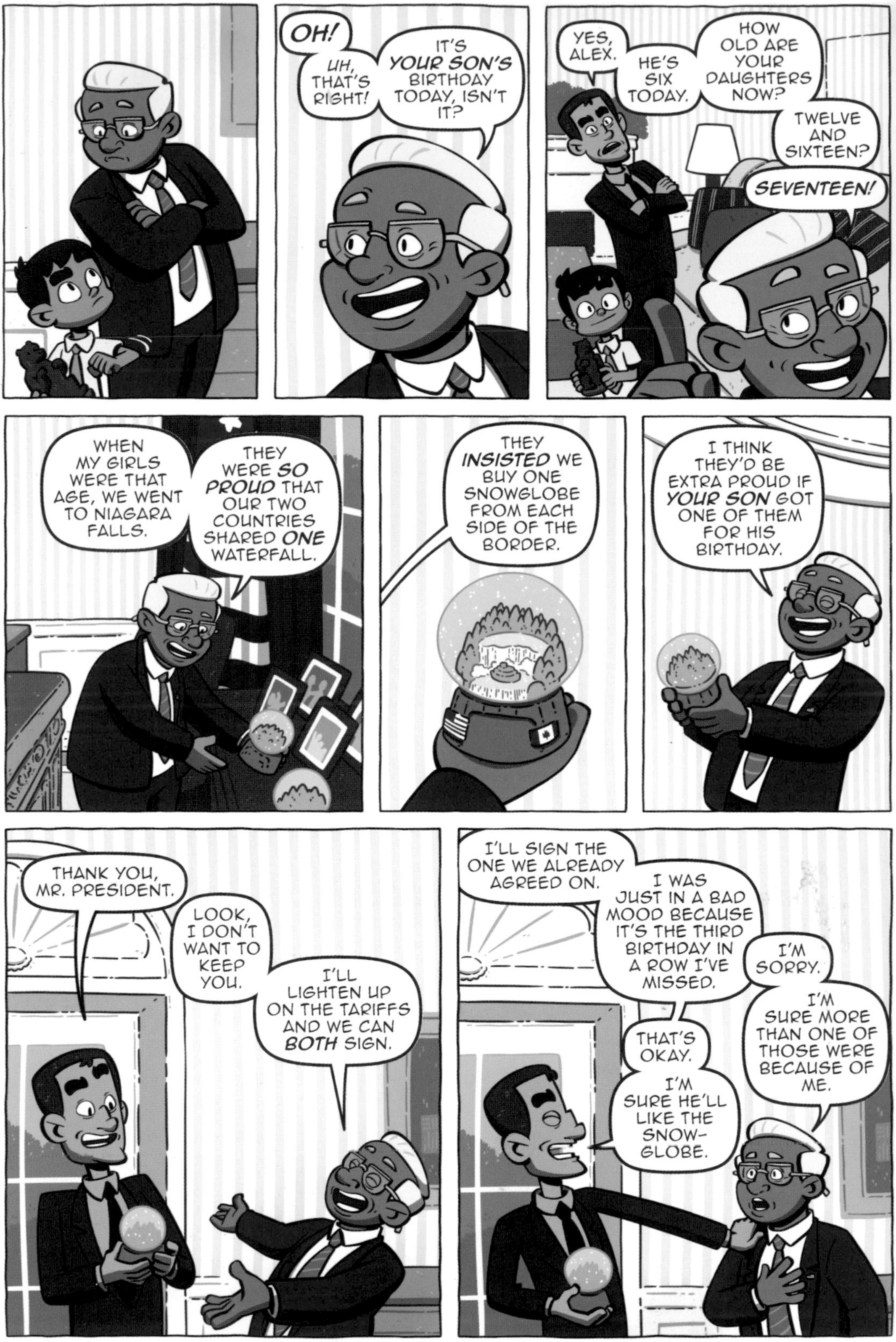
OH!
UH, THAT'S RIGHT!
IT'S YOUR SON'S BIRTHDAY TODAY, ISN'T IT?
YES, ALEX.
HE'S SIX TODAY.
HOW OLD ARE YOUR DAUGHTERS NOW?
TWELVE AND SIXTEEN?
SEVENTEEN!
WHEN MY GIRLS WERE THAT AGE, WE WENT TO NIAGARA FALLS.
THEY WERE SO PROUD THAT OUR TWO COUNTRIES SHARED ONE WATERFALL.
THEY INSISTED WE BUY ONE SNOWGLOBE FROM EACH SIDE OF THE BORDER.
I THINK THEY'D BE EXTRA PROUD IF YOUR SON GOT ONE OF THEM FOR HIS BIRTHDAY.
THANK YOU, MR. PRESIDENT.
LOOK, I DON'T WANT TO KEEP YOU.
I'LL LIGHTEN UP ON THE TARIFFS AND WE CAN BOTH SIGN.
I'LL SIGN THE ONE WE ALREADY AGREED ON.
I WAS JUST IN A BAD MOOD BECAUSE IT'S THE THIRD BIRTHDAY IN A ROW I'VE MISSED.
I'M SORRY.
THAT'S OKAY.
I'M SURE HE'LL LIKE THE SNOW-GLOBE.
I'M SURE MORE THAN ONE OF THOSE WERE BECAUSE OF ME.

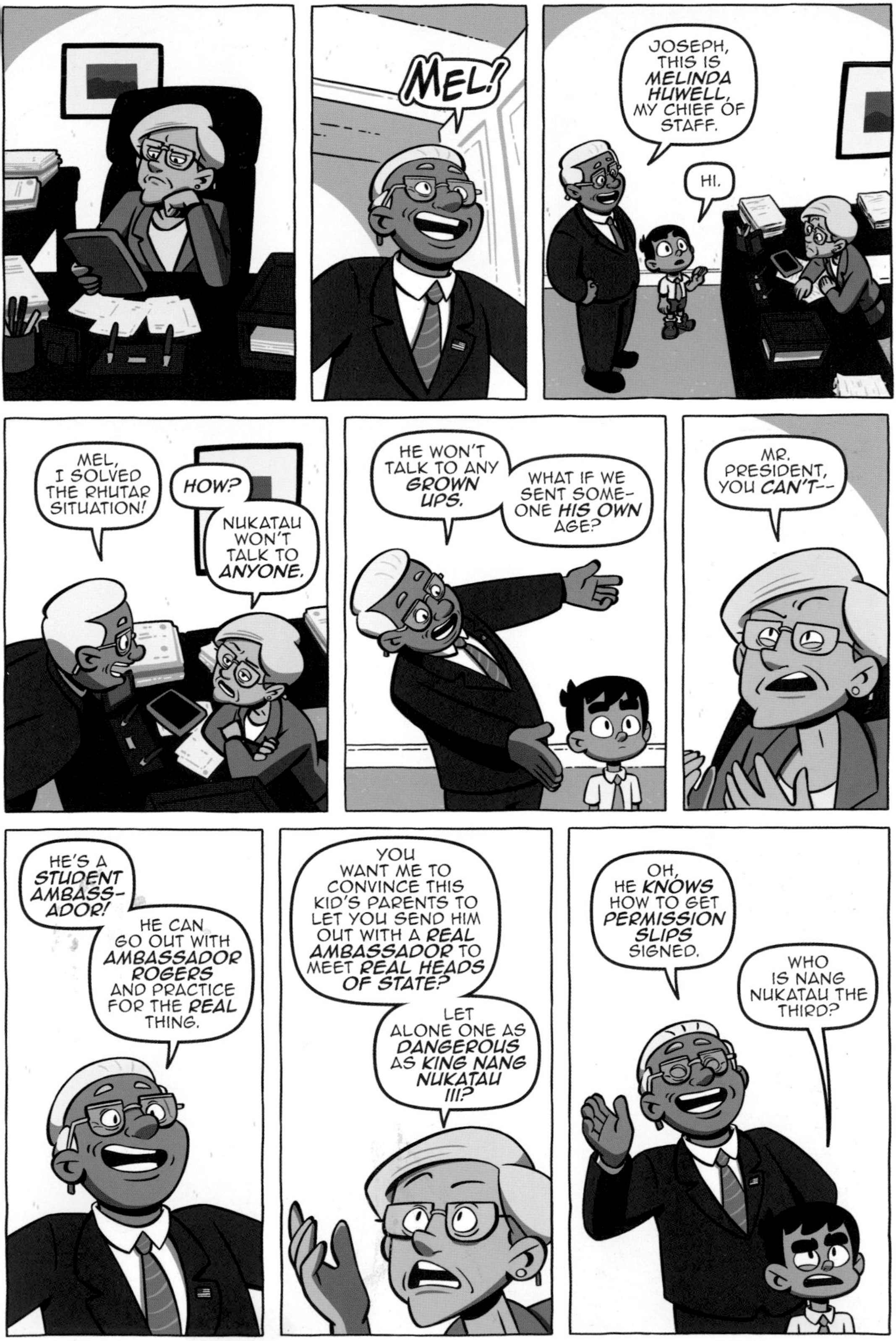
MEL!
JOSEPH, THIS IS MELINDA HUWELL, MY CHIEF OF STAFF.
HI.
MEL, I SOLVED THE RHUTAR SITUATION!
HOW?
NUKATAU WON'T TALK TO ANYONE.
HE WON'T TALK TO ANY GROWN UPS.
WHAT IF WE SENT SOME-ONE HIS OWN AGE?
MR. PRESIDENT, YOU CAN'T--
HE'S A STUDENT AMBASS-ADOR!
HE CAN GO OUT WITH AMBASSADOR ROGERS AND PRACTICE FOR THE REAL THING.
YOU WANT ME TO CONVINCE THIS KID'S PARENTS TO LET YOU SEND HIM OUT WITH A REAL AMBASSADOR TO MEET REAL HEADS OF STATE?
LET ALONE ONE AS DANGEROUS AS KING NANG NUKATAU III?
OH, HE KNOWS HOW TO GET PERMISSION SLIPS SIGNED.
WHO IS NANG NUKATAU THE THIRD?

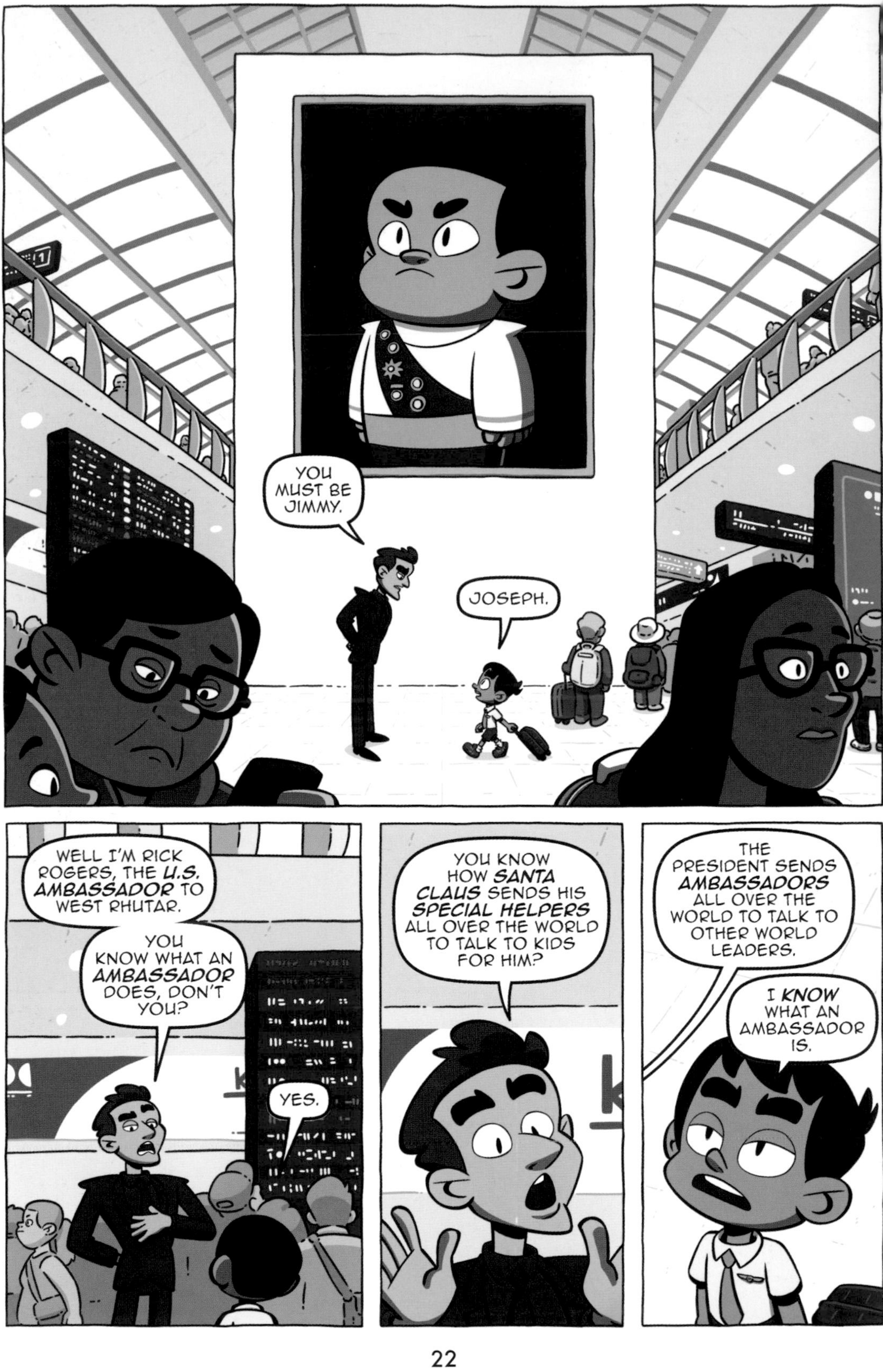
YOU MUST BE JIMMY.
JOSEPH.
WELL I'M RICK ROGERS, THE *U.S. AMBASSADOR* TO WEST RHUTAR.
YOU KNOW WHAT AN *AMBASSADOR* DOES, DON'T YOU?
YES.
YOU KNOW HOW *SANTA CLAUS* SENDS HIS *SPECIAL HELPERS* ALL OVER THE WORLD TO TALK TO KIDS FOR HIM?
THE PRESIDENT SENDS *AMBASSADORS* ALL OVER THE WORLD TO TALK TO OTHER WORLD LEADERS.
I *KNOW* WHAT AN AMBASSADOR IS.

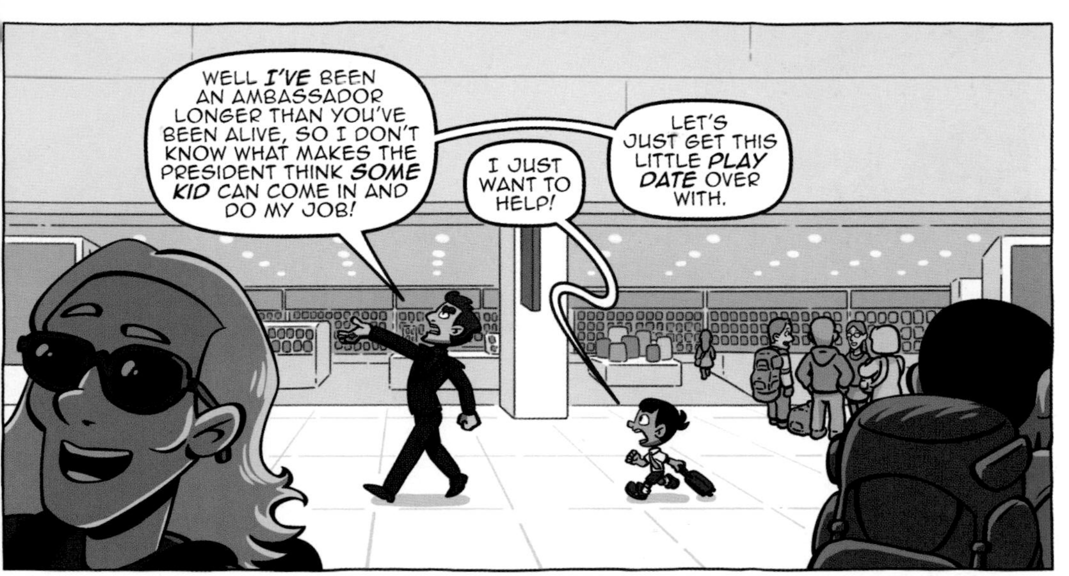
WELL I'VE BEEN AN AMBASSADOR LONGER THAN YOU'VE BEEN ALIVE, SO I DON'T KNOW WHAT MAKES THE PRESIDENT THINK SOME KID CAN COME IN AND DO MY JOB!
I JUST WANT TO HELP!
LET'S JUST GET THIS LITTLE PLAY DATE OVER WITH.

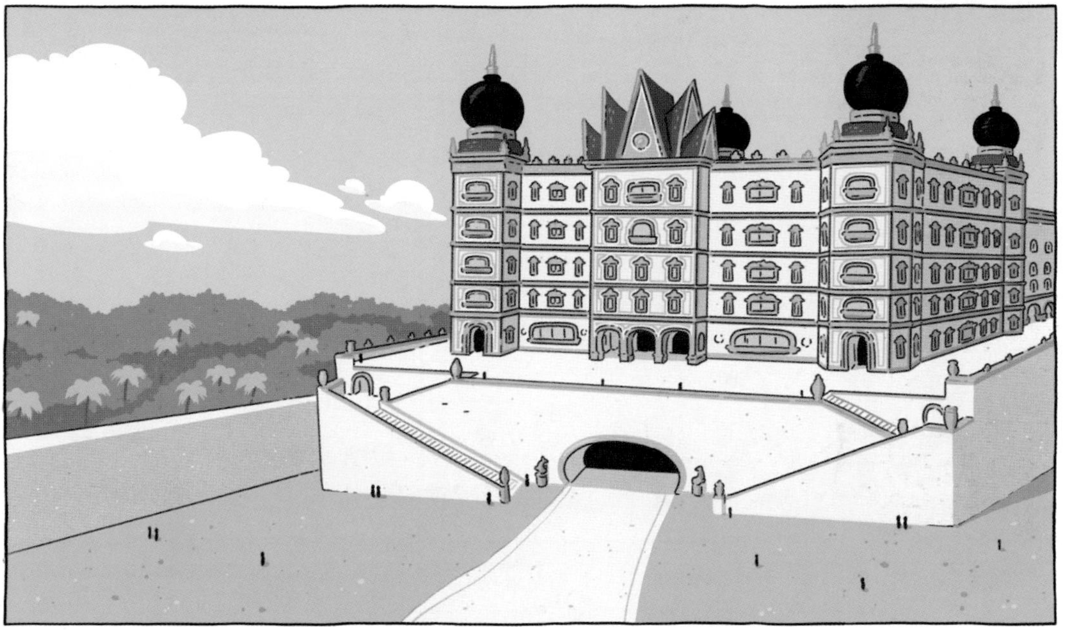

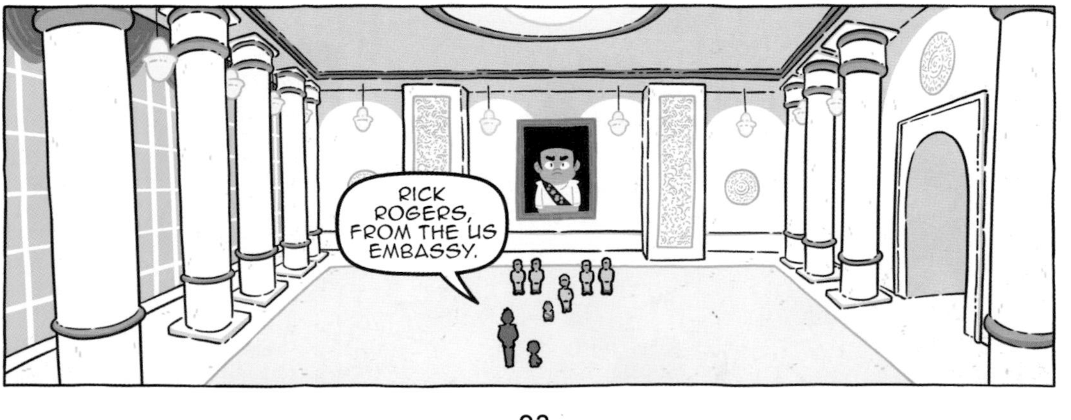
RICK ROGERS, FROM THE US EMBASSY.

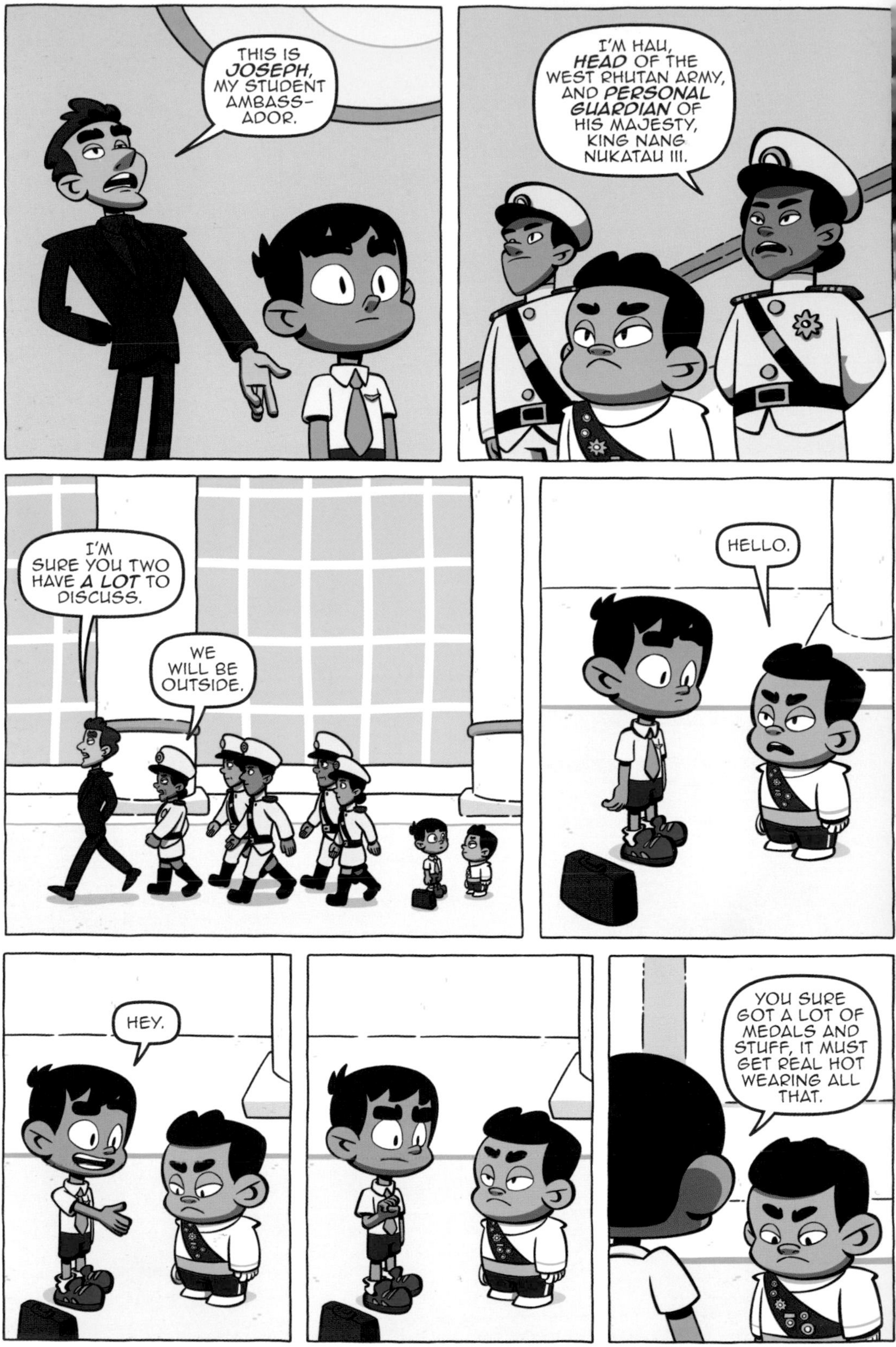
THIS IS JOSEPH, MY STUDENT AMBASS-ADOR.
I'M HAU, HEAD OF THE WEST RHUTAN ARMY, AND PERSONAL GUARDIAN OF HIS MAJESTY, KING NANG NUKATAU III.
I'M SURE YOU TWO HAVE A LOT TO DISCUSS.
WE WILL BE OUTSIDE.
HELLO.
HEY.
YOU SURE GOT A LOT OF MEDALS AND STUFF, IT MUST GET REAL HOT WEARING ALL THAT.

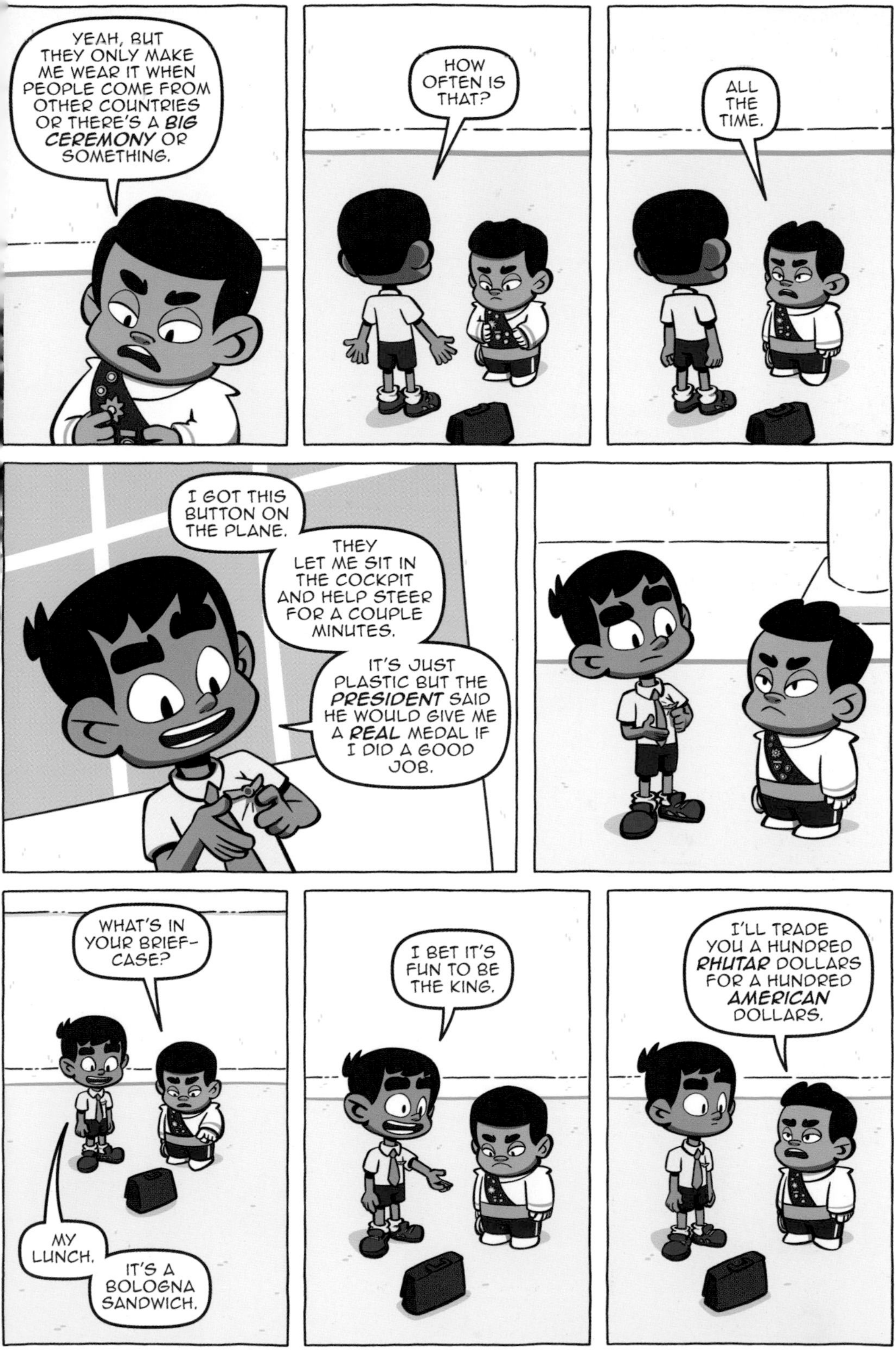
YEAH, BUT THEY ONLY MAKE ME WEAR IT WHEN PEOPLE COME FROM OTHER COUNTRIES OR THERE'S A *BIG CEREMONY* OR SOMETHING.
HOW OFTEN IS THAT?
ALL THE TIME.
I GOT THIS BUTTON ON THE PLANE.
THEY LET ME SIT IN THE COCKPIT AND HELP STEER FOR A COUPLE MINUTES.
IT'S JUST PLASTIC BUT THE *PRESIDENT* SAID HE WOULD GIVE ME A *REAL* MEDAL IF I DID A GOOD JOB.
WHAT'S IN YOUR BRIEF-CASE?
MY LUNCH.
IT'S A BOLOGNA SANDWICH.
I BET IT'S FUN TO BE THE KING.
I'LL TRADE YOU A HUNDRED *RHUTAR* DOLLARS FOR A HUNDRED *AMERICAN* DOLLARS.

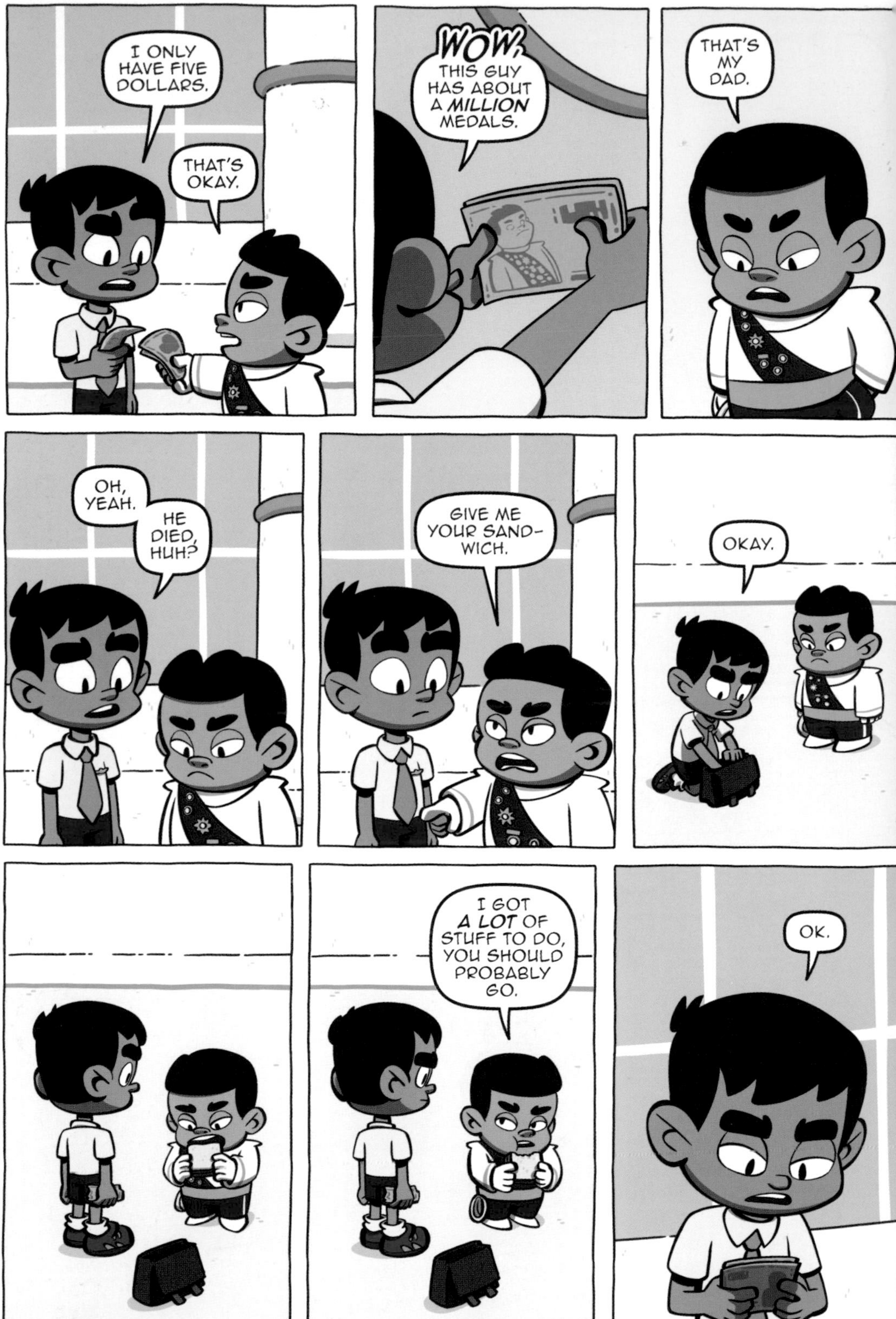
I ONLY HAVE FIVE DOLLARS.
THAT'S OKAY.
WOW. THIS GUY HAS ABOUT A **MILLION** MEDALS.
THAT'S MY DAD.
OH, YEAH.
HE DIED, HUH?
GIVE ME YOUR SAND-WICH.
OKAY.
I GOT **A LOT** OF STUFF TO DO, YOU SHOULD PROBABLY GO.
OK.

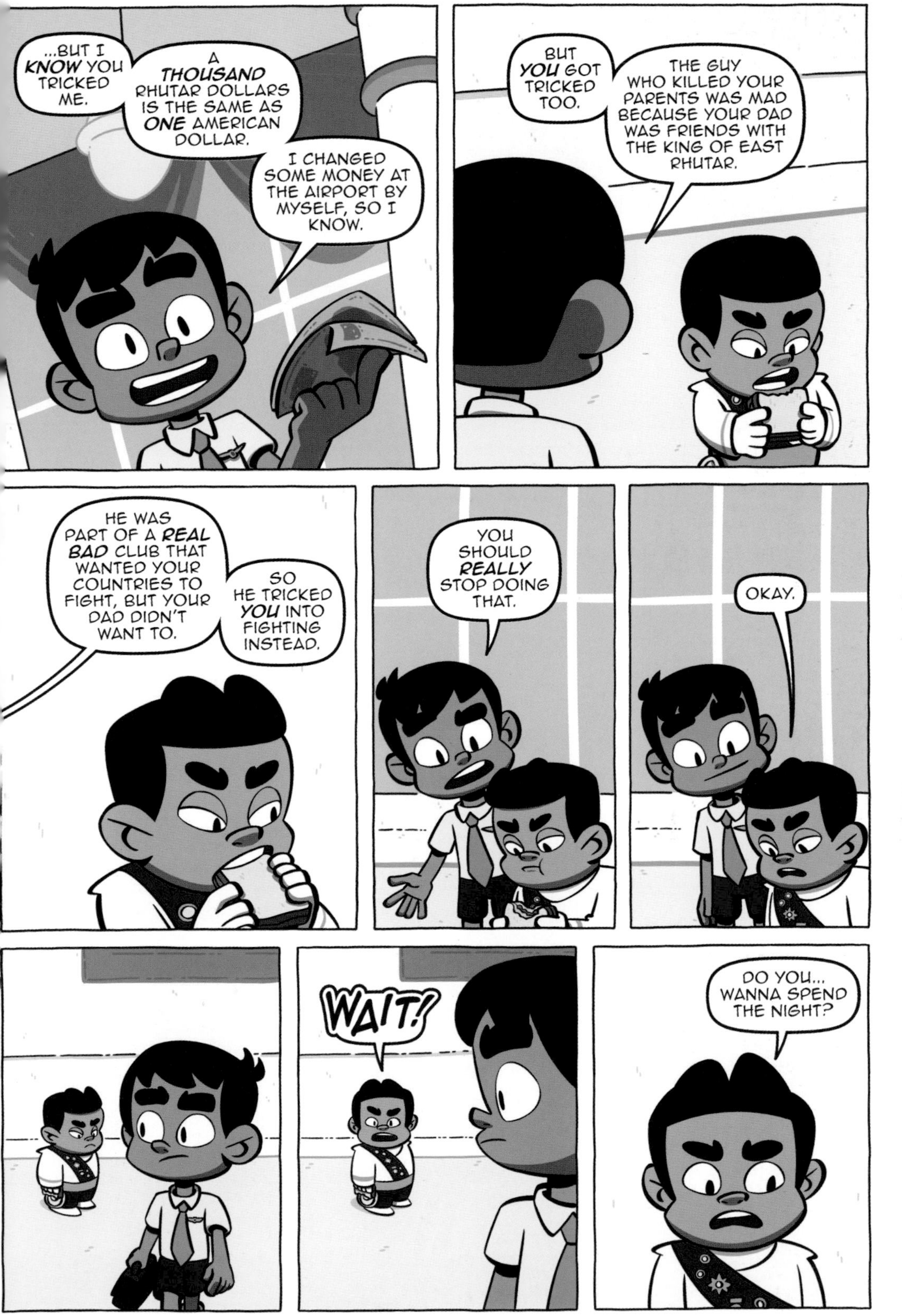
...BUT I KNOW YOU TRICKED ME.
A THOUSAND RHUTAR DOLLARS IS THE SAME AS ONE AMERICAN DOLLAR.
I CHANGED SOME MONEY AT THE AIRPORT BY MYSELF, SO I KNOW.
BUT YOU GOT TRICKED TOO.
THE GUY WHO KILLED YOUR PARENTS WAS MAD BECAUSE YOUR DAD WAS FRIENDS WITH THE KING OF EAST RHUTAR.
HE WAS PART OF A REAL BAD CLUB THAT WANTED YOUR COUNTRIES TO FIGHT, BUT YOUR DAD DIDN'T WANT TO.
SO HE TRICKED YOU INTO FIGHTING INSTEAD.
YOU SHOULD REALLY STOP DOING THAT.
OKAY.
WAIT!
DO YOU... WANNA SPEND THE NIGHT?

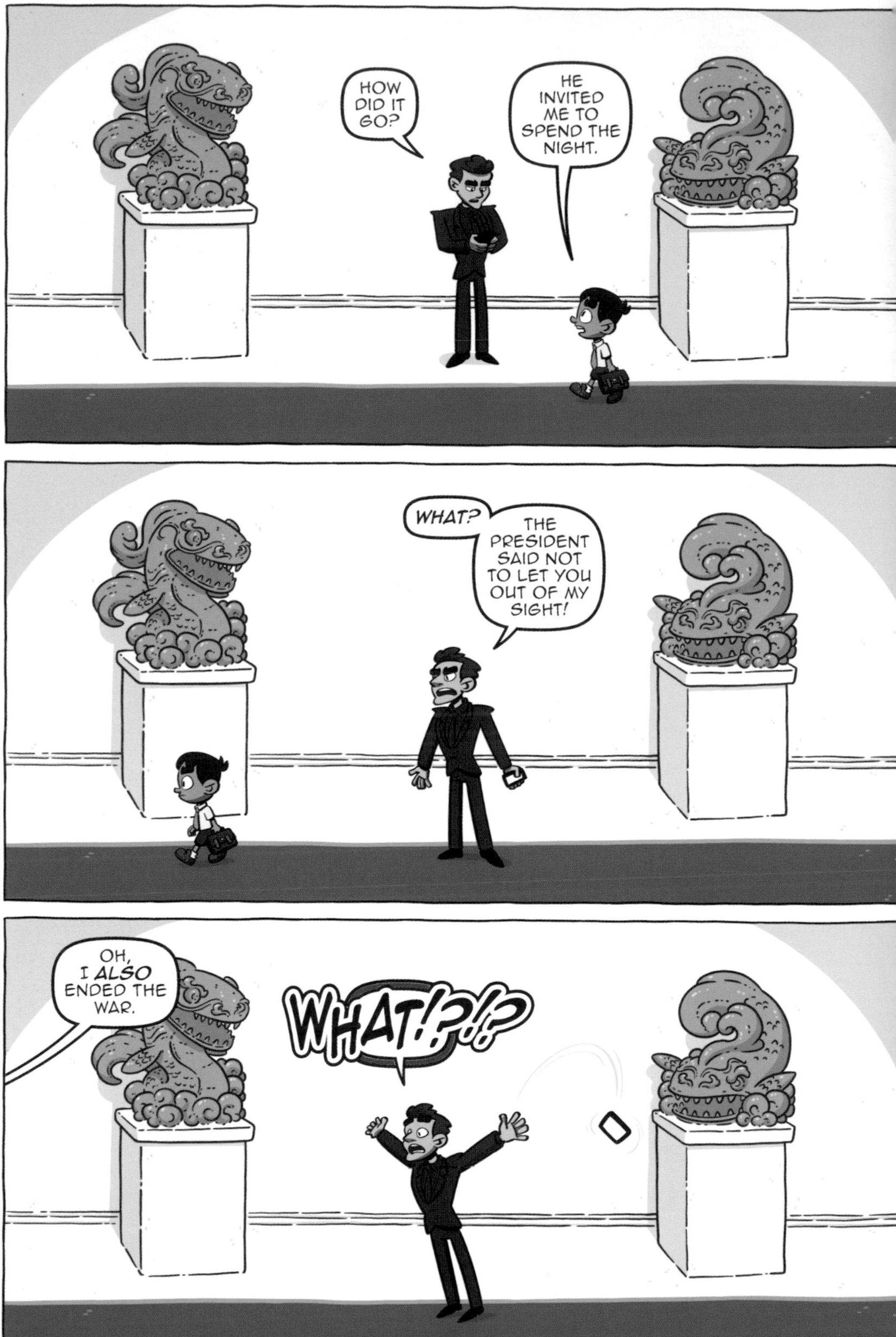
HOW DID IT GO?
HE INVITED ME TO SPEND THE NIGHT.
WHAT?
THE PRESIDENT SAID NOT TO LET YOU OUT OF MY SIGHT!
OH, I *ALSO* ENDED THE WAR.
WHAT!?!?

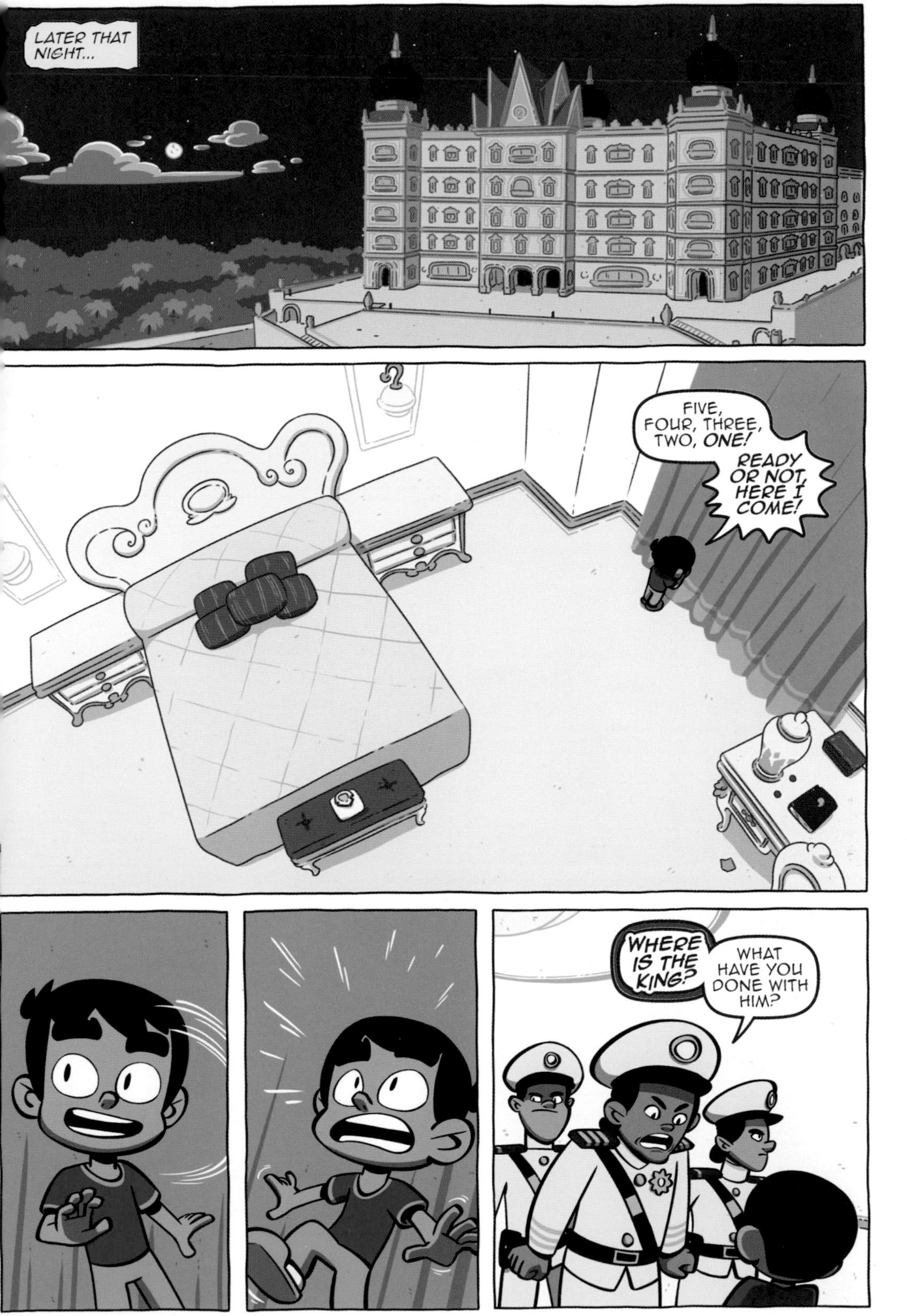
LATER THAT NIGHT...
FIVE, FOUR, THREE, TWO, ONE!
READY OR NOT, HERE I COME!
WHERE IS THE KING?
WHAT HAVE YOU DONE WITH HIM?

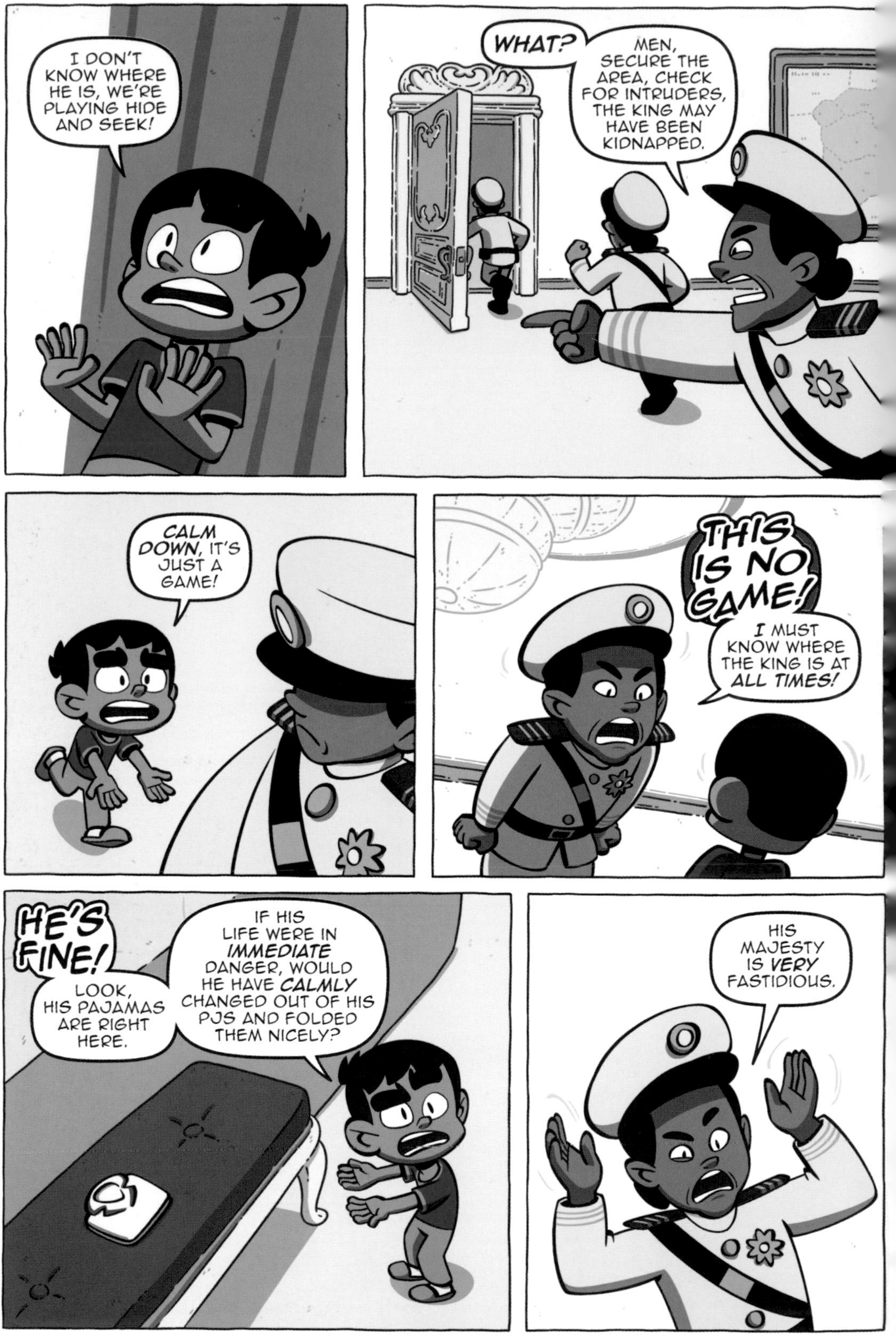
I DON'T KNOW WHERE HE IS, WE'RE PLAYING HIDE AND SEEK!
WHAT?
MEN, SECURE THE AREA, CHECK FOR INTRUDERS, THE KING MAY HAVE BEEN KIDNAPPED.
CALM DOWN, IT'S JUST A GAME!
THIS IS NO GAME!
I MUST KNOW WHERE THE KING IS AT ALL TIMES!
HE'S FINE!
LOOK, HIS PAJAMAS ARE RIGHT HERE.
IF HIS LIFE WERE IN IMMEDIATE DANGER, WOULD HE HAVE CALMLY CHANGED OUT OF HIS PJS AND FOLDED THEM NICELY?
HIS MAJESTY IS VERY FASTIDIOUS.

JUST
HELP
ME FIND
HIM.

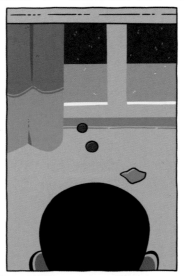

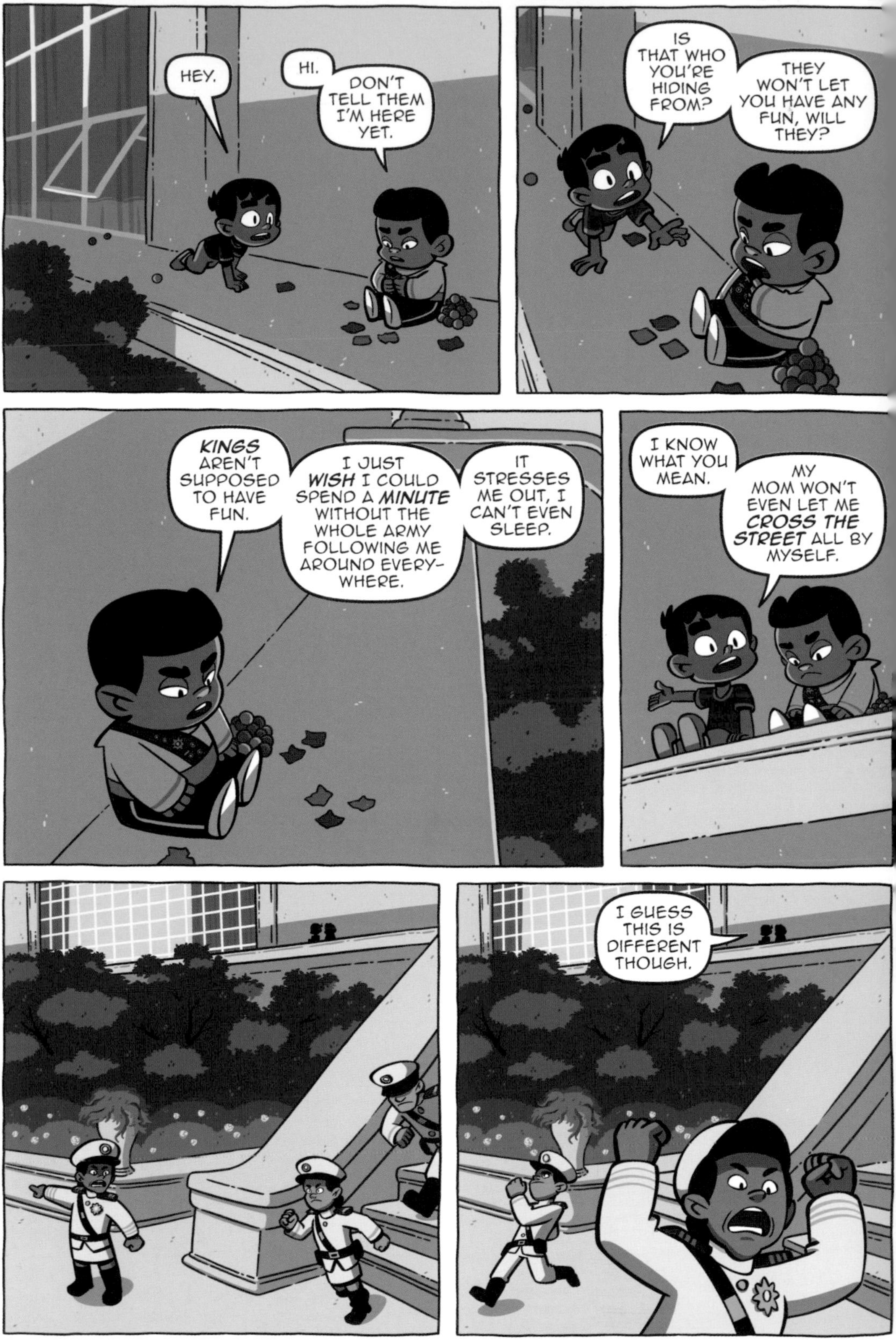
HEY.
HI.
DON'T TELL THEM I'M HERE YET.
IS THAT WHO YOU'RE HIDING FROM?
THEY WON'T LET YOU HAVE ANY FUN, WILL THEY?
KINGS AREN'T SUPPOSED TO HAVE FUN.
I JUST WISH I COULD SPEND A MINUTE WITHOUT THE WHOLE ARMY FOLLOWING ME AROUND EVERY-WHERE.
IT STRESSES ME OUT, I CAN'T EVEN SLEEP.
I KNOW WHAT YOU MEAN.
MY MOM WON'T EVEN LET ME CROSS THE STREET ALL BY MYSELF.
I GUESS THIS IS DIFFERENT THOUGH.

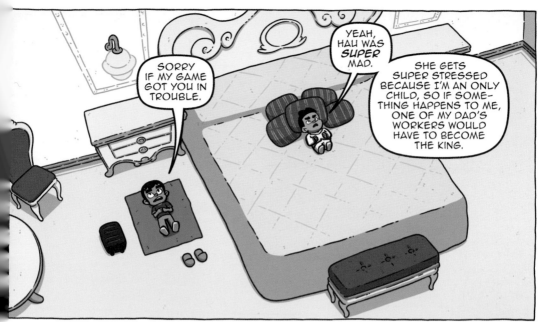

SORRY IF MY GAME GOT YOU IN TROUBLE.

YEAH, HAU WAS *SUPER* MAD.

SHE GETS SUPER STRESSED BECAUSE I'M AN ONLY CHILD, SO IF SOMETHING HAPPENS TO ME, ONE OF MY DAD'S WORKERS WOULD HAVE TO BECOME THE KING.

DID YOU PROMISE NEVER TO DO IT AGAIN?

NO, I FIRED HER.

BUT WE GOTTA STAY IN HERE NOW.

DID YOU BRING ANY COOL STUFF?

JUST SOME COMIC BOOKS.

KINGS *DON'T* READ COMIC BOOKS.

WE ONLY READ *REAL* BOOKS WHERE WE CAN LEARN STUFF.

DID YOU BRING ANYTHING ELSE?

I BROUGHT SOME MANHWA THAT MY BABYSITTER GAVE ME.

WHAT'S A *MANHWA?*

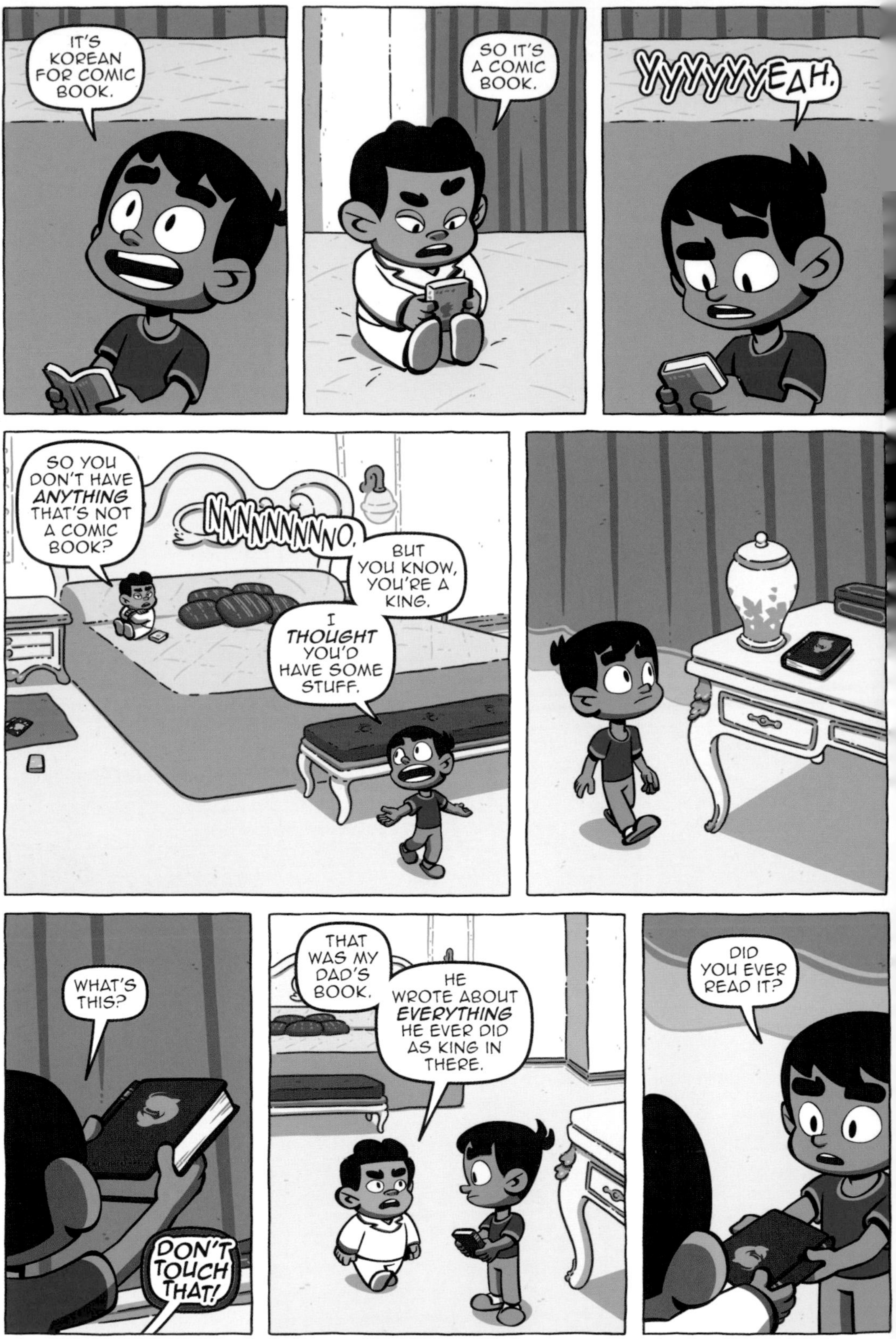
IT'S KOREAN FOR COMIC BOOK.
SO IT'S A COMIC BOOK.
YYYYYYEAH.
SO YOU DON'T HAVE ANYTHING THAT'S NOT A COMIC BOOK?
NNNNNNNNNO.
BUT YOU KNOW, YOU'RE A KING.
I THOUGHT YOU'D HAVE SOME STUFF.
WHAT'S THIS?
DON'T TOUCH THAT!
THAT WAS MY DAD'S BOOK.
HE WROTE ABOUT EVERYTHING HE EVER DID AS KING IN THERE.
DID YOU EVER READ IT?

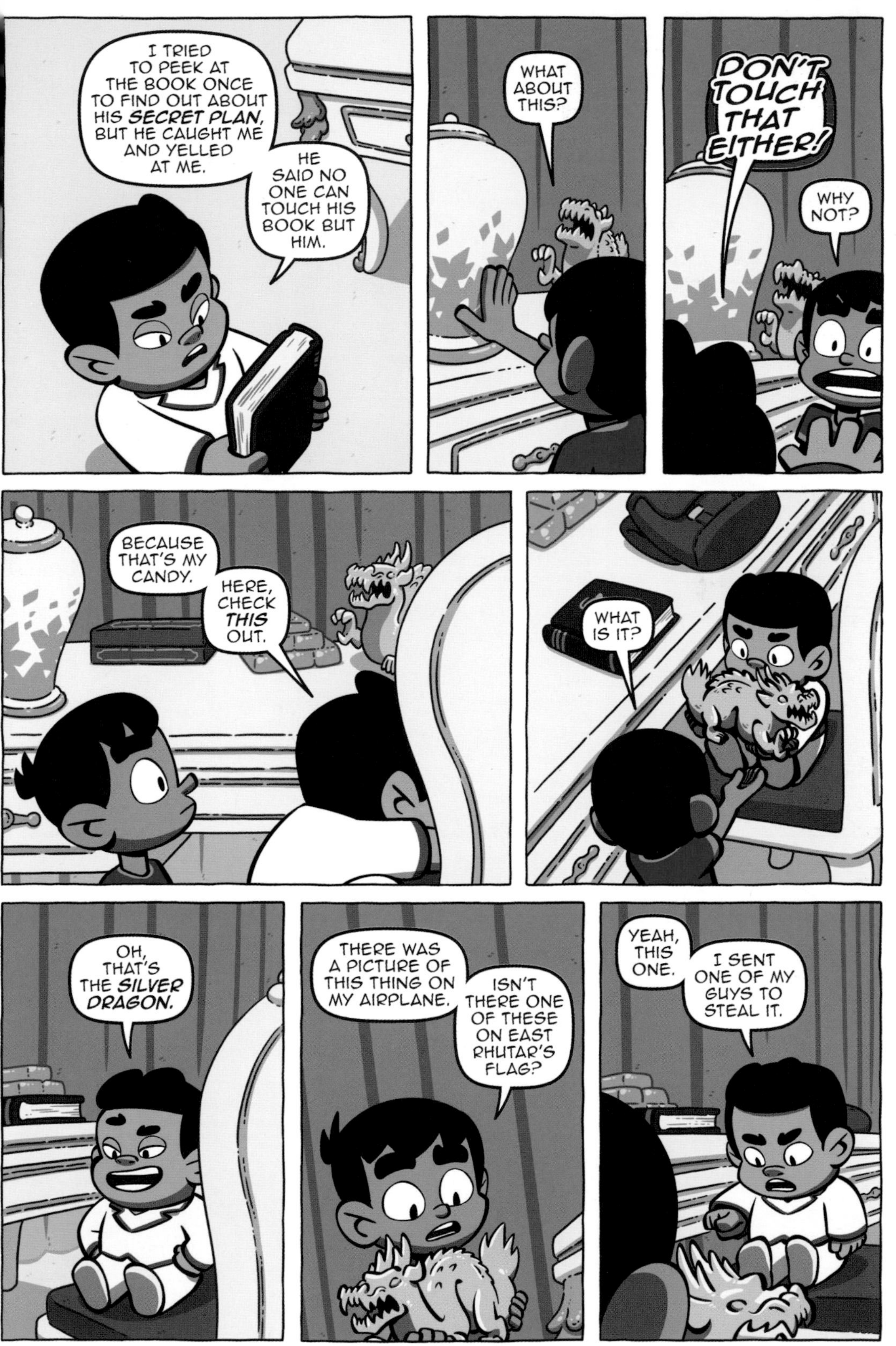
I TRIED TO PEEK AT THE BOOK ONCE TO FIND OUT ABOUT HIS SECRET PLAN, BUT HE CAUGHT ME AND YELLED AT ME.
HE SAID NO ONE CAN TOUCH HIS BOOK BUT HIM.
WHAT ABOUT THIS?
DON'T TOUCH THAT EITHER!
WHY NOT?
BECAUSE THAT'S MY CANDY.
HERE, CHECK THIS OUT.
WHAT IS IT?
OH, THAT'S THE SILVER DRAGON.
THERE WAS A PICTURE OF THIS THING ON MY AIRPLANE.
ISN'T THERE ONE OF THESE ON EAST RHUTAR'S FLAG?
YEAH, THIS ONE.
I SENT ONE OF MY GUYS TO STEAL IT.

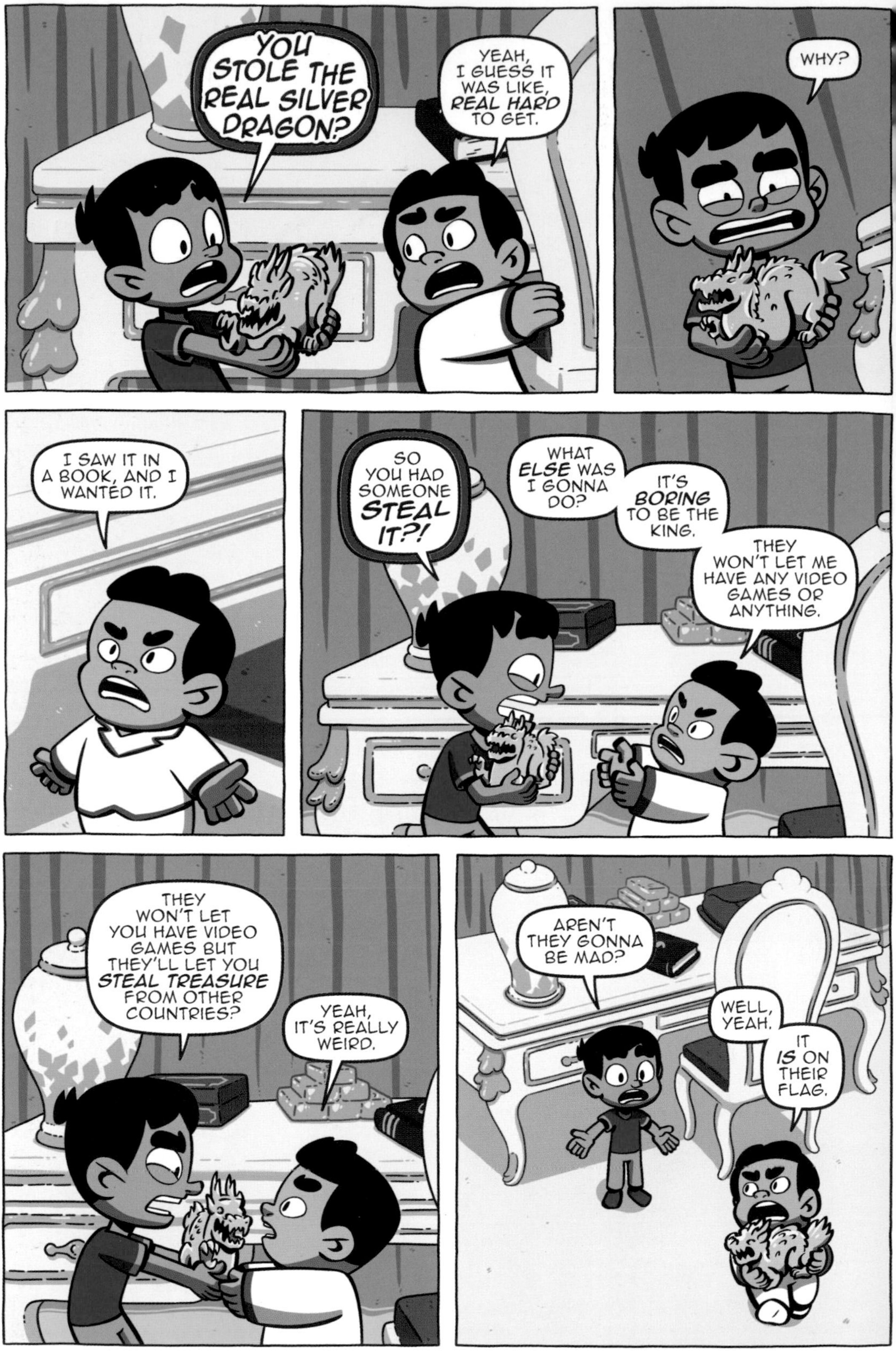
YOU STOLE THE REAL SILVER DRAGON?
YEAH, I GUESS IT WAS LIKE, REAL HARD TO GET.
WHY?
I SAW IT IN A BOOK, AND I WANTED IT.
SO YOU HAD SOMEONE STEAL IT?!
WHAT ELSE WAS I GONNA DO?
IT'S BORING TO BE THE KING.
THEY WON'T LET ME HAVE ANY VIDEO GAMES OR ANYTHING.
THEY WON'T LET YOU HAVE VIDEO GAMES BUT THEY'LL LET YOU STEAL TREASURE FROM OTHER COUNTRIES?
YEAH, IT'S REALLY WEIRD.
AREN'T THEY GONNA BE MAD?
WELL, YEAH.
IT IS ON THEIR FLAG.

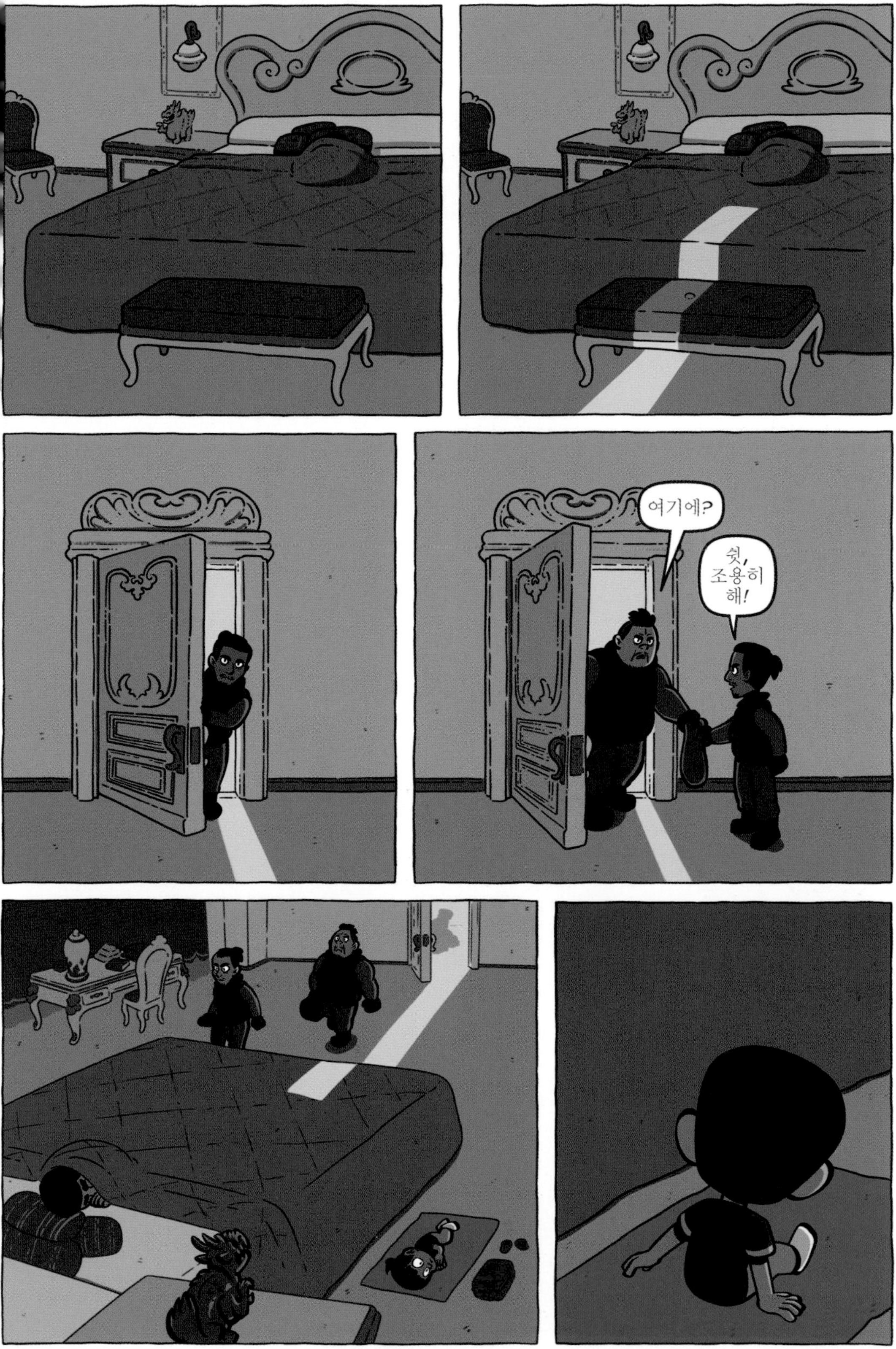
여기에?
쉿, 조용히 해!

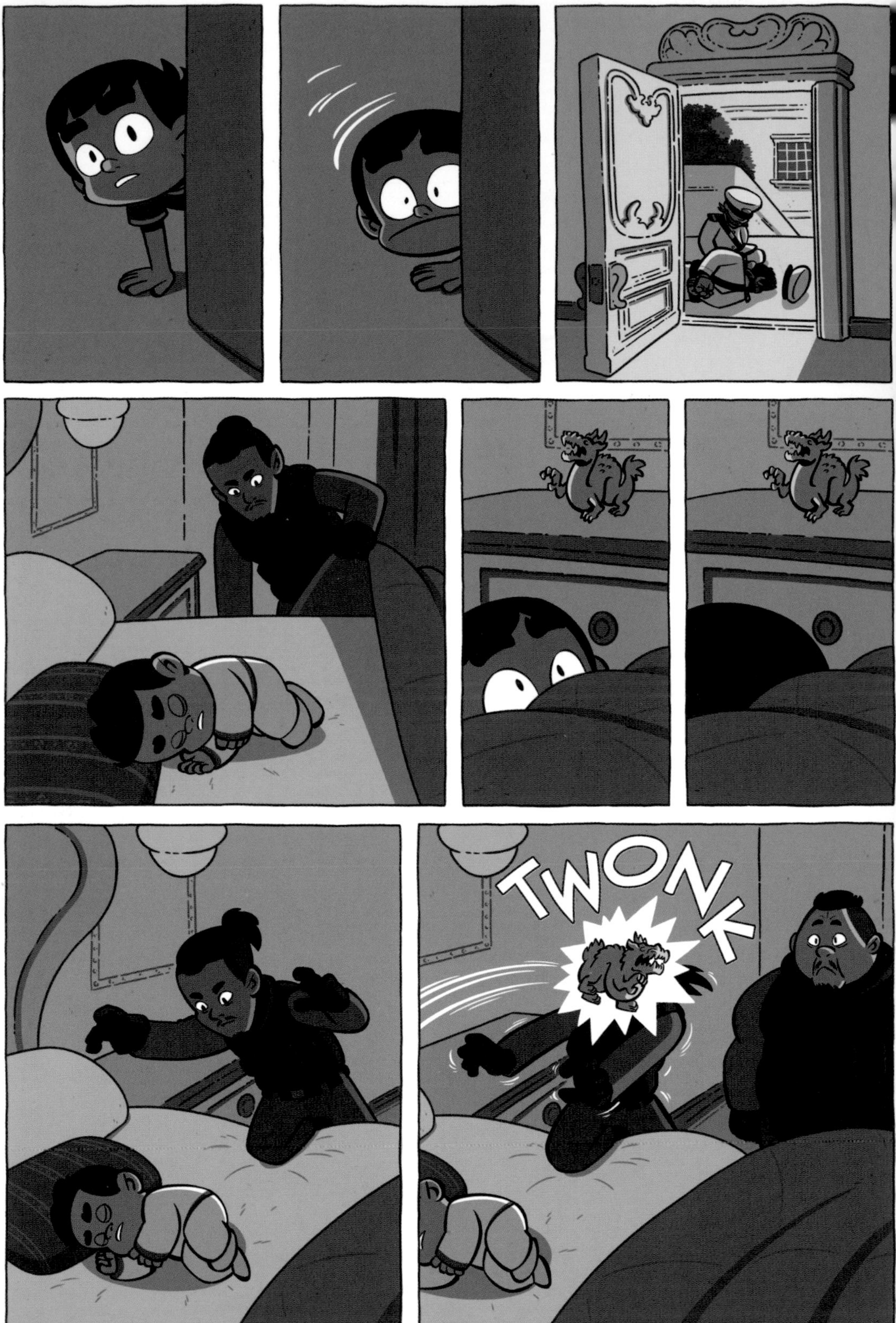
TWONK

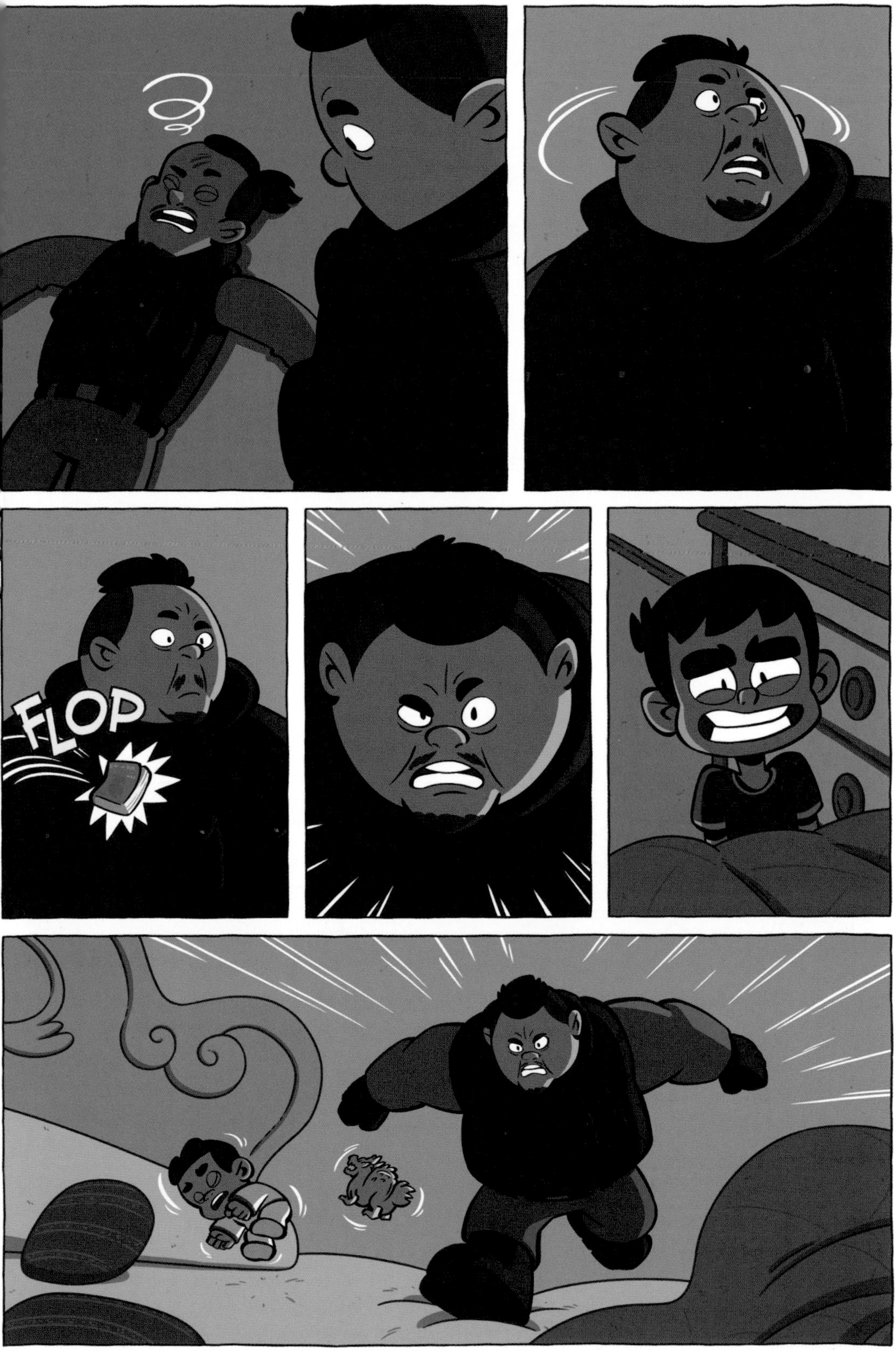
FLOP

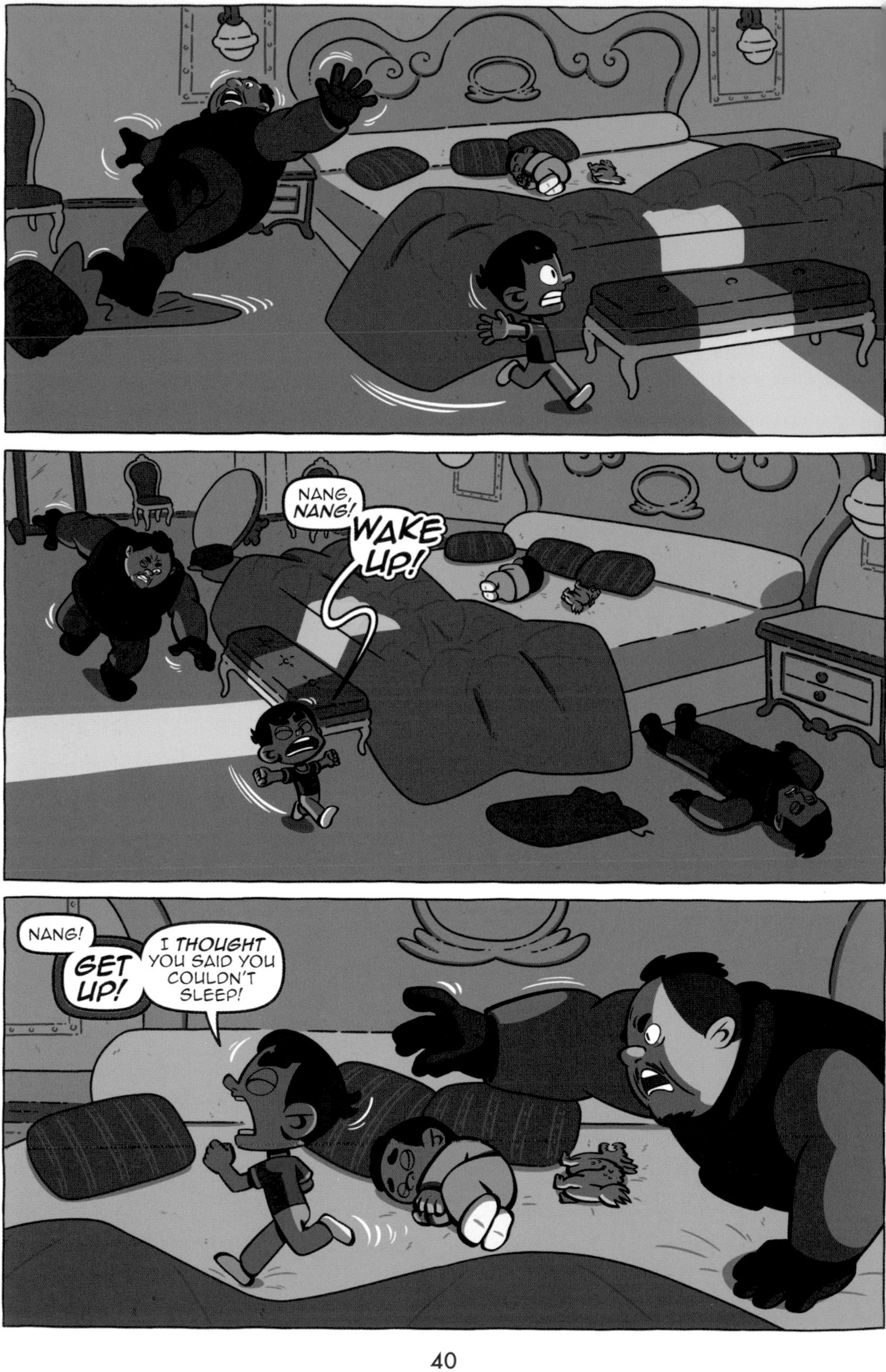
NANG, NANG!
WAKE UP!
NANG!
GET UP!
I THOUGHT YOU SAID YOU COULDN'T SLEEP!

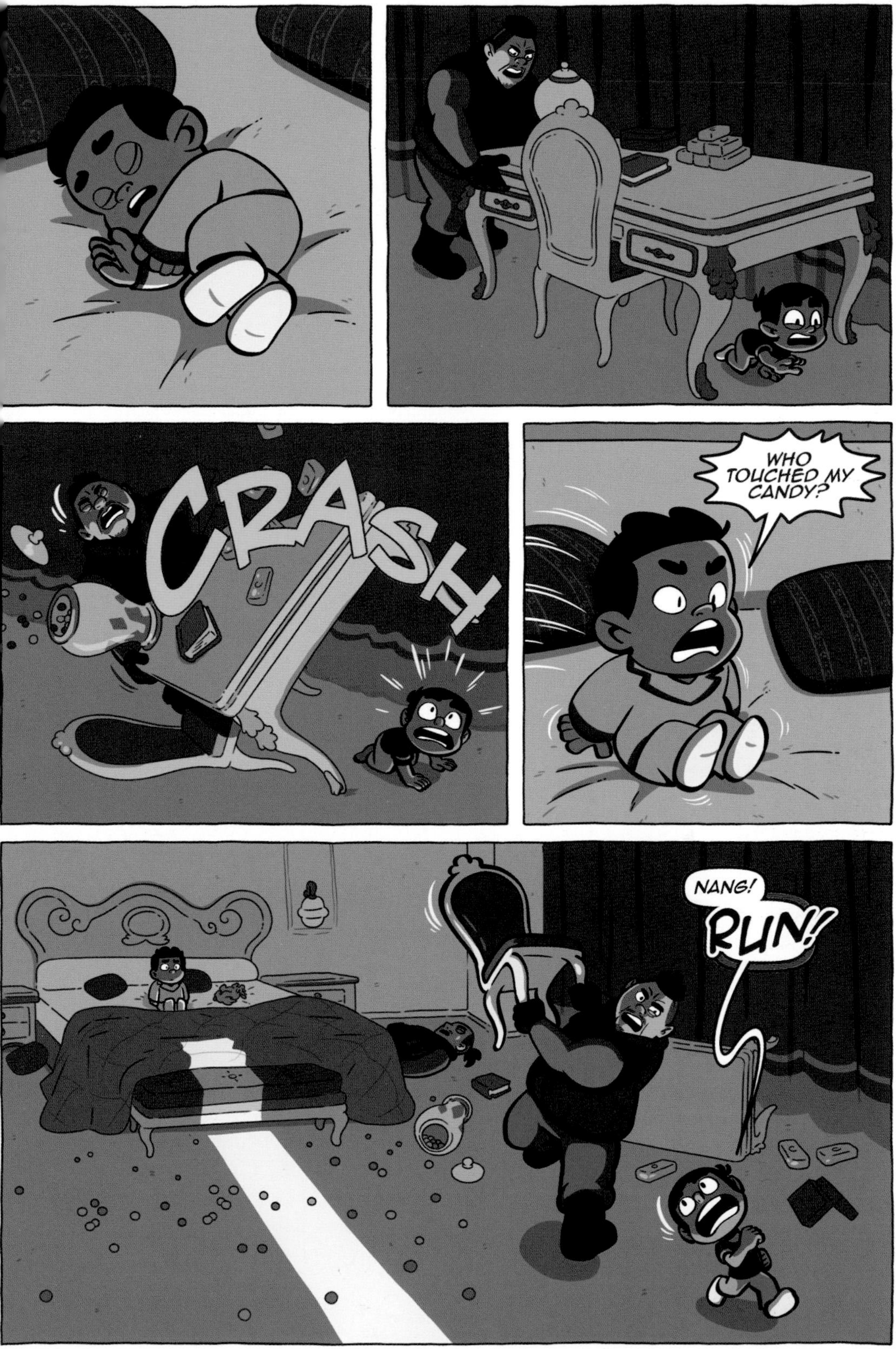
CRASH
WHO TOUCHED MY CANDY?
NANG!
RUN!

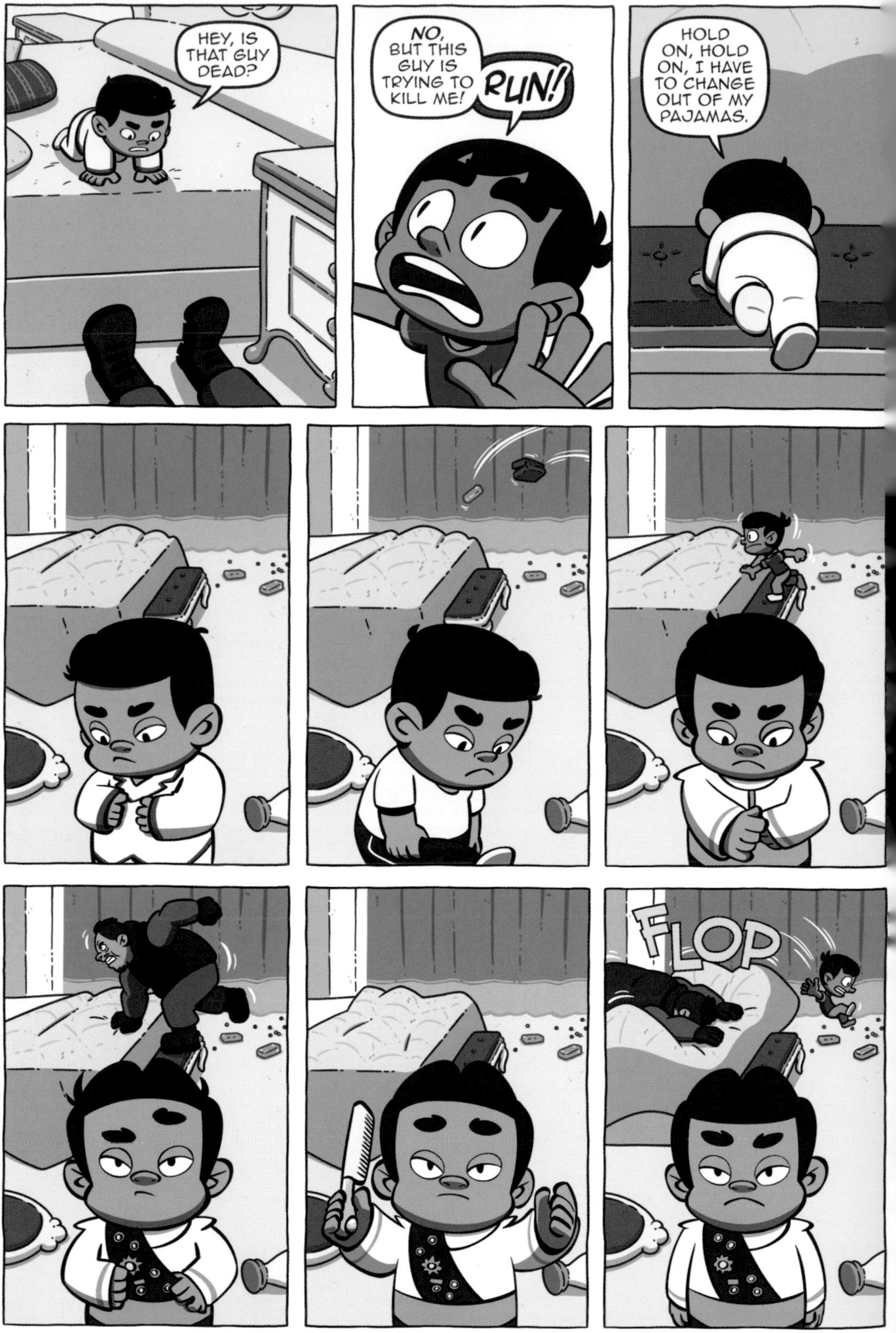
HEY, IS THAT GUY DEAD?
NO, BUT THIS GUY IS TRYING TO KILL ME!
RUN!
HOLD ON, HOLD ON, I HAVE TO CHANGE OUT OF MY PAJAMAS.
FLOP

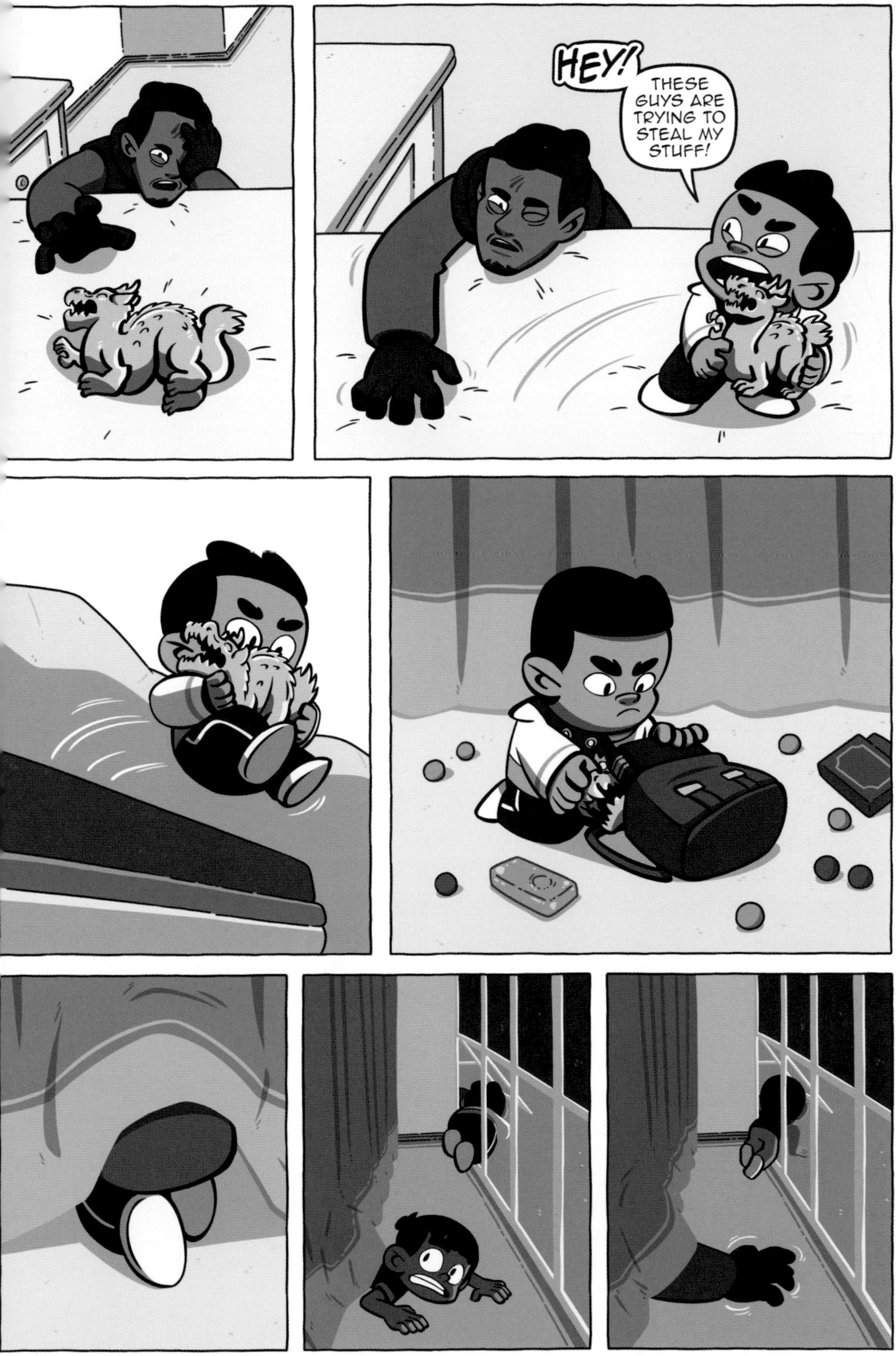
HEY!
THESE GUYS ARE TRYING TO STEAL MY STUFF!

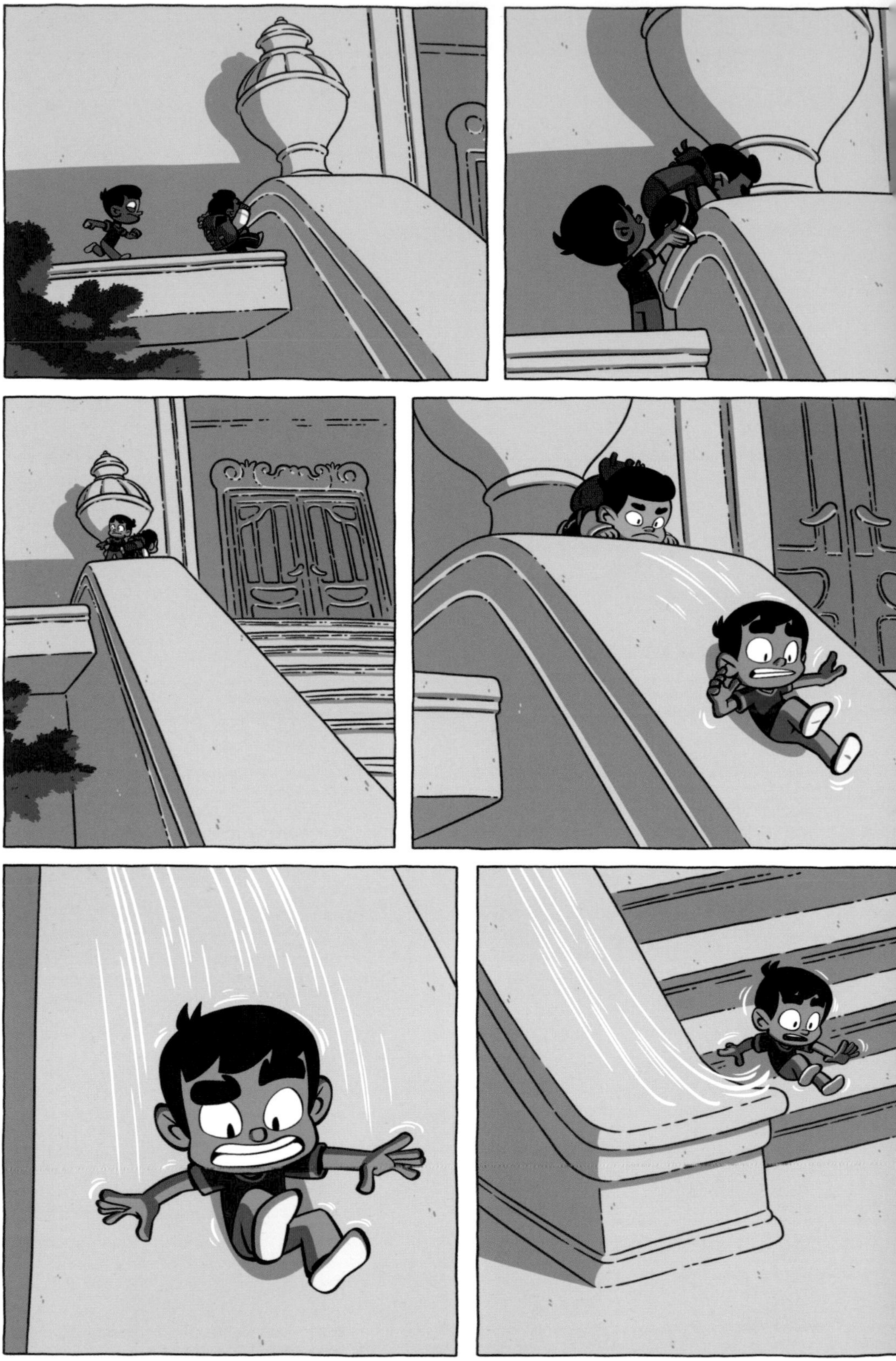

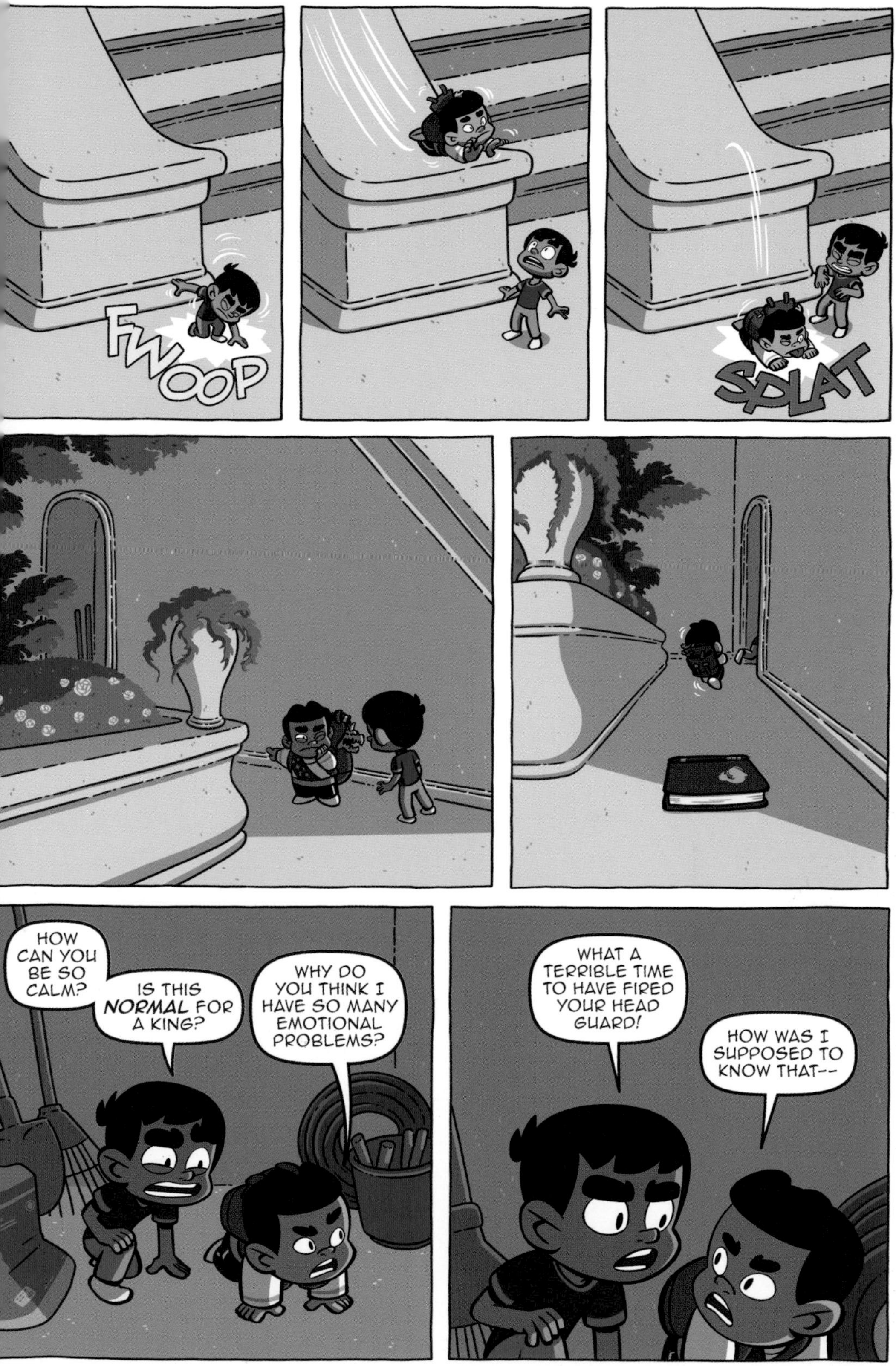
FWOOP
SPLAT
HOW CAN YOU BE SO CALM?
IS THIS NORMAL FOR A KING?
WHY DO YOU THINK I HAVE SO MANY EMOTIONAL PROBLEMS?
WHAT A TERRIBLE TIME TO HAVE FIRED YOUR HEAD GUARD!
HOW WAS I SUPPOSED TO KNOW THAT--

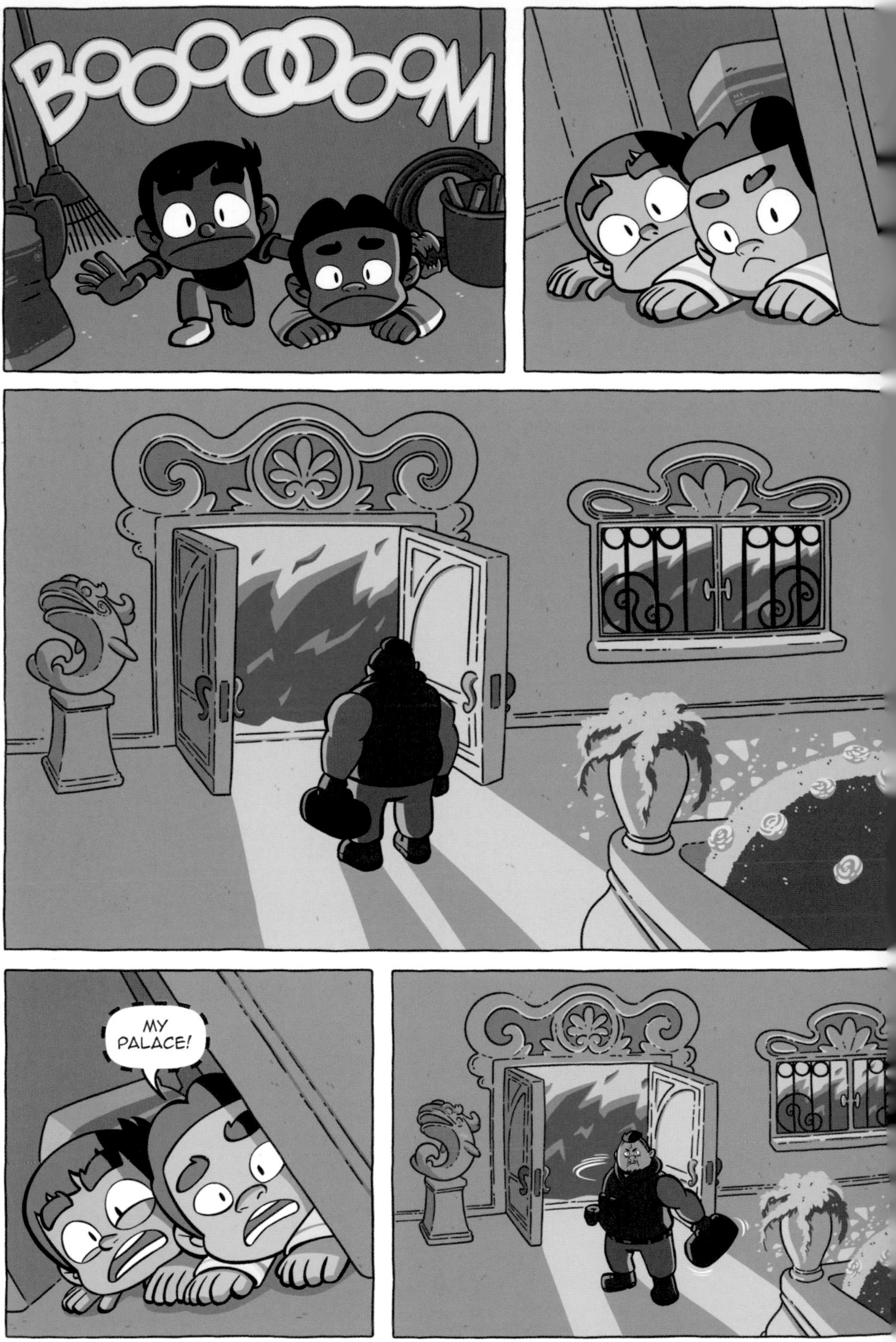
BOOOOOOOM
MY PALACE!

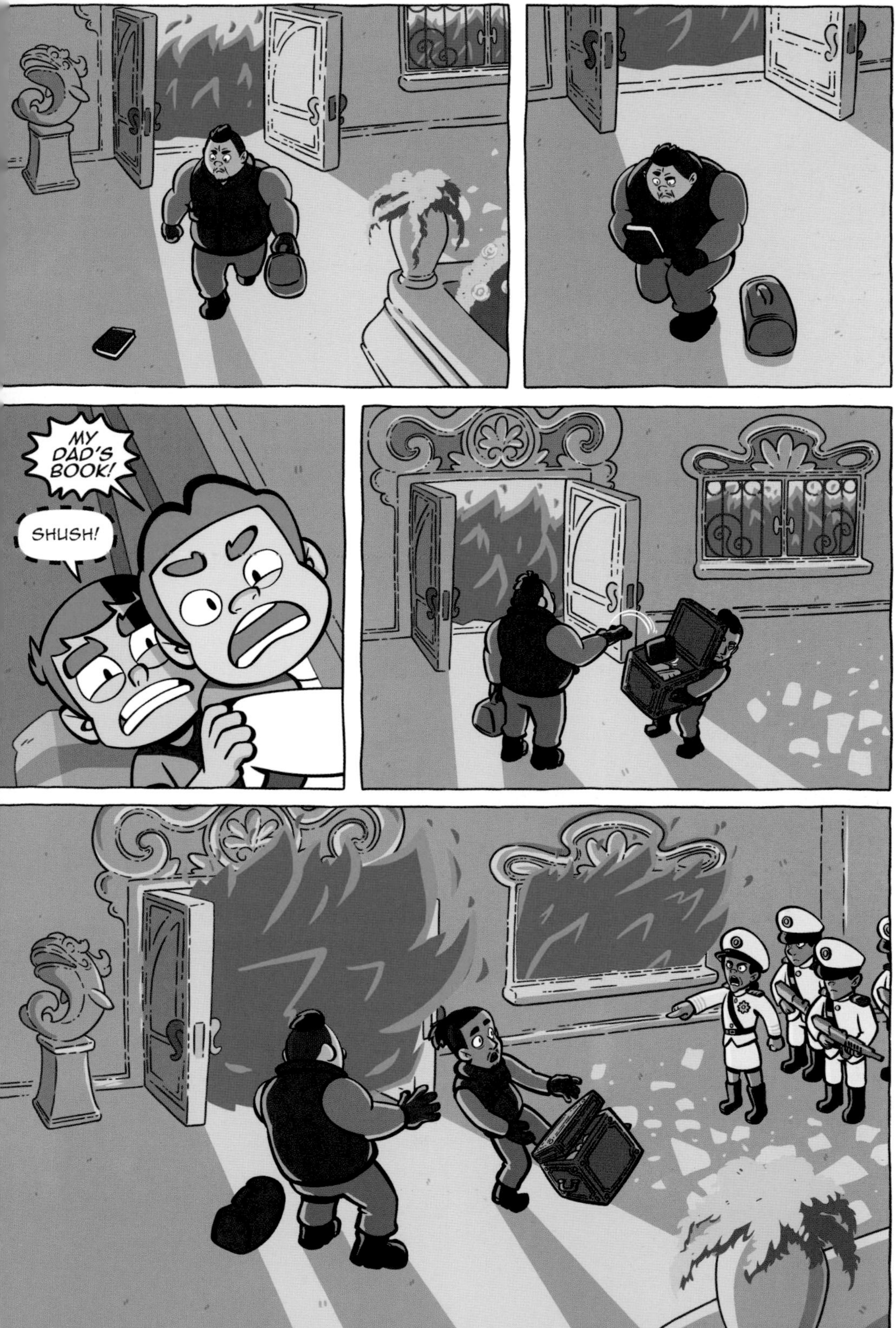
MY DAD'S BOOK!
SHUSH!

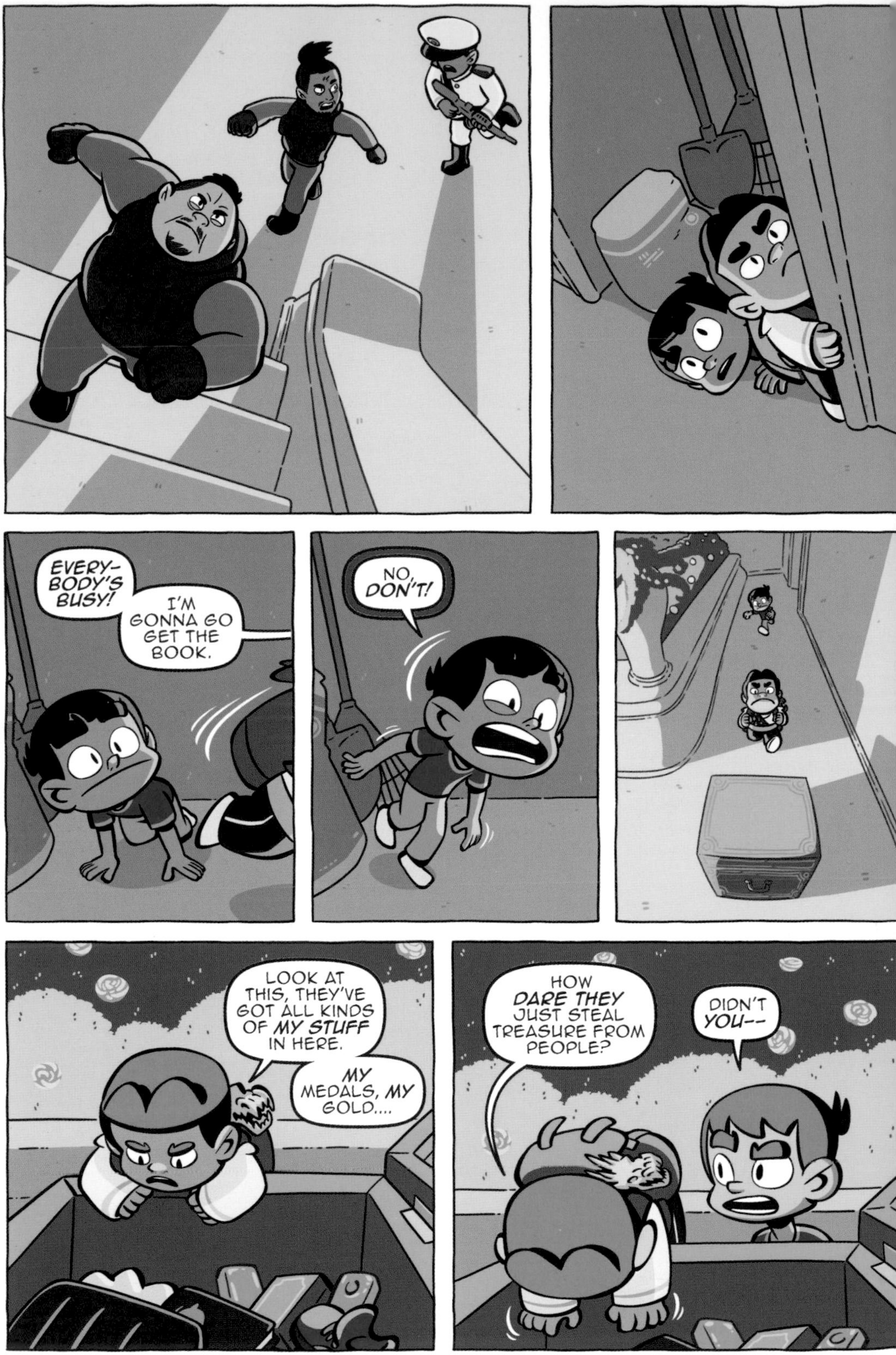
EVERY-BODY'S BUSY!
I'M GONNA GO GET THE BOOK.
NO, DON'T!
LOOK AT THIS, THEY'VE GOT ALL KINDS OF MY STUFF IN HERE.
MY MEDALS, MY GOLD....
HOW DARE THEY JUST STEAL TREASURE FROM PEOPLE?
DIDN'T YOU--

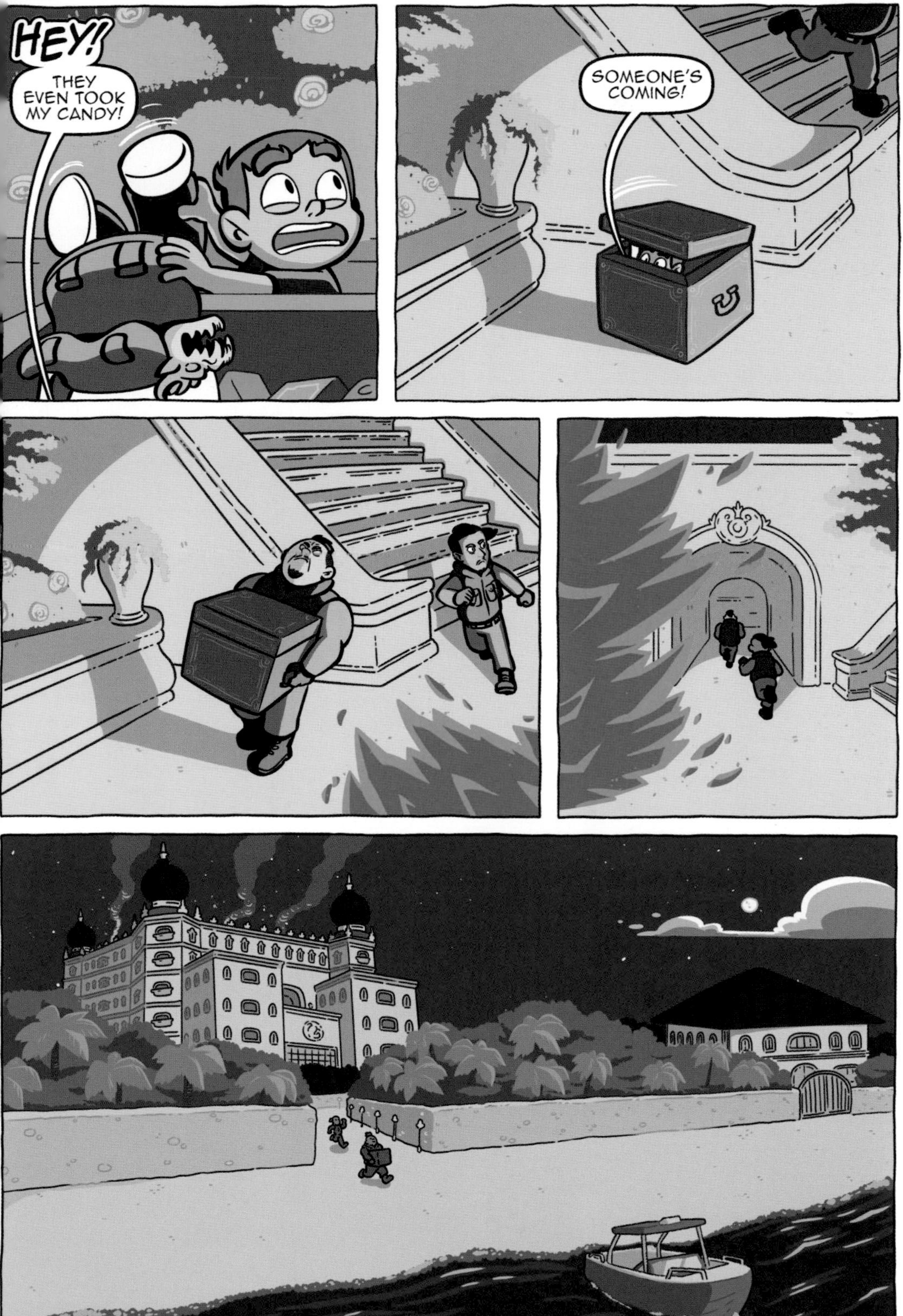
HEY!
THEY EVEN TOOK MY CANDY!
SOMEONE'S COMING!

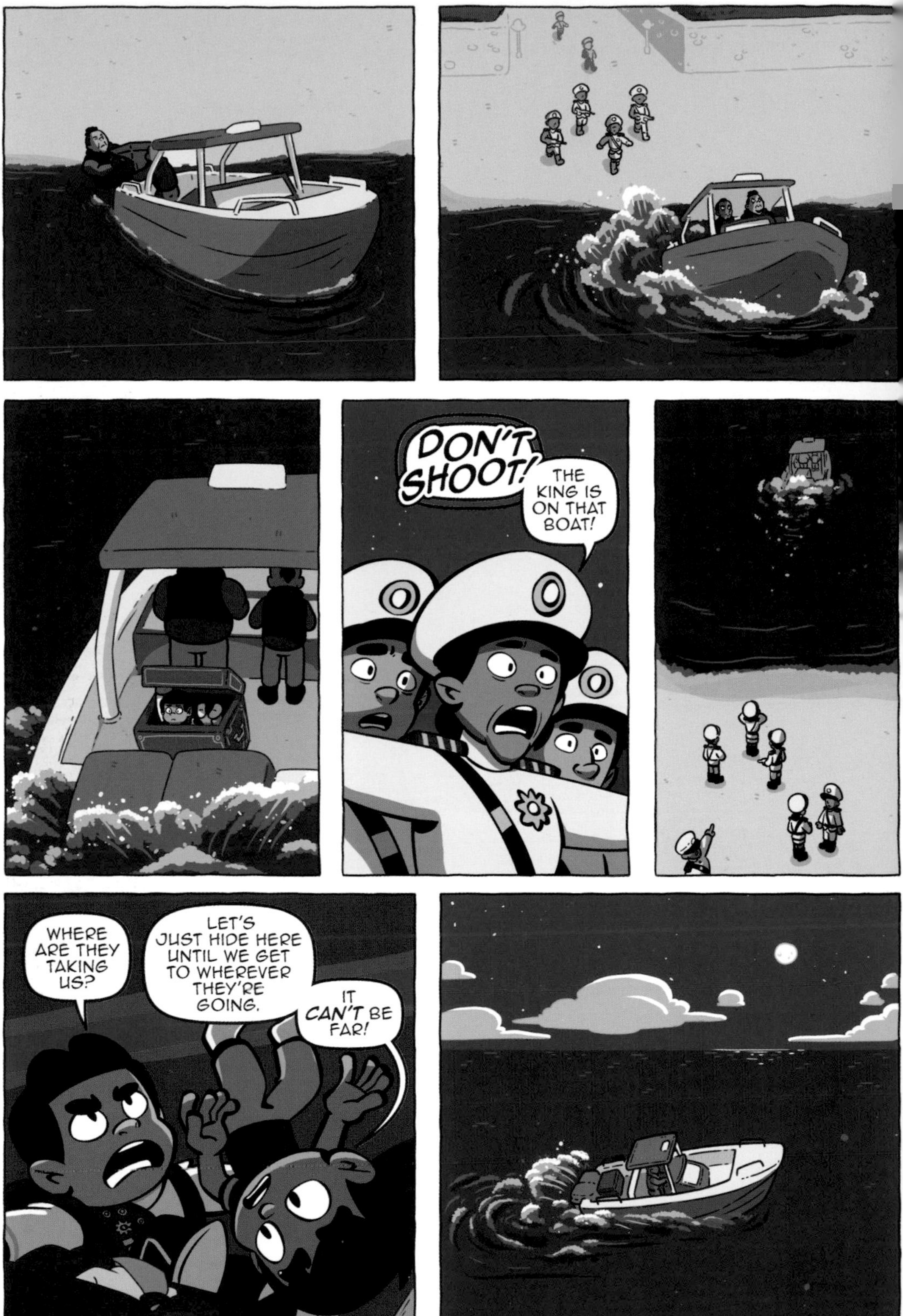
DON'T SHOOT!
THE KING IS ON THAT BOAT!
WHERE ARE THEY TAKING US?
LET'S JUST HIDE HERE UNTIL WE GET TO WHEREVER THEY'RE GOING.
IT CAN'T BE FAR!

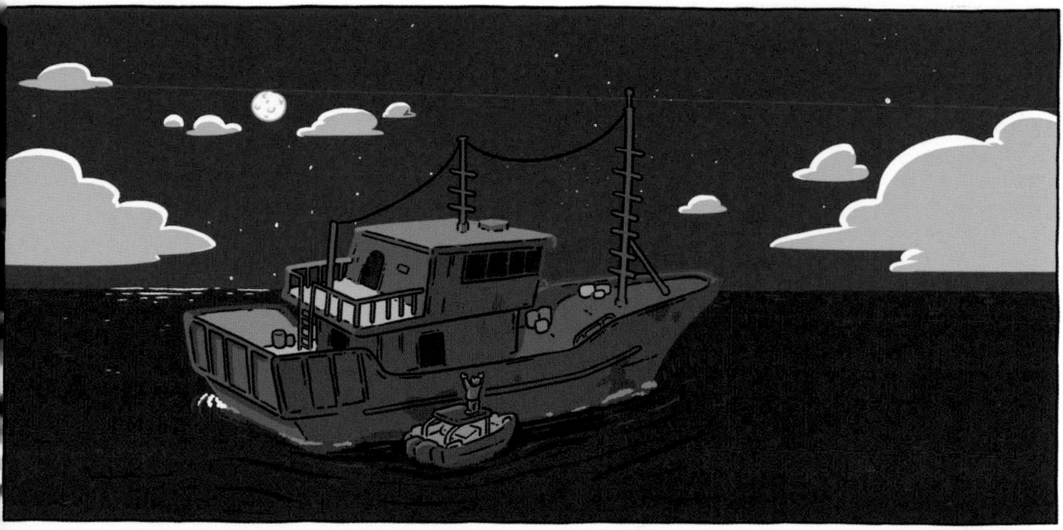

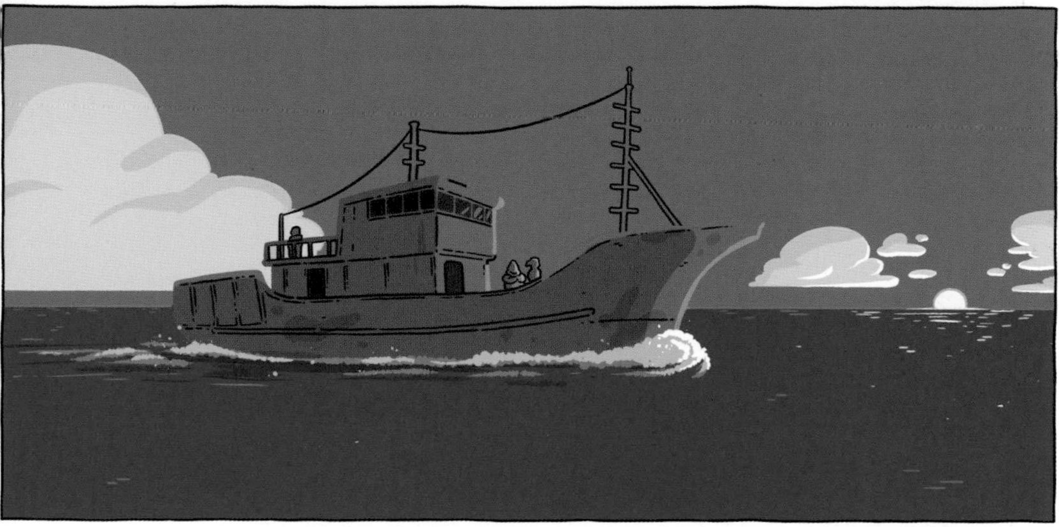

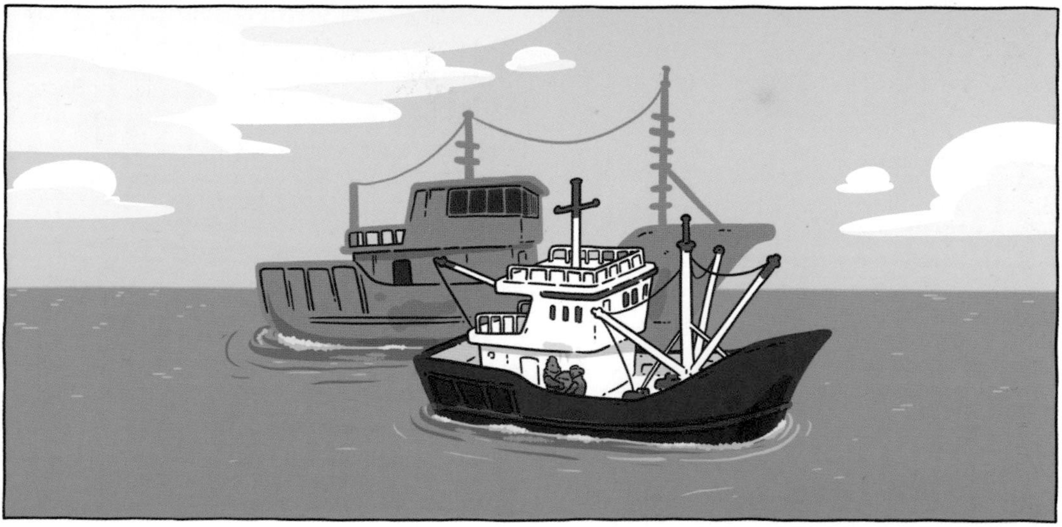

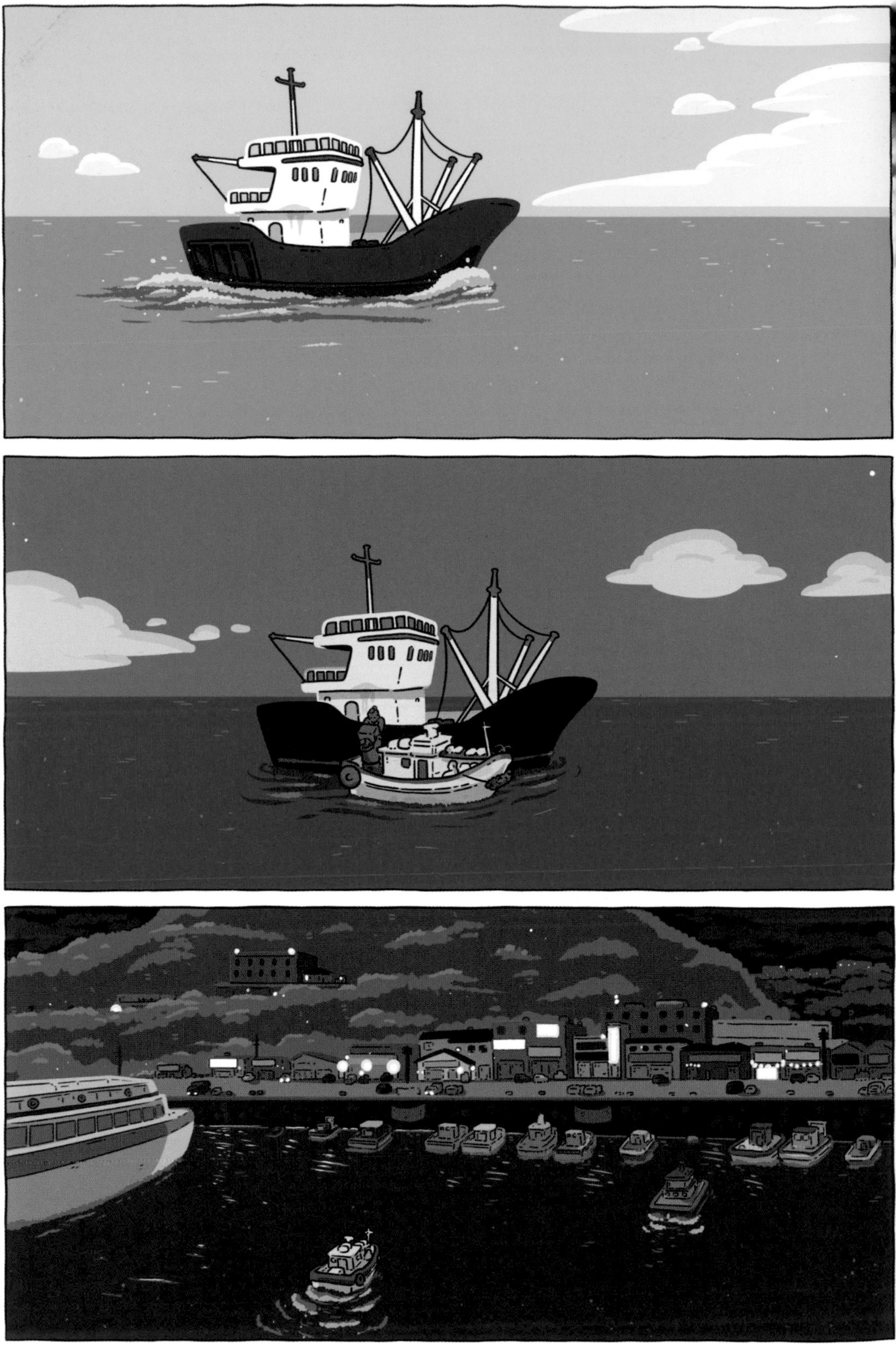

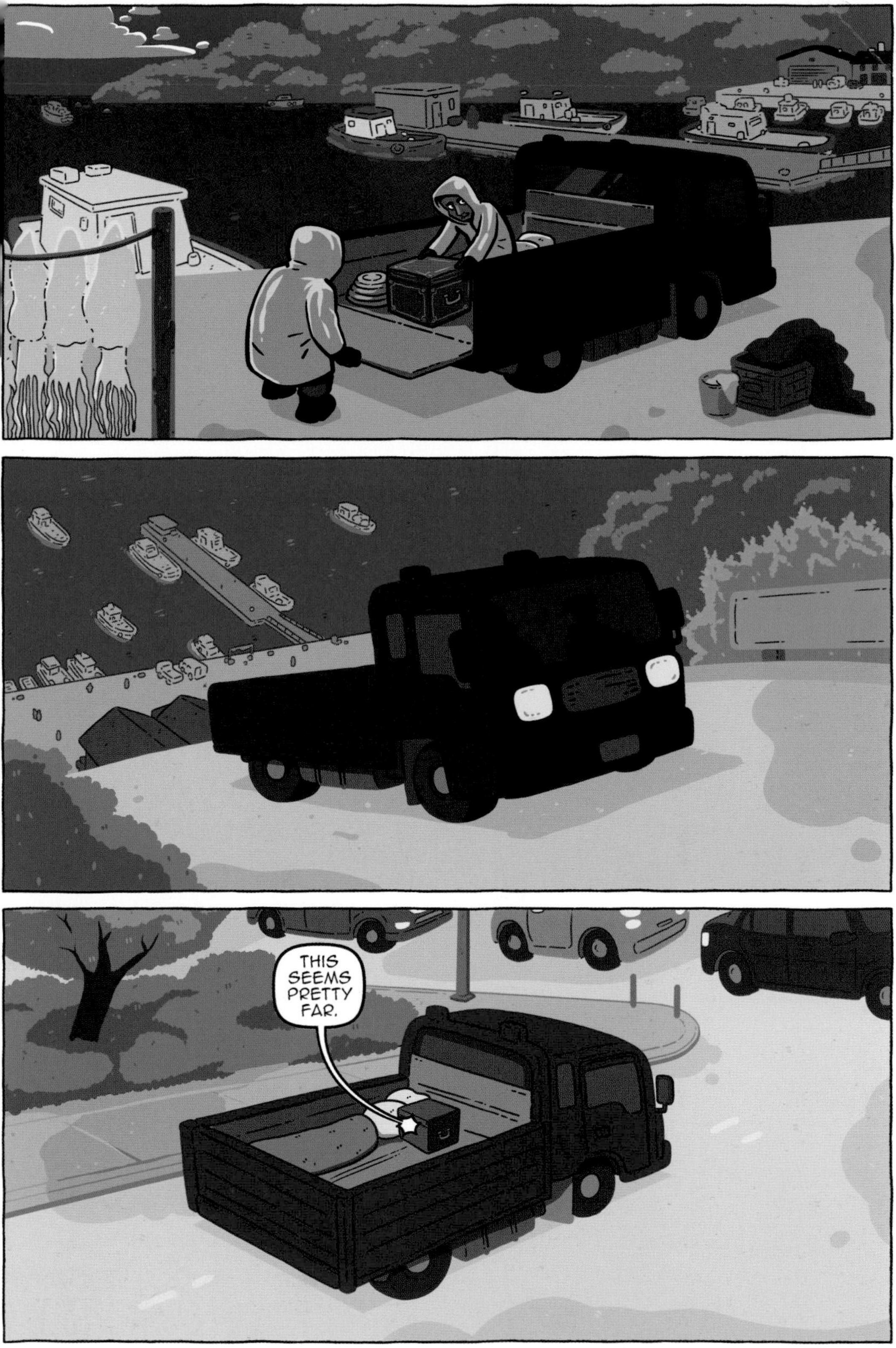
THIS SEEMS PRETTY FAR.

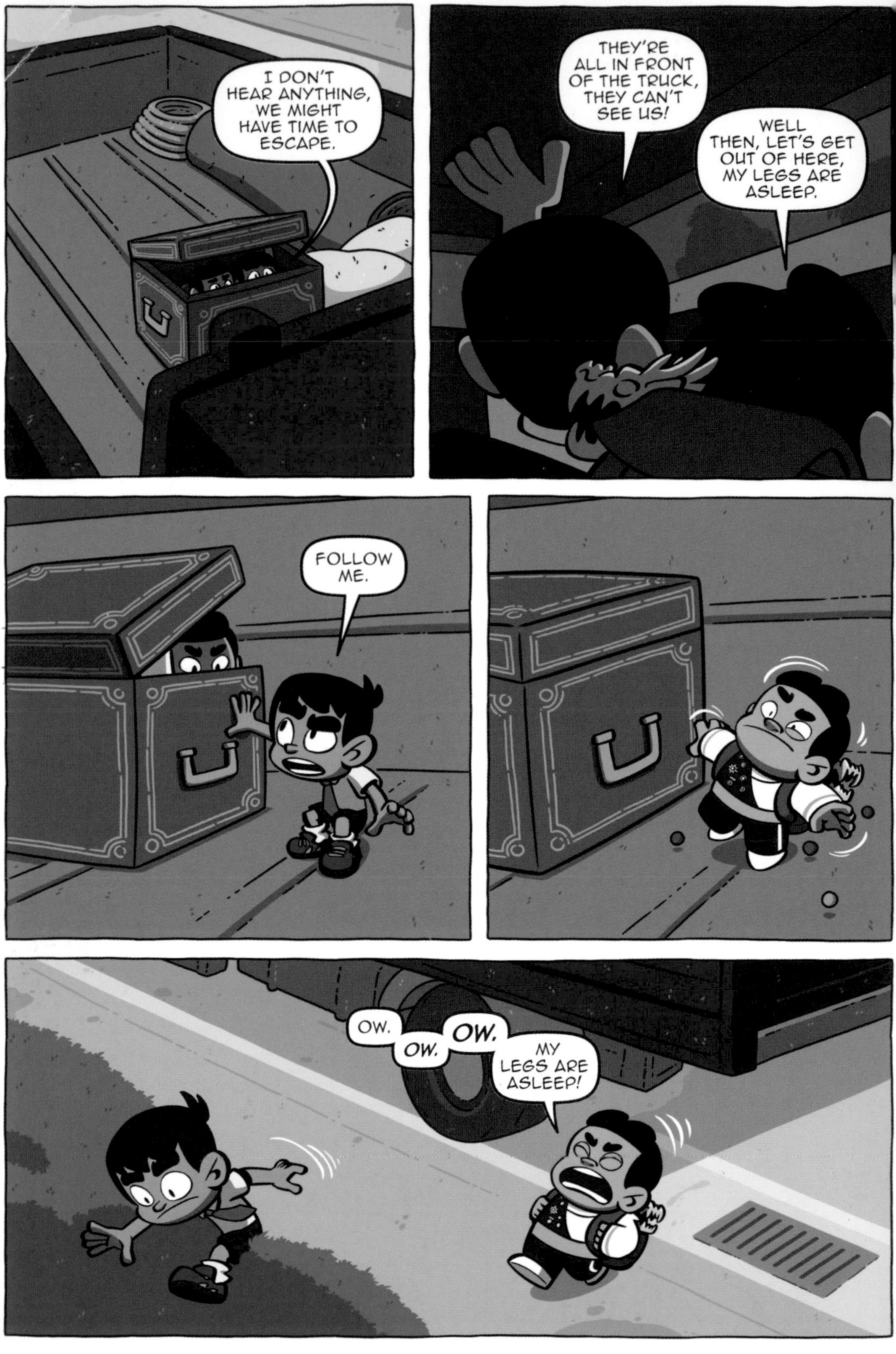
I DON'T HEAR ANYTHING, WE MIGHT HAVE TIME TO ESCAPE.
THEY'RE ALL IN FRONT OF THE TRUCK, THEY CAN'T SEE US!
WELL THEN, LET'S GET OUT OF HERE, MY LEGS ARE ASLEEP.
FOLLOW ME.
OW.
OW.
OW.
MY LEGS ARE ASLEEP!

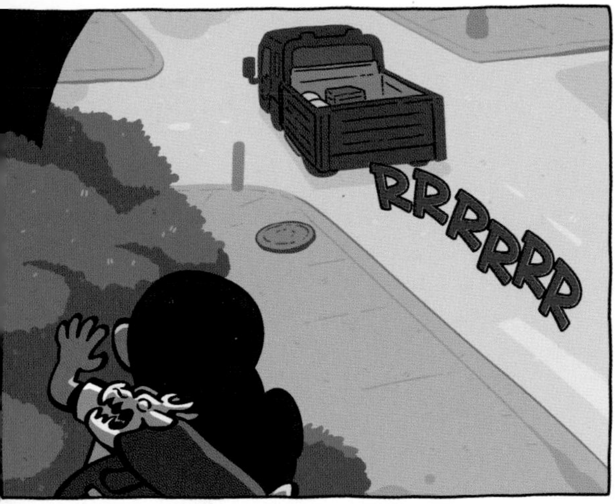
RRRRRRR

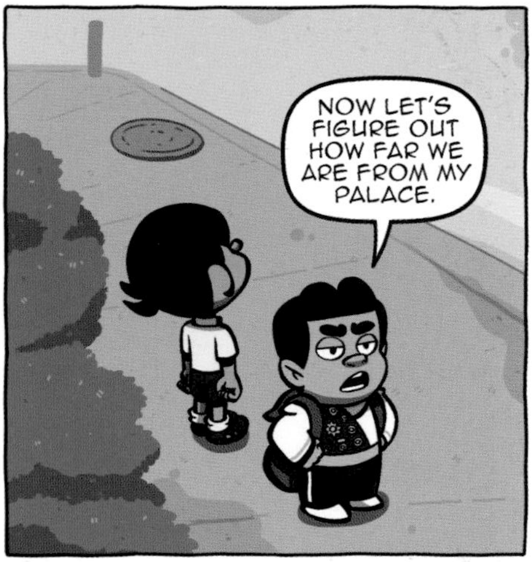
NOW LET'S FIGURE OUT HOW FAR WE ARE FROM MY PALACE.

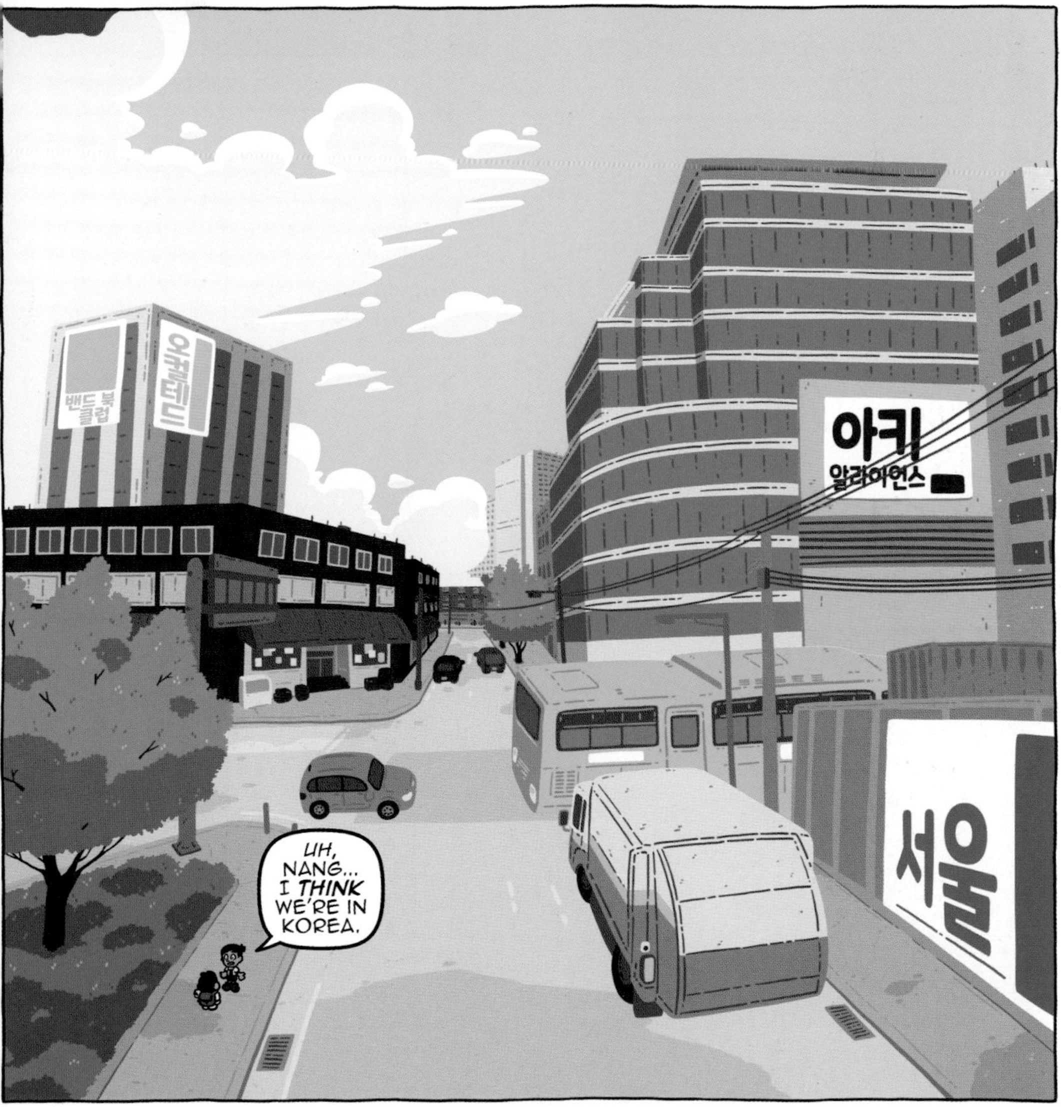
밴드 북 클럽
오컬테드
아키
알라이언스
서울
UH, NANG... I *THINK* WE'RE IN KOREA.

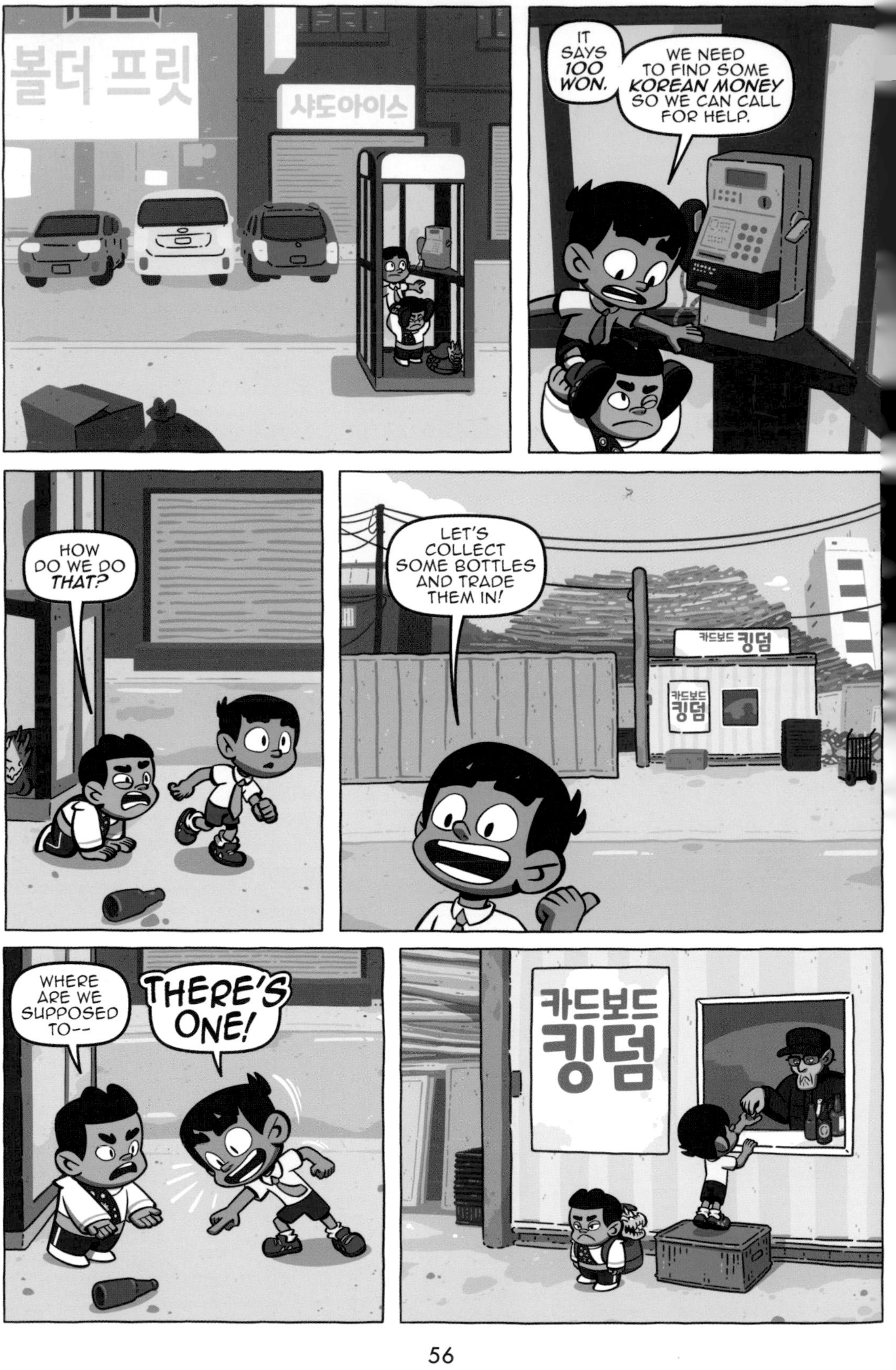
볼더 프릿
샤도아이스
IT SAYS 100 WON.
WE NEED TO FIND SOME KOREAN MONEY SO WE CAN CALL FOR HELP.
HOW DO WE DO THAT?
LET'S COLLECT SOME BOTTLES AND TRADE THEM IN!
카드보드 킹덤
카드보드 킹덤
WHERE ARE WE SUPPOSED TO--
THERE'S ONE!
카드보드 킹덤

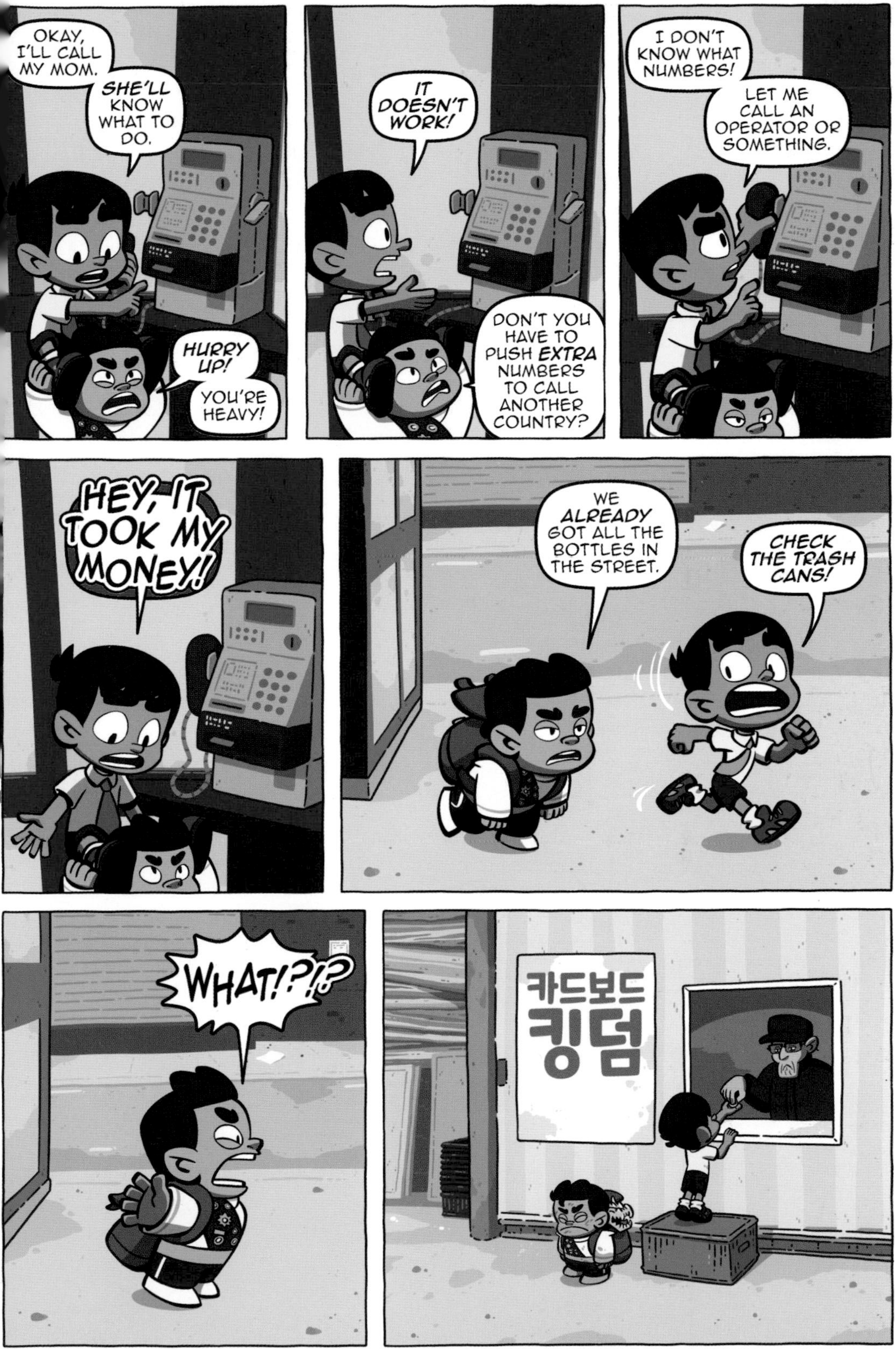
OKAY, I'LL CALL MY MOM.
SHE'LL KNOW WHAT TO DO.
HURRY UP!
YOU'RE HEAVY!
IT DOESN'T WORK!
DON'T YOU HAVE TO PUSH EXTRA NUMBERS TO CALL ANOTHER COUNTRY?
I DON'T KNOW WHAT NUMBERS!
LET ME CALL AN OPERATOR OR SOMETHING.
HEY, IT TOOK MY MONEY!
WE ALREADY GOT ALL THE BOTTLES IN THE STREET.
CHECK THE TRASH CANS!
WHAT!?!?
카드보드
킹덤

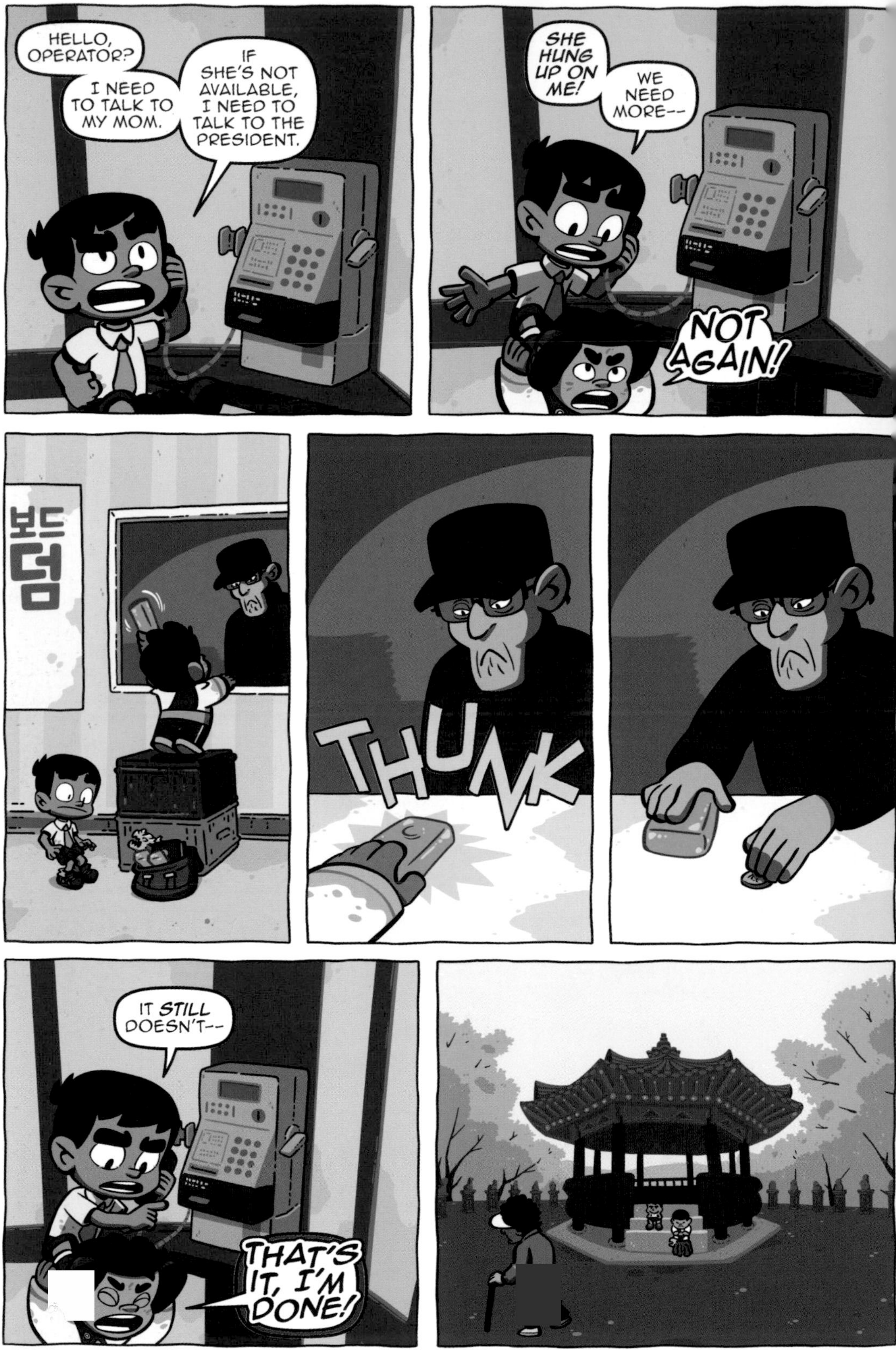

HELLO, OPERATOR?
I NEED TO TALK TO MY MOM.
IF SHE'S NOT AVAILABLE, I NEED TO TALK TO THE PRESIDENT.
SHE HUNG UP ON ME!
WE NEED MORE--
NOT AGAIN!
보드
덤
THUNK
IT STILL DOESN'T--
THAT'S IT, I'M DONE!

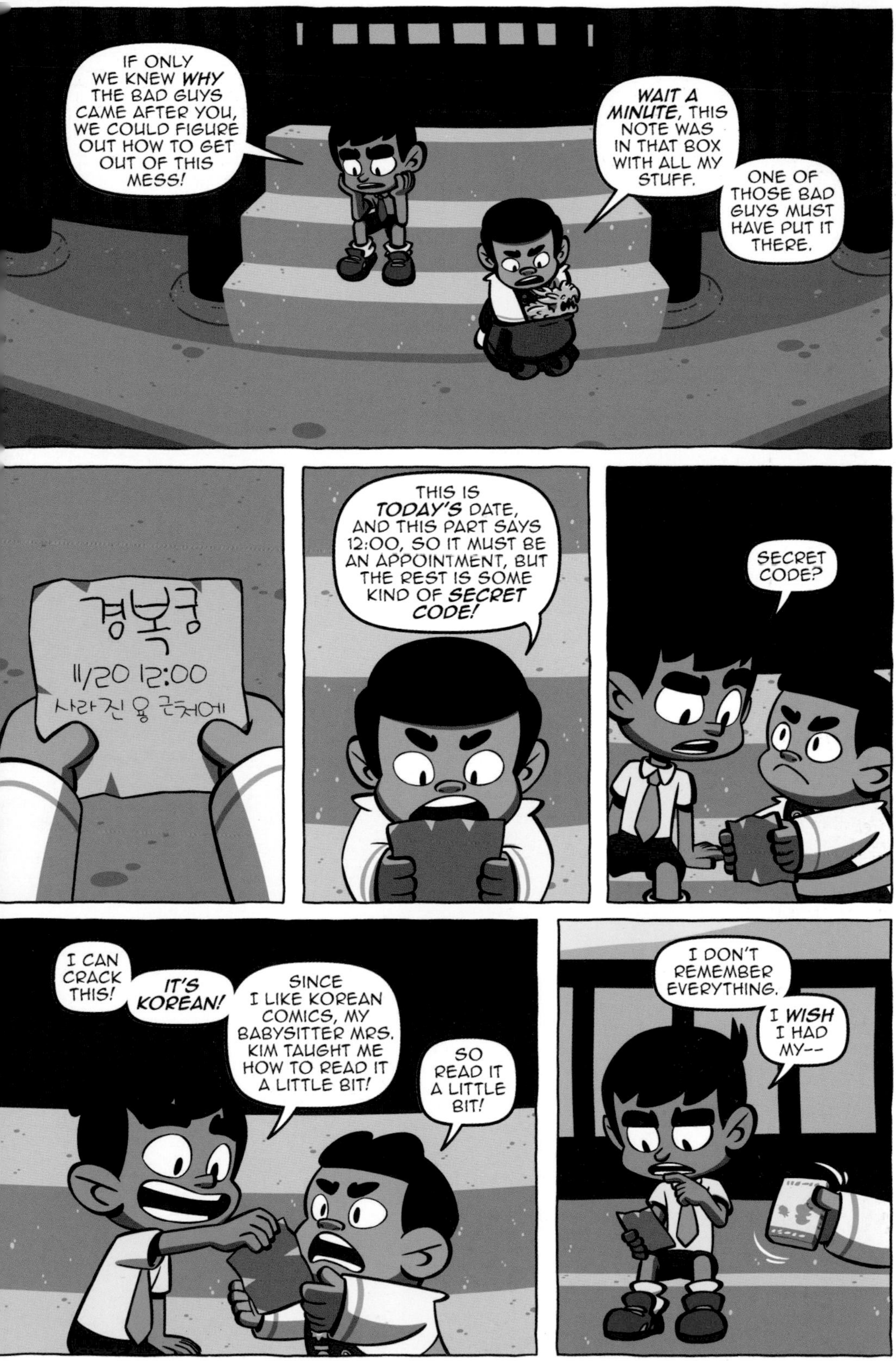
IF ONLY WE KNEW WHY THE BAD GUYS CAME AFTER YOU, WE COULD FIGURE OUT HOW TO GET OUT OF THIS MESS!
WAIT A MINUTE, THIS NOTE WAS IN THAT BOX WITH ALL MY STUFF.
ONE OF THOSE BAD GUYS MUST HAVE PUT IT THERE.
경복궁
11/20 12:00
사라진 용 근처에
THIS IS TODAY'S DATE, AND THIS PART SAYS 12:00, SO IT MUST BE AN APPOINTMENT, BUT THE REST IS SOME KIND OF SECRET CODE!
SECRET CODE?
I CAN CRACK THIS!
IT'S KOREAN!
SINCE I LIKE KOREAN COMICS, MY BABYSITTER MRS. KIM TAUGHT ME HOW TO READ IT A LITTLE BIT!
SO READ IT A LITTLE BIT!
I DON'T REMEMBER EVERYTHING.
I WISH I HAD MY--

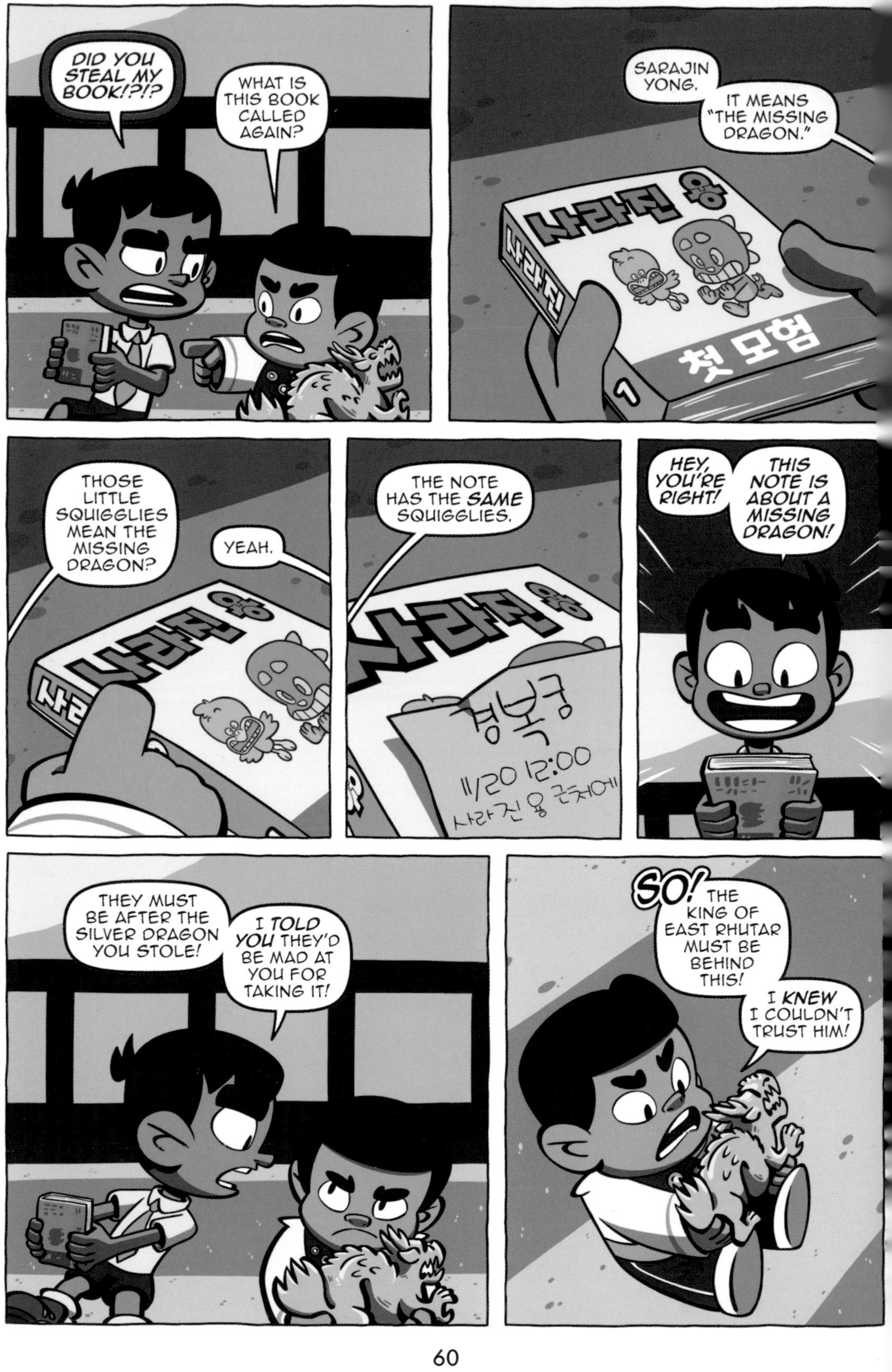
DID YOU STEAL MY BOOK!?!?
WHAT IS THIS BOOK CALLED AGAIN?
SARAJIN YONG.
IT MEANS "THE MISSING DRAGON."
사라진 용
첫 모험
THOSE LITTLE SQUIGGLIES MEAN THE MISSING DRAGON?
YEAH.
THE NOTE HAS THE SAME SQUIGGLIES.
경복궁
11/20 12:00
사라진 용 근처에
HEY, YOU'RE RIGHT!
THIS NOTE IS ABOUT A MISSING DRAGON!
THEY MUST BE AFTER THE SILVER DRAGON YOU STOLE!
I TOLD YOU THEY'D BE MAD AT YOU FOR TAKING IT!
SO! THE KING OF EAST RHUTAR MUST BE BEHIND THIS!
I KNEW I COULDN'T TRUST HIM!

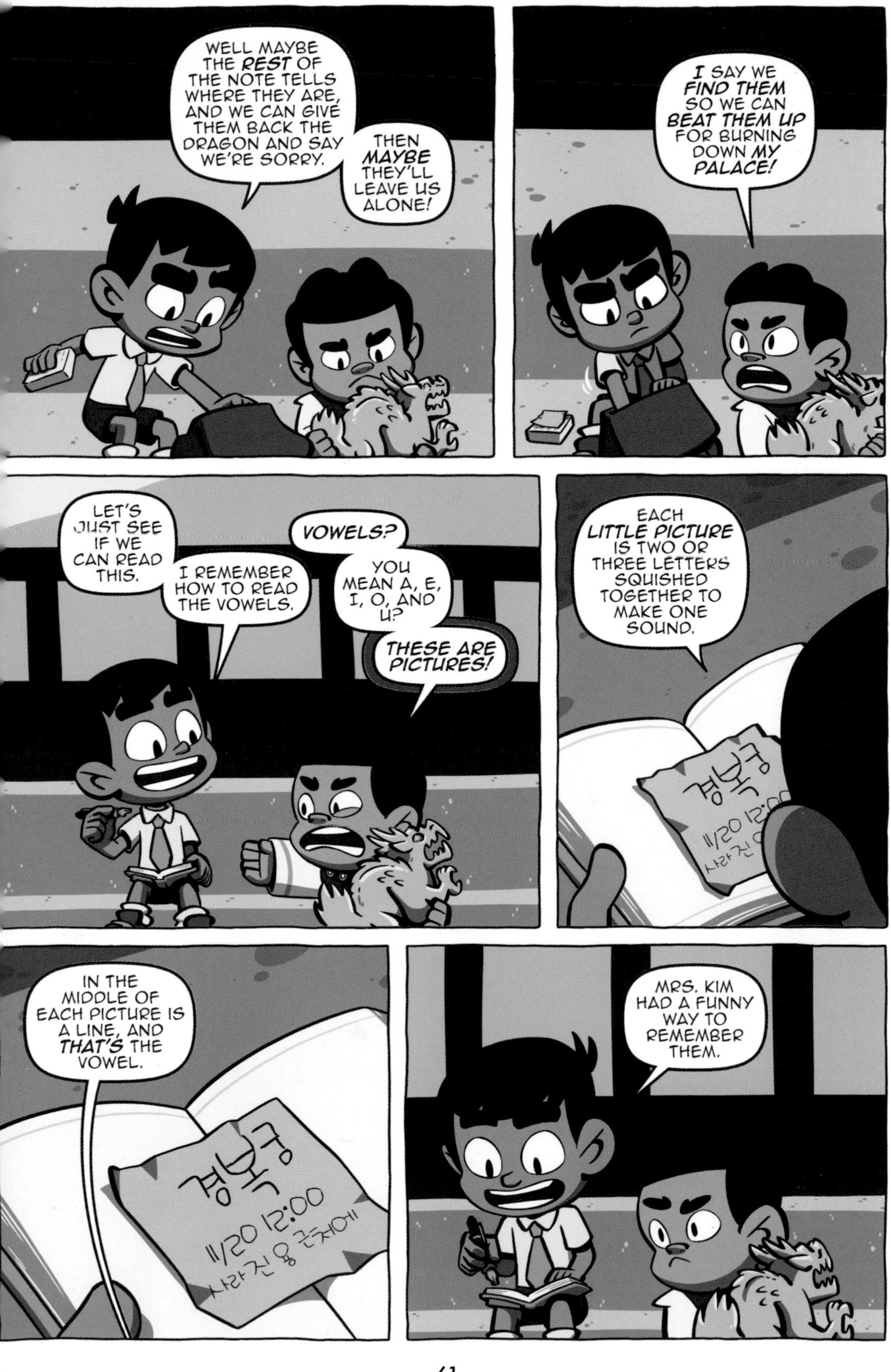
WELL MAYBE THE REST OF THE NOTE TELLS WHERE THEY ARE, AND WE CAN GIVE THEM BACK THE DRAGON AND SAY WE'RE SORRY.
THEN MAYBE THEY'LL LEAVE US ALONE!
I SAY WE FIND THEM SO WE CAN BEAT THEM UP FOR BURNING DOWN MY PALACE!
LET'S JUST SEE IF WE CAN READ THIS.
I REMEMBER HOW TO READ THE VOWELS.
VOWELS?
YOU MEAN A, E, I, O, AND U?
THESE ARE PICTURES!
EACH LITTLE PICTURE IS TWO OR THREE LETTERS SQUISHED TOGETHER TO MAKE ONE SOUND.
IN THE MIDDLE OF EACH PICTURE IS A LINE, AND THAT'S THE VOWEL.
경복궁
11/20 12:00
사라진 용 근처에
MRS. KIM HAD A FUNNY WAY TO REMEMBER THEM.

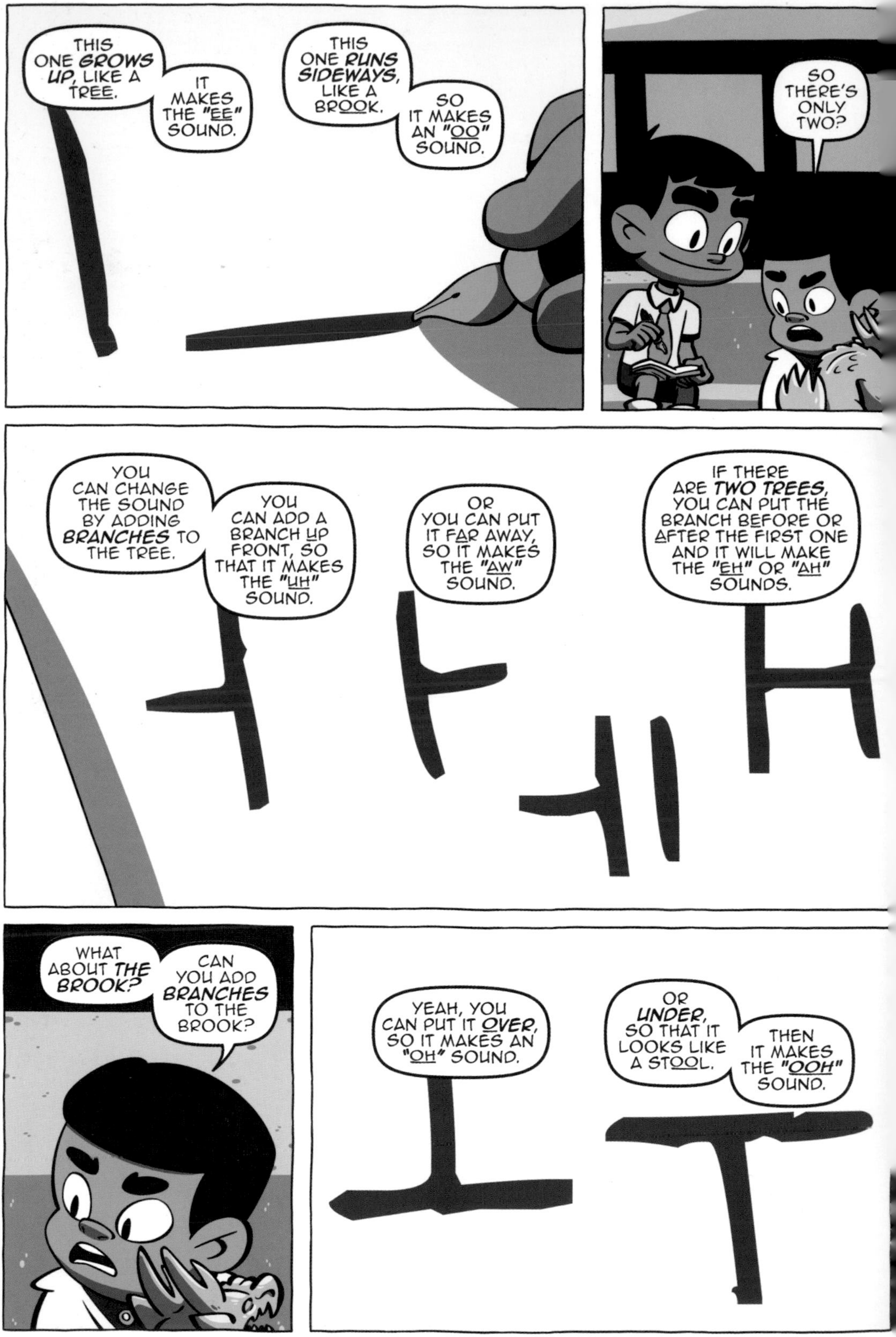
THIS ONE GROWS UP, LIKE A TREE.
IT MAKES THE "EE" SOUND.
THIS ONE RUNS SIDEWAYS, LIKE A BROOK.
SO IT MAKES AN "OO" SOUND.
SO THERE'S ONLY TWO?
YOU CAN CHANGE THE SOUND BY ADDING BRANCHES TO THE TREE.
YOU CAN ADD A BRANCH UP FRONT, SO THAT IT MAKES THE "UH" SOUND.
OR YOU CAN PUT IT FAR AWAY, SO IT MAKES THE "AW" SOUND.
IF THERE ARE TWO TREES, YOU CAN PUT THE BRANCH BEFORE OR AFTER THE FIRST ONE AND IT WILL MAKE THE "EH" OR "AH" SOUNDS.
WHAT ABOUT THE BROOK?
CAN YOU ADD BRANCHES TO THE BROOK?
YEAH, YOU CAN PUT IT OVER, SO IT MAKES AN "OH" SOUND.
OR UNDER, SO THAT IT LOOKS LIKE A STOOL.
THEN IT MAKES THE "OOH" SOUND.

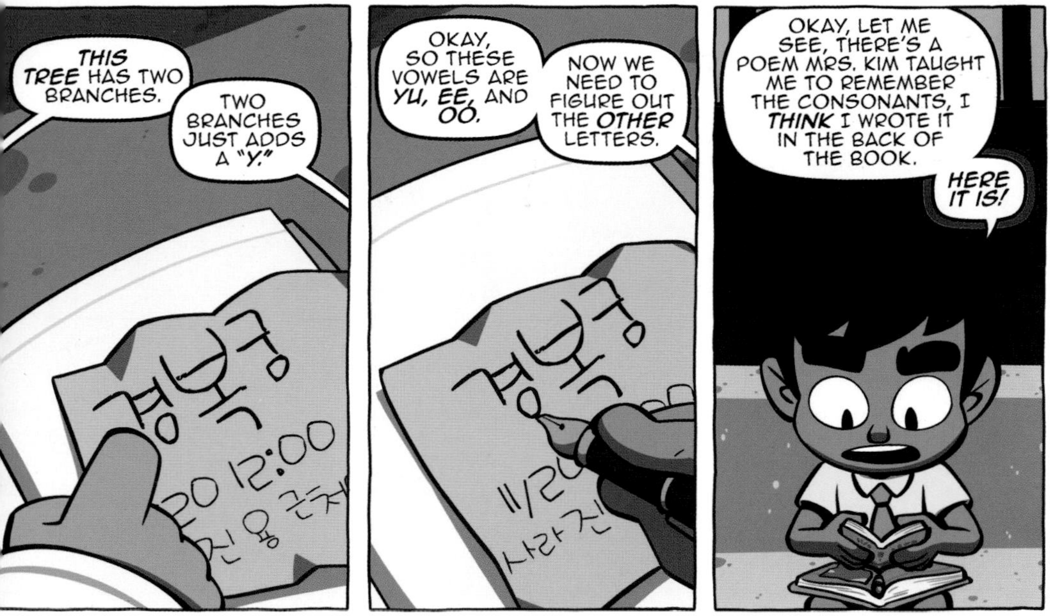
THIS TREE HAS TWO BRANCHES.
TWO BRANCHES JUST ADDS A "Y."
OKAY, SO THESE VOWELS ARE YU, EE, AND OO.
NOW WE NEED TO FIGURE OUT THE OTHER LETTERS.
OKAY, LET ME SEE, THERE'S A POEM MRS. KIM TAUGHT ME TO REMEMBER THE CONSONANTS, I THINK I WROTE IT IN THE BACK OF THE BOOK.
HERE IT IS!

ㅂ LOOKS LIKE A BUCKET, SO IT'S THE SAME AS B.

ㅍ MEANS PART TWO, SO IT'S THE SAME AS P.

ㄱ LOOKS LIKE A GUN, AND SO IT EQUALS G.

ㄷ LOOKS LIKE A DESK, AND SO IT EQUALS D.

ㅁ 'S SHAPED LIKE A MAP, SO IT SOUNDS LIKE M.

ㄴ LOOKS LIKE A NOSE, SO IT SOUNDS LIKE N.

ㄹ IS R FOR RUNNER UP BECAUSE IT LOOKS LIKE A TWO.

ㅅ IS LIKE A SLICE OF PIZZA. THAT S IS YOUR CLUE!

ㅇ CAN BE CALLED NOTHING. LIKE A ZERO, IT'S ROUND.

AT THE END, IT MAKES NG.

AT THE START, IT MAKES NO SOUND.

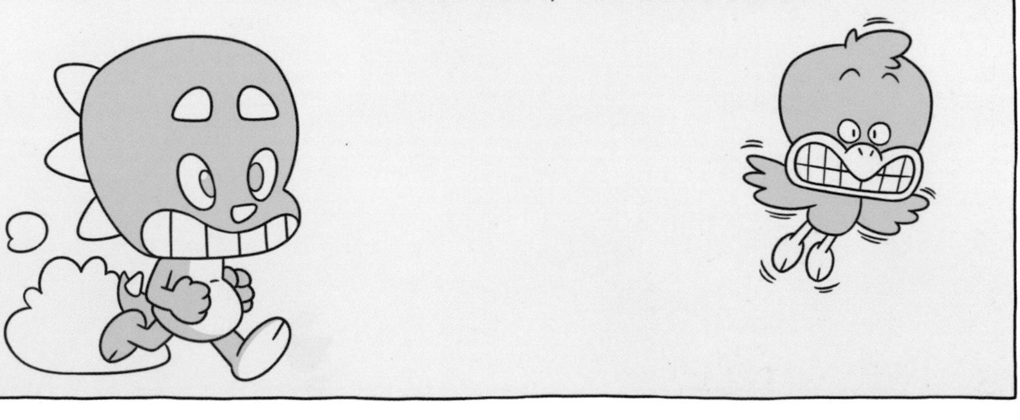

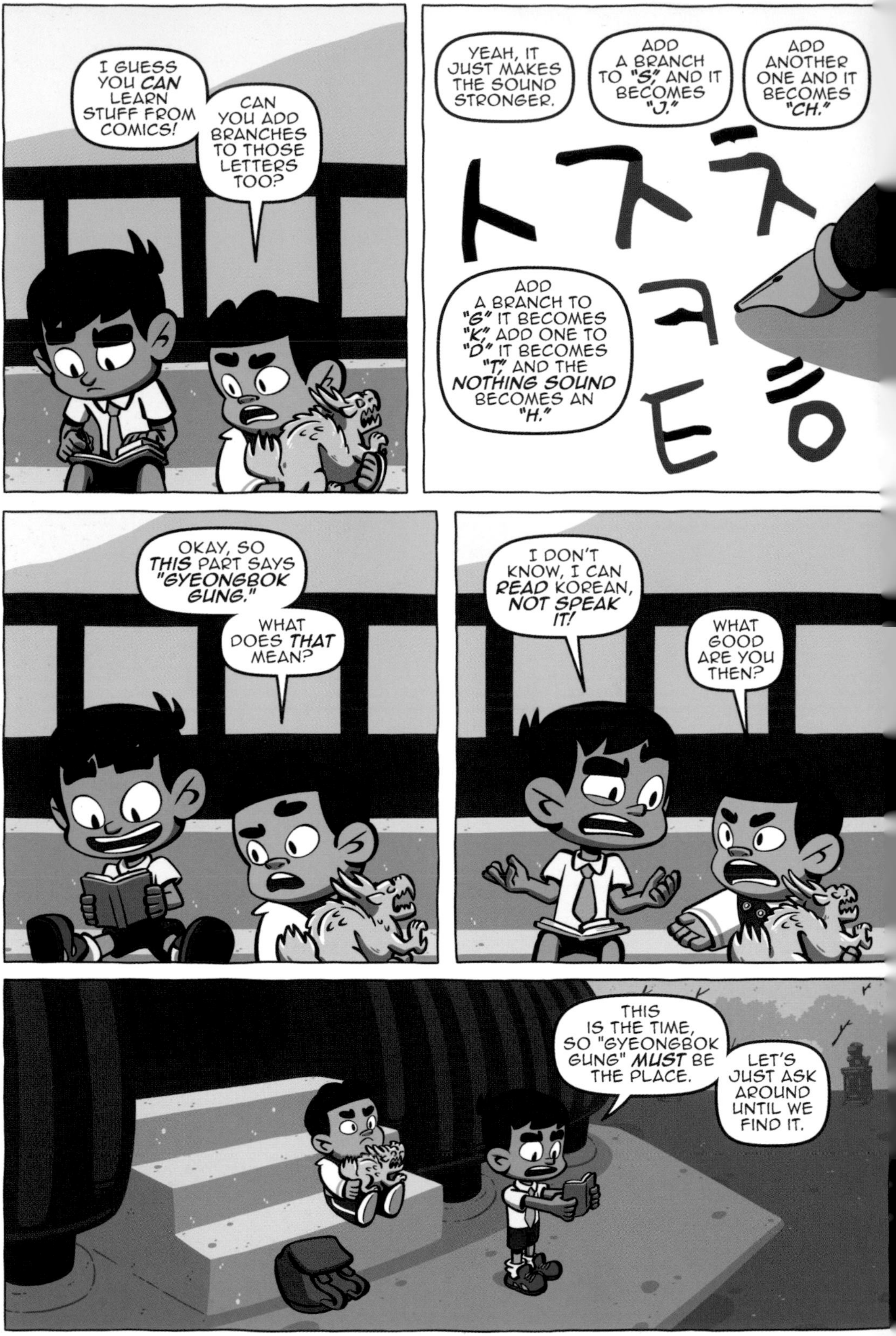
I GUESS YOU CAN LEARN STUFF FROM COMICS!
CAN YOU ADD BRANCHES TO THOSE LETTERS TOO?
YEAH, IT JUST MAKES THE SOUND STRONGER.
ADD A BRANCH TO "S," AND IT BECOMES "J."
ADD ANOTHER ONE AND IT BECOMES "CH."
ㅅ ㅈ ㅊ
ADD A BRANCH TO "G" IT BECOMES "K," ADD ONE TO "D" IT BECOMES "T," AND THE NOTHING SOUND BECOMES AN "H."
ㅋ ㅌ ㅎ
OKAY, SO THIS PART SAYS "GYEONGBOK GUNG."
WHAT DOES THAT MEAN?
I DON'T KNOW, I CAN READ KOREAN, NOT SPEAK IT!
WHAT GOOD ARE YOU THEN?
THIS IS THE TIME, SO "GYEONGBOK GUNG" MUST BE THE PLACE.
LET'S JUST ASK AROUND UNTIL WE FIND IT.

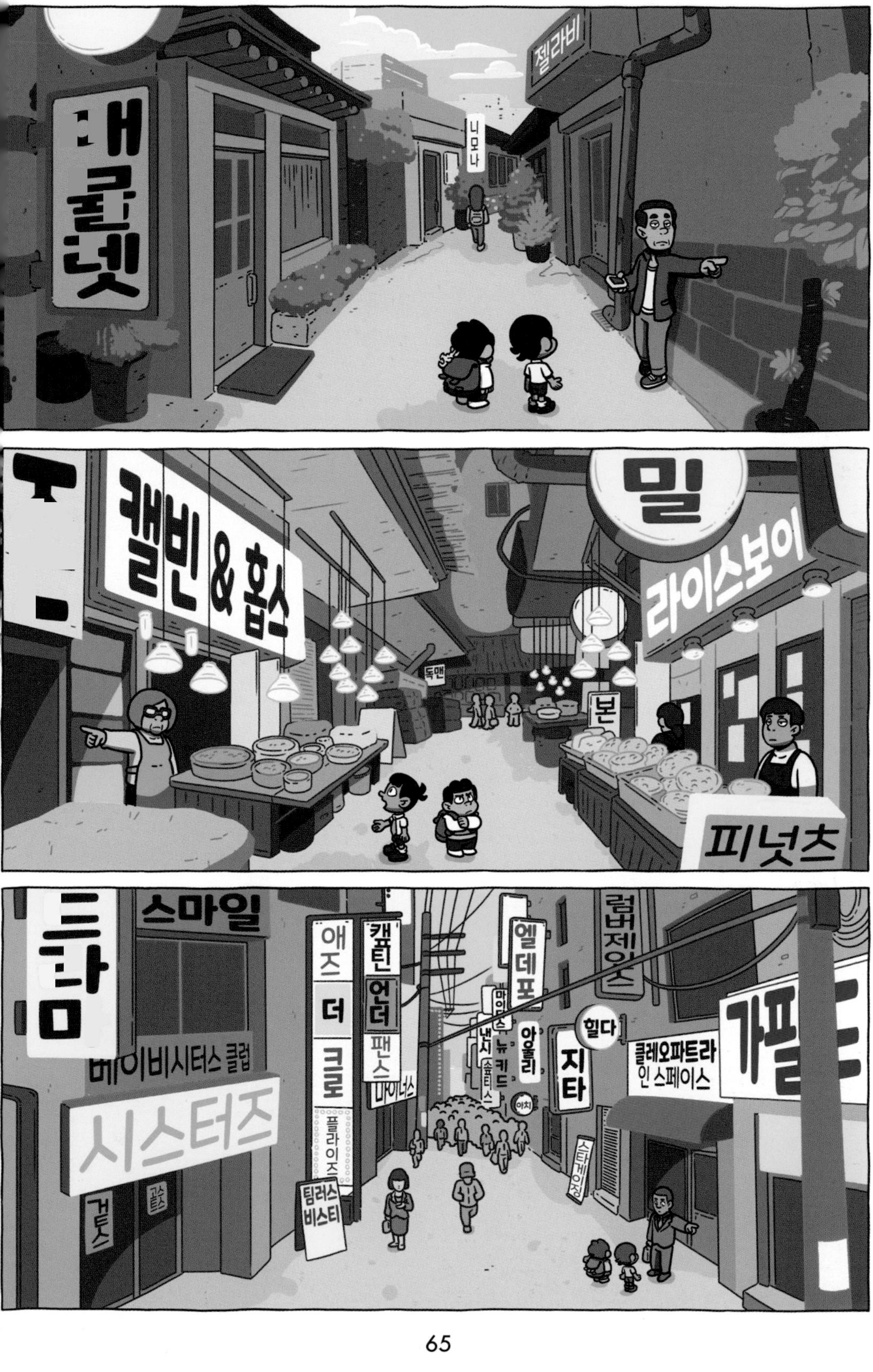
젤라비
니모나
캘빈 & 홉스
밀
라이스보이
독맨
본
피넛츠
스마일
베이비시터스 클럽
시스터즈
애즈 더 크로
캡틴 언더팬스
마이너스
플라이즈
팀러스 비스티
엘데포
낸시
뉴 키드
아울리
아치
힐다
지타
스타게이징
럼버제인스
클레오파트라 인 스페이스
가필드

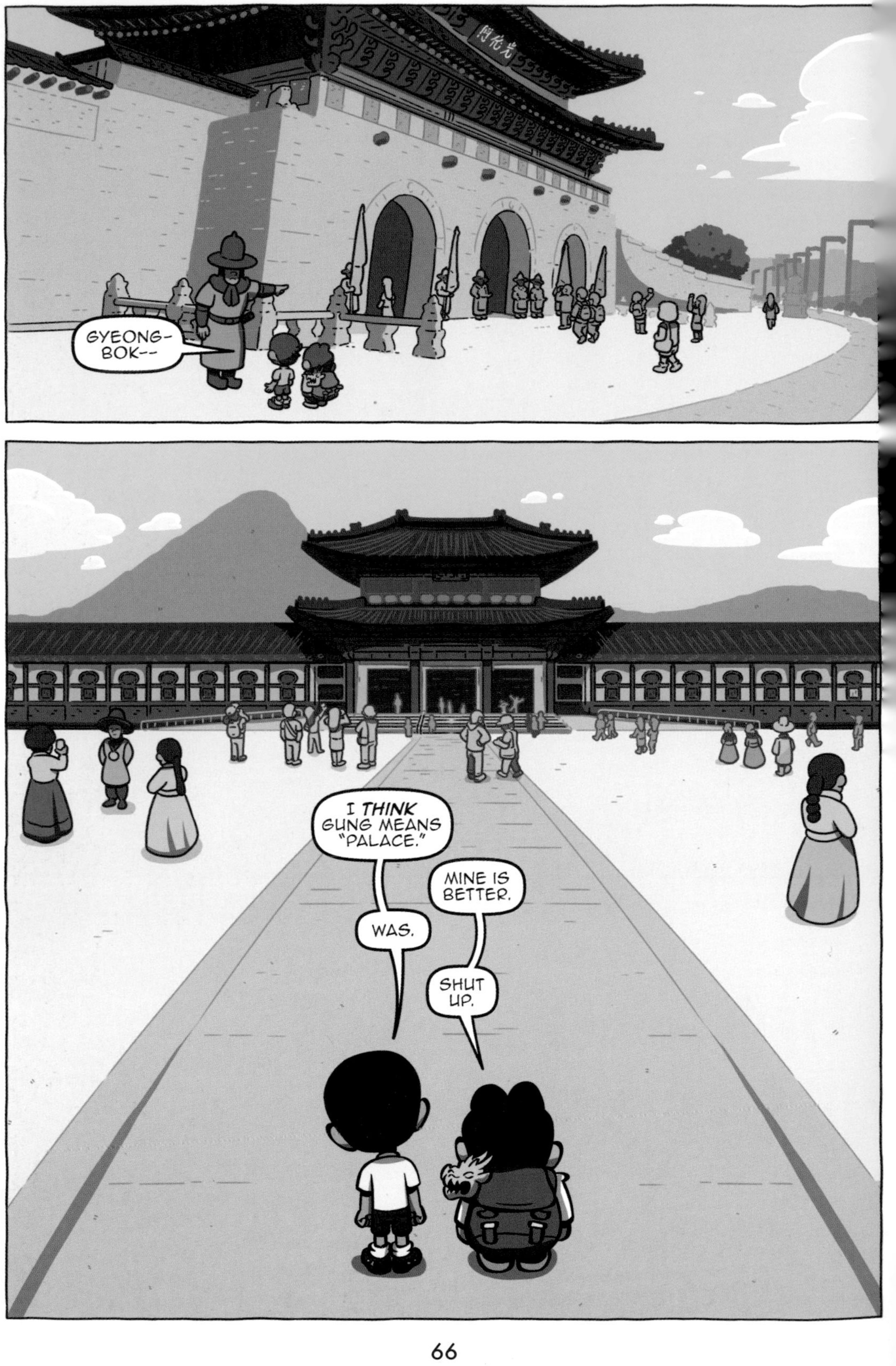
GYEONG-BOK--
I THINK GUNG MEANS "PALACE."
WAS.
MINE IS BETTER.
SHUT UP.

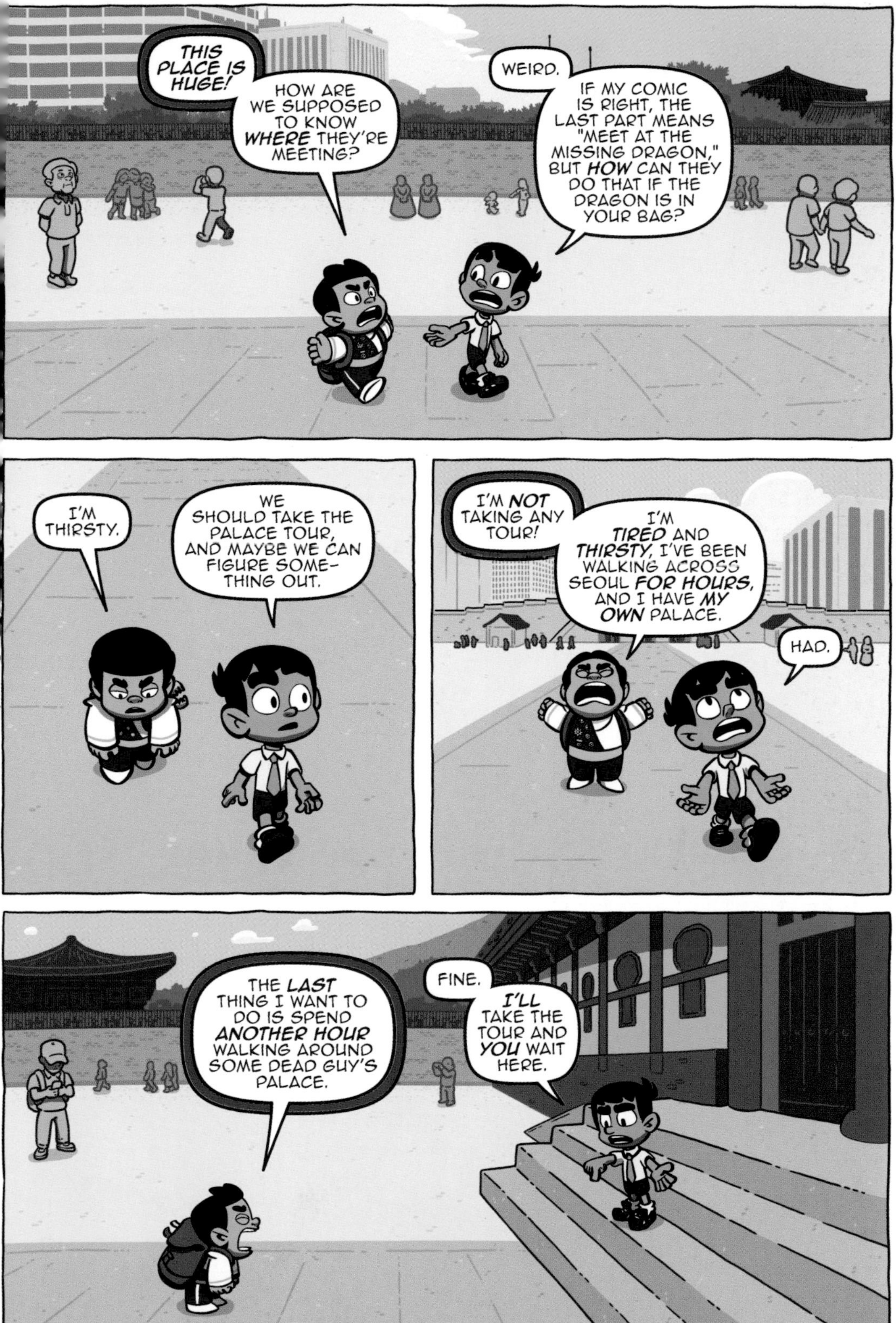

THIS PLACE IS HUGE!
HOW ARE WE SUPPOSED TO KNOW WHERE THEY'RE MEETING?
WEIRD.
IF MY COMIC IS RIGHT, THE LAST PART MEANS "MEET AT THE MISSING DRAGON," BUT HOW CAN THEY DO THAT IF THE DRAGON IS IN YOUR BAG?
I'M THIRSTY.
WE SHOULD TAKE THE PALACE TOUR, AND MAYBE WE CAN FIGURE SOMETHING OUT.
I'M NOT TAKING ANY TOUR!
I'M TIRED AND THIRSTY, I'VE BEEN WALKING ACROSS SEOUL FOR HOURS, AND I HAVE MY OWN PALACE.
HAD.
THE LAST THING I WANT TO DO IS SPEND ANOTHER HOUR WALKING AROUND SOME DEAD GUY'S PALACE.
FINE.
I'LL TAKE THE TOUR AND YOU WAIT HERE.

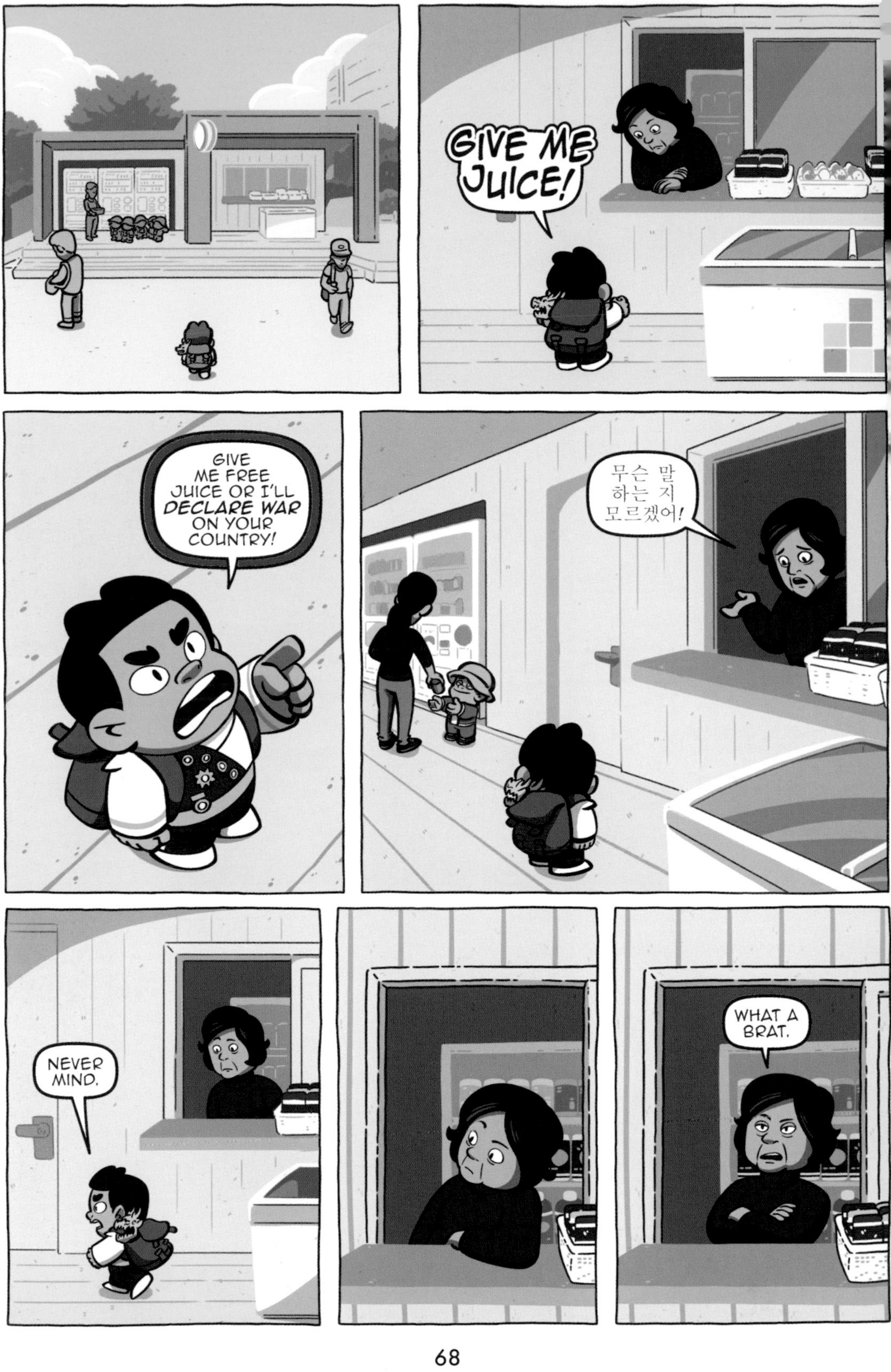
GIVE ME JUICE!
GIVE ME FREE JUICE OR I'LL DECLARE WAR ON YOUR COUNTRY!
무슨 말 하는 지 모르겠어!
NEVER MIND.
WHAT A BRAT.

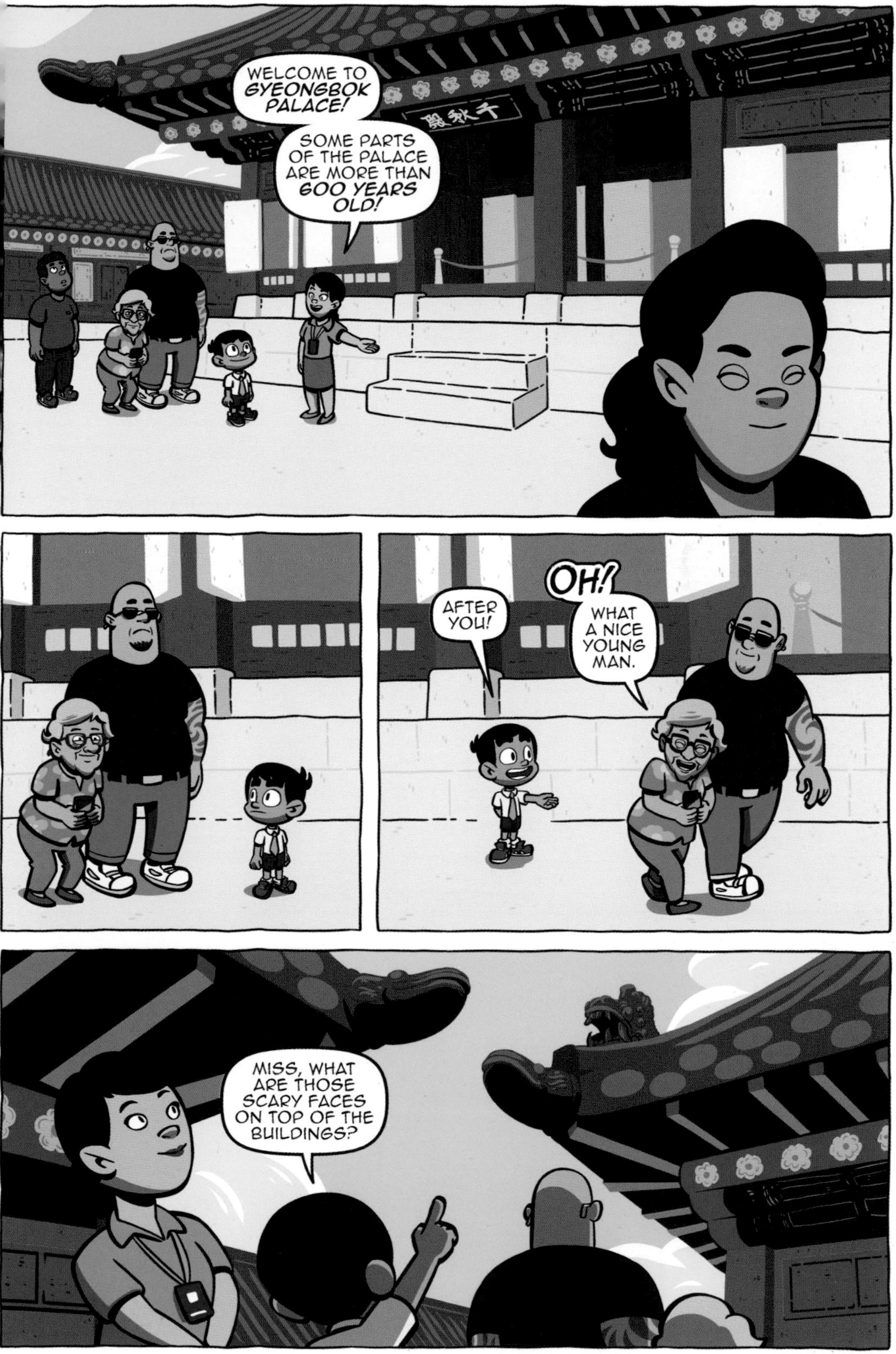
WELCOME TO GYEONGBOK PALACE!
SOME PARTS OF THE PALACE ARE MORE THAN 600 YEARS OLD!
AFTER YOU!
OH!
WHAT A NICE YOUNG MAN.
MISS, WHAT ARE THOSE SCARY FACES ON TOP OF THE BUILDINGS?

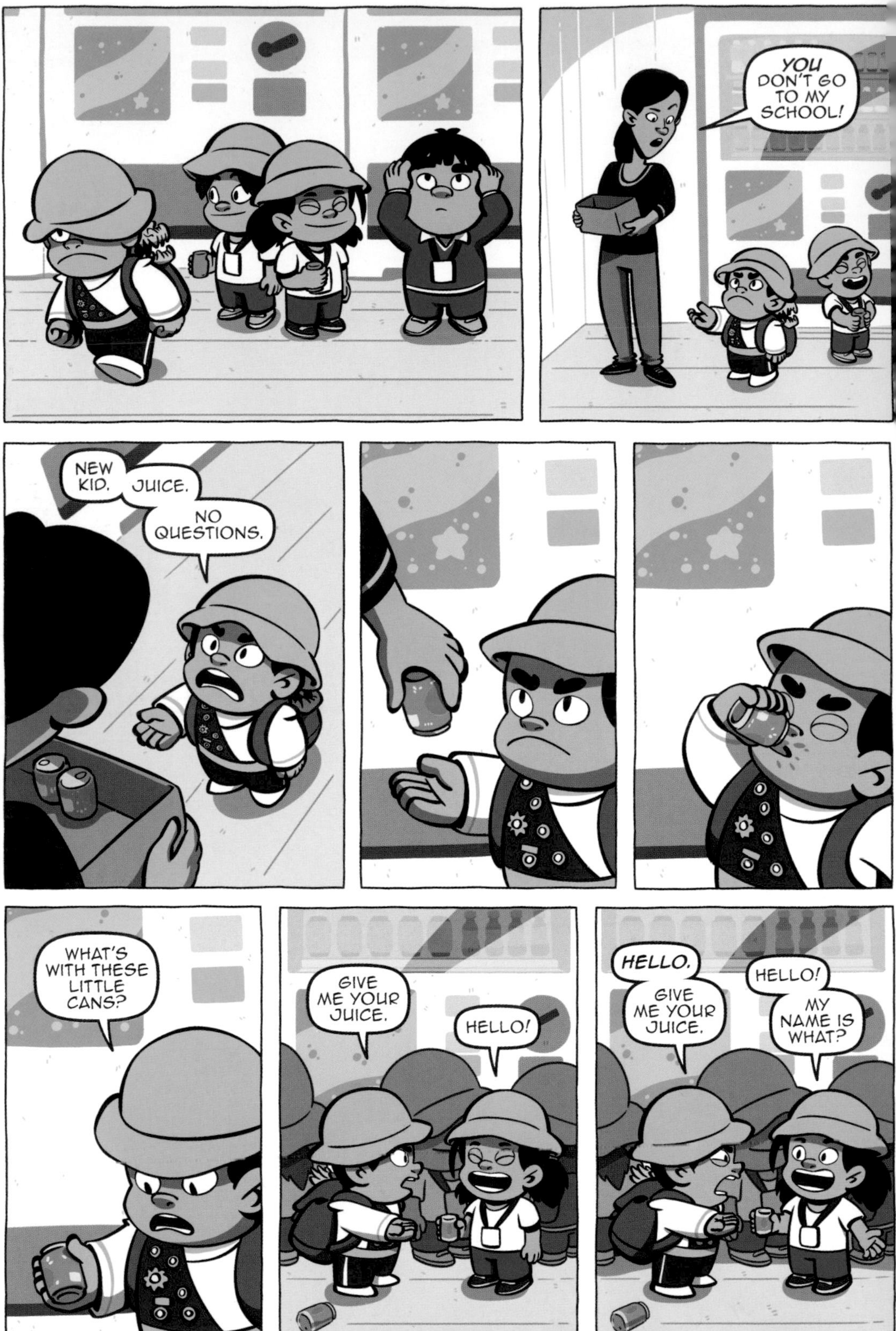
YOU DON'T GO TO MY SCHOOL!
NEW KID.
JUICE.
NO QUESTIONS.
WHAT'S WITH THESE LITTLE CANS?
GIVE ME YOUR JUICE.
HELLO!
HELLO.
GIVE ME YOUR JUICE.
HELLO!
MY NAME IS WHAT?

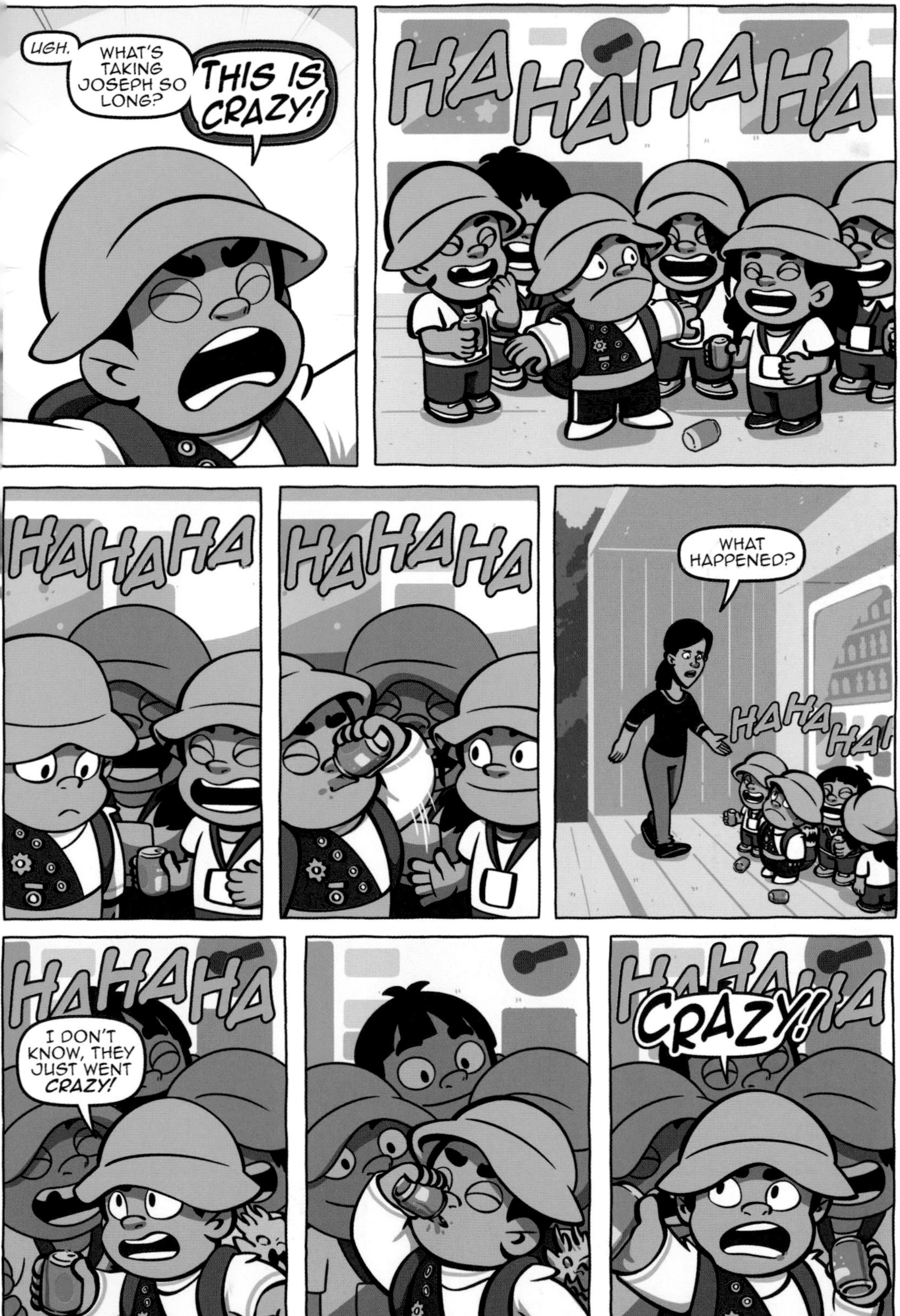
UGH.
WHAT'S TAKING JOSEPH SO LONG?
THIS IS CRAZY!
HAHAHAHAHA
HAHAHA
HAHAHA
WHAT HAPPENED?
HAHAHAHA!
HAHAHA
I DON'T KNOW, THEY JUST WENT CRAZY!
CRAZY!

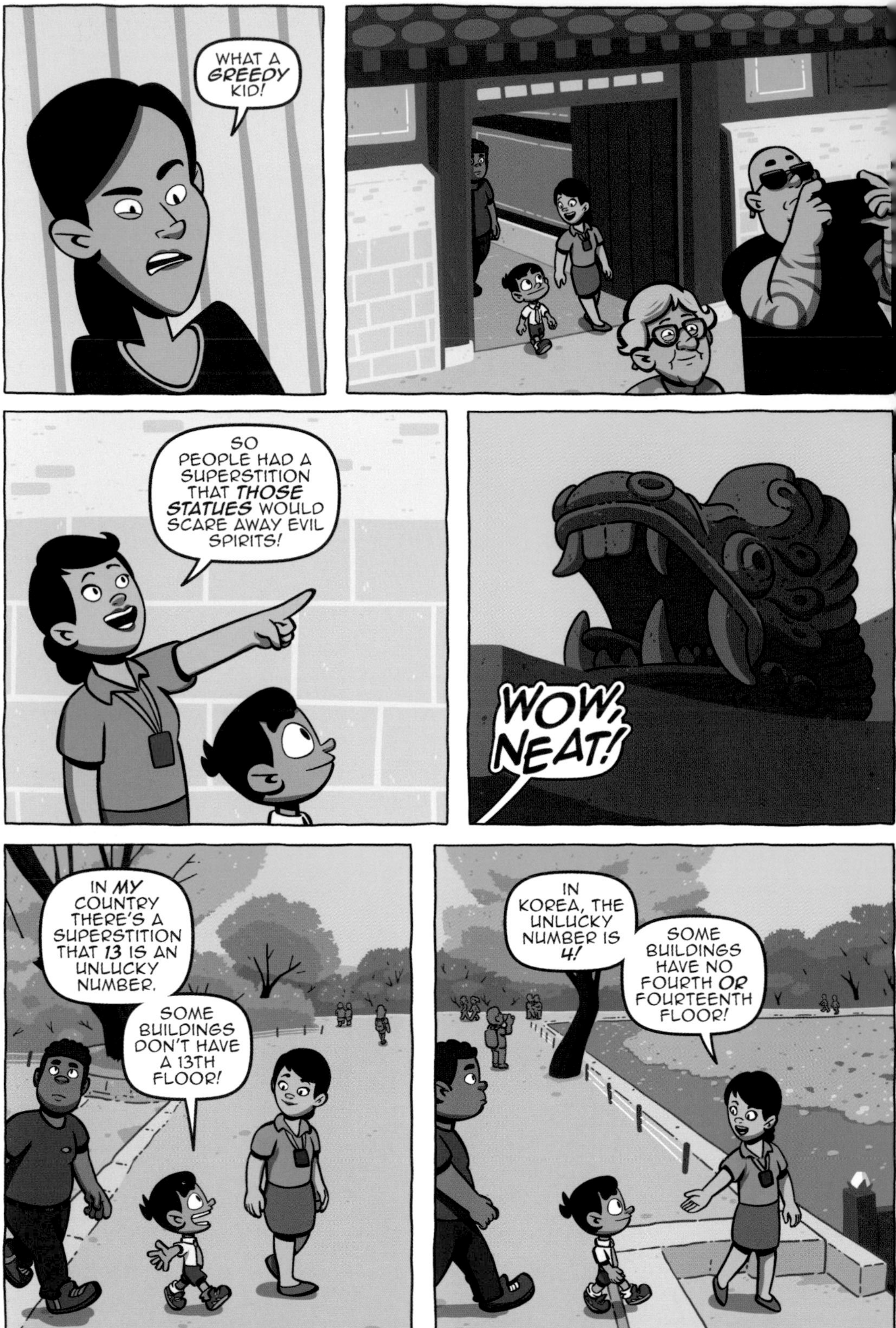
WHAT A GREEDY KID!
SO PEOPLE HAD A SUPERSTITION THAT THOSE STATUES WOULD SCARE AWAY EVIL SPIRITS!
WOW, NEAT!
IN MY COUNTRY THERE'S A SUPERSTITION THAT 13 IS AN UNLUCKY NUMBER.
SOME BUILDINGS DON'T HAVE A 13TH FLOOR!
IN KOREA, THE UNLUCKY NUMBER IS 4!
SOME BUILDINGS HAVE NO FOURTH OR FOURTEENTH FLOOR!

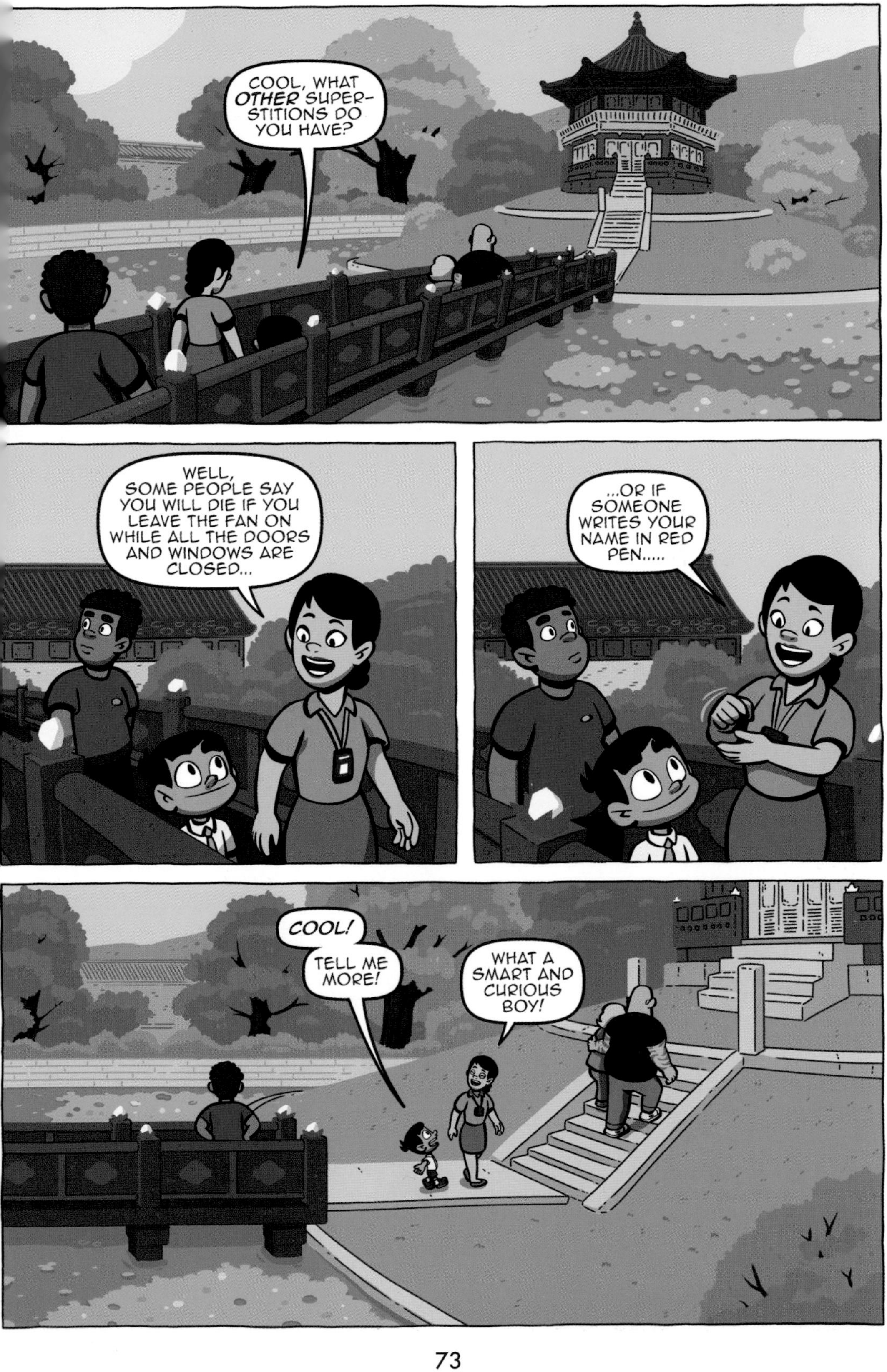
COOL, WHAT OTHER SUPER-STITIONS DO YOU HAVE?
WELL, SOME PEOPLE SAY YOU WILL DIE IF YOU LEAVE THE FAN ON WHILE ALL THE DOORS AND WINDOWS ARE CLOSED...
...OR IF SOMEONE WRITES YOUR NAME IN RED PEN.....
COOL!
TELL ME MORE!
WHAT A SMART AND CURIOUS BOY!

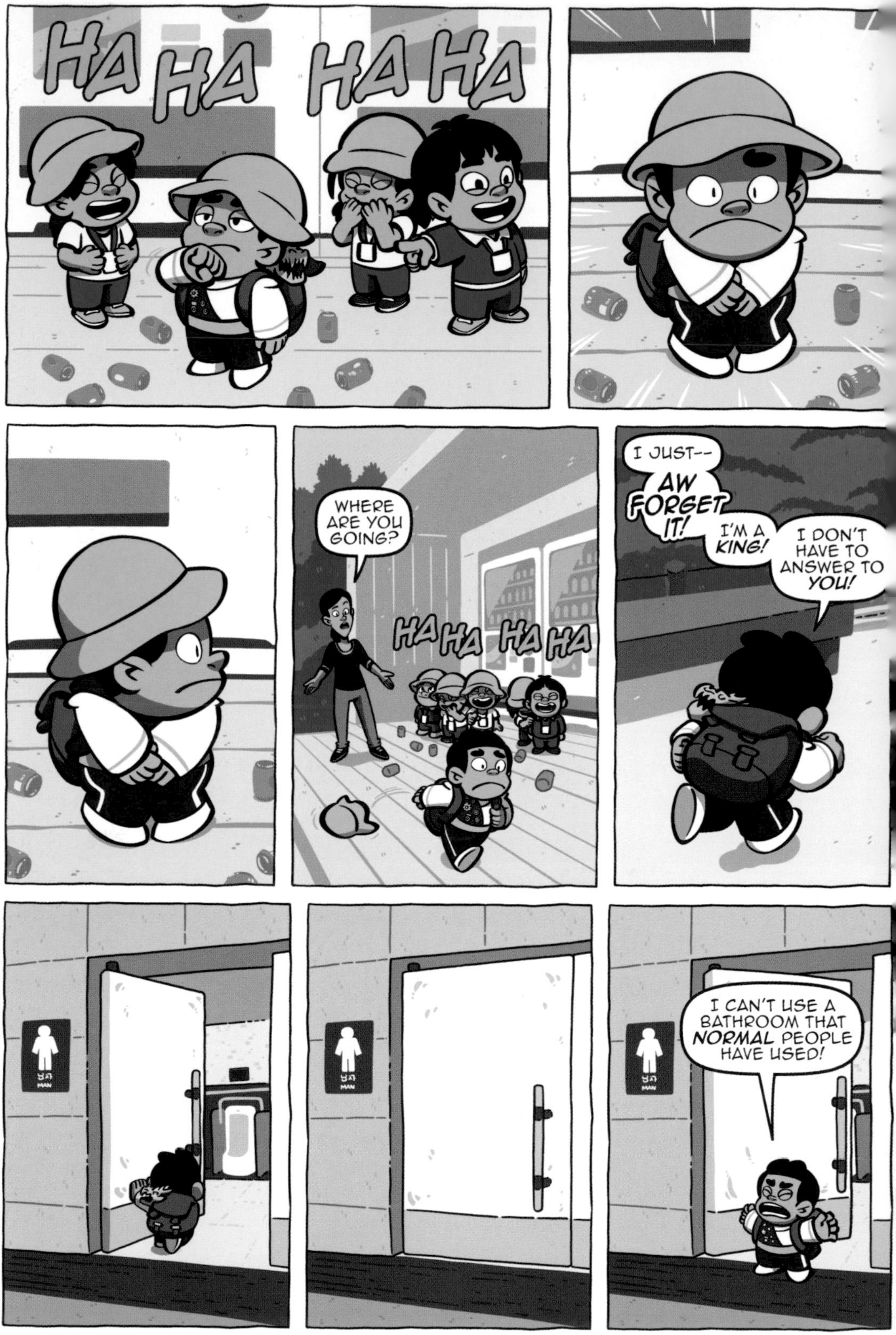
HA HA HA HA
WHERE ARE YOU GOING?
HA HA HA HA
I JUST--
AW FORGET IT!
I'M A KING!
I DON'T HAVE TO ANSWER TO YOU!
I CAN'T USE A BATHROOM THAT NORMAL PEOPLE HAVE USED!

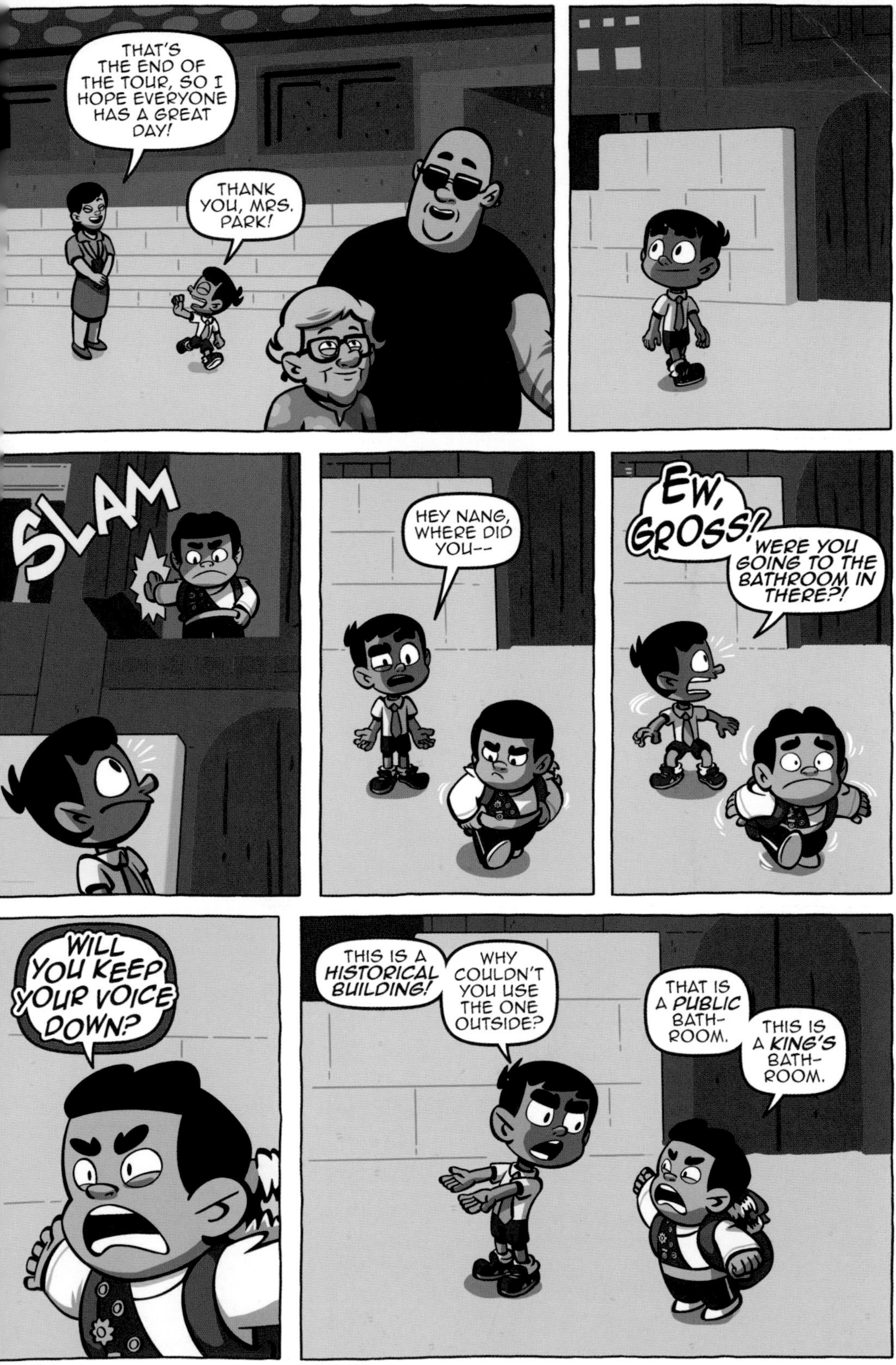
THAT'S THE END OF THE TOUR, SO I HOPE EVERYONE HAS A GREAT DAY!
THANK YOU, MRS. PARK!
SLAM
HEY NANG, WHERE DID YOU--
EW, GROSS!
WERE YOU GOING TO THE BATHROOM IN THERE?!
WILL YOU KEEP YOUR VOICE DOWN?
THIS IS A HISTORICAL BUILDING!
WHY COULDN'T YOU USE THE ONE OUTSIDE?
THAT IS A PUBLIC BATH-ROOM.
THIS IS A KING'S BATH-ROOM.

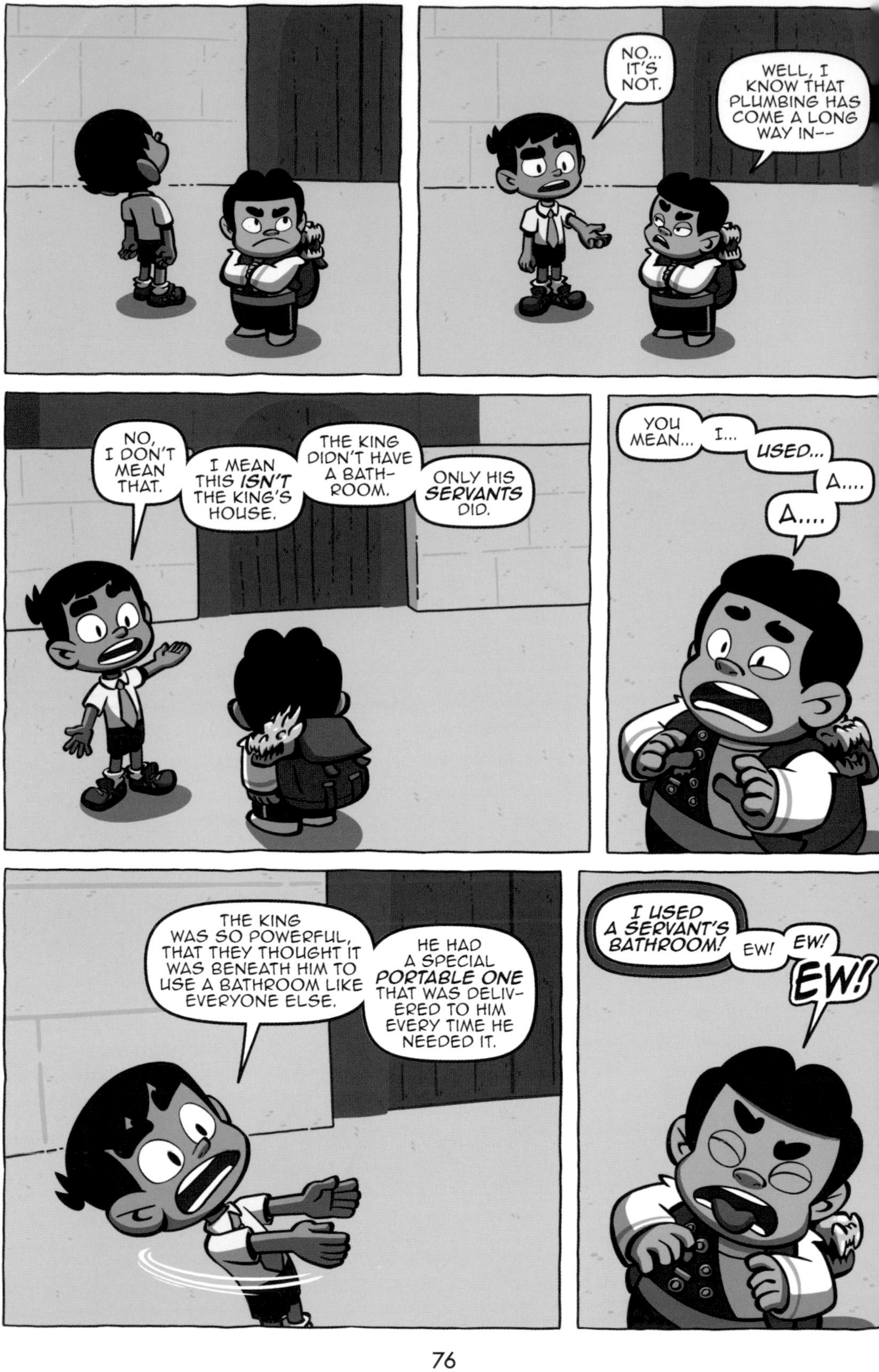
NO... IT'S NOT.
WELL, I KNOW THAT PLUMBING HAS COME A LONG WAY IN--
NO, I DON'T MEAN THAT.
I MEAN THIS ISN'T THE KING'S HOUSE.
THE KING DIDN'T HAVE A BATH-ROOM.
ONLY HIS SERVANTS DID.
YOU MEAN...
I...
USED...
A....
A....
THE KING WAS SO POWERFUL, THAT THEY THOUGHT IT WAS BENEATH HIM TO USE A BATHROOM LIKE EVERYONE ELSE.
HE HAD A SPECIAL PORTABLE ONE THAT WAS DELIV-ERED TO HIM EVERY TIME HE NEEDED IT.
I USED A SERVANT'S BATHROOM!
EW!
EW!
EW!

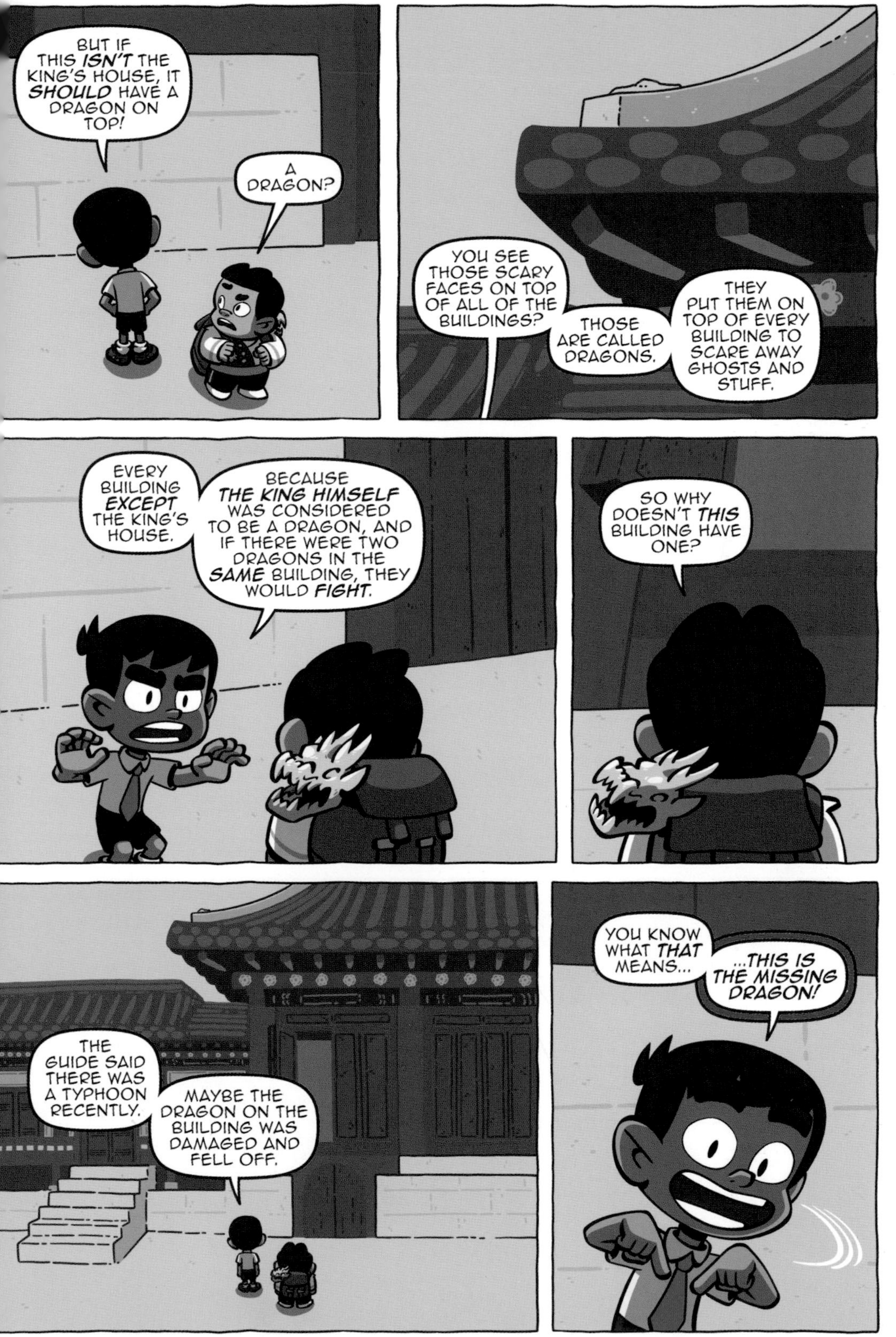
BUT IF THIS ISN'T THE KING'S HOUSE, IT SHOULD HAVE A DRAGON ON TOP!
A DRAGON?
YOU SEE THOSE SCARY FACES ON TOP OF ALL OF THE BUILDINGS?
THOSE ARE CALLED DRAGONS.
THEY PUT THEM ON TOP OF EVERY BUILDING TO SCARE AWAY GHOSTS AND STUFF.
EVERY BUILDING EXCEPT THE KING'S HOUSE.
BECAUSE THE KING HIMSELF WAS CONSIDERED TO BE A DRAGON, AND IF THERE WERE TWO DRAGONS IN THE SAME BUILDING, THEY WOULD FIGHT.
SO WHY DOESN'T THIS BUILDING HAVE ONE?
THE GUIDE SAID THERE WAS A TYPHOON RECENTLY.
MAYBE THE DRAGON ON THE BUILDING WAS DAMAGED AND FELL OFF.
YOU KNOW WHAT THAT MEANS...
...THIS IS THE MISSING DRAGON!

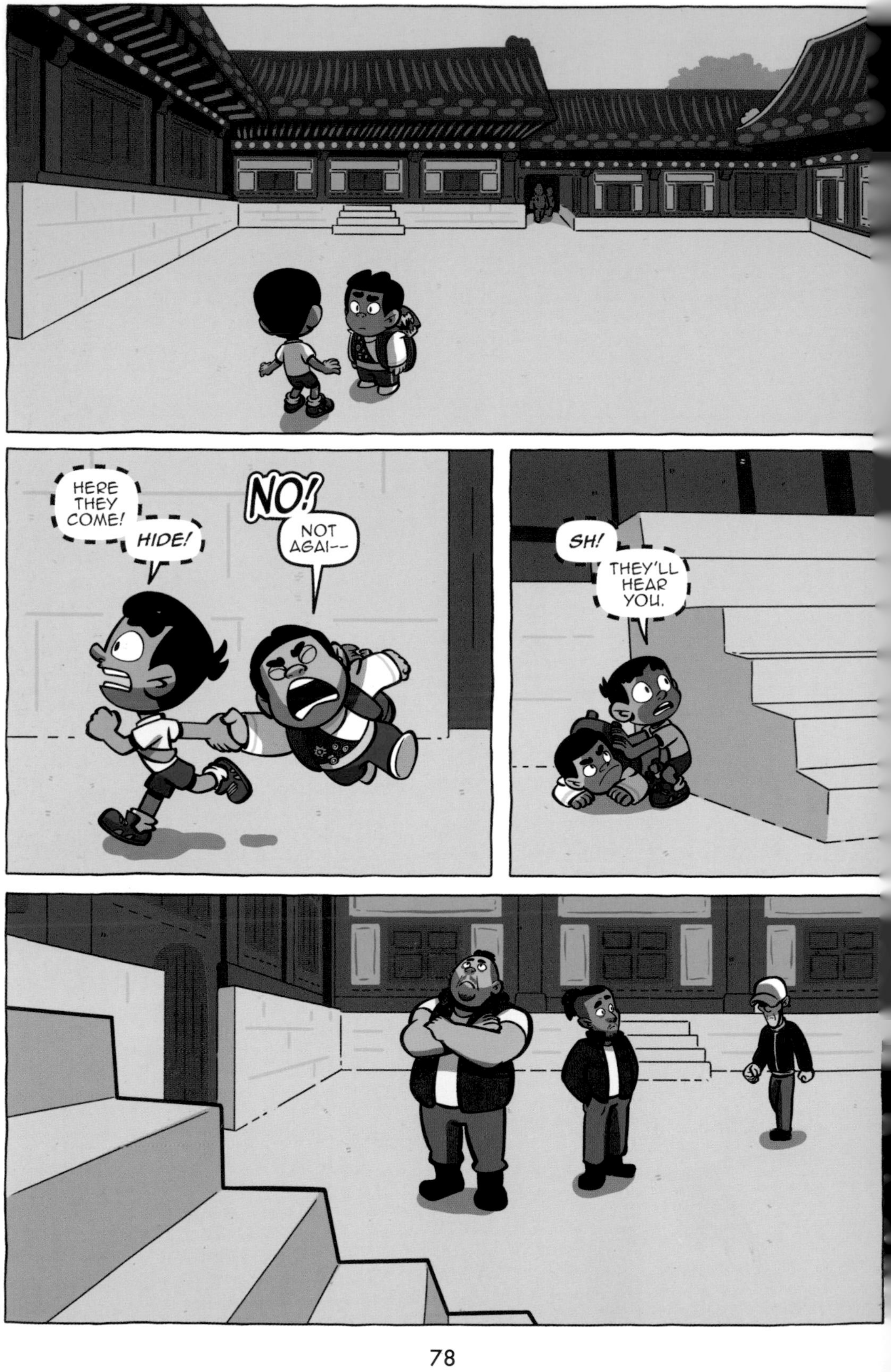
HERE THEY COME!
HIDE!
NO!
NOT AGAI--
SH!
THEY'LL HEAR YOU.

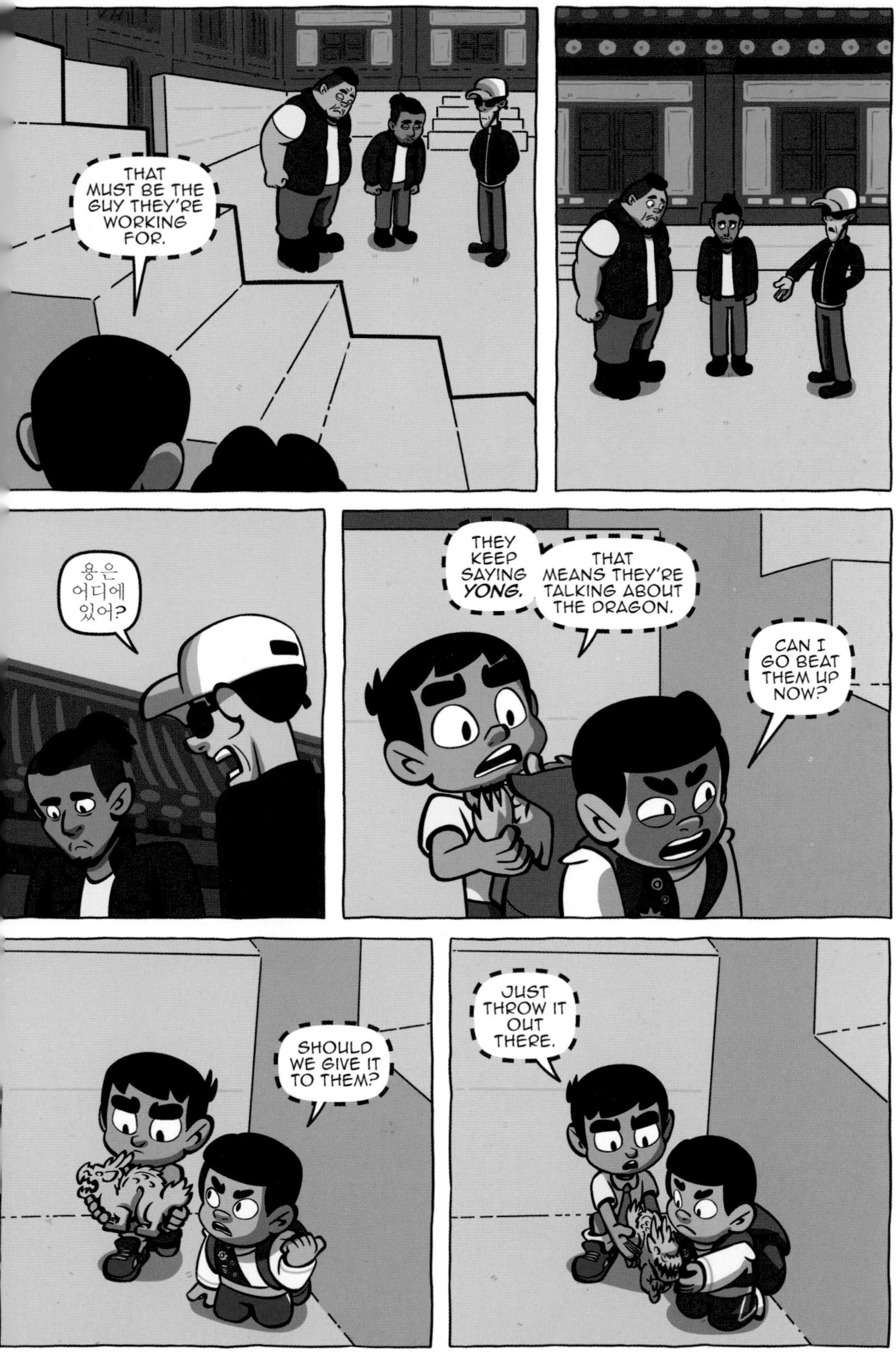
THAT MUST BE THE GUY THEY'RE WORKING FOR.
용은 어디에 있어?
THEY KEEP SAYING *YONG.*
THAT MEANS THEY'RE TALKING ABOUT THE DRAGON.
CAN I GO BEAT THEM UP NOW?
SHOULD WE GIVE IT TO THEM?
JUST THROW IT OUT THERE.

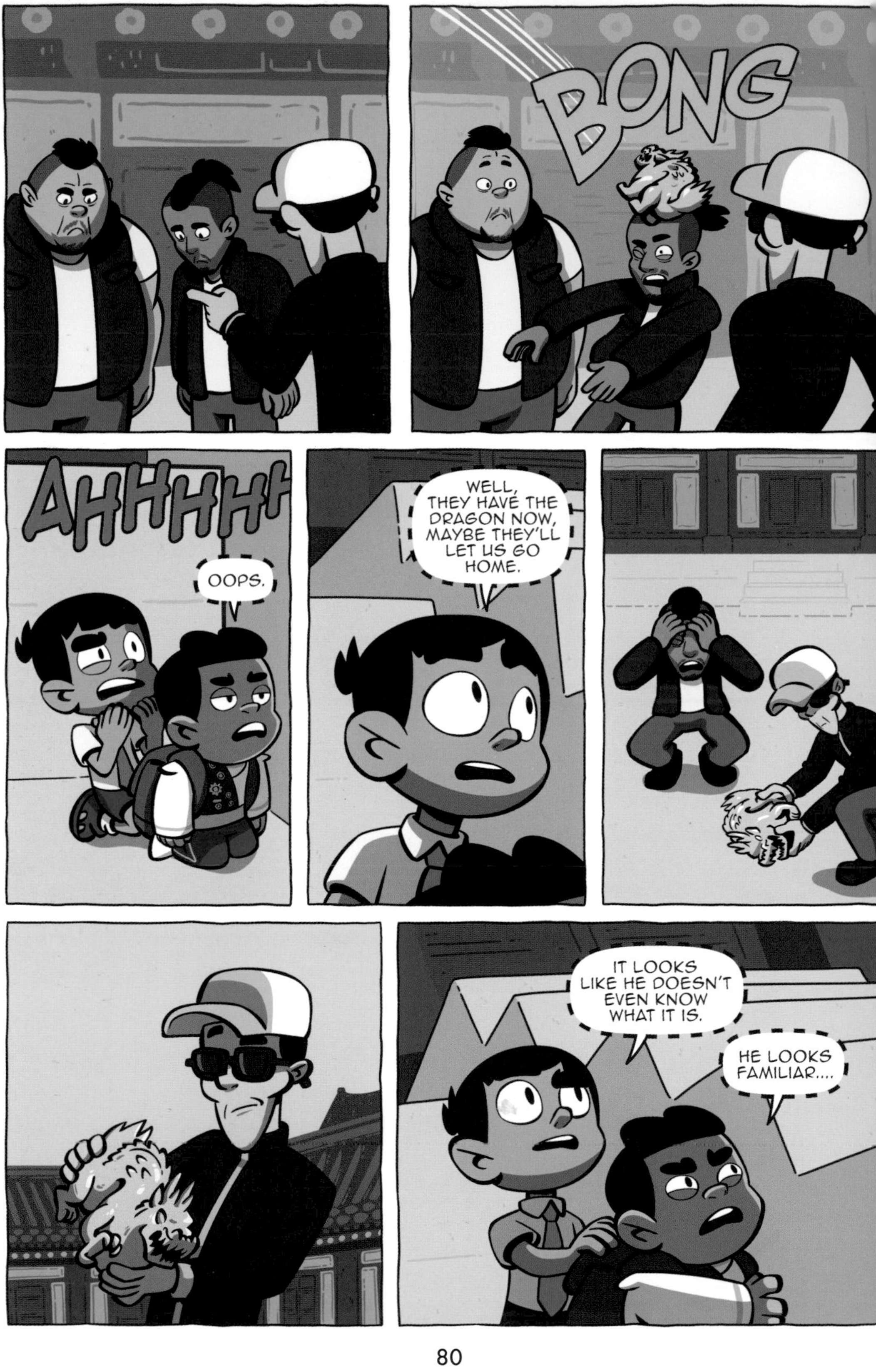
BONG
AHHHH
OOPS.
WELL, THEY HAVE THE DRAGON NOW, MAYBE THEY'LL LET US GO HOME.
IT LOOKS LIKE HE DOESN'T EVEN KNOW WHAT IT IS.
HE LOOKS FAMILIAR....

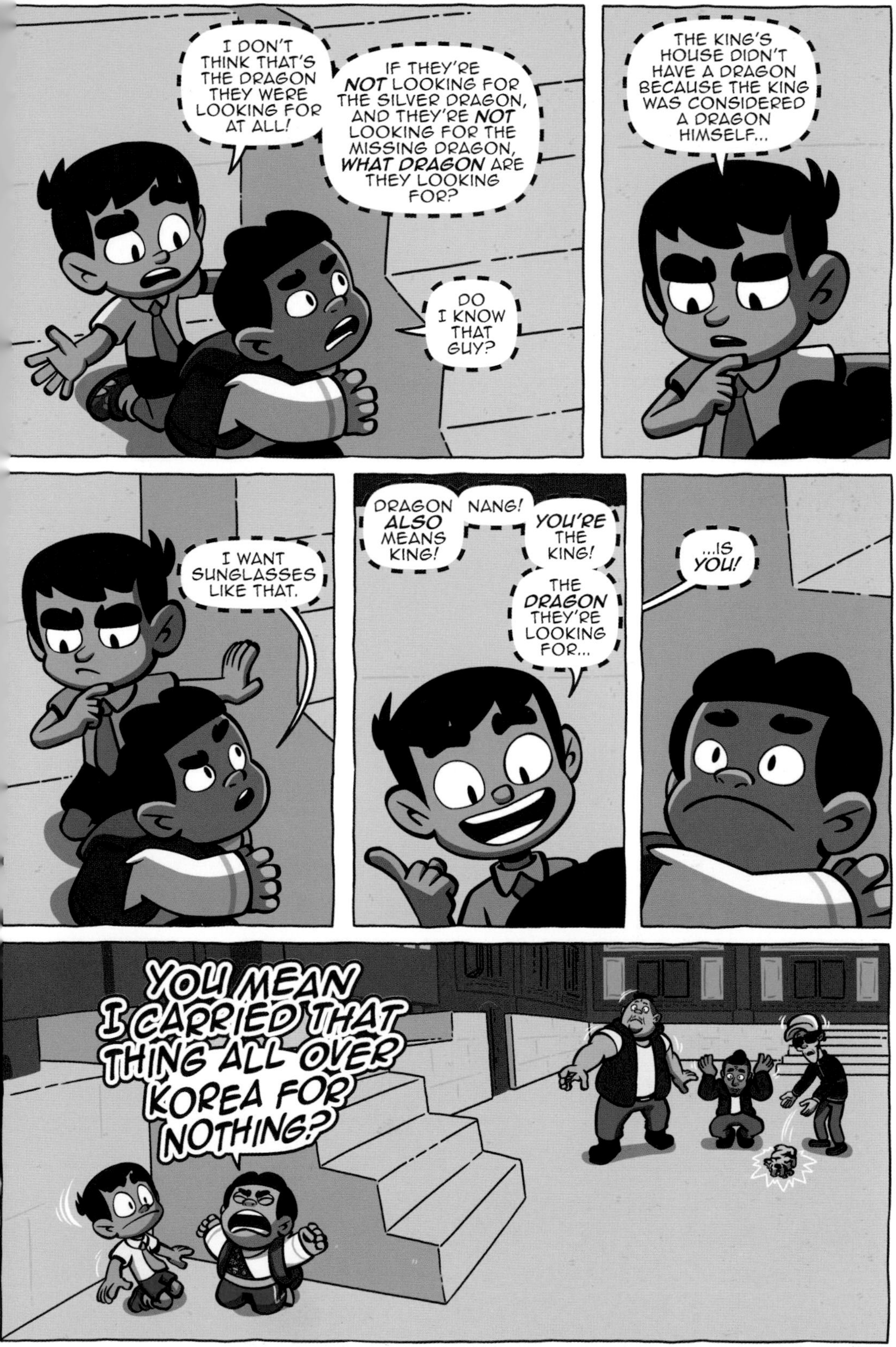
I DON'T THINK THAT'S THE DRAGON THEY WERE LOOKING FOR AT ALL!
IF THEY'RE NOT LOOKING FOR THE SILVER DRAGON, AND THEY'RE NOT LOOKING FOR THE MISSING DRAGON, WHAT DRAGON ARE THEY LOOKING FOR?
DO I KNOW THAT GUY?
THE KING'S HOUSE DIDN'T HAVE A DRAGON BECAUSE THE KING WAS CONSIDERED A DRAGON HIMSELF...
I WANT SUNGLASSES LIKE THAT.
DRAGON ALSO MEANS KING!
NANG!
YOU'RE THE KING!
THE DRAGON THEY'RE LOOKING FOR...
...IS YOU!
YOU MEAN I CARRIED THAT THING ALL OVER KOREA FOR NOTHING?

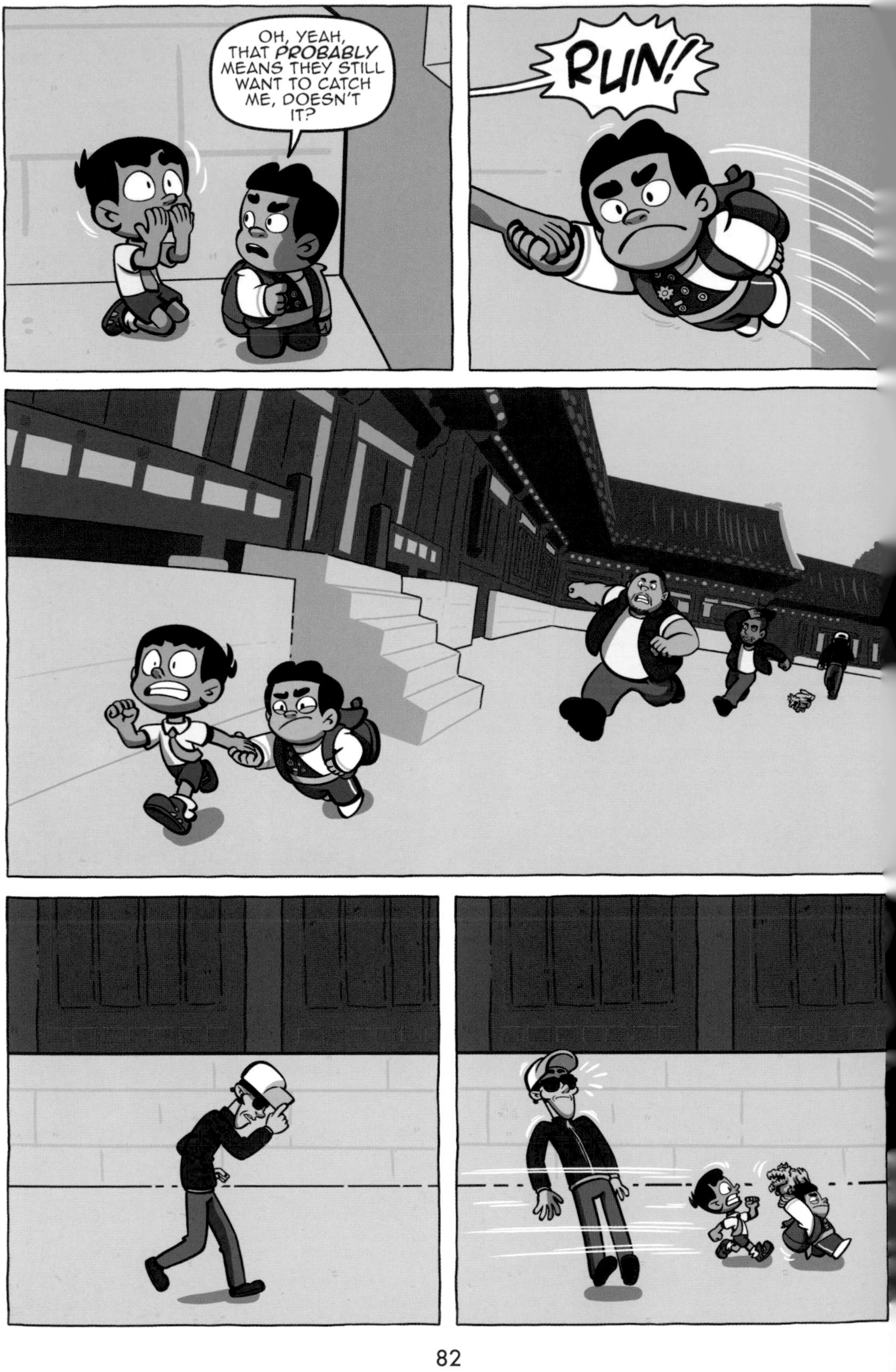
OH, YEAH, THAT PROBABLY MEANS THEY STILL WANT TO CATCH ME, DOESN'T IT?
RUN!

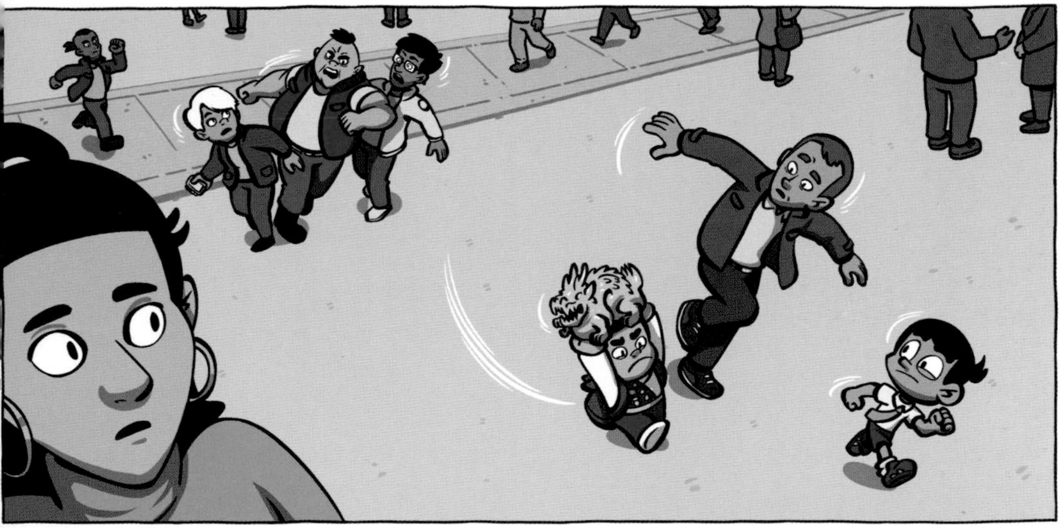

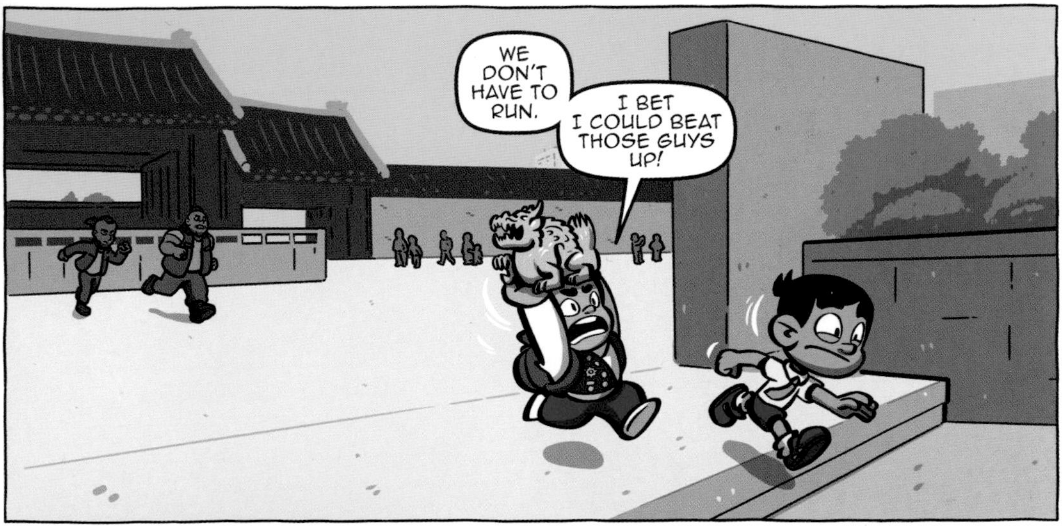

WE DON'T HAVE TO RUN.
I BET I COULD BEAT THOSE GUYS UP!

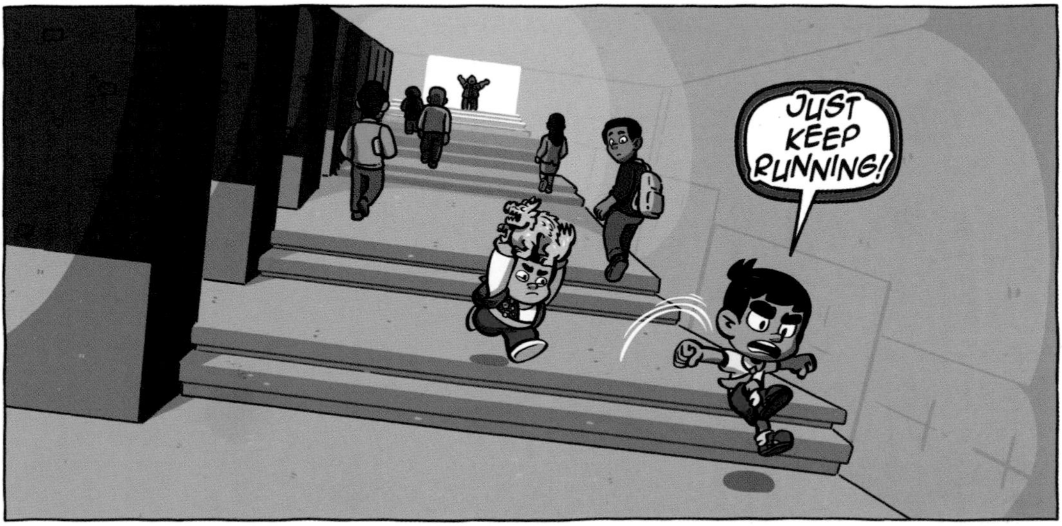

JUST KEEP RUNNING!

IT'S LIKE YOU SAID!

THE KING OF KOREA DIDN'T *NEED* ANY STATUE TO PROTECT HIM!

KINGS AREN'T SCARED OF *ANY-THING!*

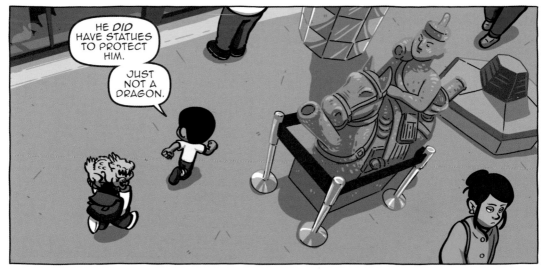

HE *DID* HAVE STATUES TO PROTECT HIM.

JUST NOT A DRAGON.

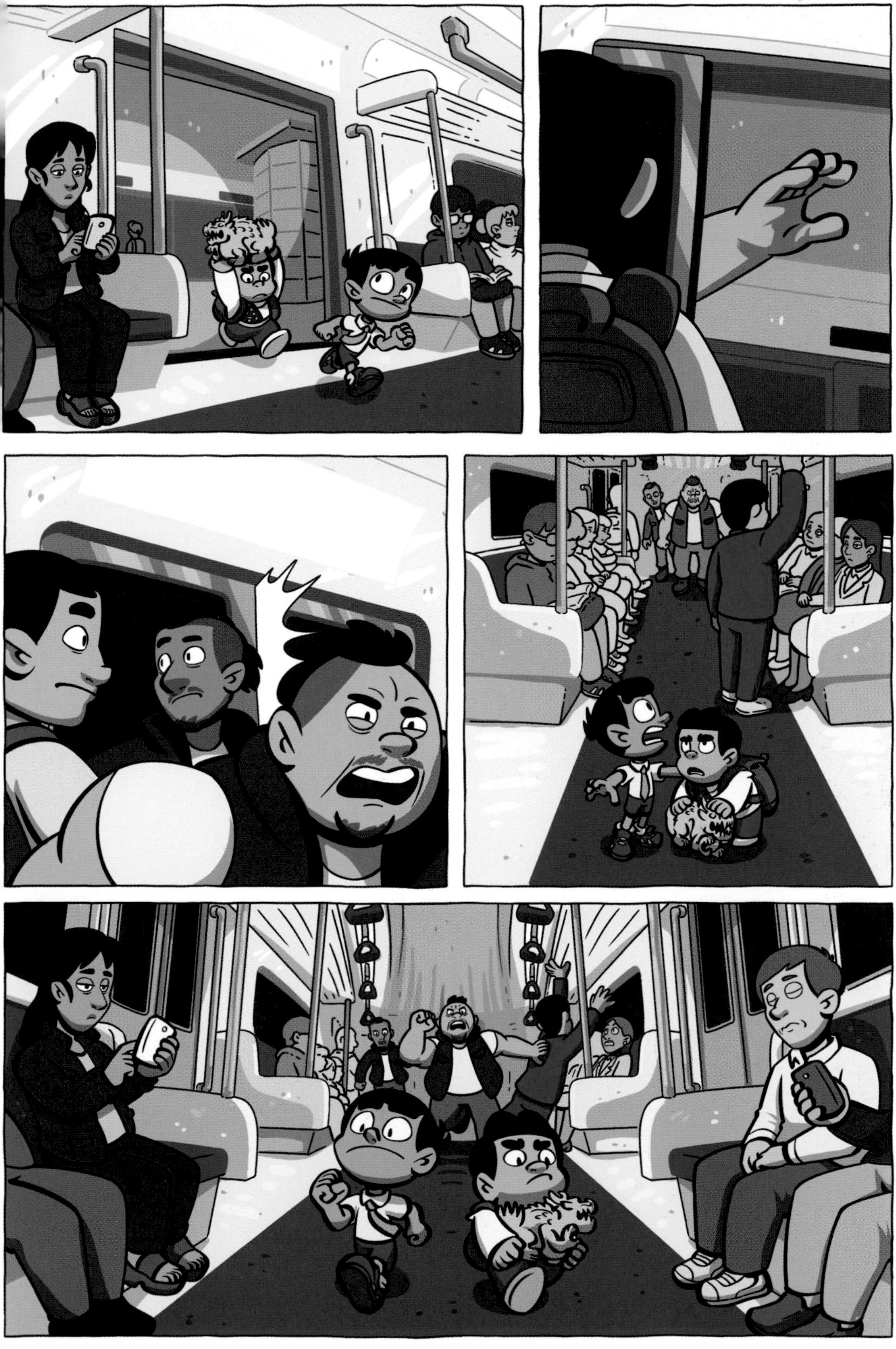

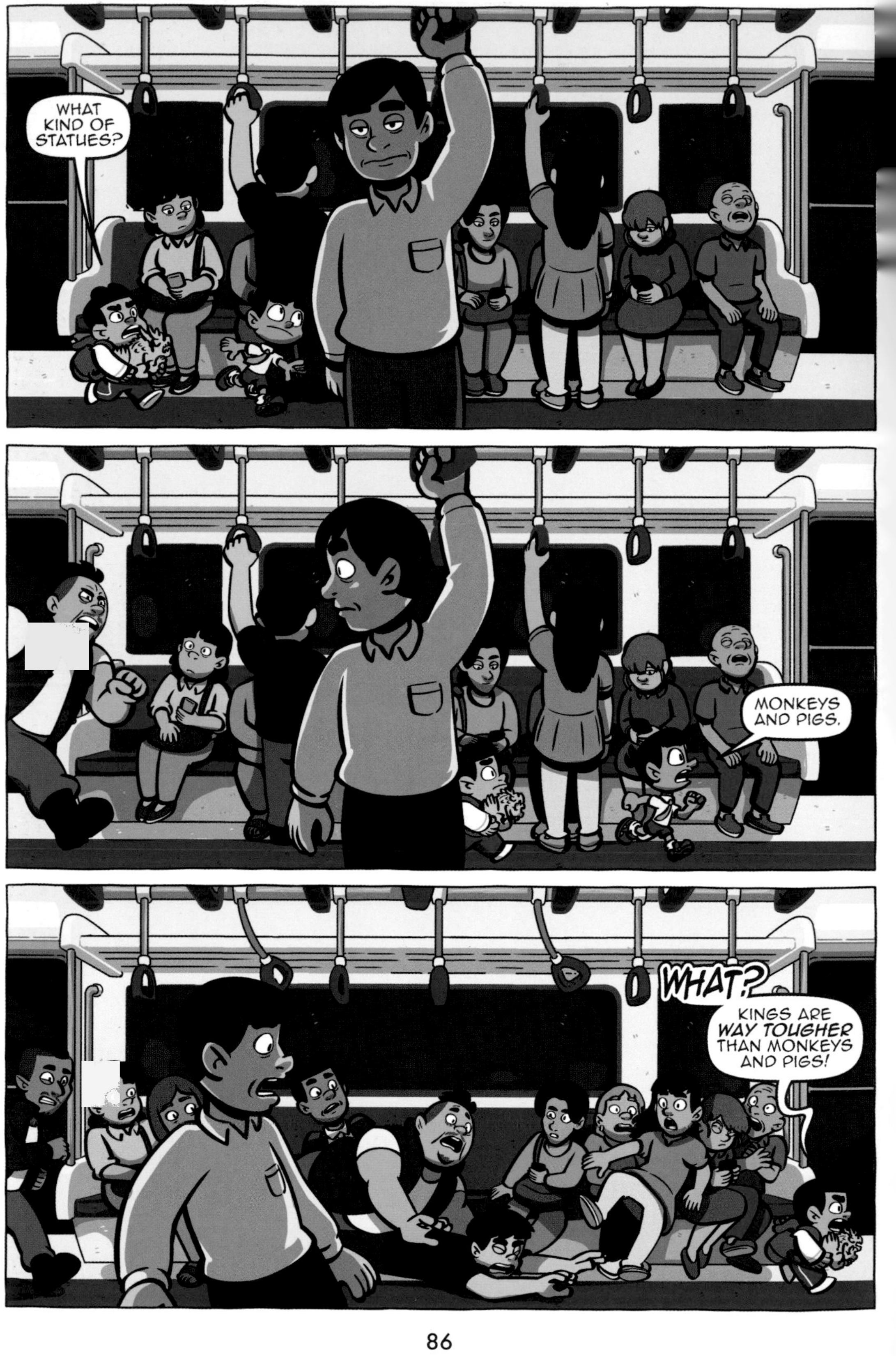
WHAT KIND OF STATUES?
MONKEYS AND PIGS.
WHAT?
KINGS ARE *WAY TOUGHER* THAN MONKEYS AND PIGS!

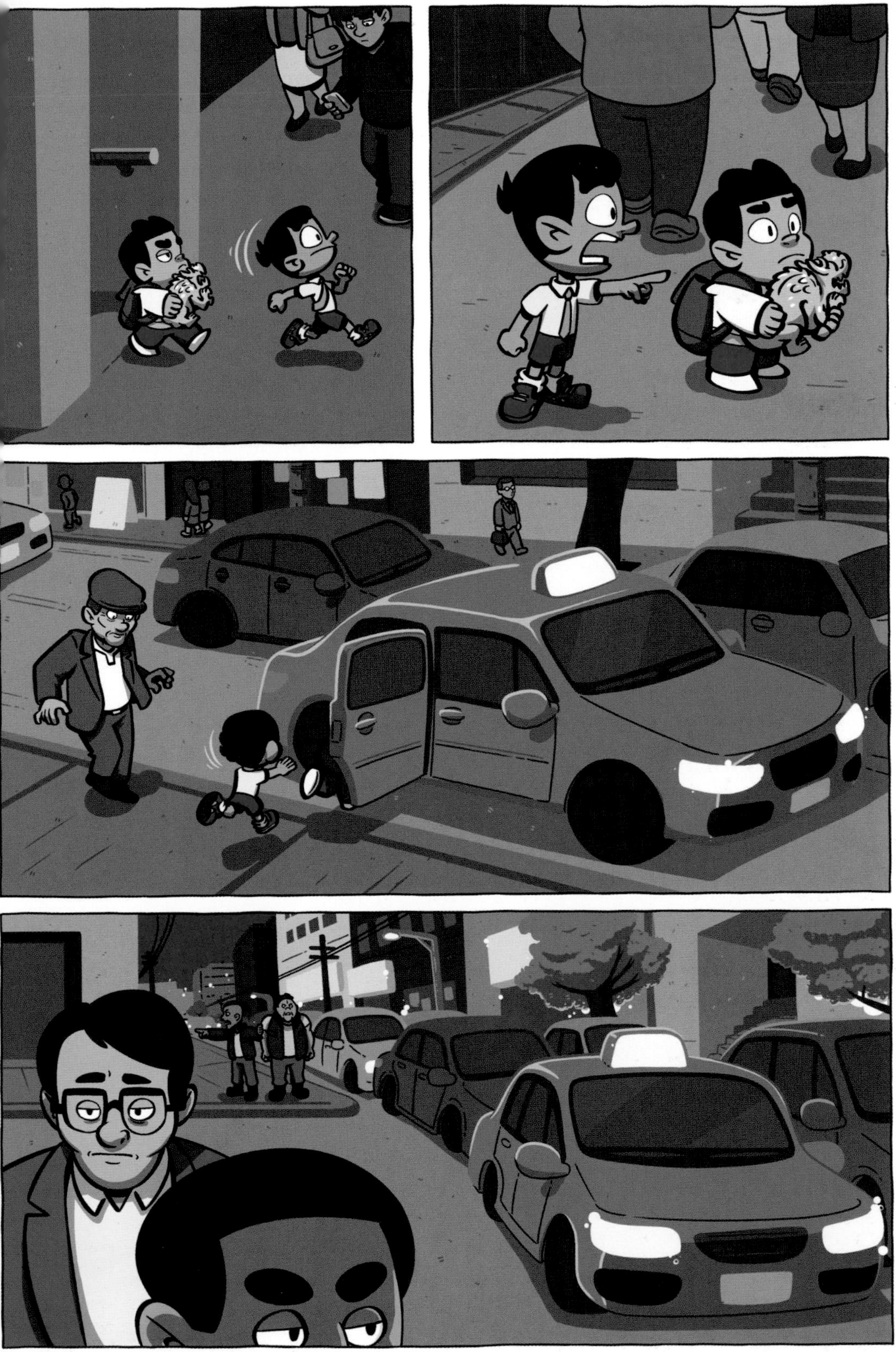

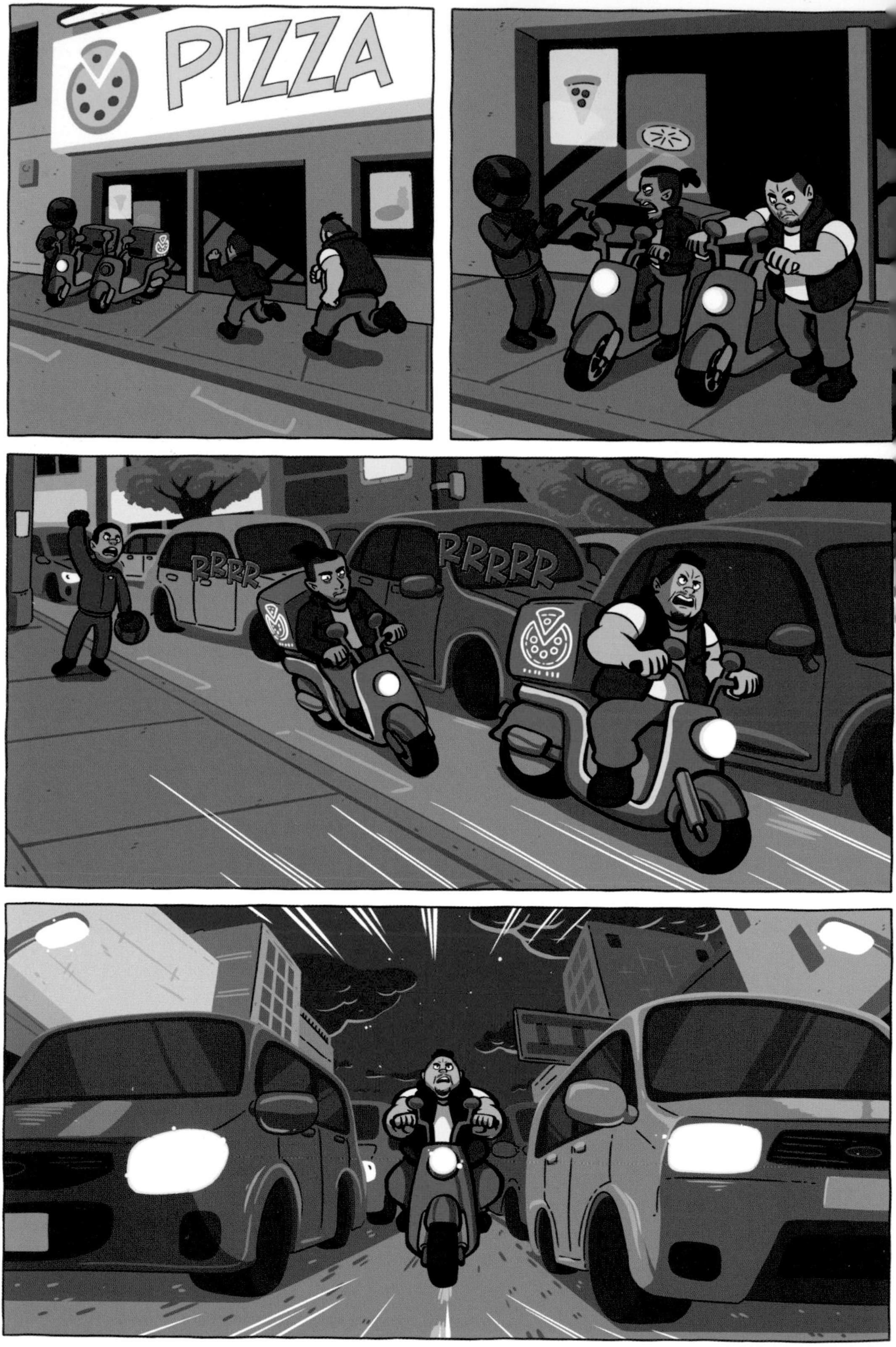
PIZZA
RRRR
RRRRR

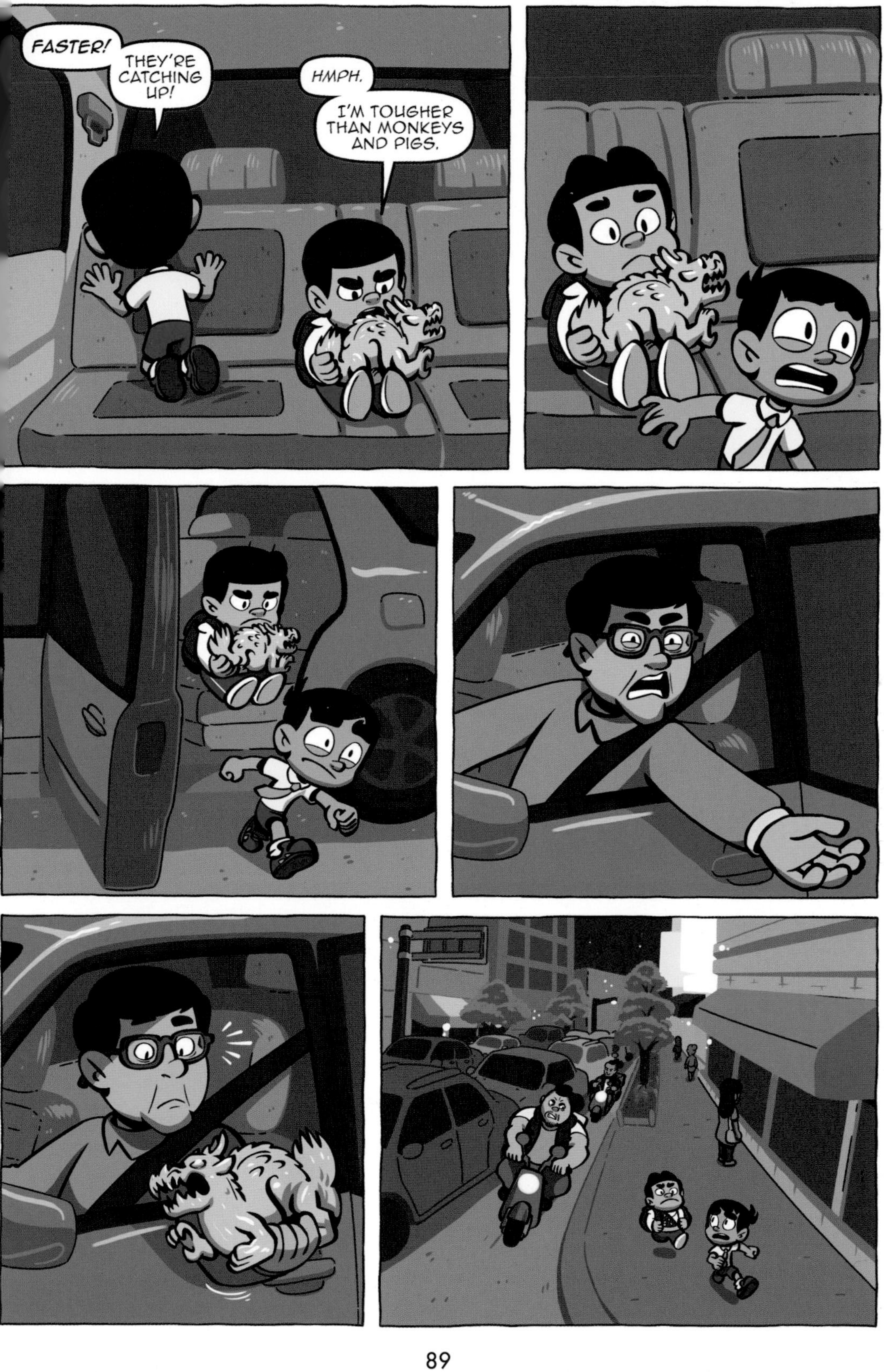
FASTER!
THEY'RE CATCHING UP!
HMPH.
I'M TOUGHER THAN MONKEYS AND PIGS.

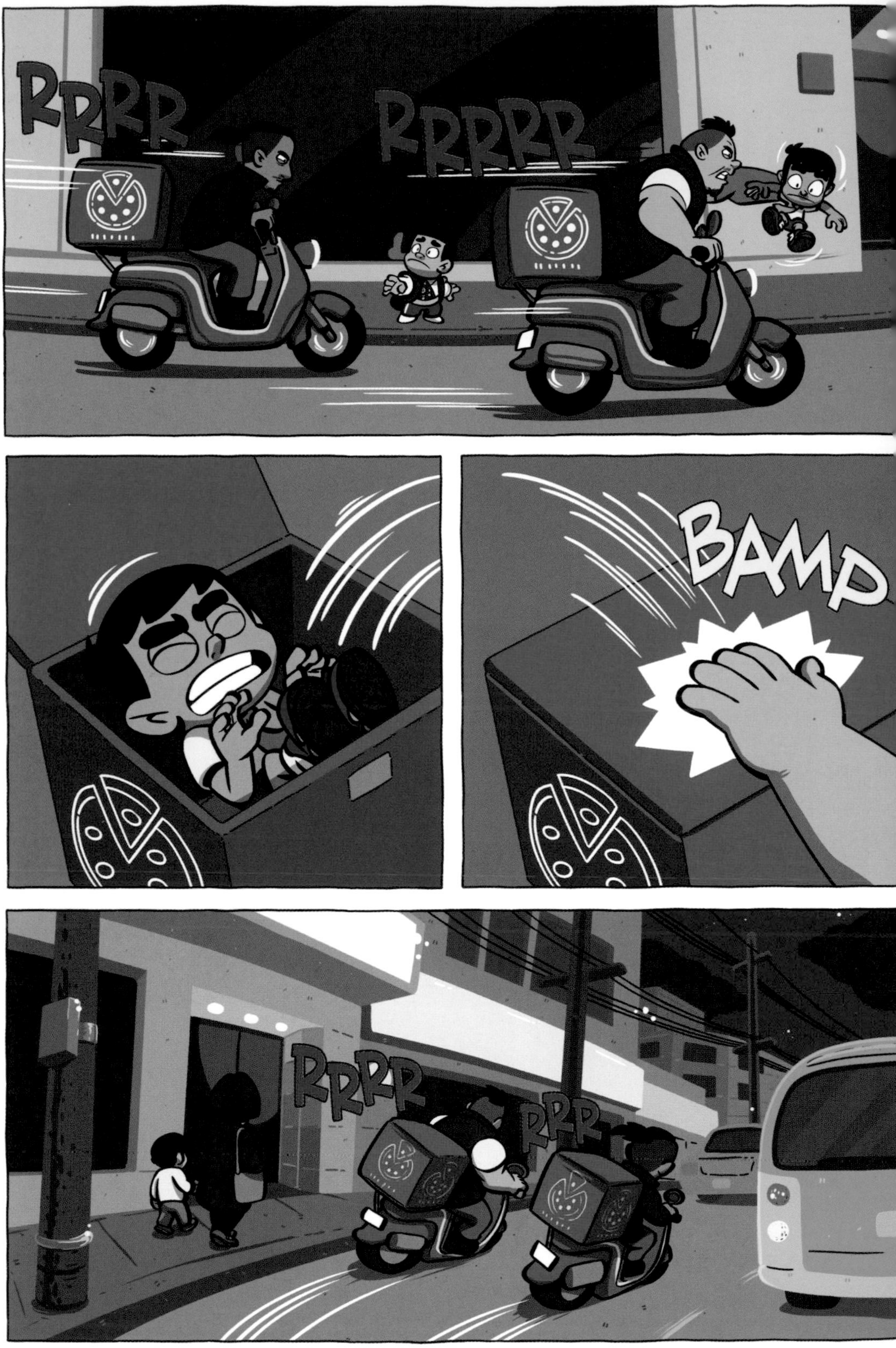
RRRR
RRRRR
BAMP
RRRR
RRR

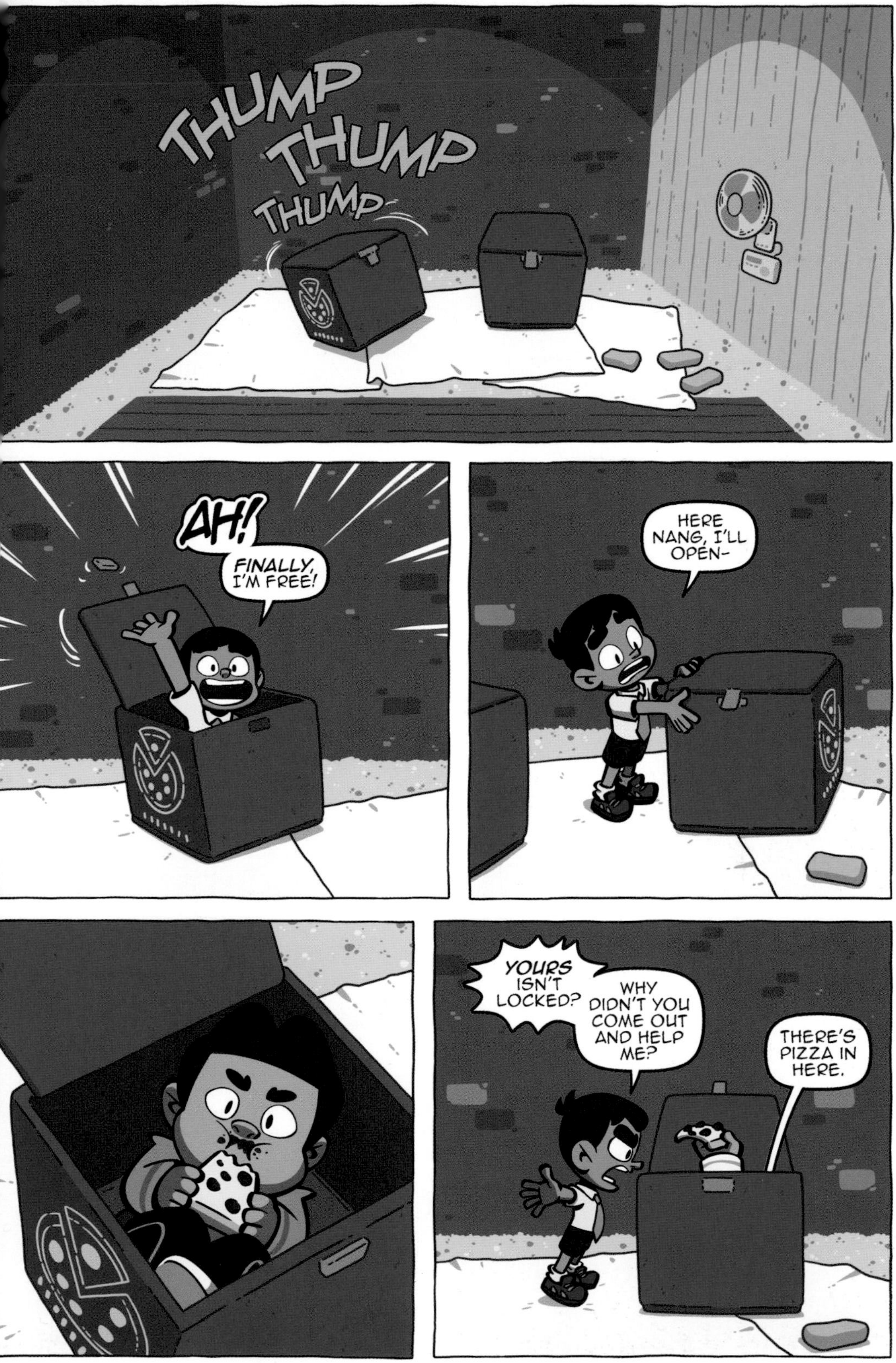
THUMP THUMP THUMP
AH!
FINALLY, I'M FREE!
HERE NANG, I'LL OPEN-
YOURS ISN'T LOCKED?
WHY DIDN'T YOU COME OUT AND HELP ME?
THERE'S PIZZA IN HERE.

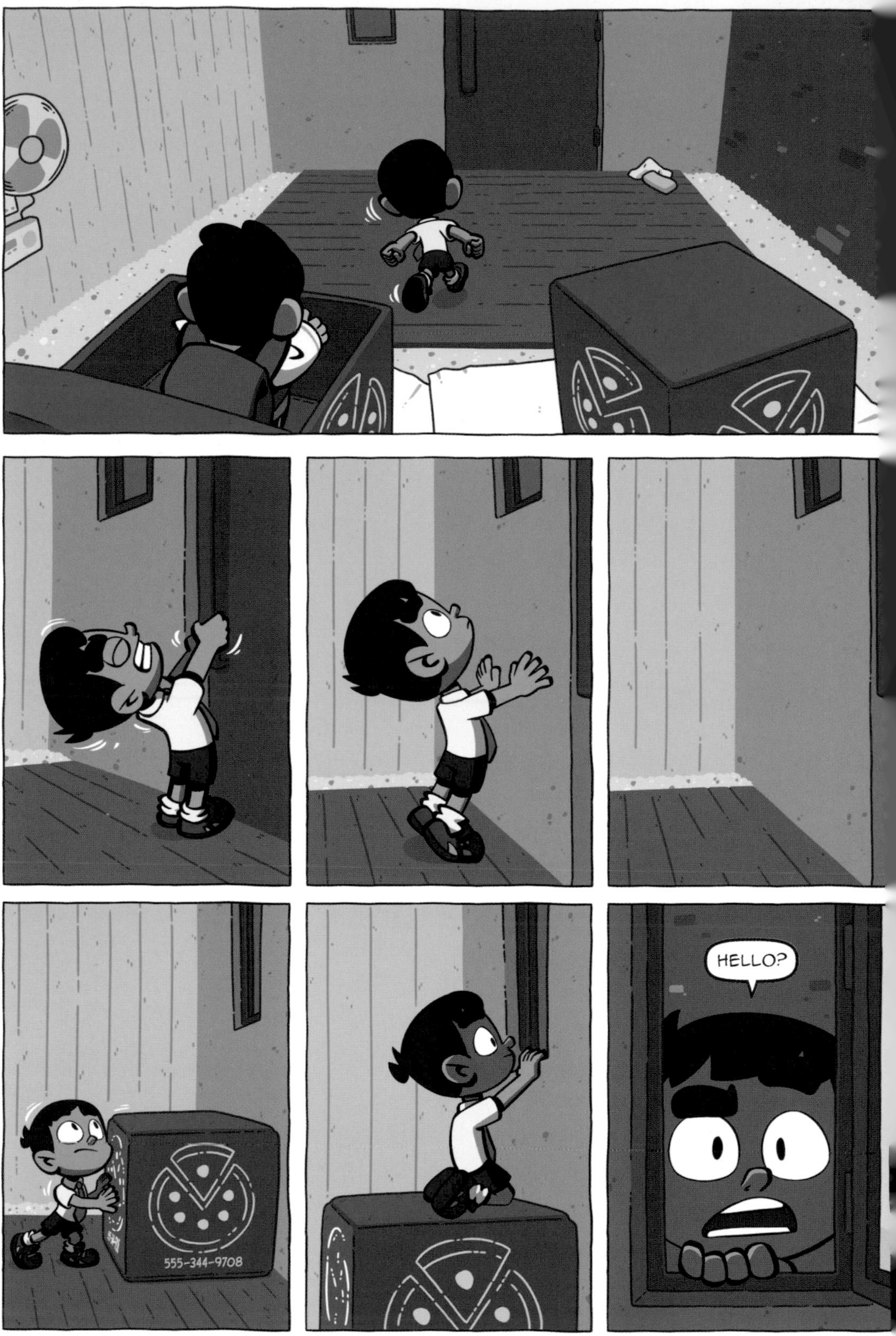
555-344-9708
HELLO?

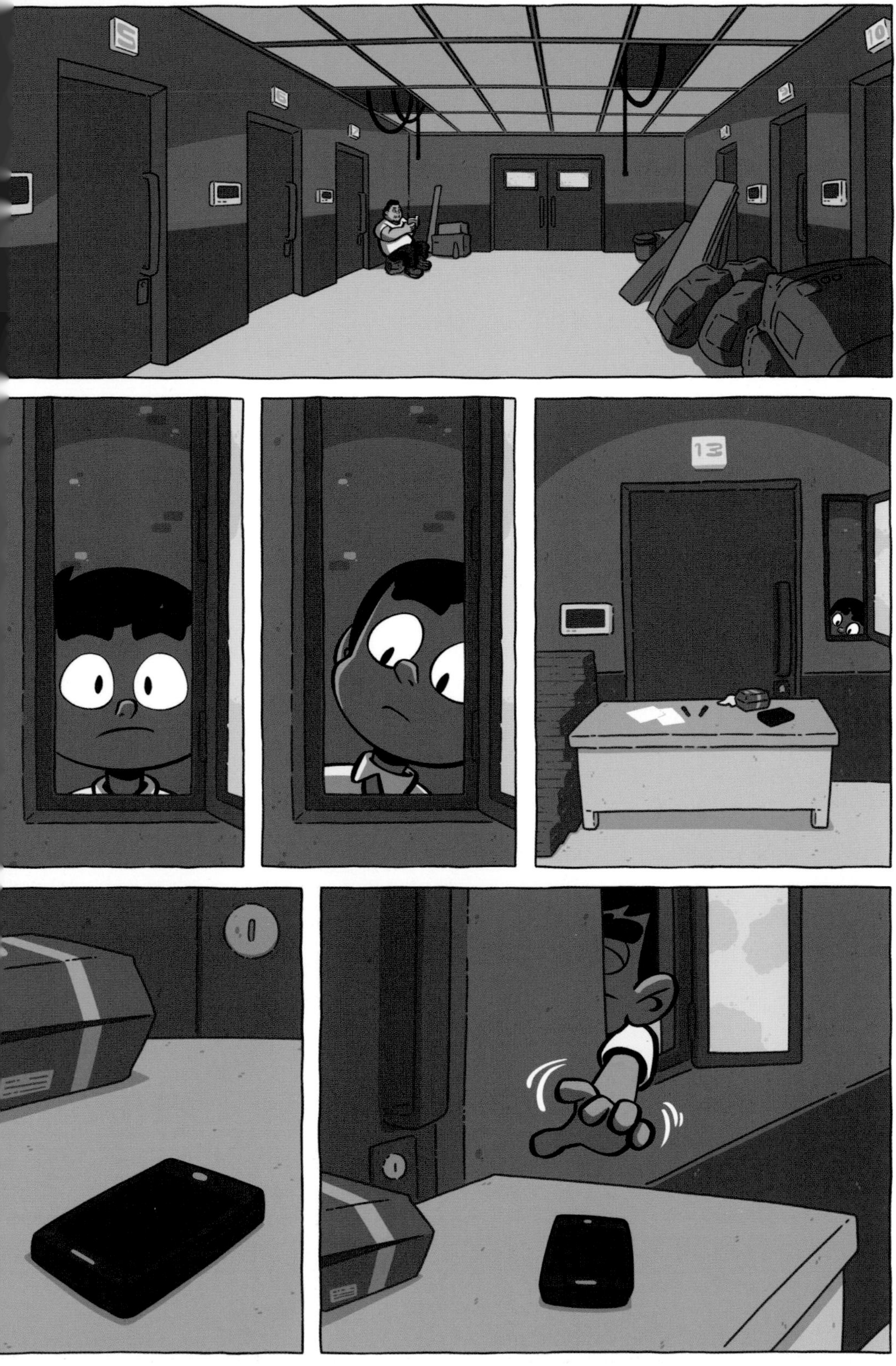
13

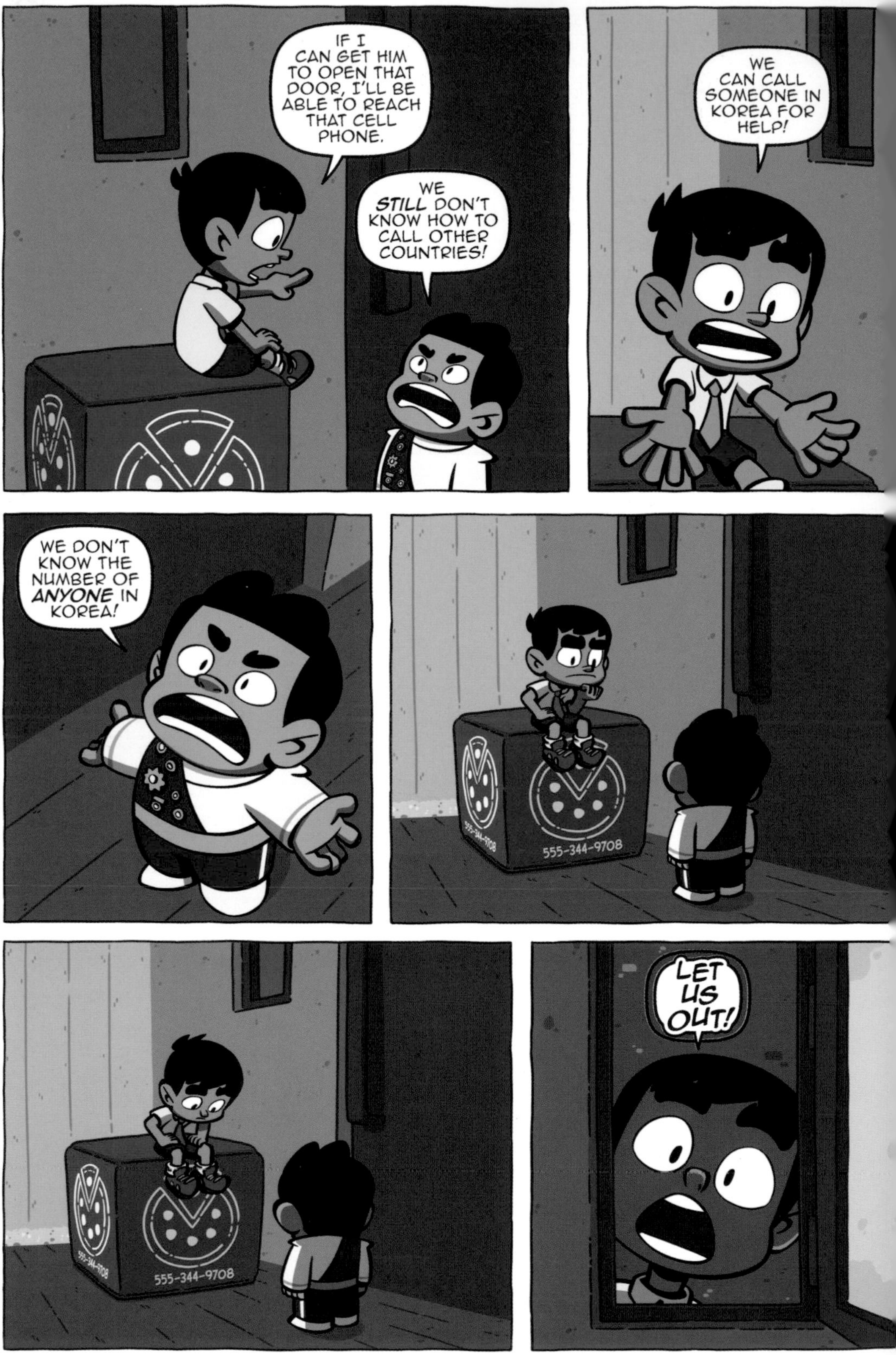
IF I CAN GET HIM TO OPEN THAT DOOR, I'LL BE ABLE TO REACH THAT CELL PHONE.
WE STILL DON'T KNOW HOW TO CALL OTHER COUNTRIES!
WE CAN CALL SOMEONE IN KOREA FOR HELP!
WE DON'T KNOW THE NUMBER OF ANYONE IN KOREA!
555-344-9708
555-344-9708
555-344-9708
555-344-9708
LET US OUT!

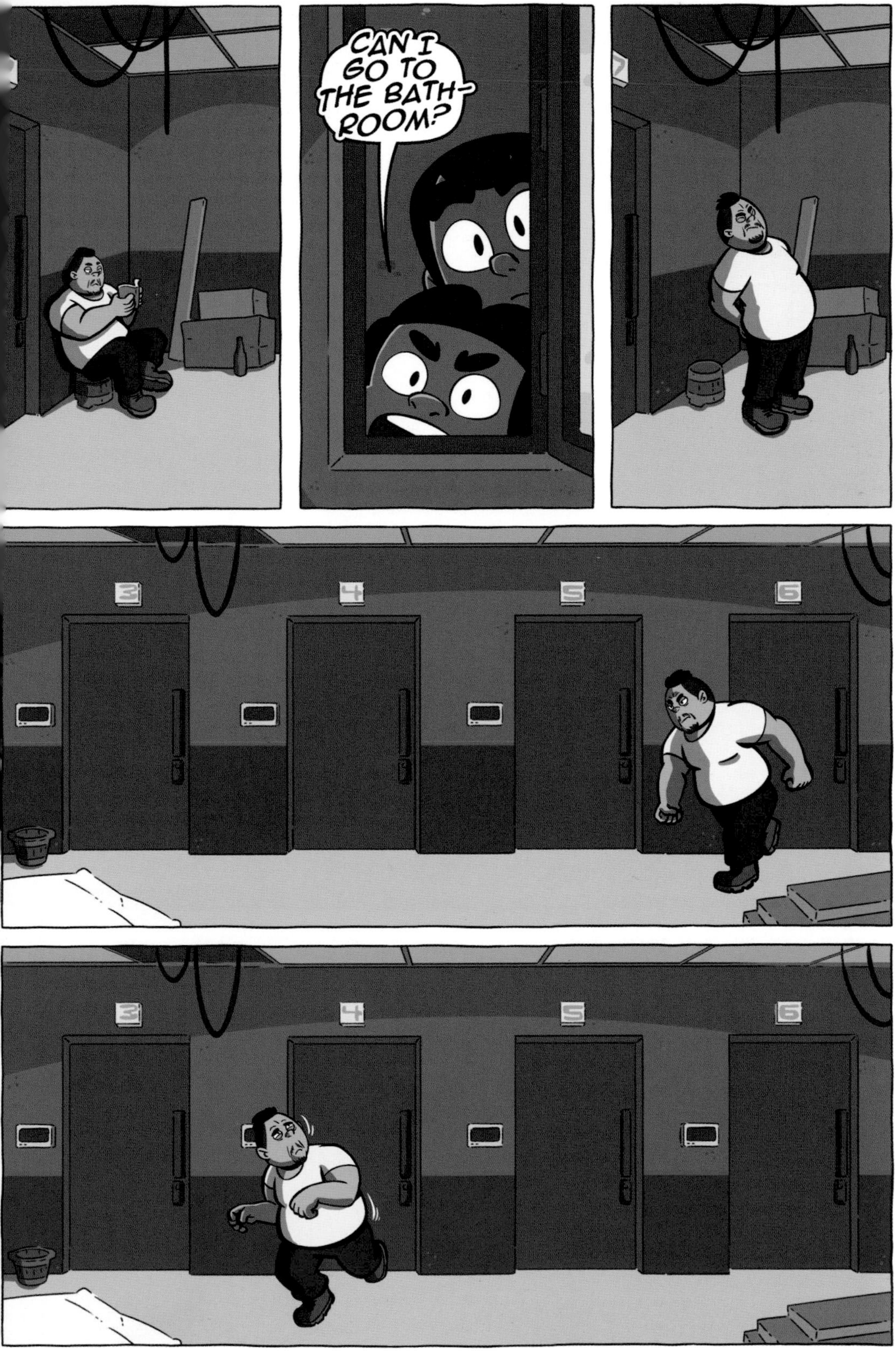
CAN I GO TO THE BATH-ROOM?
3
4
5
6
3
4
5
6

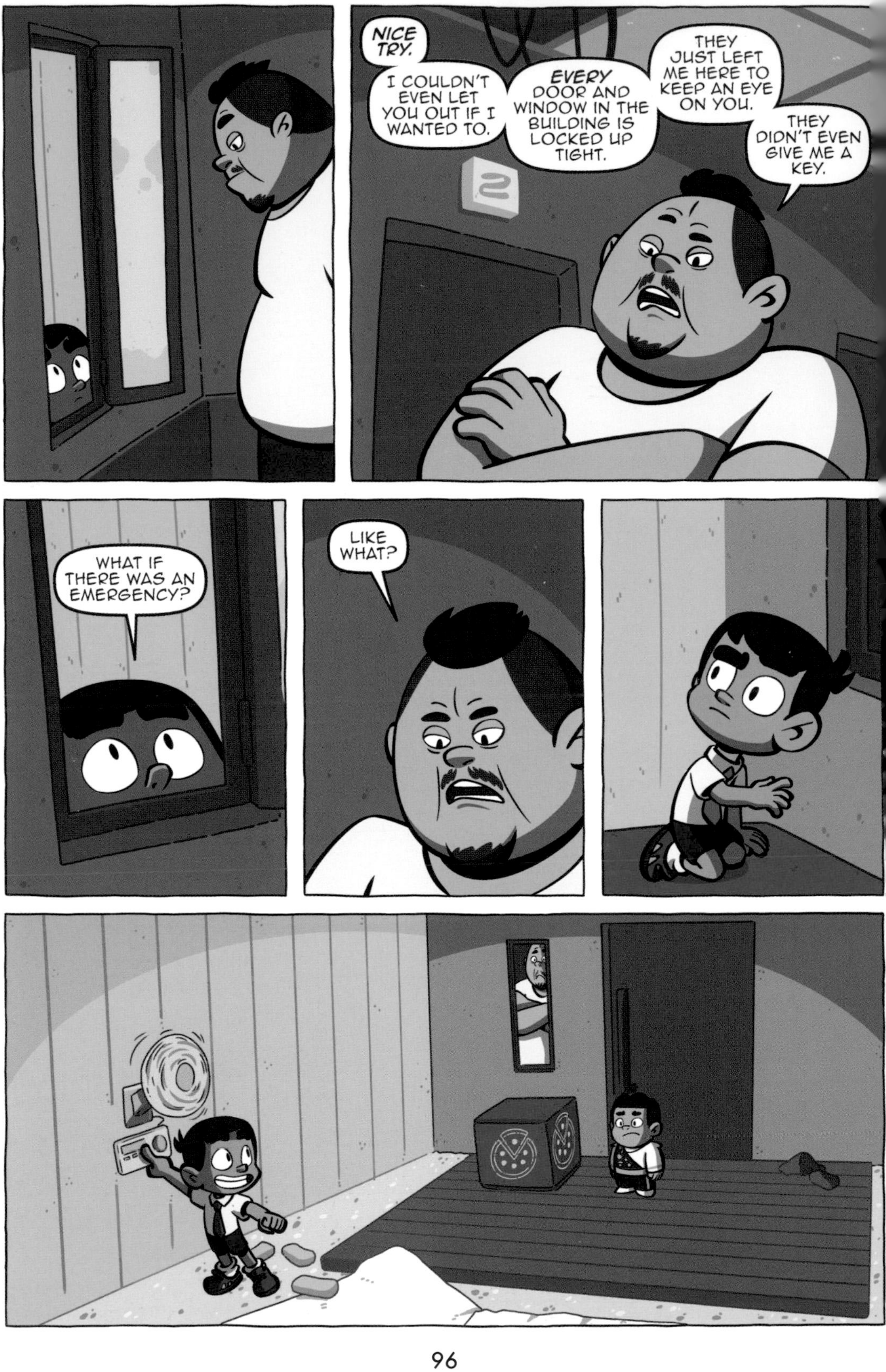
NICE TRY.
I COULDN'T EVEN LET YOU OUT IF I WANTED TO.
EVERY DOOR AND WINDOW IN THE BUILDING IS LOCKED UP TIGHT.
THEY JUST LEFT ME HERE TO KEEP AN EYE ON YOU.
THEY DIDN'T EVEN GIVE ME A KEY.
WHAT IF THERE WAS AN EMERGENCY?
LIKE WHAT?

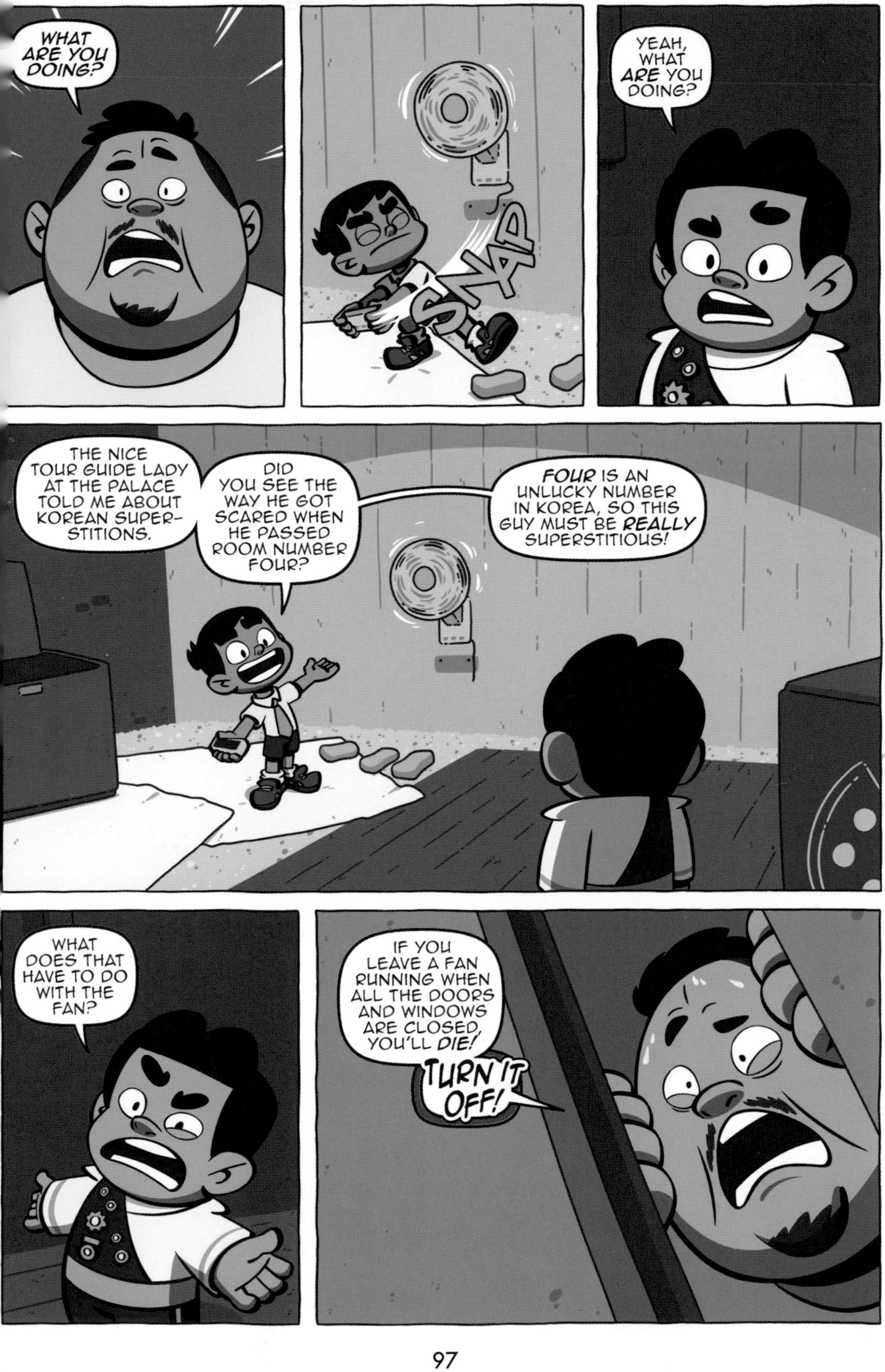
WHAT ARE YOU DOING?
SNAP
YEAH, WHAT ARE YOU DOING?
THE NICE TOUR GUIDE LADY AT THE PALACE TOLD ME ABOUT KOREAN SUPER-STITIONS.
DID YOU SEE THE WAY HE GOT SCARED WHEN HE PASSED ROOM NUMBER FOUR?
FOUR IS AN UNLUCKY NUMBER IN KOREA, SO THIS GUY MUST BE REALLY SUPERSTITIOUS!
WHAT DOES THAT HAVE TO DO WITH THE FAN?
IF YOU LEAVE A FAN RUNNING WHEN ALL THE DOORS AND WINDOWS ARE CLOSED, YOU'LL DIE!
TURN IT OFF!

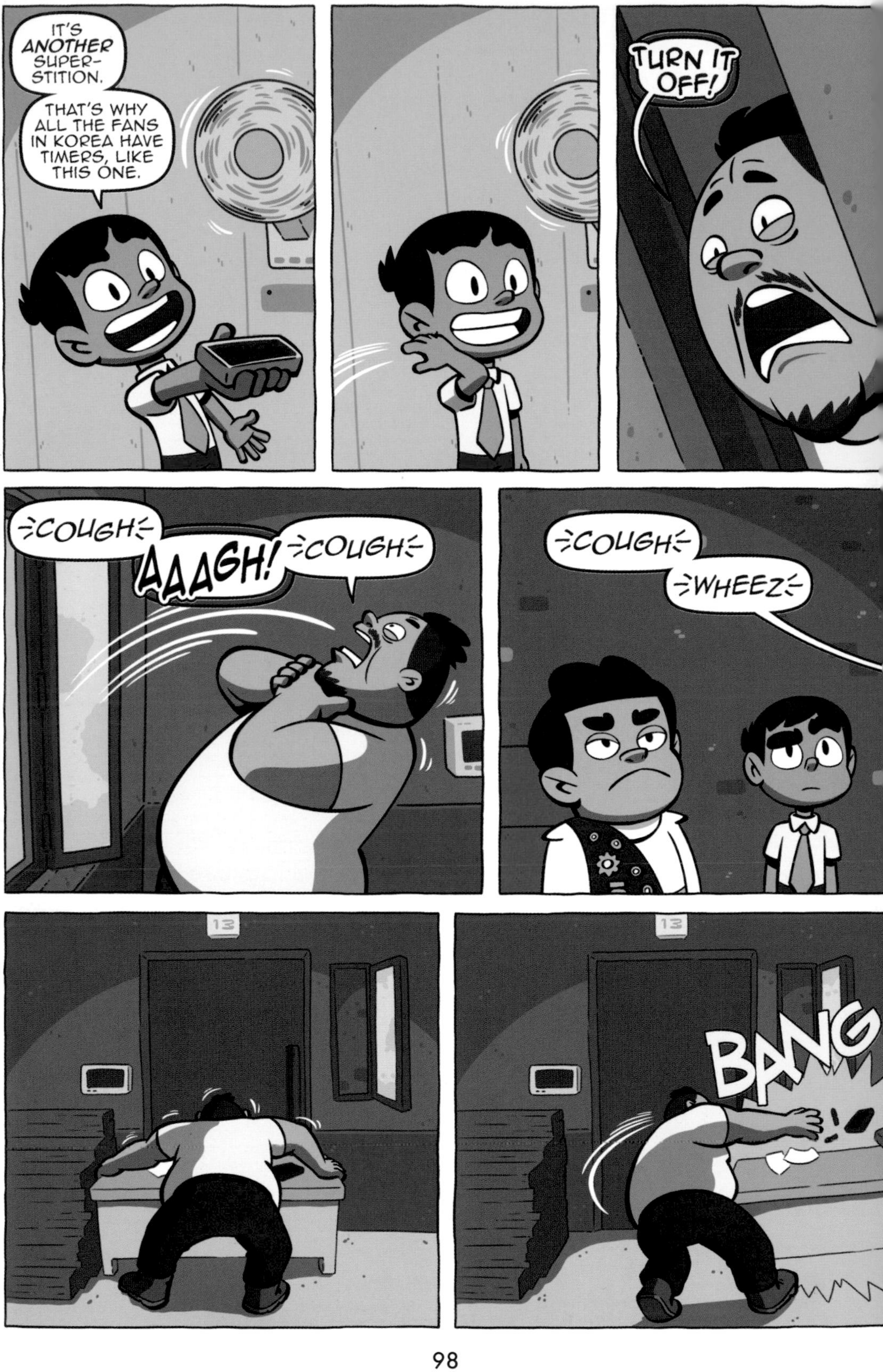
IT'S ANOTHER SUPERSTITION.
THAT'S WHY ALL THE FANS IN KOREA HAVE TIMERS, LIKE THIS ONE.
TURN IT OFF!
COUGH
AAAGH!
COUGH
COUGH
WHEEZ
13
13
BANG

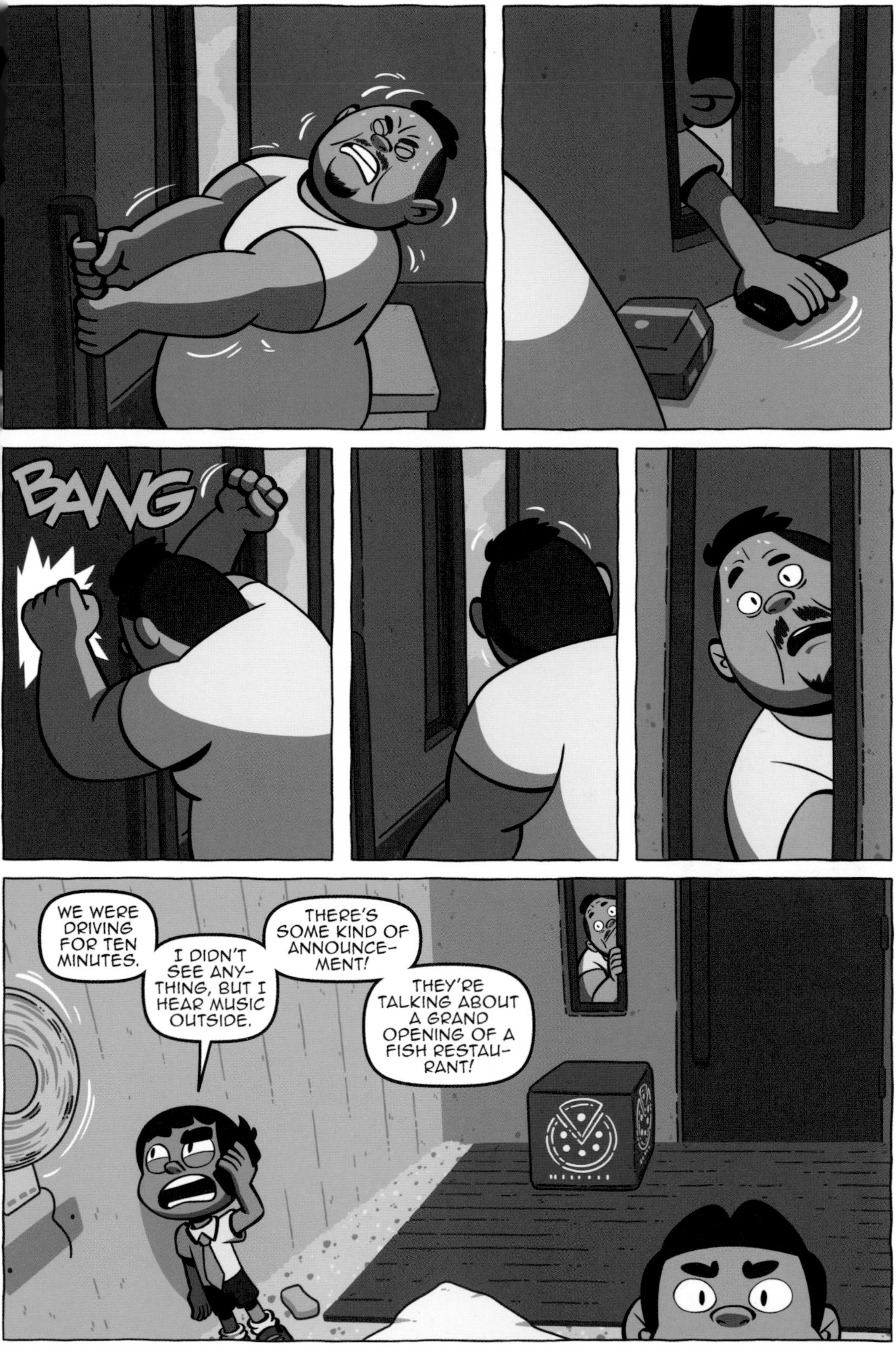
BANG
WE WERE DRIVING FOR TEN MINUTES.
I DIDN'T SEE ANY-THING, BUT I HEAR MUSIC OUTSIDE.
THERE'S SOME KIND OF ANNOUNCE-MENT!
THEY'RE TALKING ABOUT A GRAND OPENING OF A FISH RESTAU-RANT!

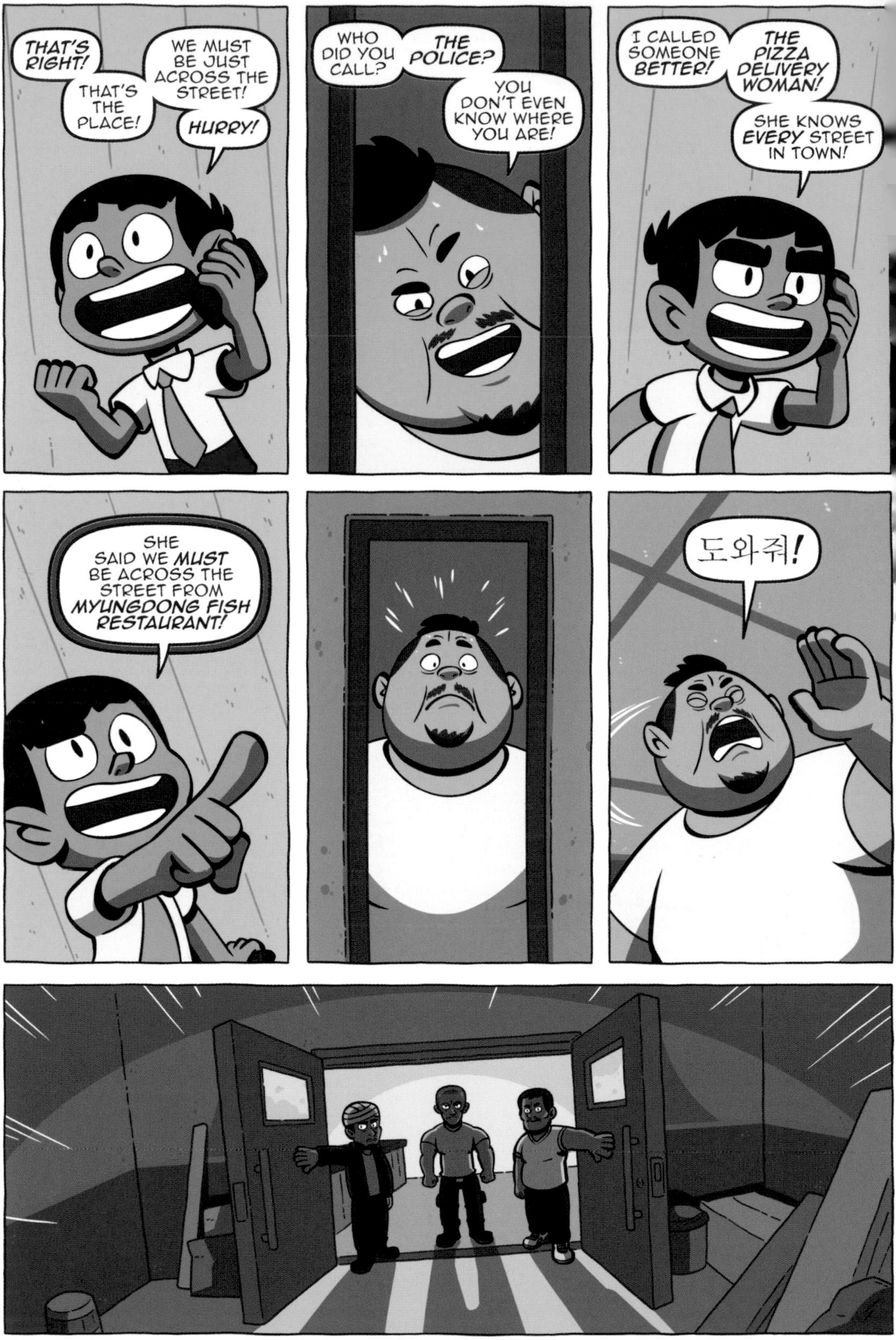
THAT'S RIGHT!
THAT'S THE PLACE!
WE MUST BE JUST ACROSS THE STREET!
HURRY!
WHO DID YOU CALL?
THE POLICE?
YOU DON'T EVEN KNOW WHERE YOU ARE!
I CALLED SOMEONE BETTER!
THE PIZZA DELIVERY WOMAN!
SHE KNOWS EVERY STREET IN TOWN!
SHE SAID WE MUST BE ACROSS THE STREET FROM MYUNGDONG FISH RESTAURANT!
도와줘!

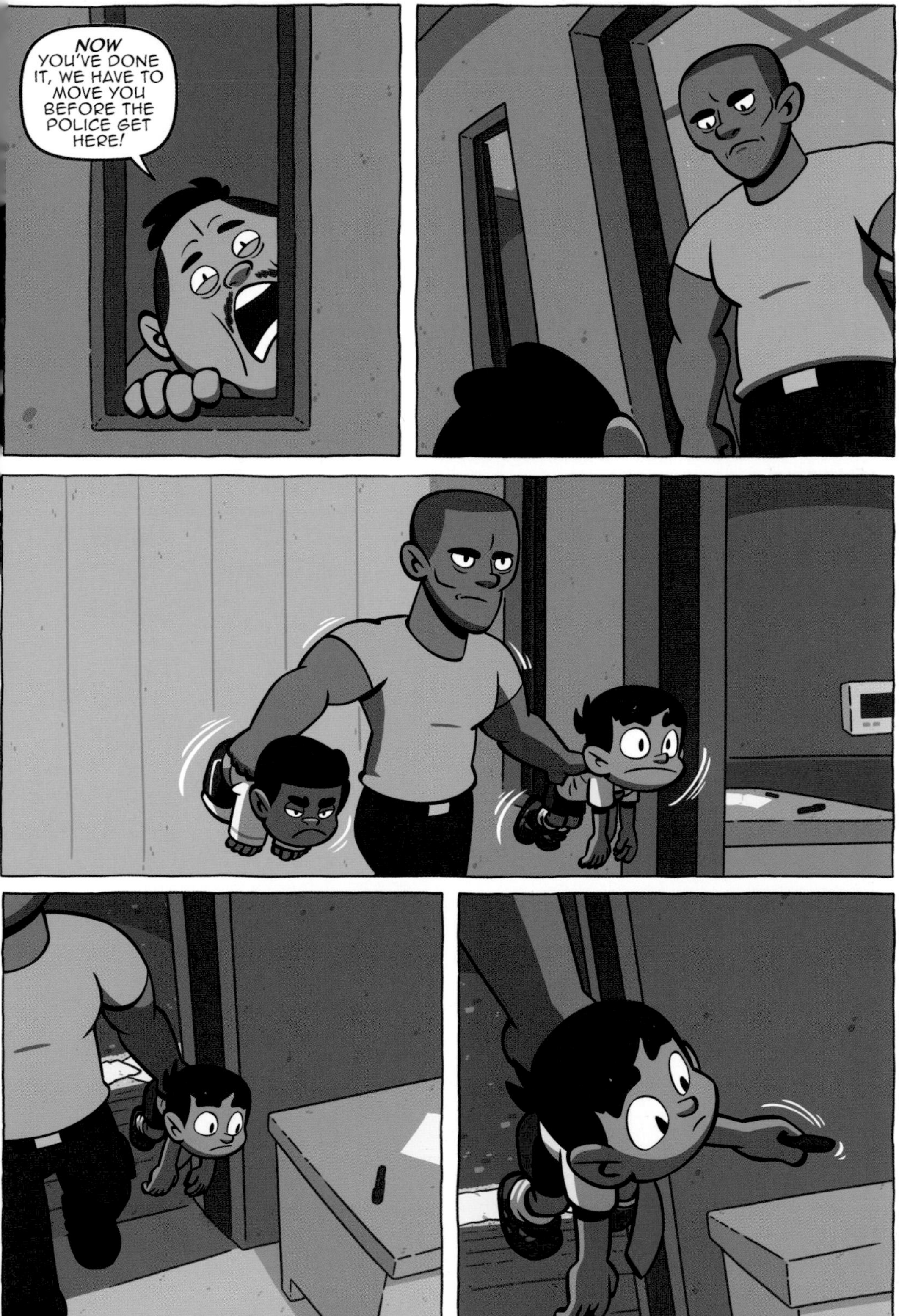
NOW YOU'VE DONE IT, WE HAVE TO MOVE YOU BEFORE THE POLICE GET HERE!

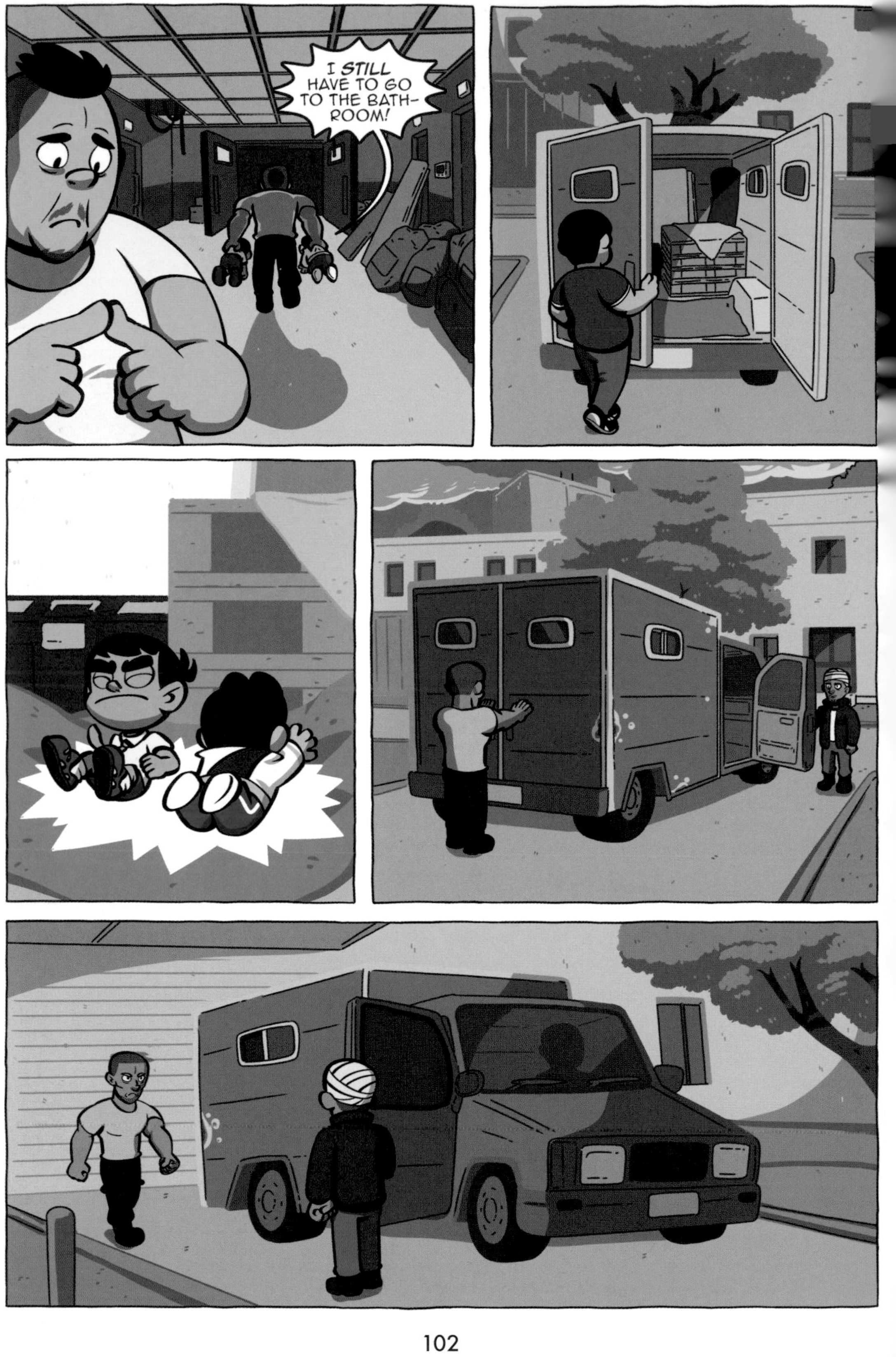
I STILL HAVE TO GO TO THE BATH-ROOM!

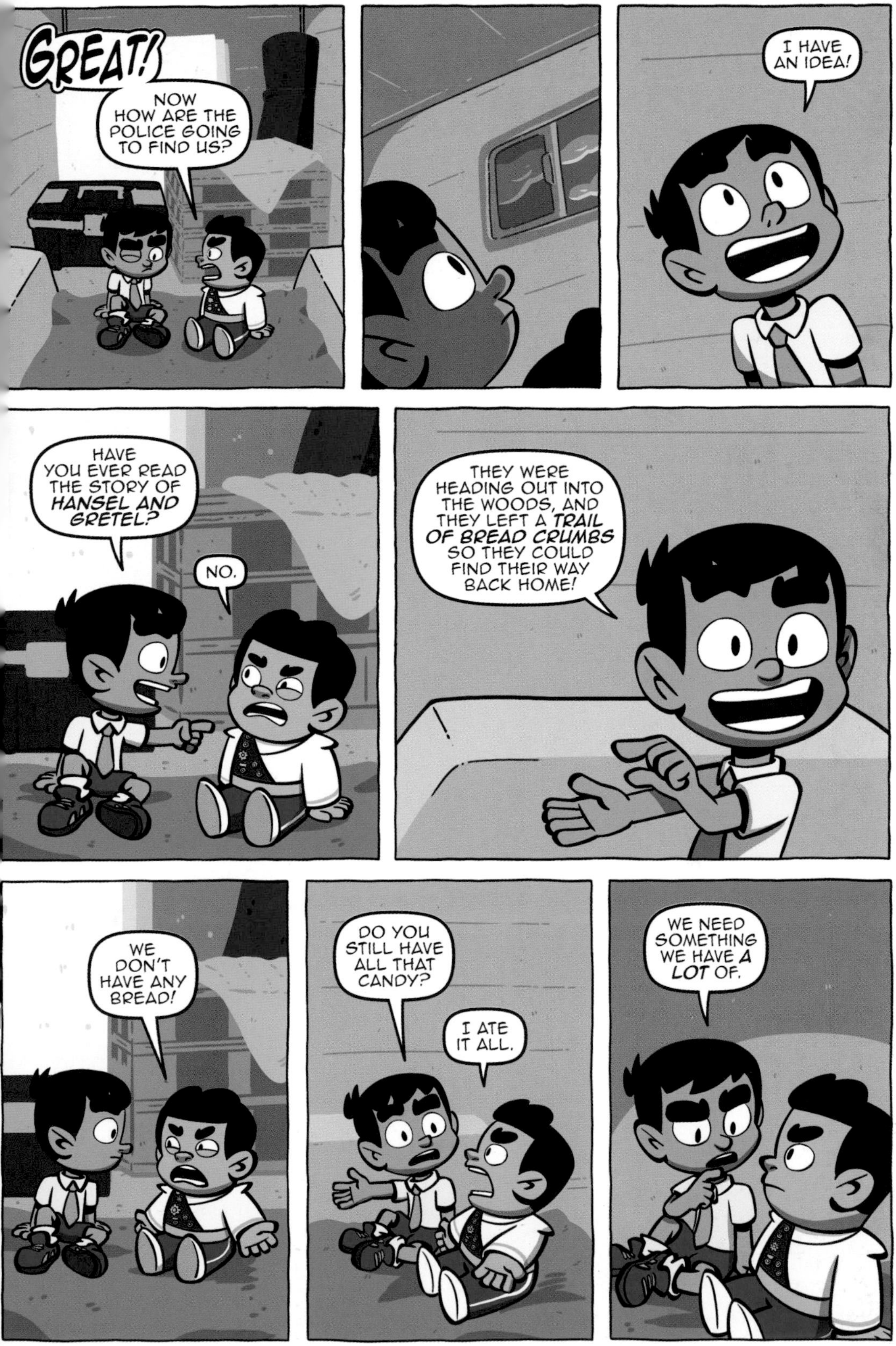
GREAT!
NOW HOW ARE THE POLICE GOING TO FIND US?
I HAVE AN IDEA!
HAVE YOU EVER READ THE STORY OF *HANSEL AND GRETEL?*
NO.
THEY WERE HEADING OUT INTO THE WOODS, AND THEY LEFT A *TRAIL OF BREAD CRUMBS* SO THEY COULD FIND THEIR WAY BACK HOME!
WE DON'T HAVE ANY BREAD!
DO YOU STILL HAVE ALL THAT CANDY?
I ATE IT ALL.
WE NEED SOMETHING WE HAVE A *LOT* OF.

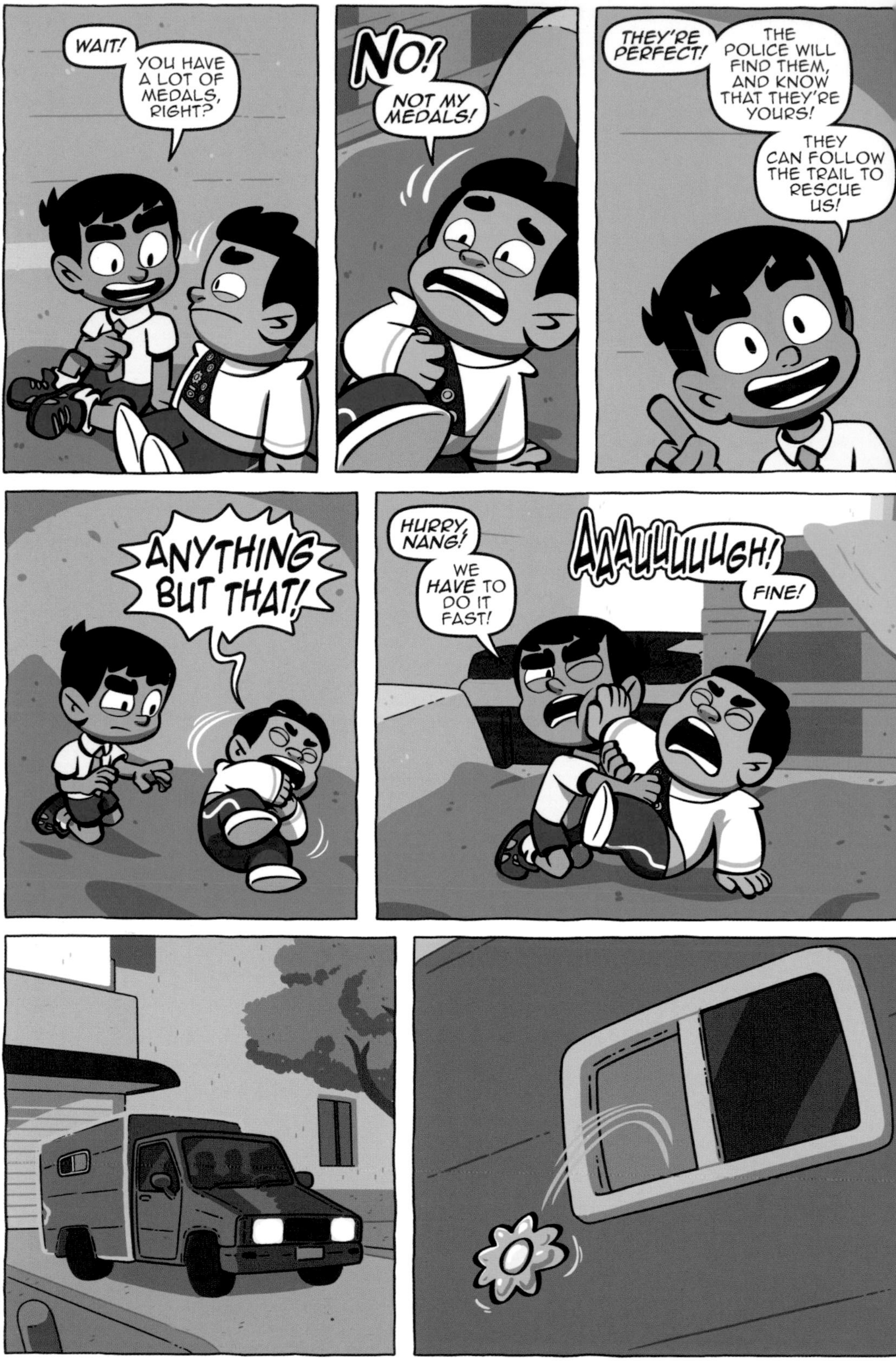
WAIT!
YOU HAVE A LOT OF MEDALS, RIGHT?
NO!
NOT MY MEDALS!
THEY'RE PERFECT!
THE POLICE WILL FIND THEM, AND KNOW THAT THEY'RE YOURS!
THEY CAN FOLLOW THE TRAIL TO RESCUE US!
ANYTHING BUT THAT!
HURRY, NANG!
WE HAVE TO DO IT FAST!
AAAUUUUUGH!
FINE!

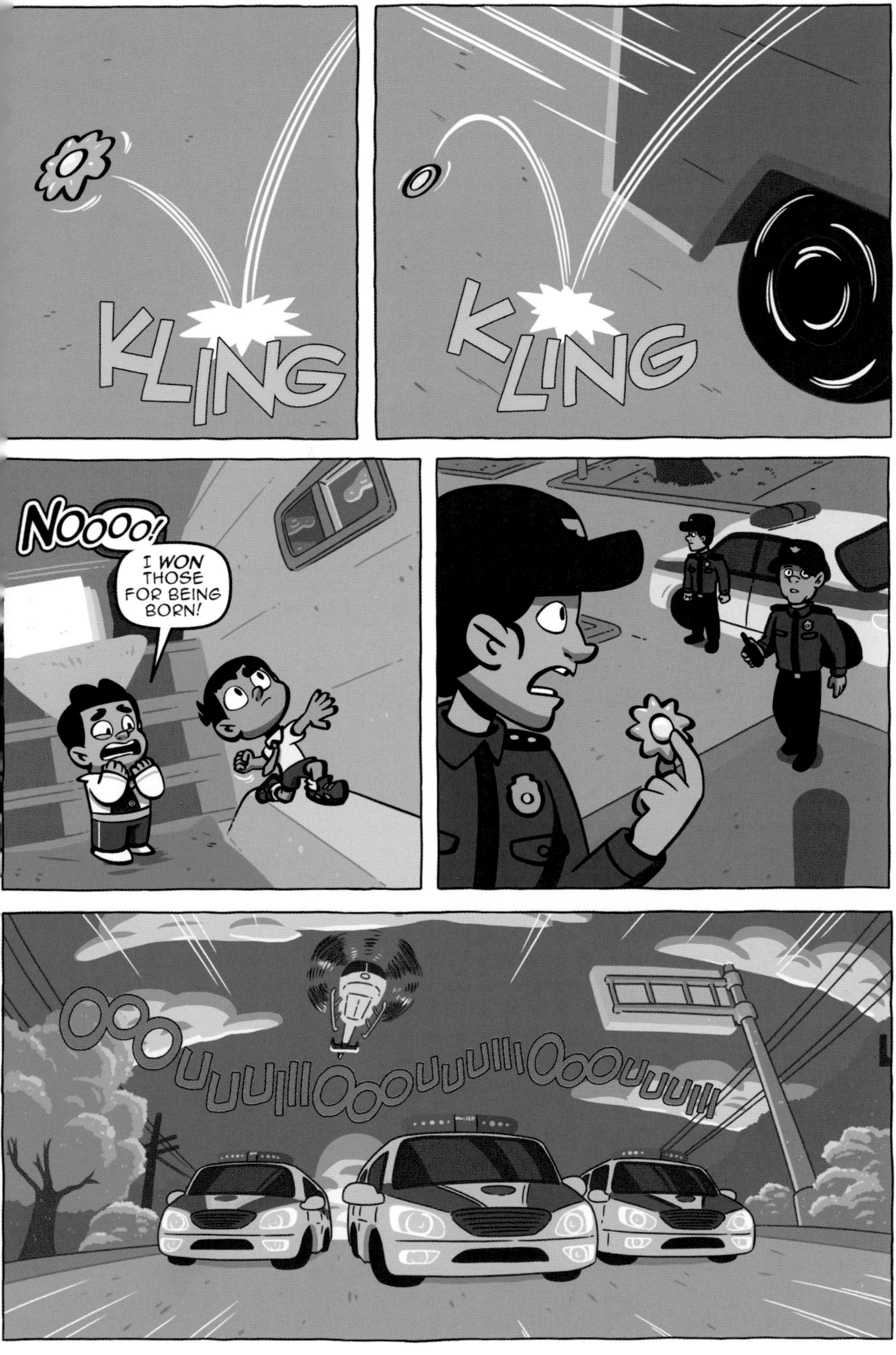
KLING
KLING
NOOOO!
I WON THOSE FOR BEING BORN!
OOOUUUIIIOOOUUUIIIOOOUUUIII

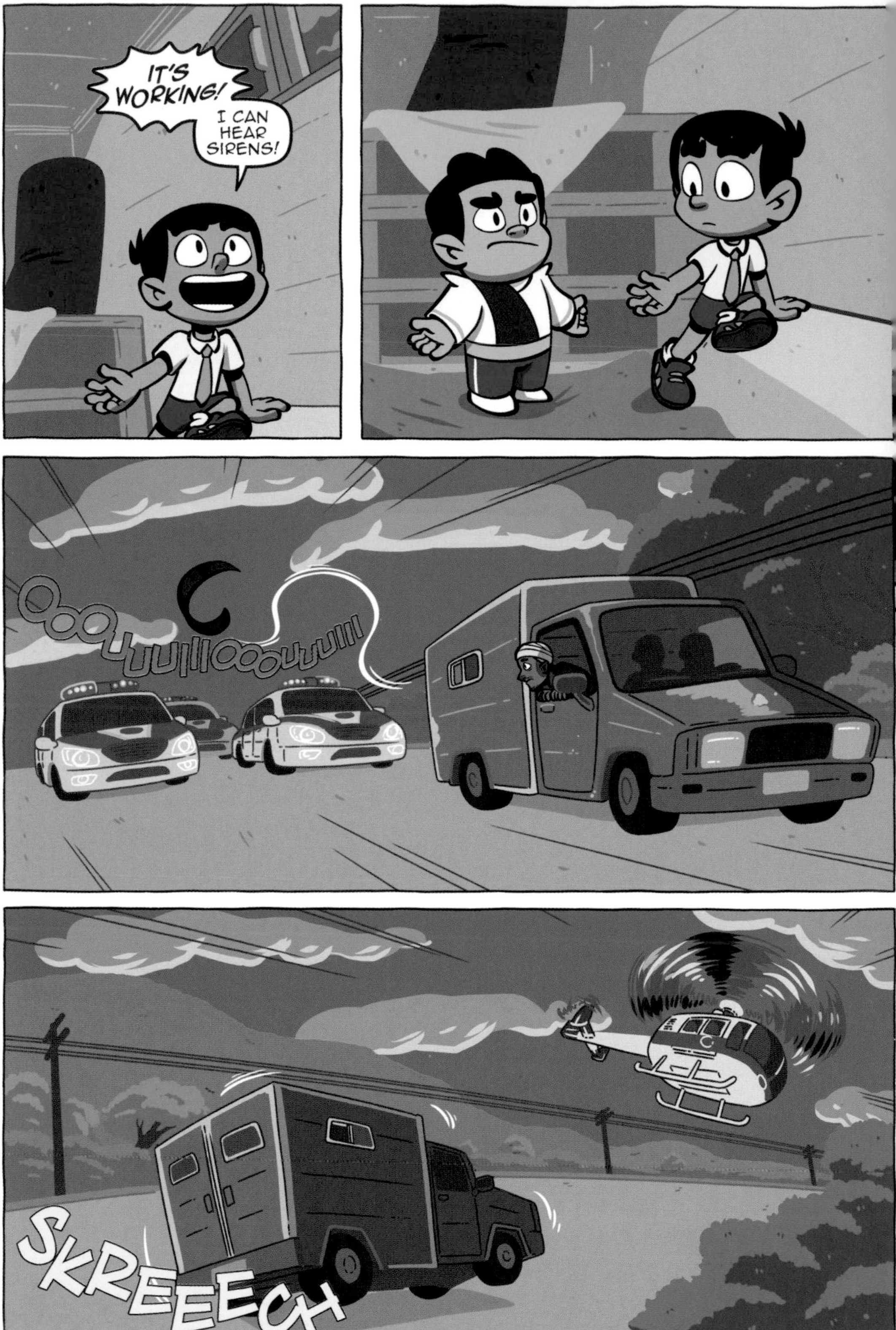
IT'S WORKING!
I CAN HEAR SIRENS!
OOOUUUIIIOOOUUUIII
SKREEECH

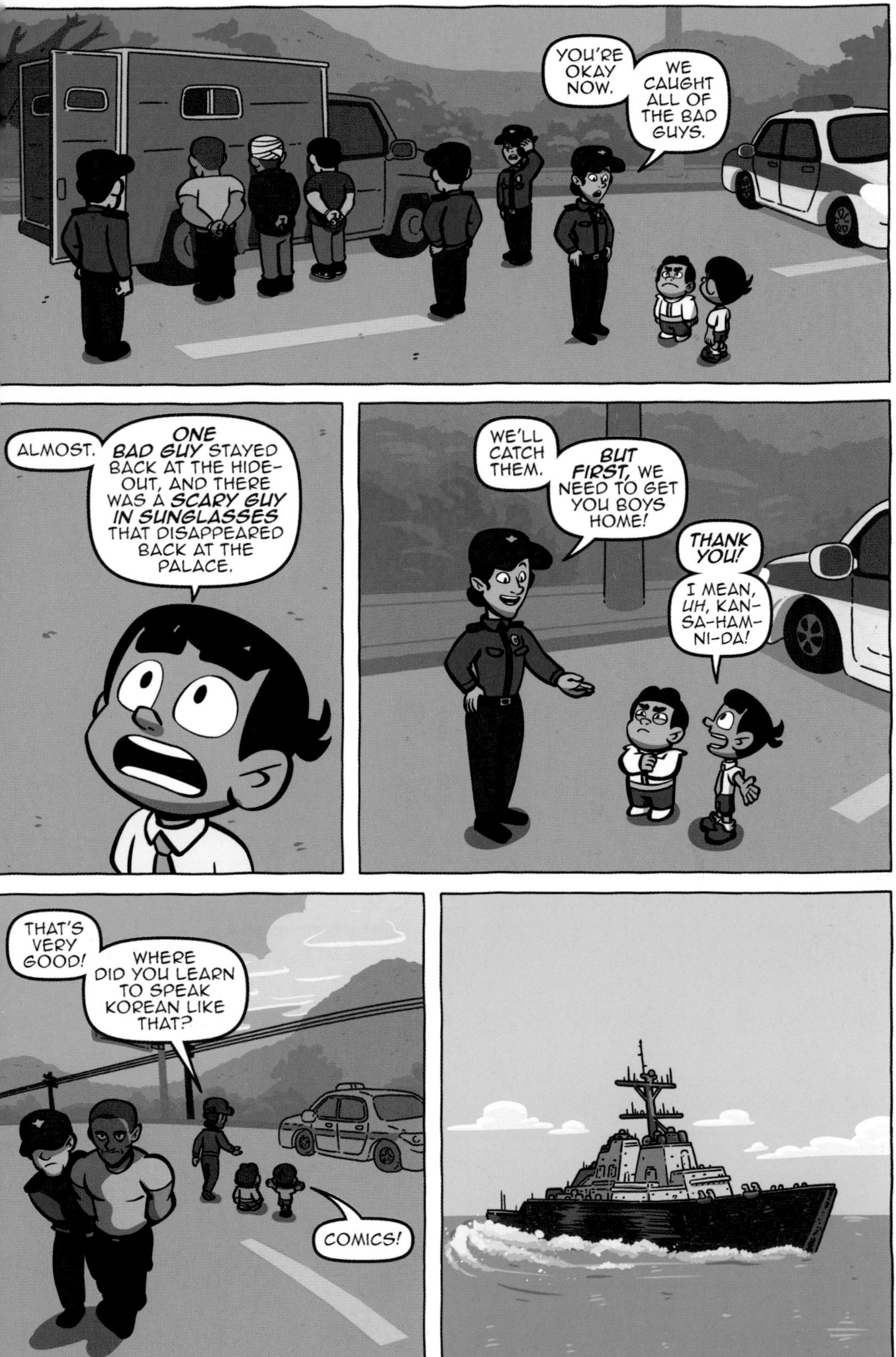
YOU'RE OKAY NOW.
WE CAUGHT ALL OF THE BAD GUYS.
ALMOST.
ONE BAD GUY STAYED BACK AT THE HIDE-OUT, AND THERE WAS A SCARY GUY IN SUNGLASSES THAT DISAPPEARED BACK AT THE PALACE.
WE'LL CATCH THEM.
BUT FIRST, WE NEED TO GET YOU BOYS HOME!
THANK YOU!
I MEAN, UH, KAN-SA-HAM-NI-DA!
THAT'S VERY GOOD!
WHERE DID YOU LEARN TO SPEAK KOREAN LIKE THAT?
COMICS!

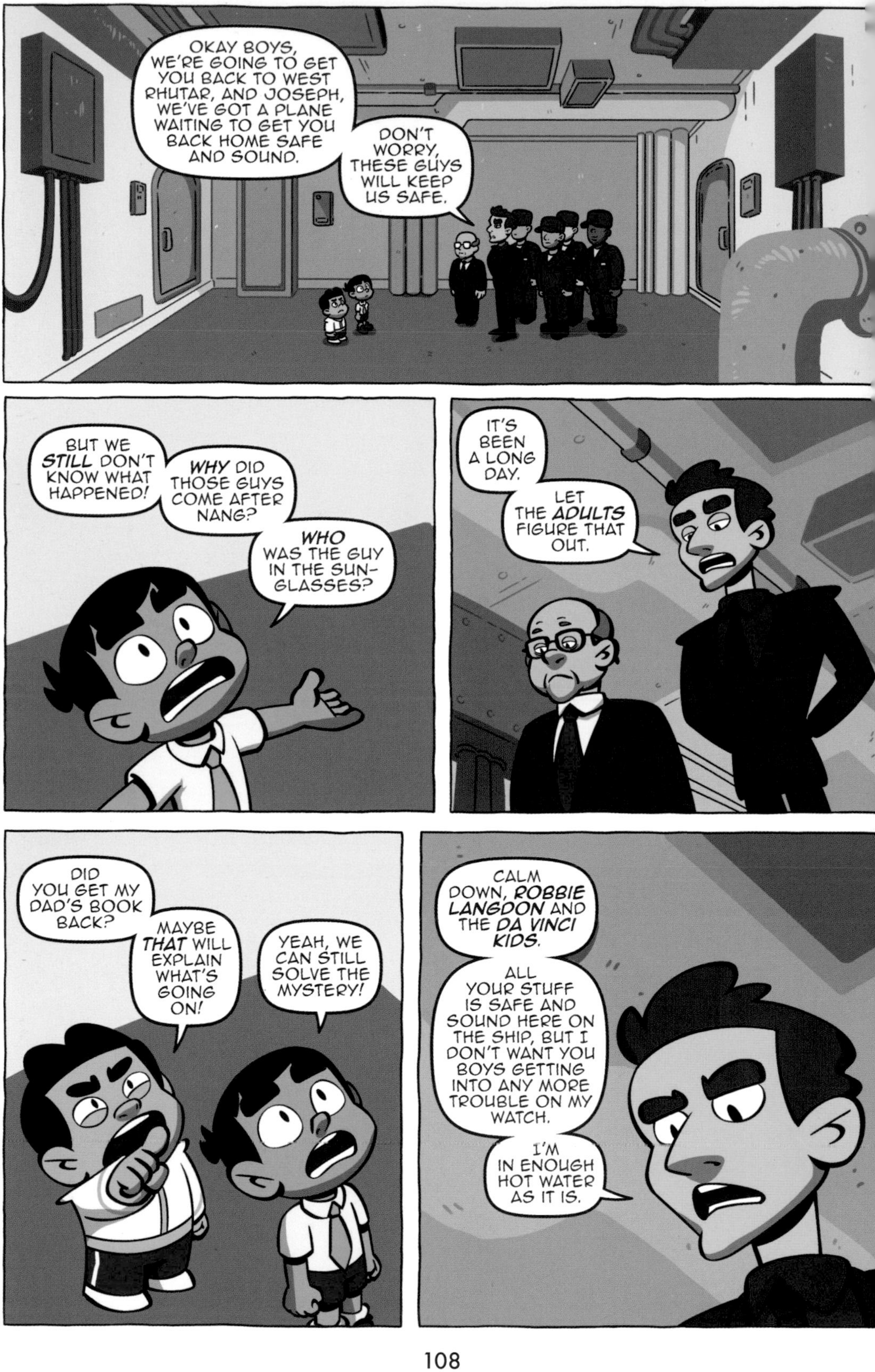
OKAY BOYS, WE'RE GOING TO GET YOU BACK TO WEST RHUTAR, AND JOSEPH, WE'VE GOT A PLANE WAITING TO GET YOU BACK HOME SAFE AND SOUND.
DON'T WORRY, THESE GUYS WILL KEEP US SAFE.
BUT WE STILL DON'T KNOW WHAT HAPPENED!
WHY DID THOSE GUYS COME AFTER NANG?
WHO WAS THE GUY IN THE SUN-GLASSES?
IT'S BEEN A LONG DAY.
LET THE ADULTS FIGURE THAT OUT.
DID YOU GET MY DAD'S BOOK BACK?
MAYBE THAT WILL EXPLAIN WHAT'S GOING ON!
YEAH, WE CAN STILL SOLVE THE MYSTERY!
CALM DOWN, ROBBIE LANGDON AND THE DA VINCI KIDS.
ALL YOUR STUFF IS SAFE AND SOUND HERE ON THE SHIP, BUT I DON'T WANT YOU BOYS GETTING INTO ANY MORE TROUBLE ON MY WATCH.
I'M IN ENOUGH HOT WATER AS IT IS.

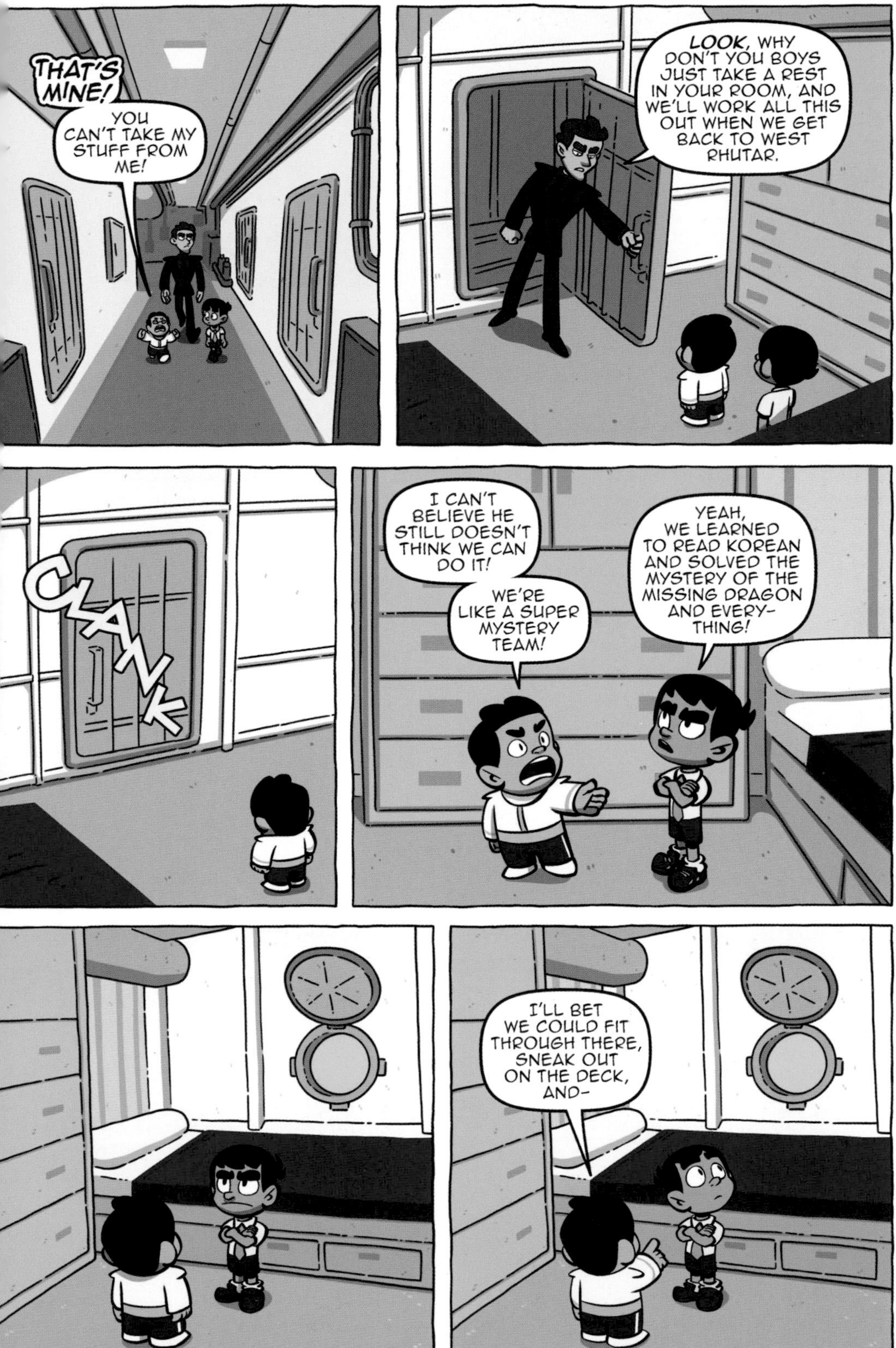
THAT'S MINE!
YOU CAN'T TAKE MY STUFF FROM ME!
LOOK, WHY DON'T YOU BOYS JUST TAKE A REST IN YOUR ROOM, AND WE'LL WORK ALL THIS OUT WHEN WE GET BACK TO WEST RHUTAR.
CLANK
I CAN'T BELIEVE HE STILL DOESN'T THINK WE CAN DO IT!
WE'RE LIKE A SUPER MYSTERY TEAM!
YEAH, WE LEARNED TO READ KOREAN AND SOLVED THE MYSTERY OF THE MISSING DRAGON AND EVERY-THING!
I'LL BET WE COULD FIT THROUGH THERE, SNEAK OUT ON THE DECK, AND-

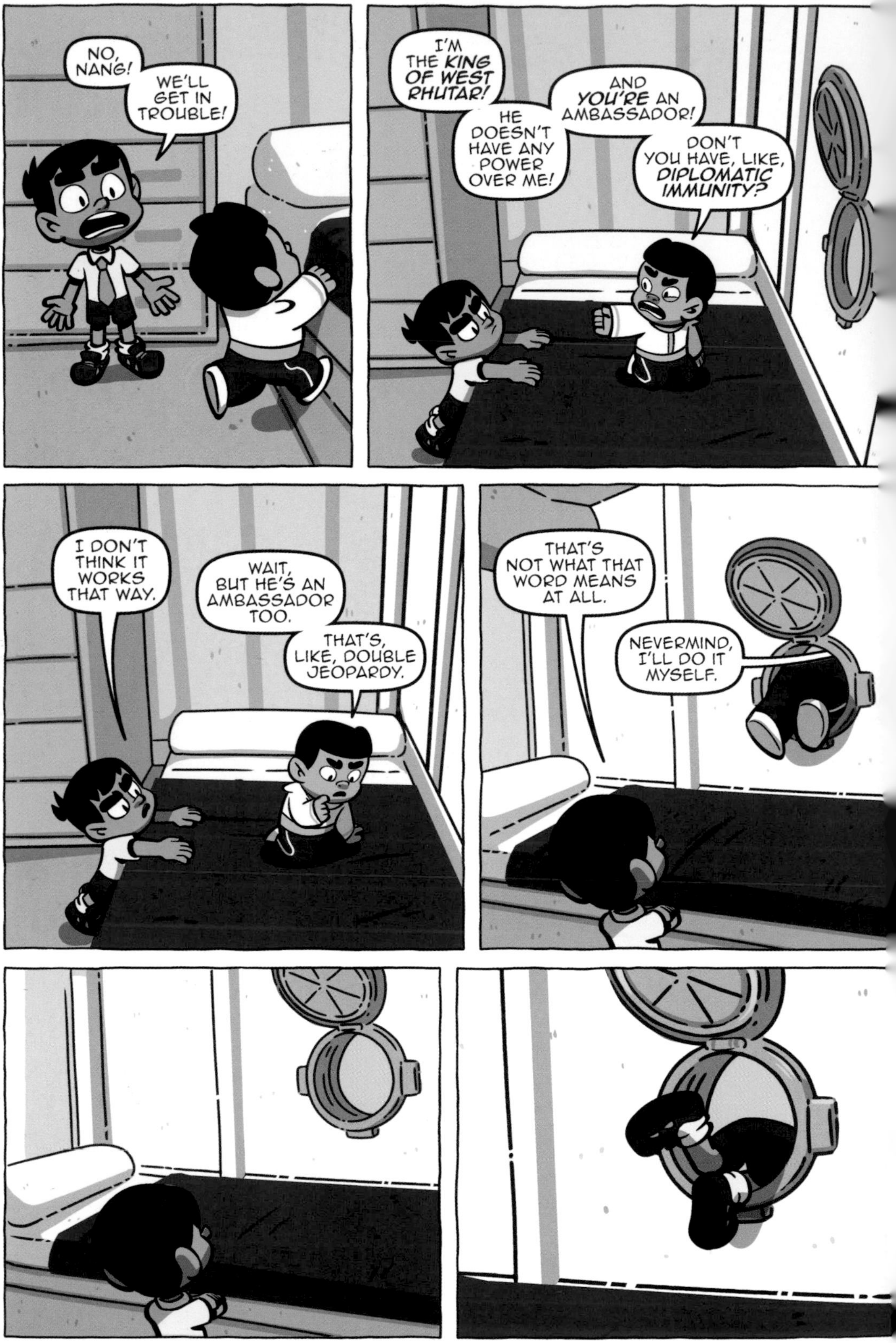
NO, NANG!
WE'LL GET IN TROUBLE!
I'M THE **KING OF WEST RHUTAR!**
HE DOESN'T HAVE ANY POWER OVER ME!
AND **YOU'RE** AN AMBASSADOR!
DON'T YOU HAVE, LIKE, **DIPLOMATIC IMMUNITY?**
I DON'T THINK IT WORKS THAT WAY.
WAIT, BUT HE'S AN AMBASSADOR TOO.
THAT'S, LIKE, DOUBLE JEOPARDY.
THAT'S NOT WHAT THAT WORD MEANS AT ALL.
NEVERMIND, I'LL DO IT MYSELF.

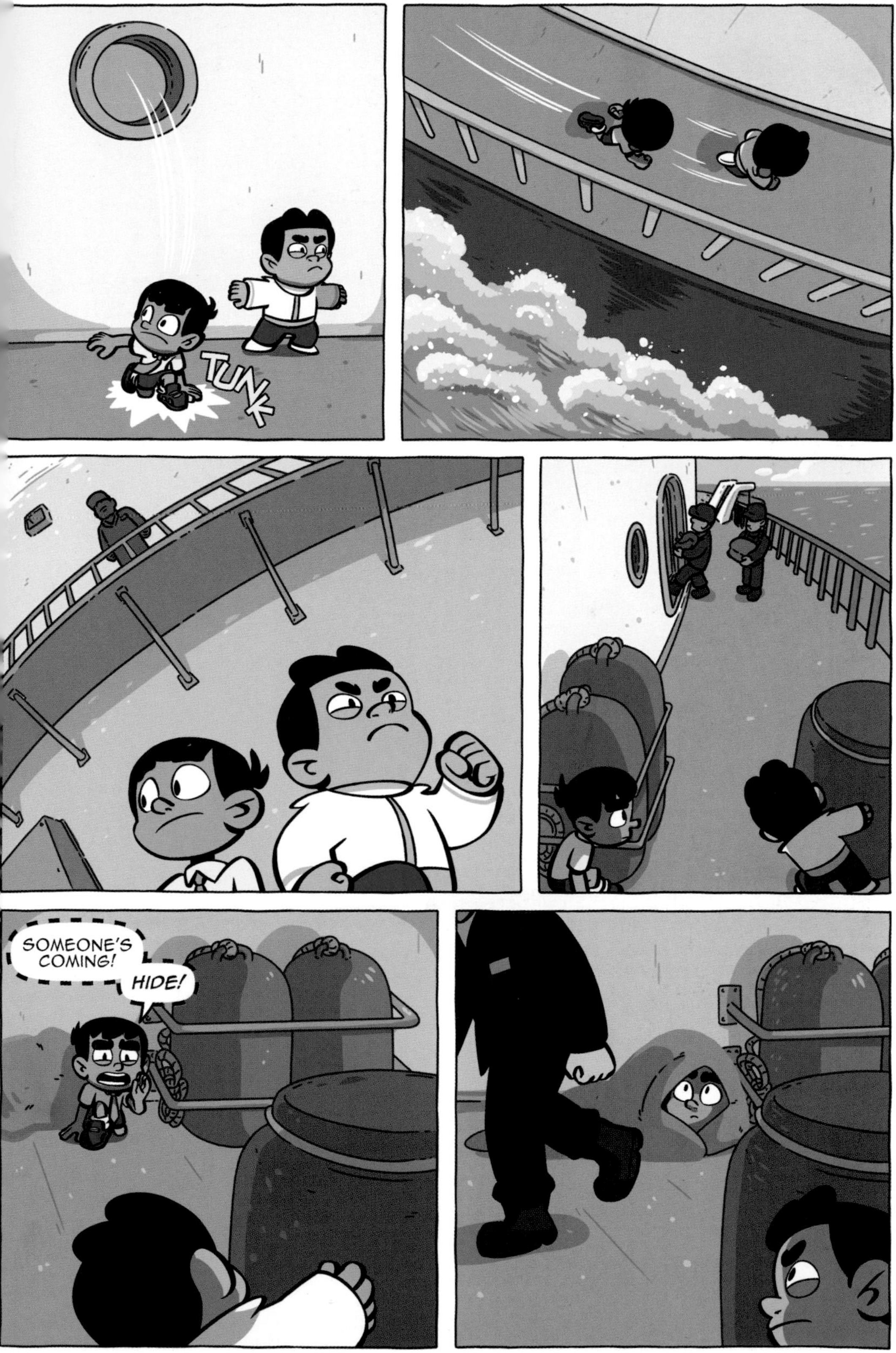
TUNK
SOMEONE'S COMING!
HIDE!

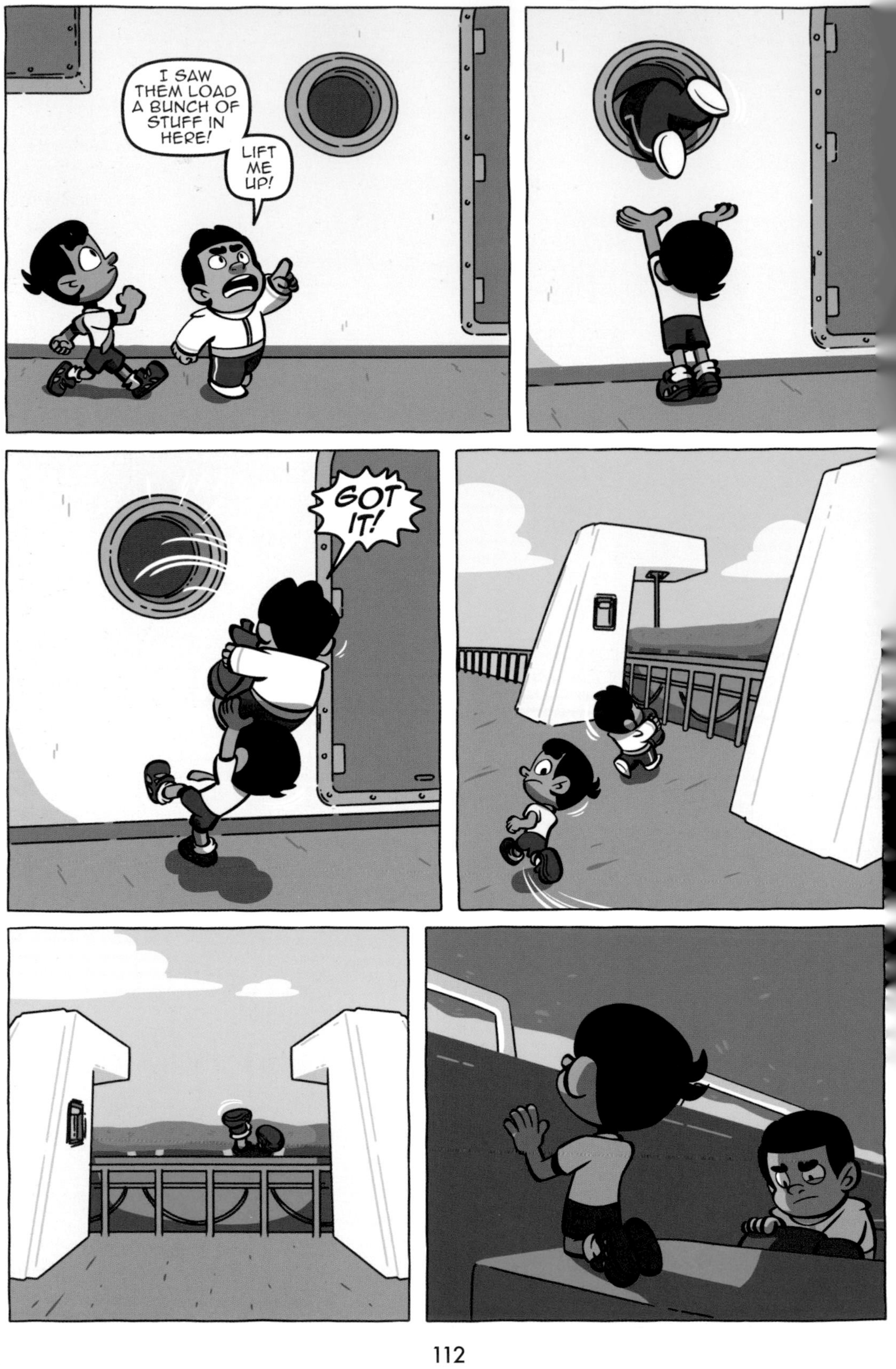
I SAW THEM LOAD A BUNCH OF STUFF IN HERE!
LIFT ME UP!
GOT IT!

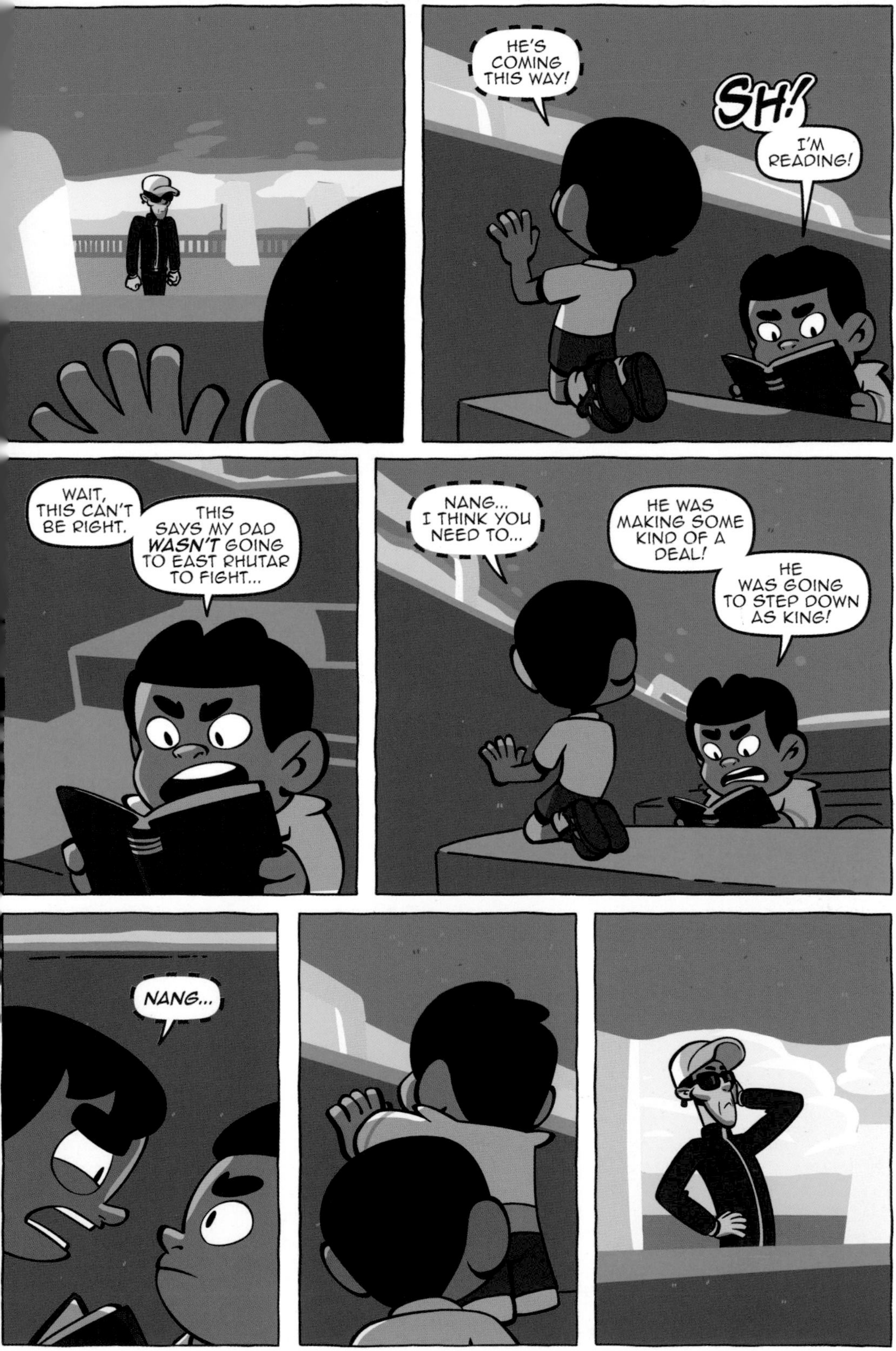
HE'S COMING THIS WAY!
SH!
I'M READING!
WAIT, THIS CAN'T BE RIGHT.
THIS SAYS MY DAD WASN'T GOING TO EAST RHUTAR TO FIGHT...
NANG... I THINK YOU NEED TO...
HE WAS MAKING SOME KIND OF A DEAL!
HE WAS GOING TO STEP DOWN AS KING!
NANG...

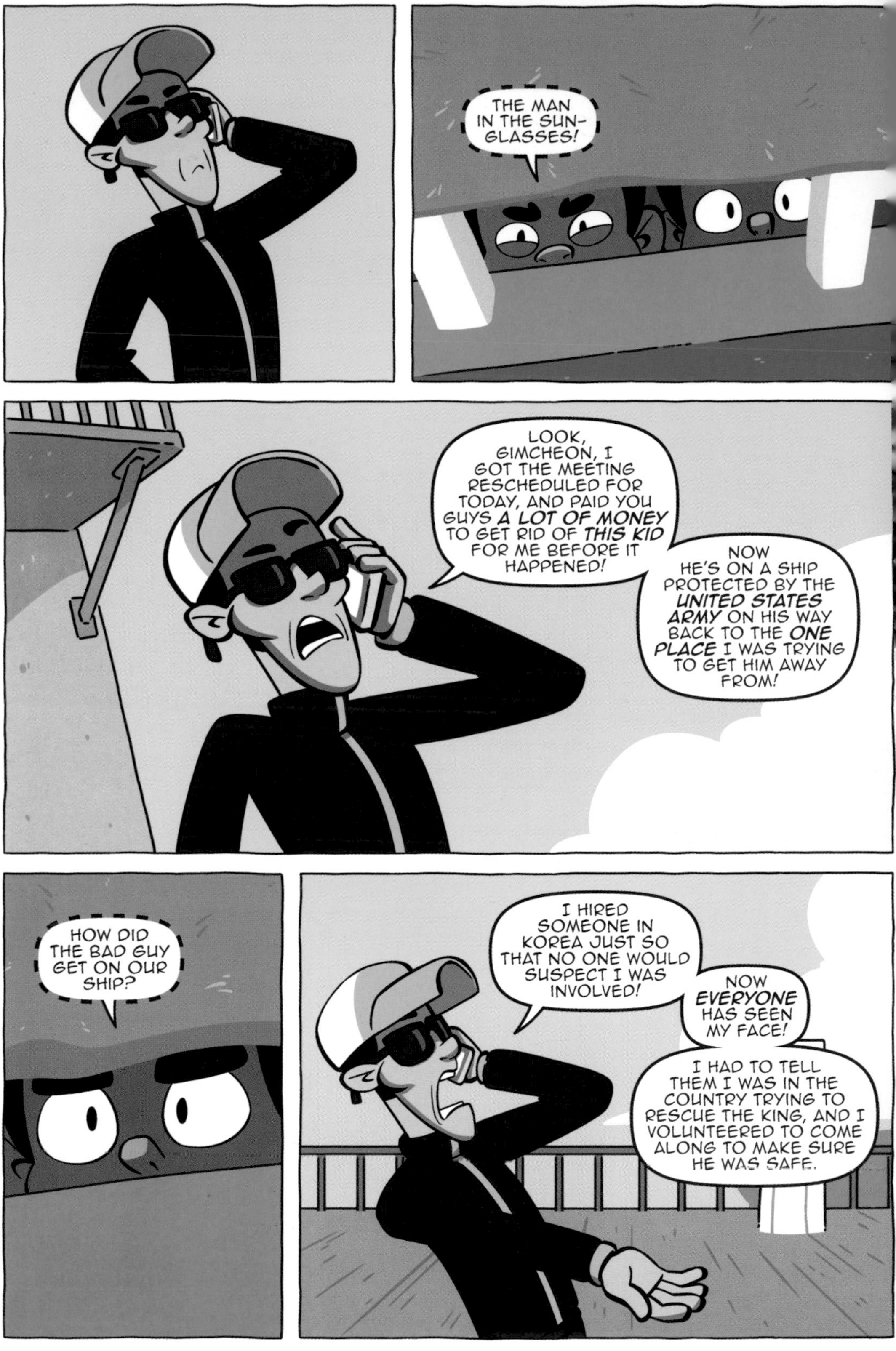
THE MAN IN THE SUN-GLASSES!
LOOK, GIMCHEON, I GOT THE MEETING RESCHEDULED FOR TODAY, AND PAID YOU GUYS *A LOT OF MONEY* TO GET RID OF *THIS KID* FOR ME BEFORE IT HAPPENED!
NOW HE'S ON A SHIP PROTECTED BY THE *UNITED STATES ARMY* ON HIS WAY BACK TO THE *ONE PLACE* I WAS TRYING TO GET HIM AWAY FROM!
HOW DID THE BAD GUY GET ON OUR SHIP?
I HIRED SOMEONE IN KOREA JUST SO THAT NO ONE WOULD SUSPECT I WAS INVOLVED!
NOW *EVERYONE* HAS SEEN MY FACE!
I HAD TO TELL THEM I WAS IN THE COUNTRY TRYING TO RESCUE THE KING, AND I VOLUNTEERED TO COME ALONG TO MAKE SURE HE WAS SAFE.

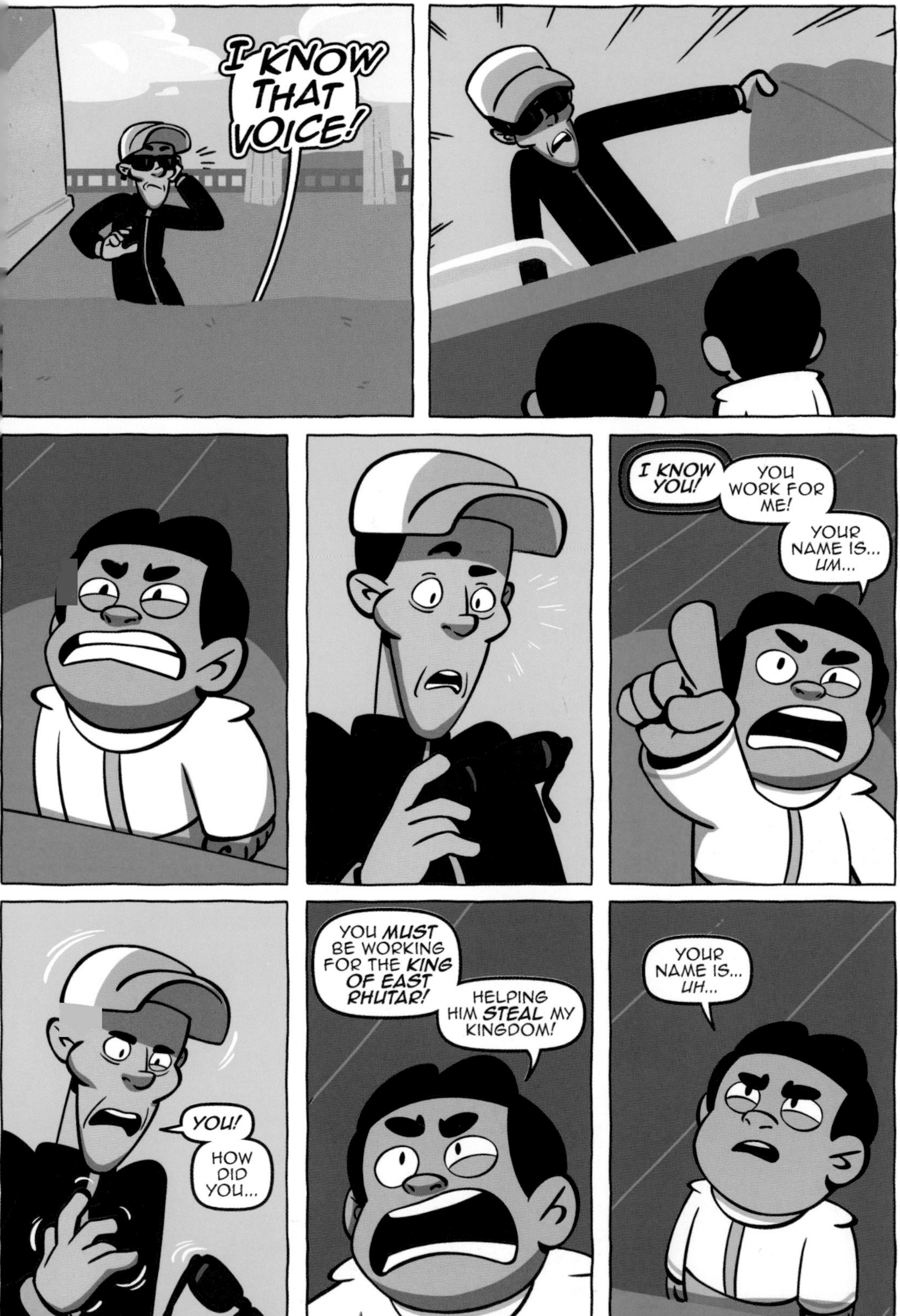
I KNOW THAT VOICE!
I KNOW YOU!
YOU WORK FOR ME!
YOUR NAME IS... UM...
YOU! HOW DID YOU...
YOU MUST BE WORKING FOR THE KING OF EAST RHUTAR!
HELPING HIM STEAL MY KINGDOM!
YOUR NAME IS... UH...

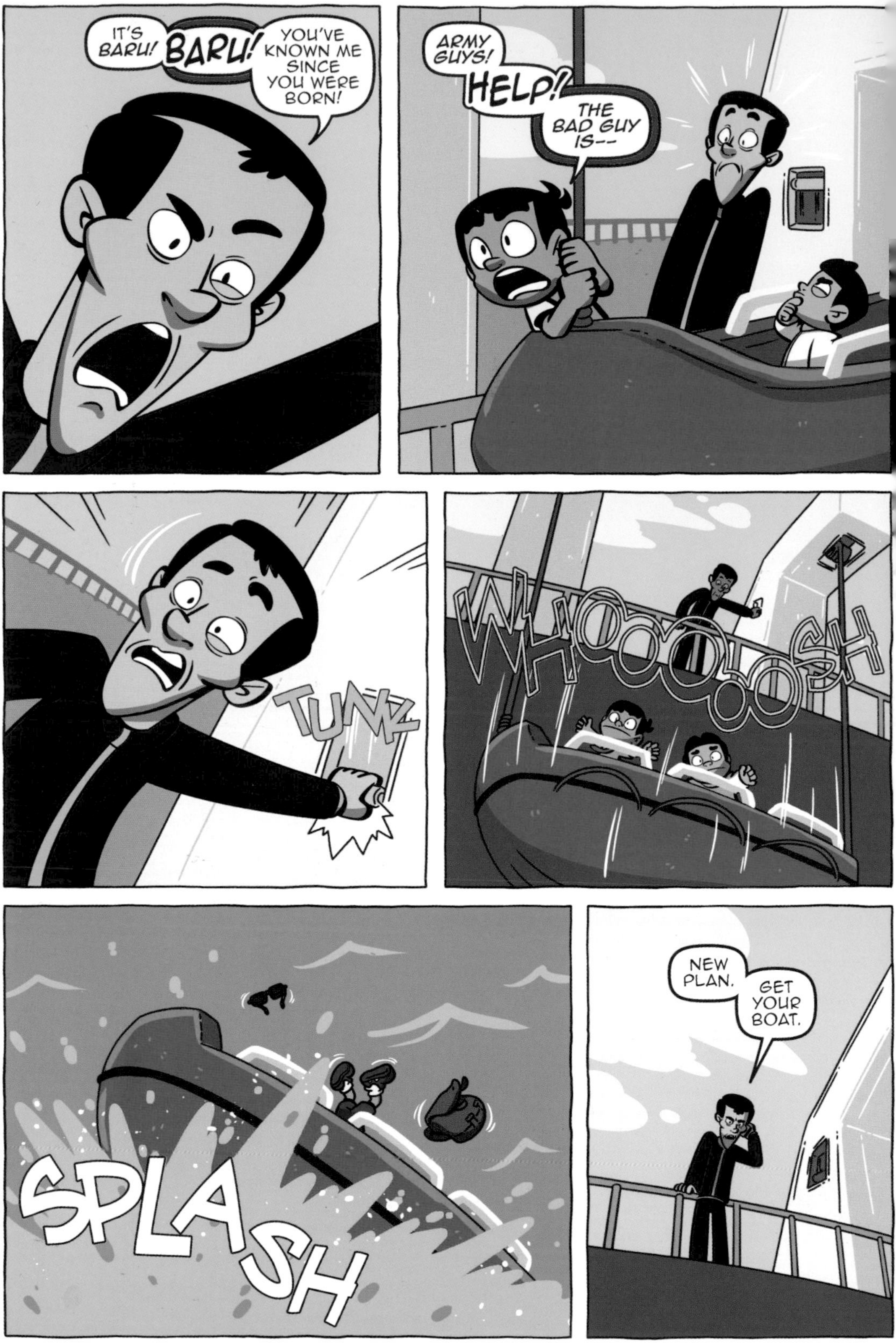
IT'S BARU!
BARU!
YOU'VE KNOWN ME SINCE YOU WERE BORN!
ARMY GUYS!
HELP!
THE BAD GUY IS--
TUNK
WHOOOOOOOSH
SPLASH
NEW PLAN.
GET YOUR BOAT.

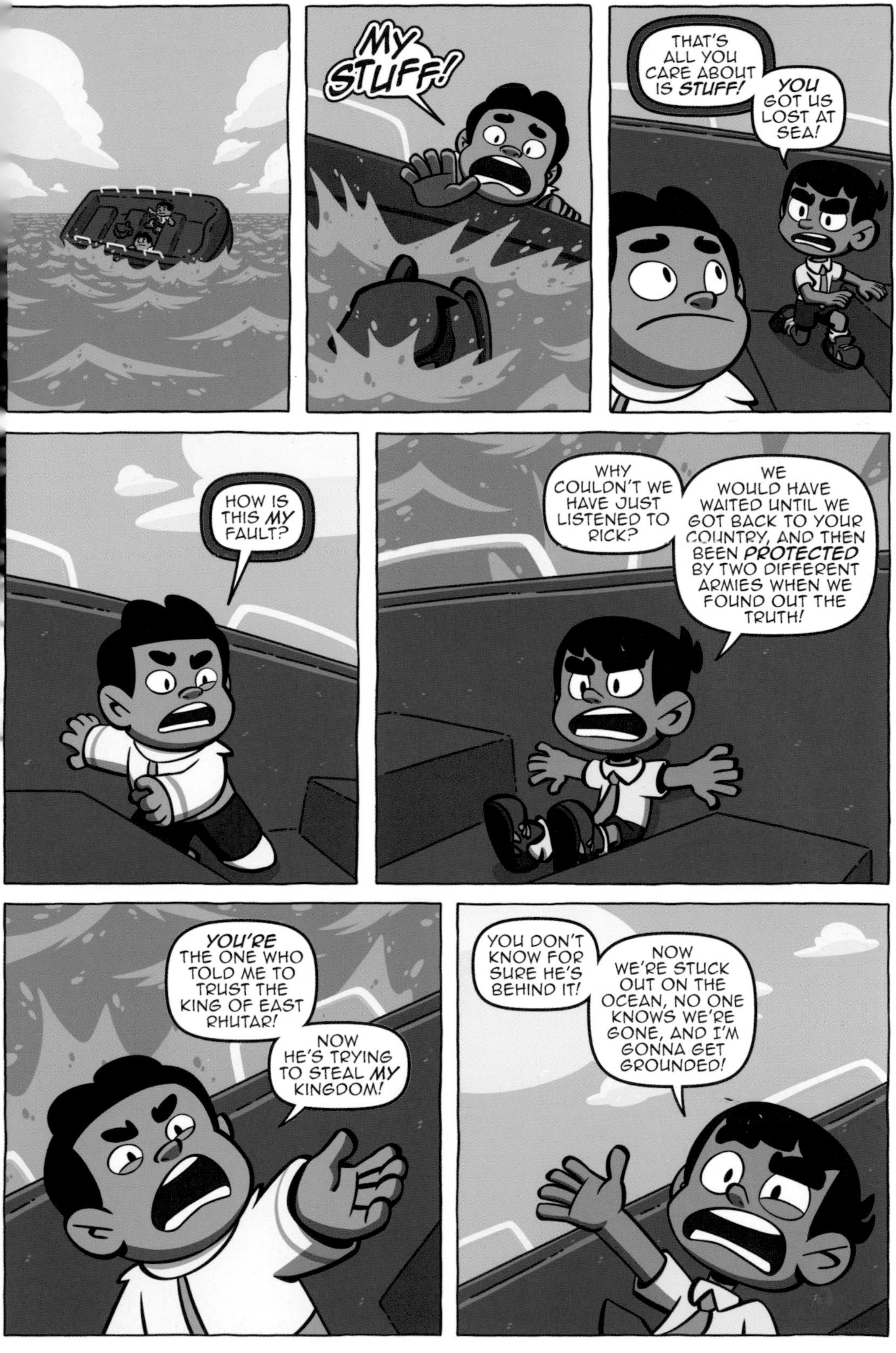
MY STUFF!
THAT'S ALL YOU CARE ABOUT IS STUFF!
YOU GOT US LOST AT SEA!
HOW IS THIS MY FAULT?
WHY COULDN'T WE HAVE JUST LISTENED TO RICK?
WE WOULD HAVE WAITED UNTIL WE GOT BACK TO YOUR COUNTRY, AND THEN BEEN PROTECTED BY TWO DIFFERENT ARMIES WHEN WE FOUND OUT THE TRUTH!
YOU'RE THE ONE WHO TOLD ME TO TRUST THE KING OF EAST RHUTAR!
NOW HE'S TRYING TO STEAL MY KINGDOM!
YOU DON'T KNOW FOR SURE HE'S BEHIND IT!
NOW WE'RE STUCK OUT ON THE OCEAN, NO ONE KNOWS WE'RE GONE, AND I'M GONNA GET GROUNDED!

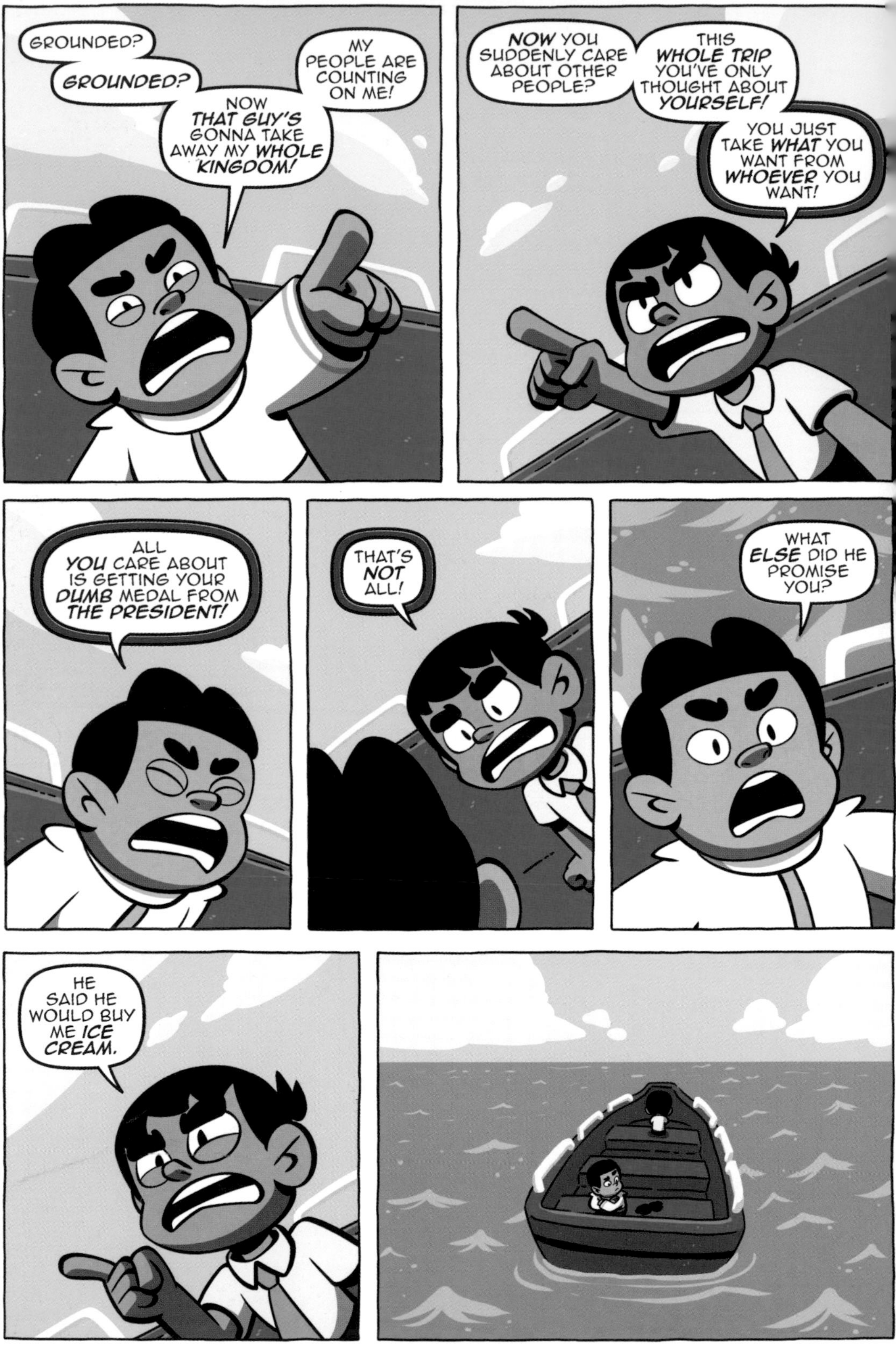
GROUNDED?
GROUNDED?
NOW THAT GUY'S GONNA TAKE AWAY MY WHOLE KINGDOM!
MY PEOPLE ARE COUNTING ON ME!
NOW YOU SUDDENLY CARE ABOUT OTHER PEOPLE?
THIS WHOLE TRIP YOU'VE ONLY THOUGHT ABOUT YOURSELF!
YOU JUST TAKE WHAT YOU WANT FROM WHOEVER YOU WANT!
ALL YOU CARE ABOUT IS GETTING YOUR DUMB MEDAL FROM THE PRESIDENT!
THAT'S NOT ALL!
WHAT ELSE DID HE PROMISE YOU?
HE SAID HE WOULD BUY ME ICE CREAM.

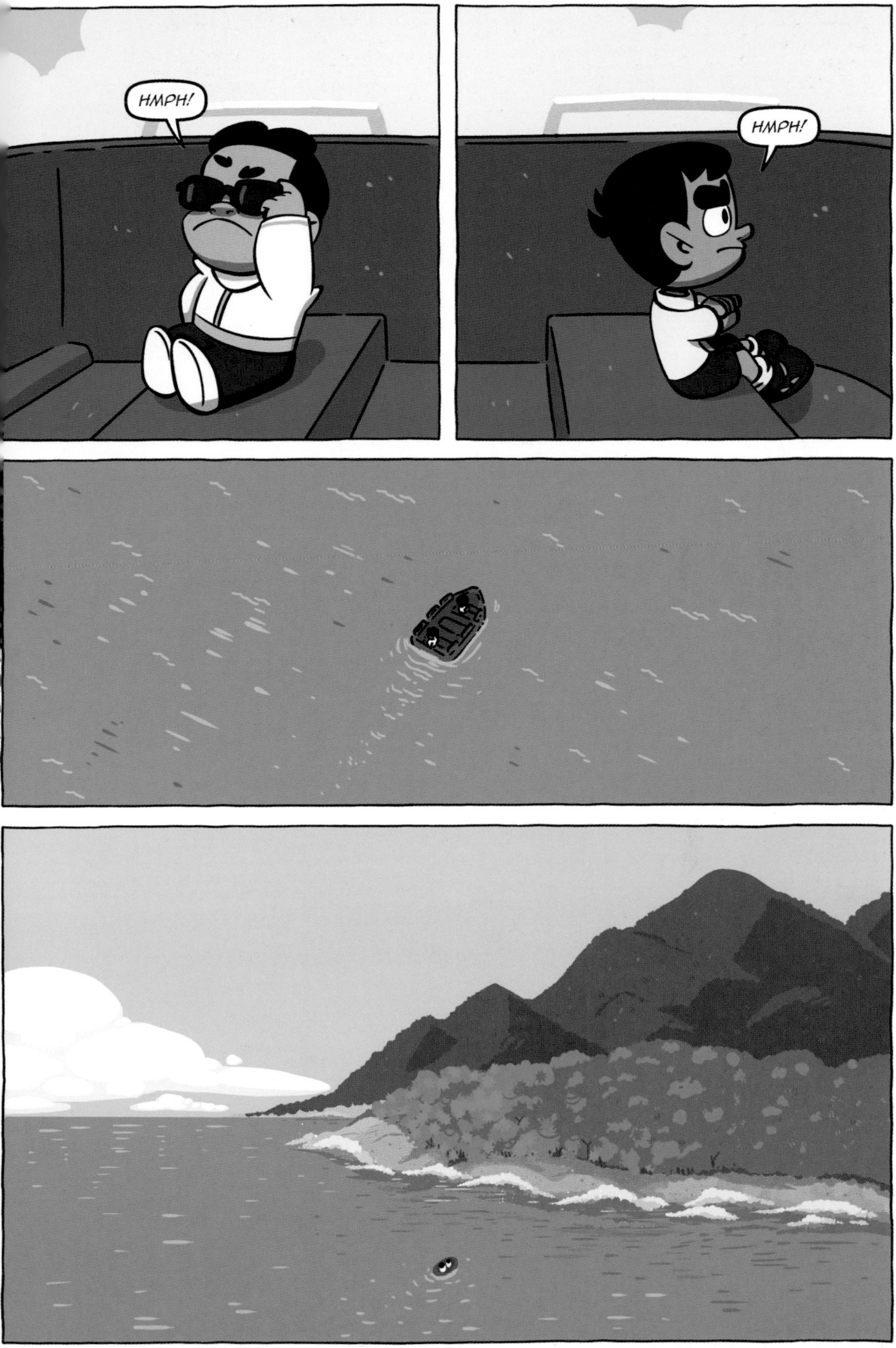
HMPH!
HMPH!

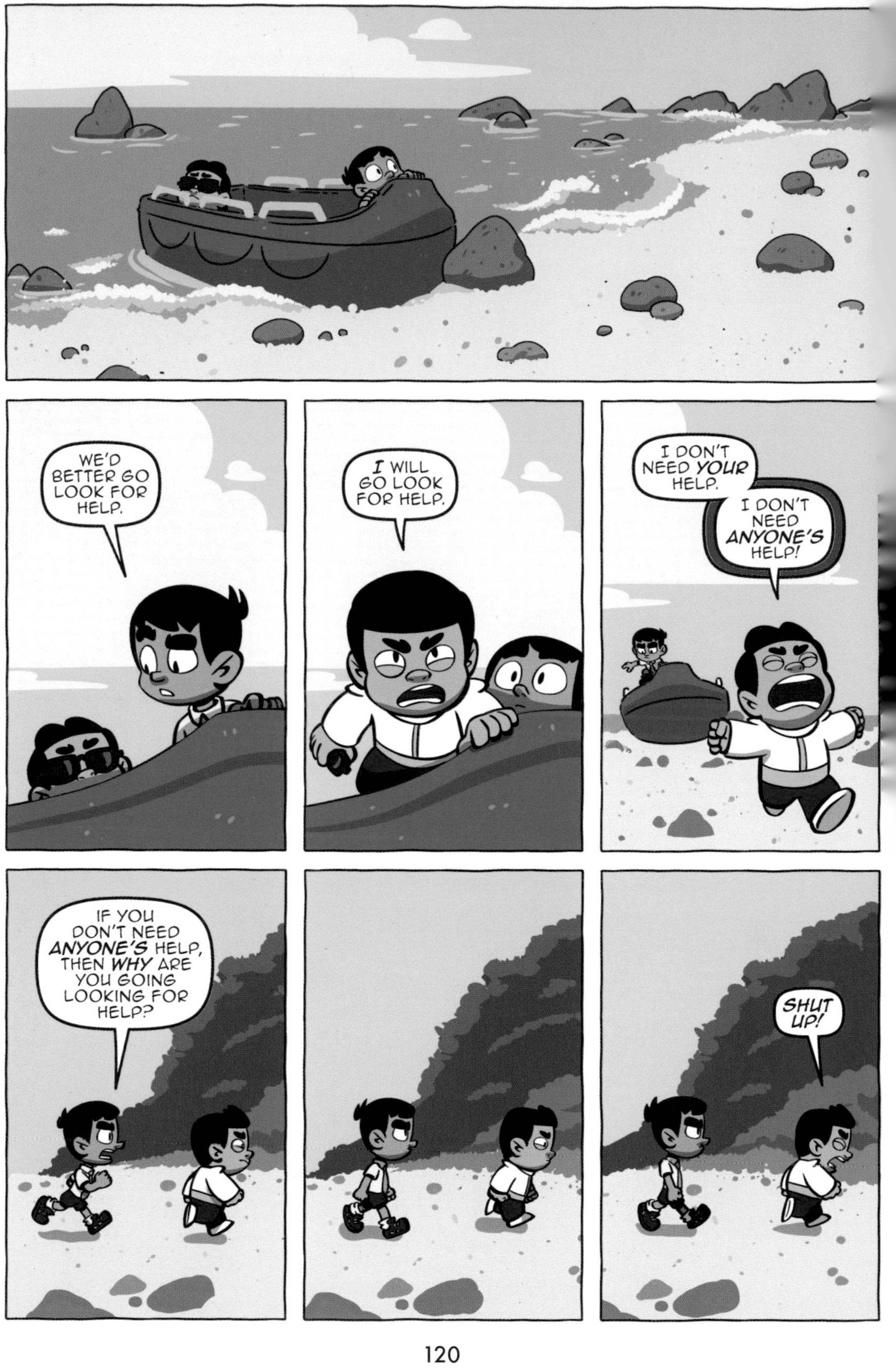
WE'D BETTER GO LOOK FOR HELP.
I WILL GO LOOK FOR HELP.
I DON'T NEED YOUR HELP.
I DON'T NEED ANYONE'S HELP!
IF YOU DON'T NEED ANYONE'S HELP, THEN WHY ARE YOU GOING LOOKING FOR HELP?
SHUT UP!

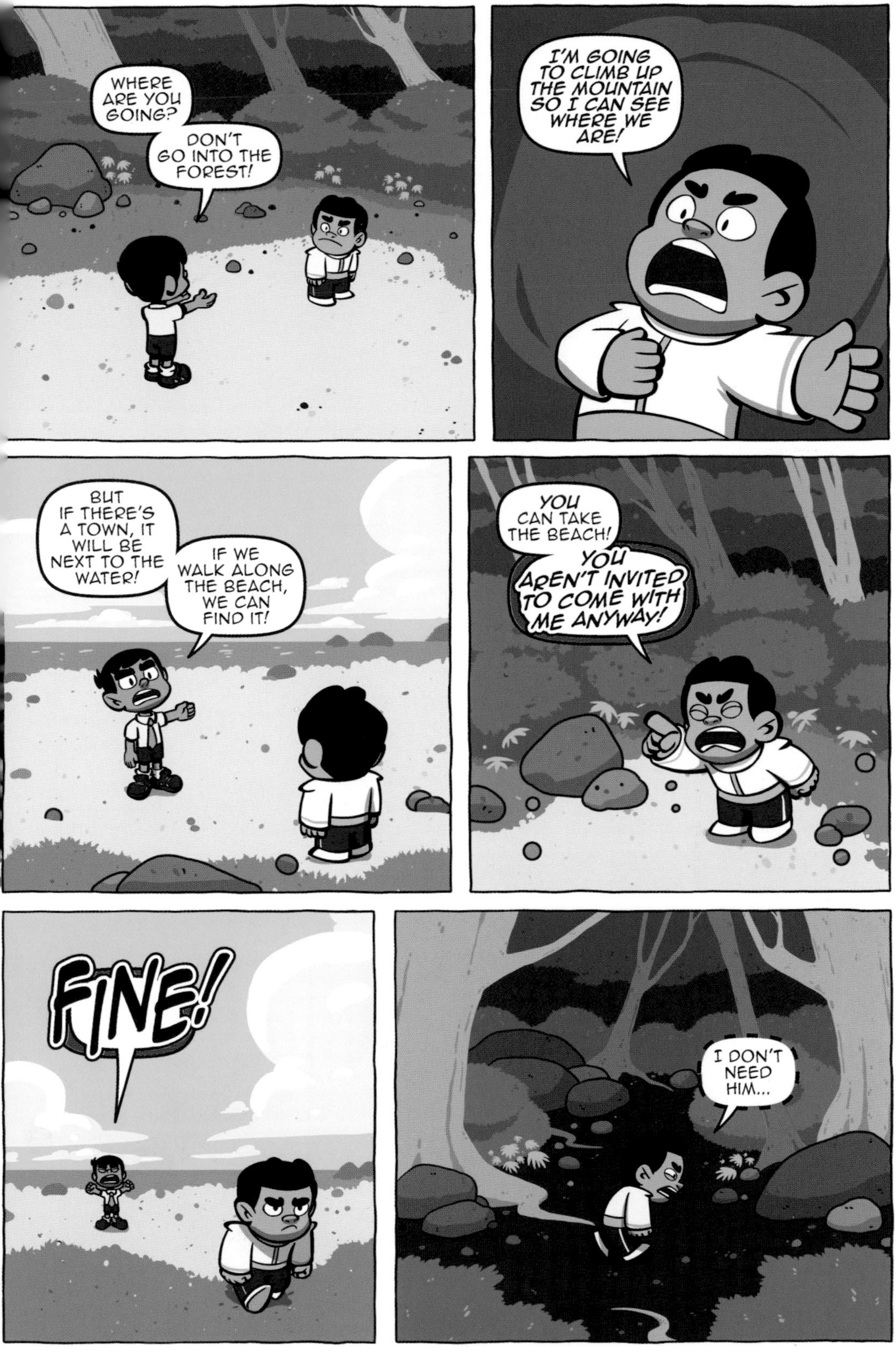
WHERE ARE YOU GOING?
DON'T GO INTO THE FOREST!
I'M GOING TO CLIMB UP THE MOUNTAIN SO I CAN SEE WHERE WE ARE!
BUT IF THERE'S A TOWN, IT WILL BE NEXT TO THE WATER!
IF WE WALK ALONG THE BEACH, WE CAN FIND IT!
YOU CAN TAKE THE BEACH!
YOU AREN'T INVITED TO COME WITH ME ANYWAY!
FINE!
I DON'T NEED HIM...

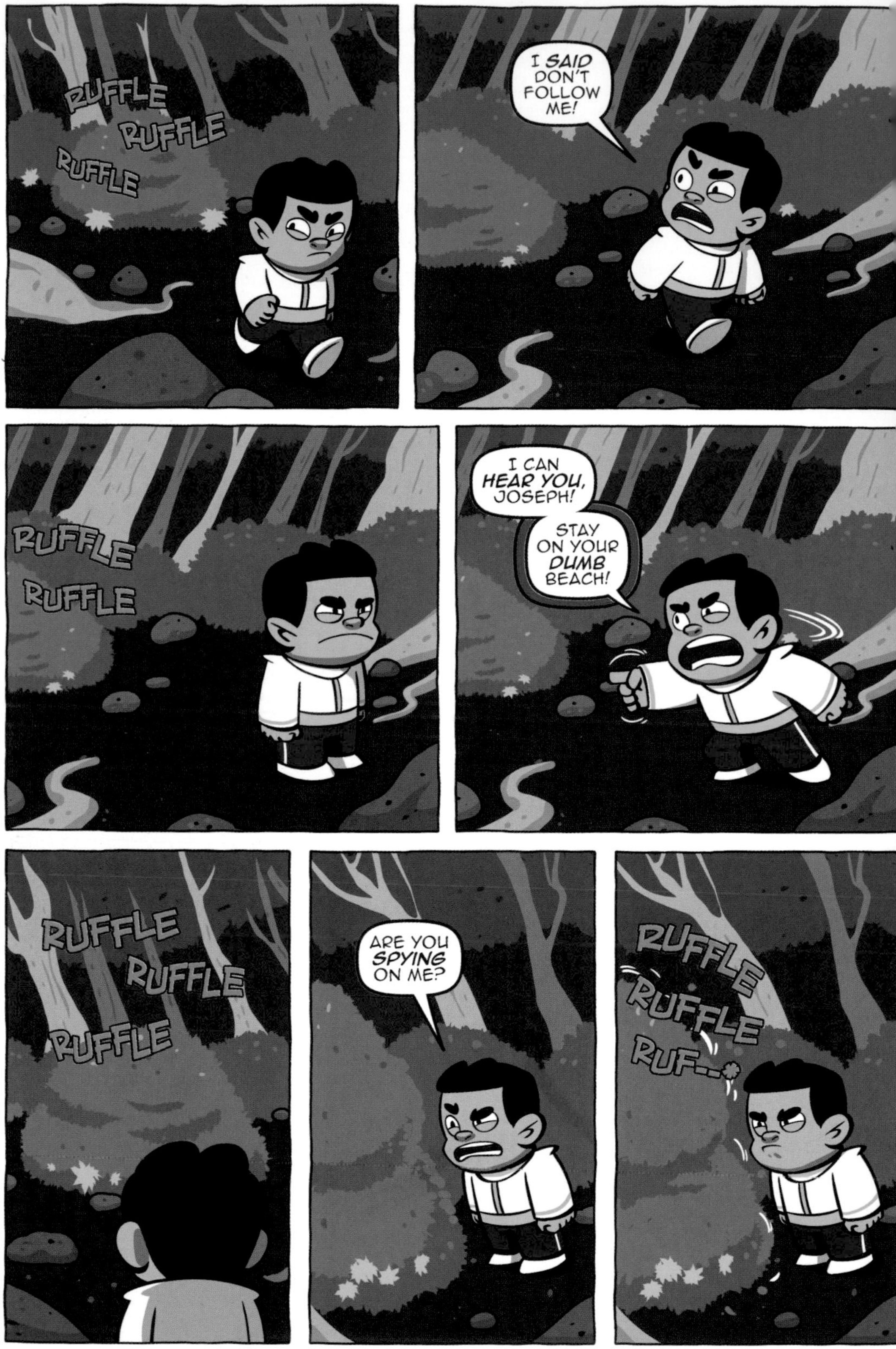
RUFFLE
RUFFLE
RUFFLE
I SAID DON'T FOLLOW ME!
RUFFLE
RUFFLE
I CAN HEAR YOU, JOSEPH!
STAY ON YOUR DUMB BEACH!
RUFFLE
RUFFLE
RUFFLE
ARE YOU SPYING ON ME?
RUFFLE
RUFFLE
RUF...

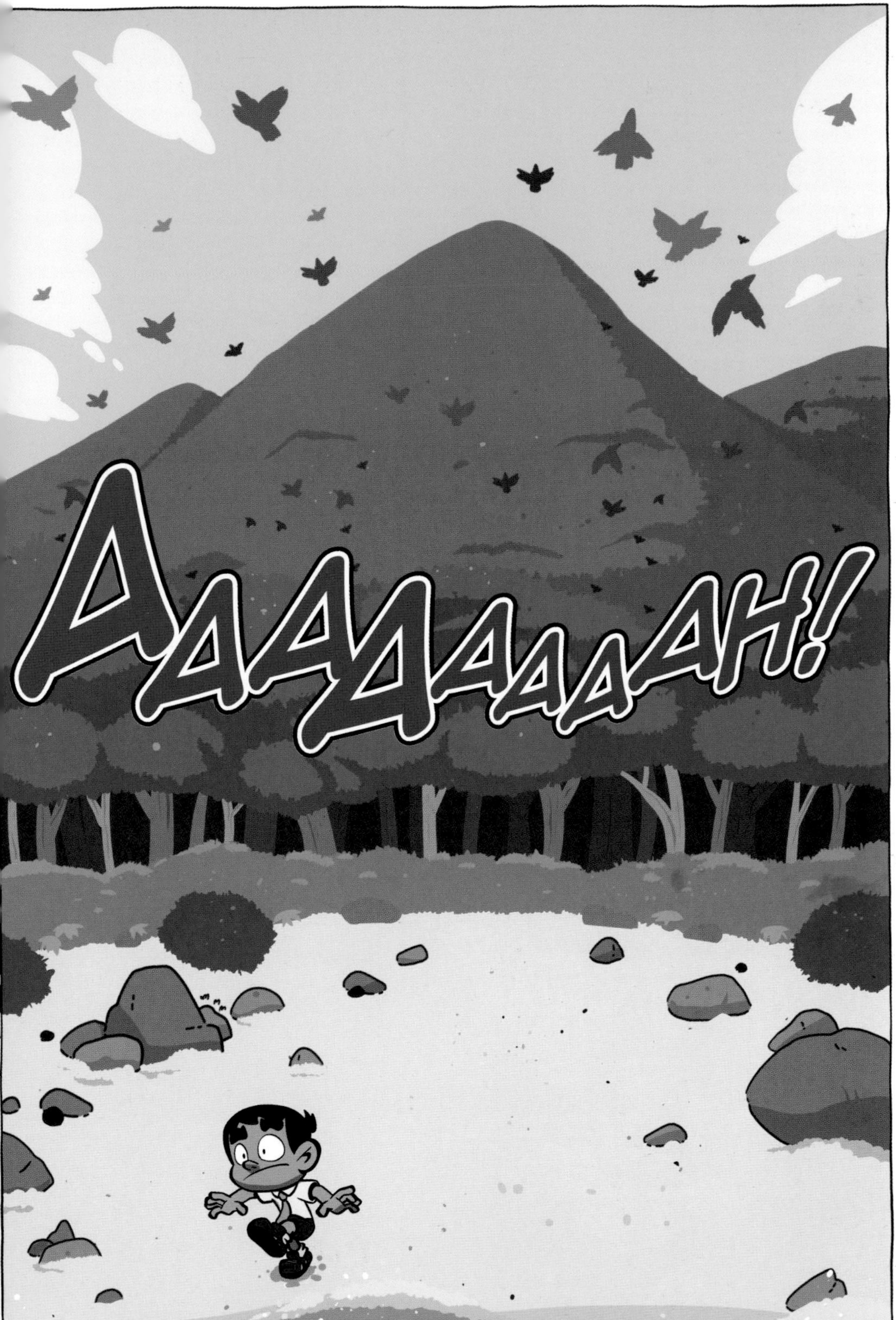
AAAAAAAAH!

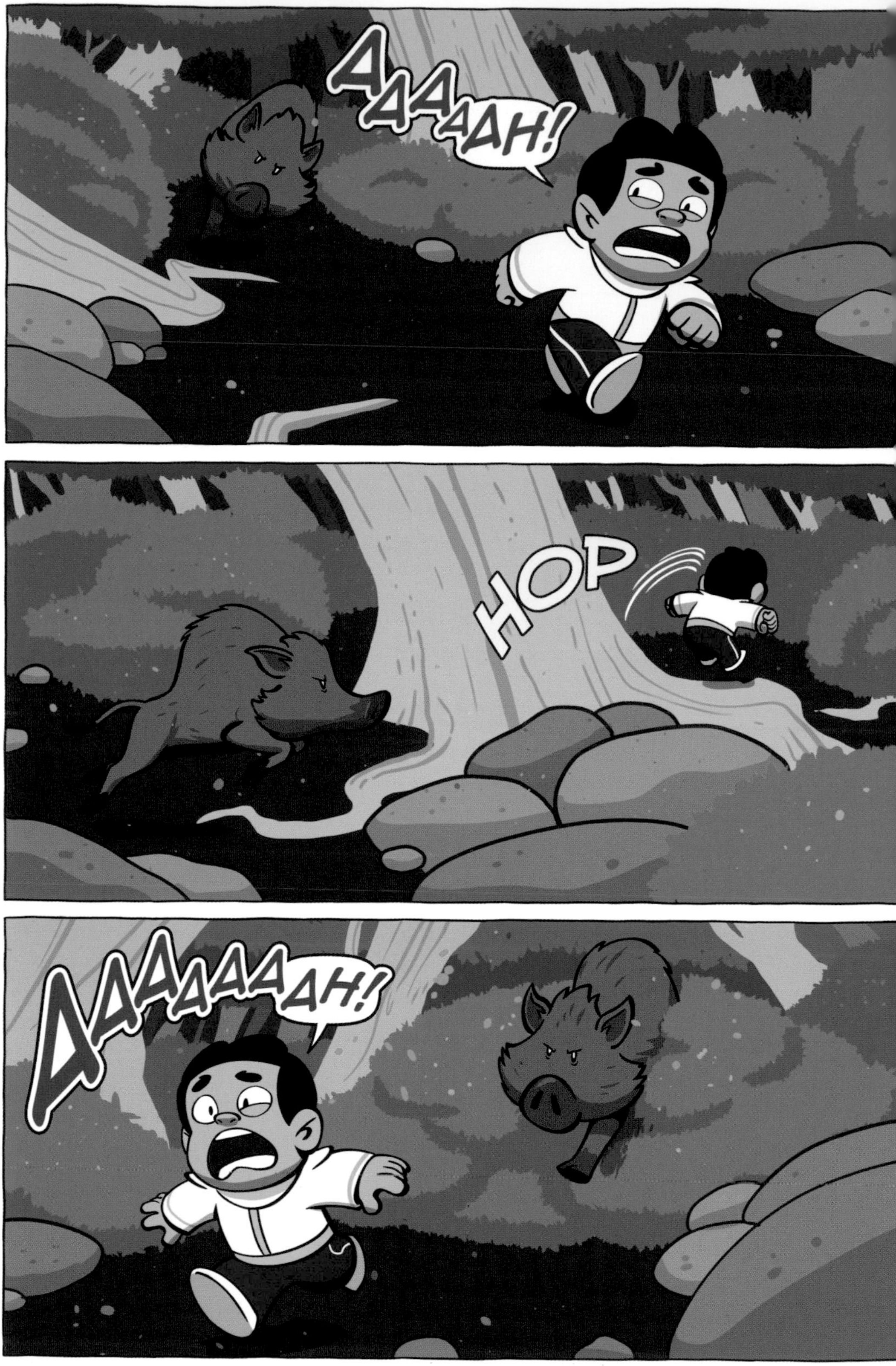
AAAAAH!
HOP
AAAAAAAH!

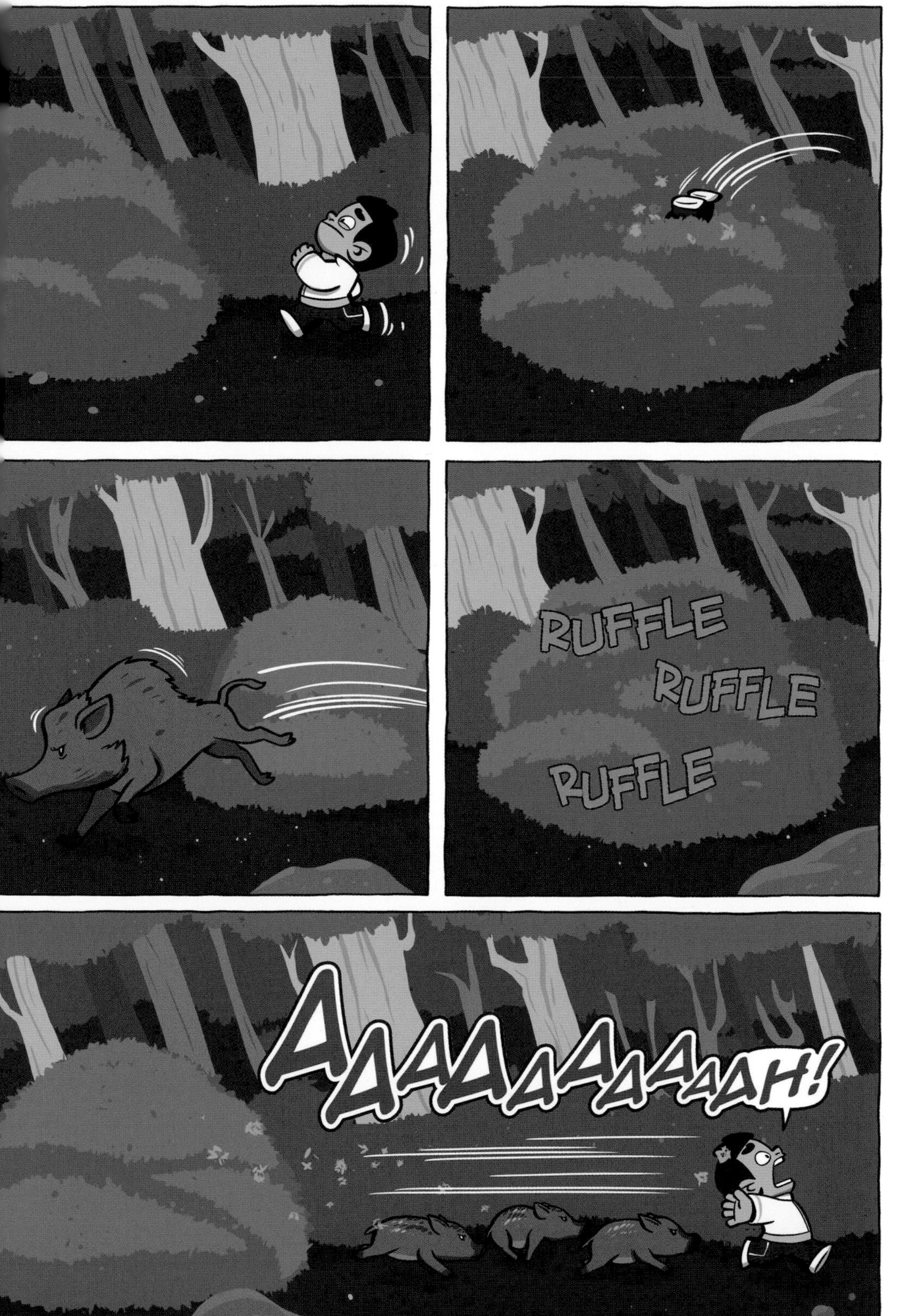
RUFFLE
RUFFLE
RUFFLE
AAAAAAAAAAH!

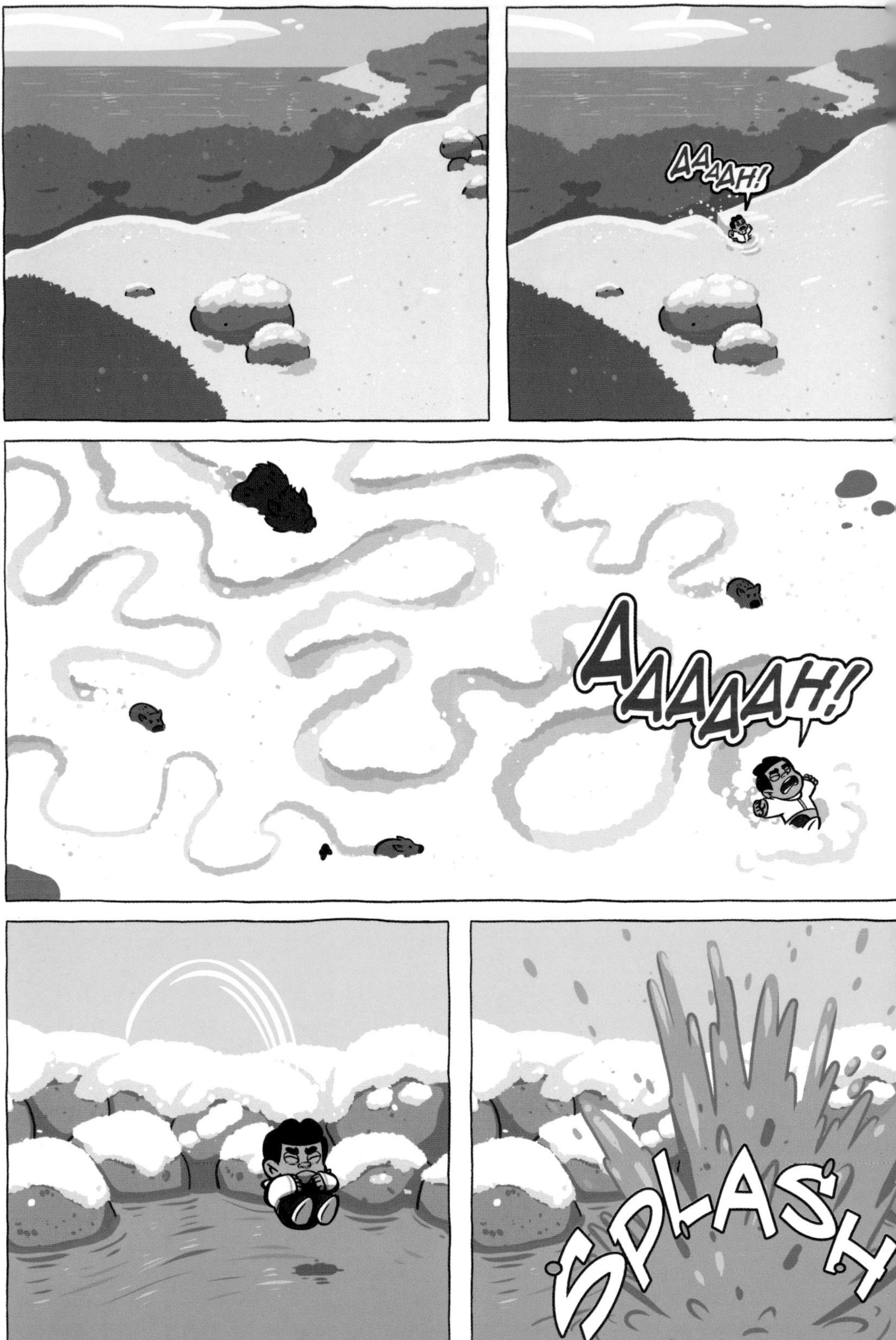
AAAAH!
AAAAAH!
SPLASH

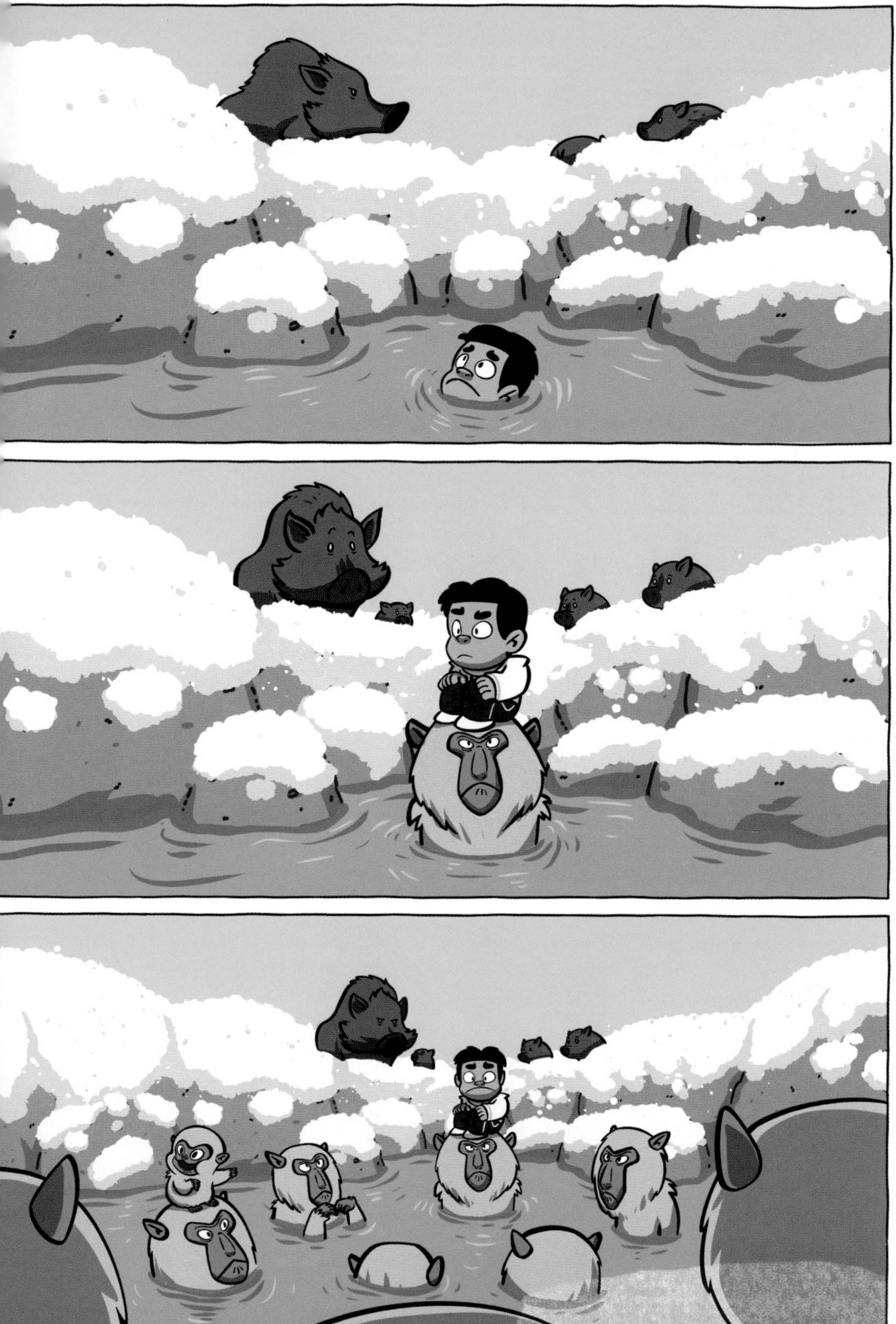

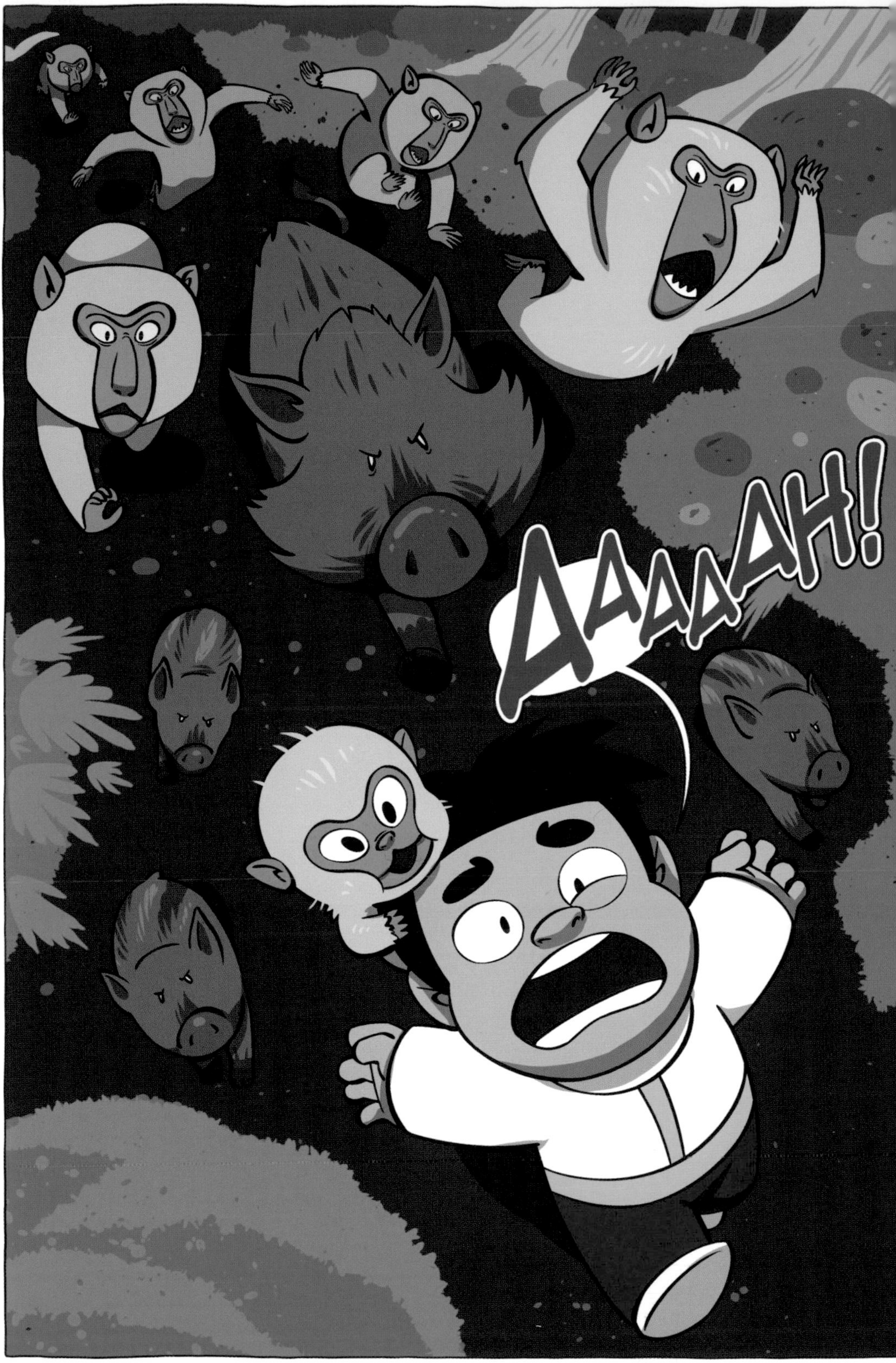
AAAAAH!

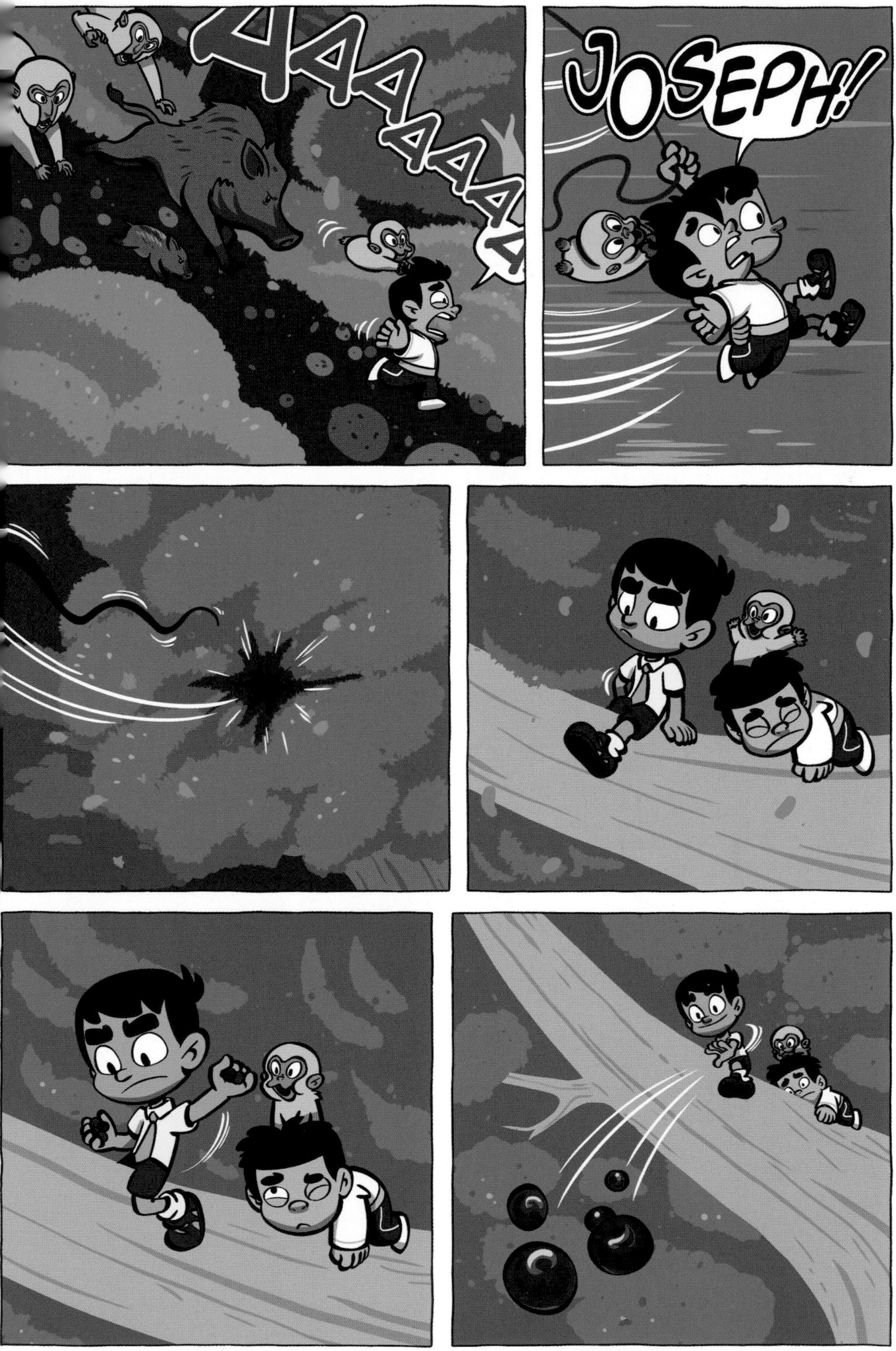
AAAAAAAA
JOSEPH!

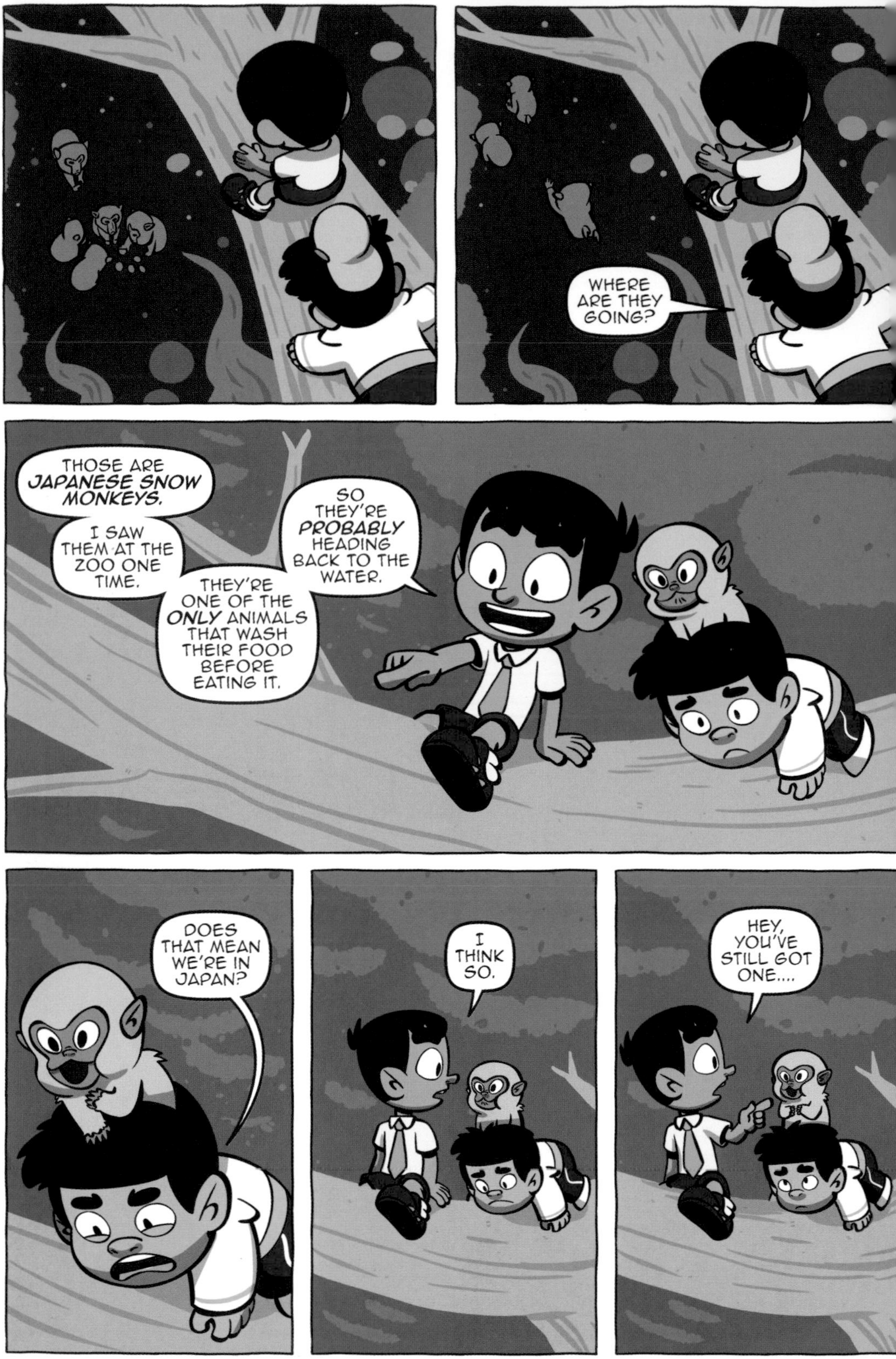
WHERE ARE THEY GOING?
THOSE ARE JAPANESE SNOW MONKEYS.
I SAW THEM AT THE ZOO ONE TIME.
THEY'RE ONE OF THE ONLY ANIMALS THAT WASH THEIR FOOD BEFORE EATING IT.
SO THEY'RE PROBABLY HEADING BACK TO THE WATER.
DOES THAT MEAN WE'RE IN JAPAN?
I THINK SO.
HEY, YOU'VE STILL GOT ONE....

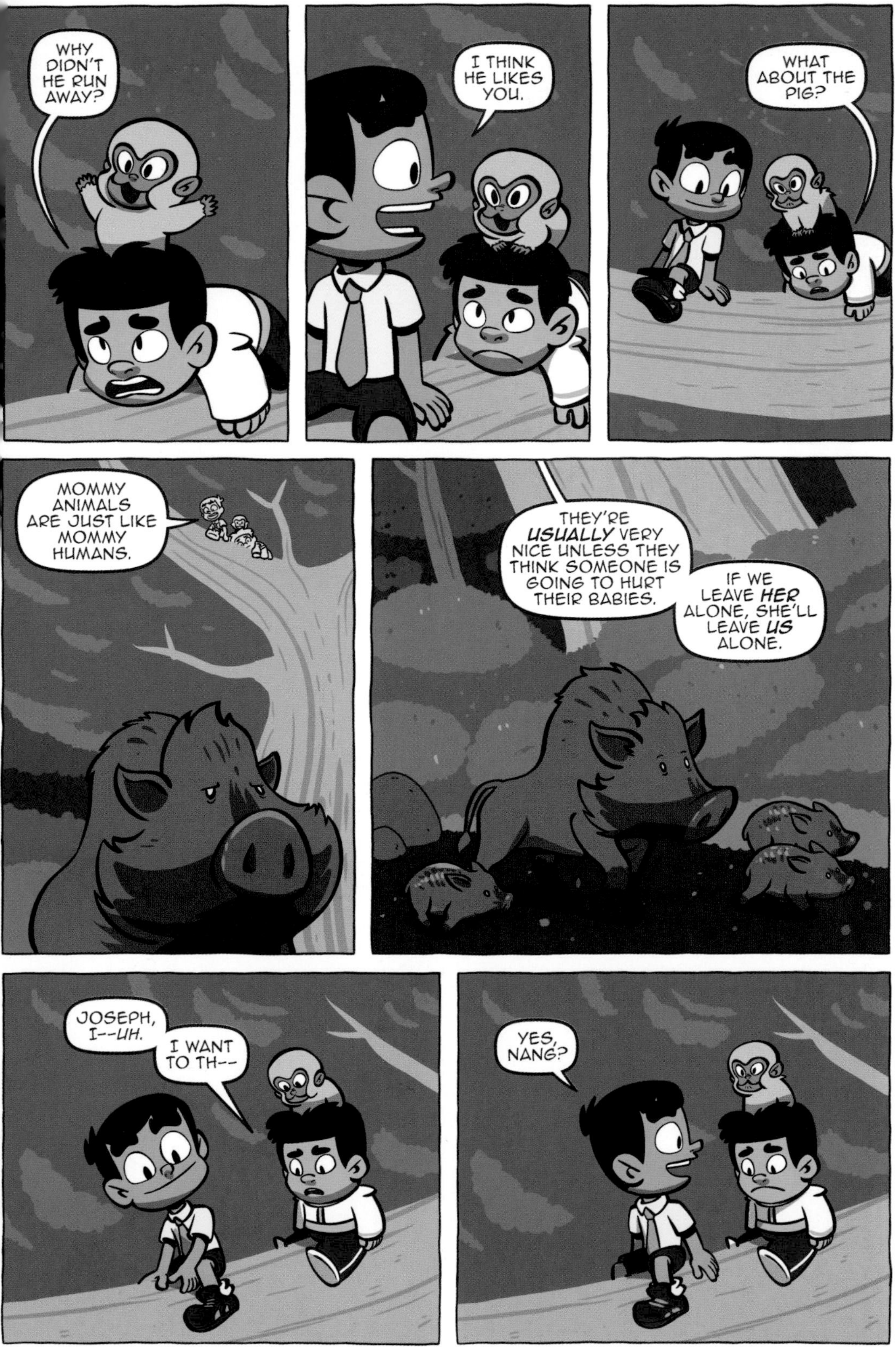
WHY DIDN'T HE RUN AWAY?
I THINK HE LIKES YOU.
WHAT ABOUT THE PIG?
MOMMY ANIMALS ARE JUST LIKE MOMMY HUMANS.
THEY'RE **USUALLY** VERY NICE UNLESS THEY THINK SOMEONE IS GOING TO HURT THEIR BABIES.
IF WE LEAVE **HER** ALONE, SHE'LL LEAVE **US** ALONE.
JOSEPH, I--UH.
I WANT TO TH--
YES, NANG?

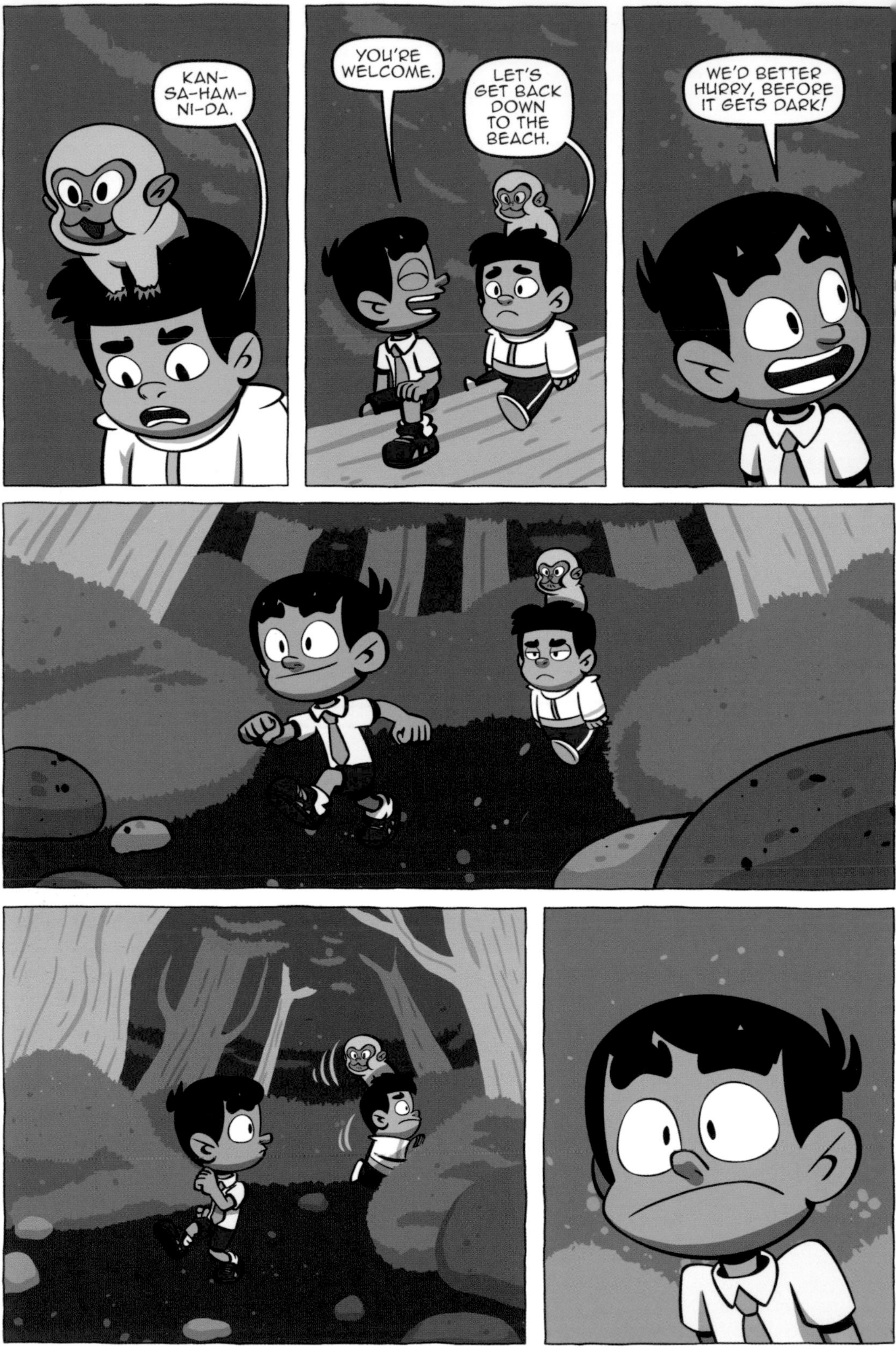
KAN-SA-HAM-NI-DA.
YOU'RE WELCOME.
LET'S GET BACK DOWN TO THE BEACH.
WE'D BETTER HURRY, BEFORE IT GETS DARK!

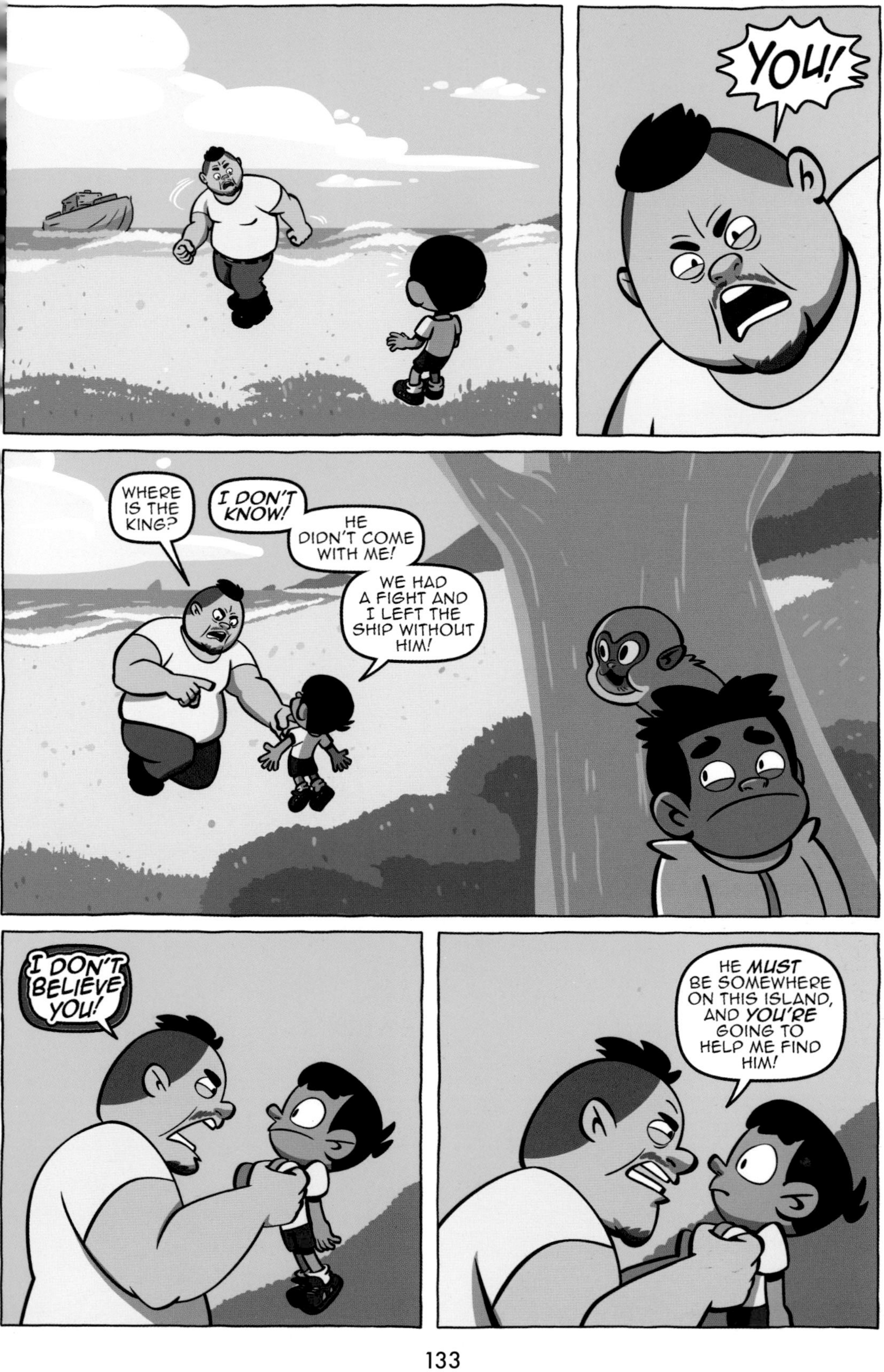
YOU!
WHERE IS THE KING?
I DON'T KNOW!
HE DIDN'T COME WITH ME!
WE HAD A FIGHT AND I LEFT THE SHIP WITHOUT HIM!
I DON'T BELIEVE YOU!
HE MUST BE SOMEWHERE ON THIS ISLAND, AND YOU'RE GOING TO HELP ME FIND HIM!

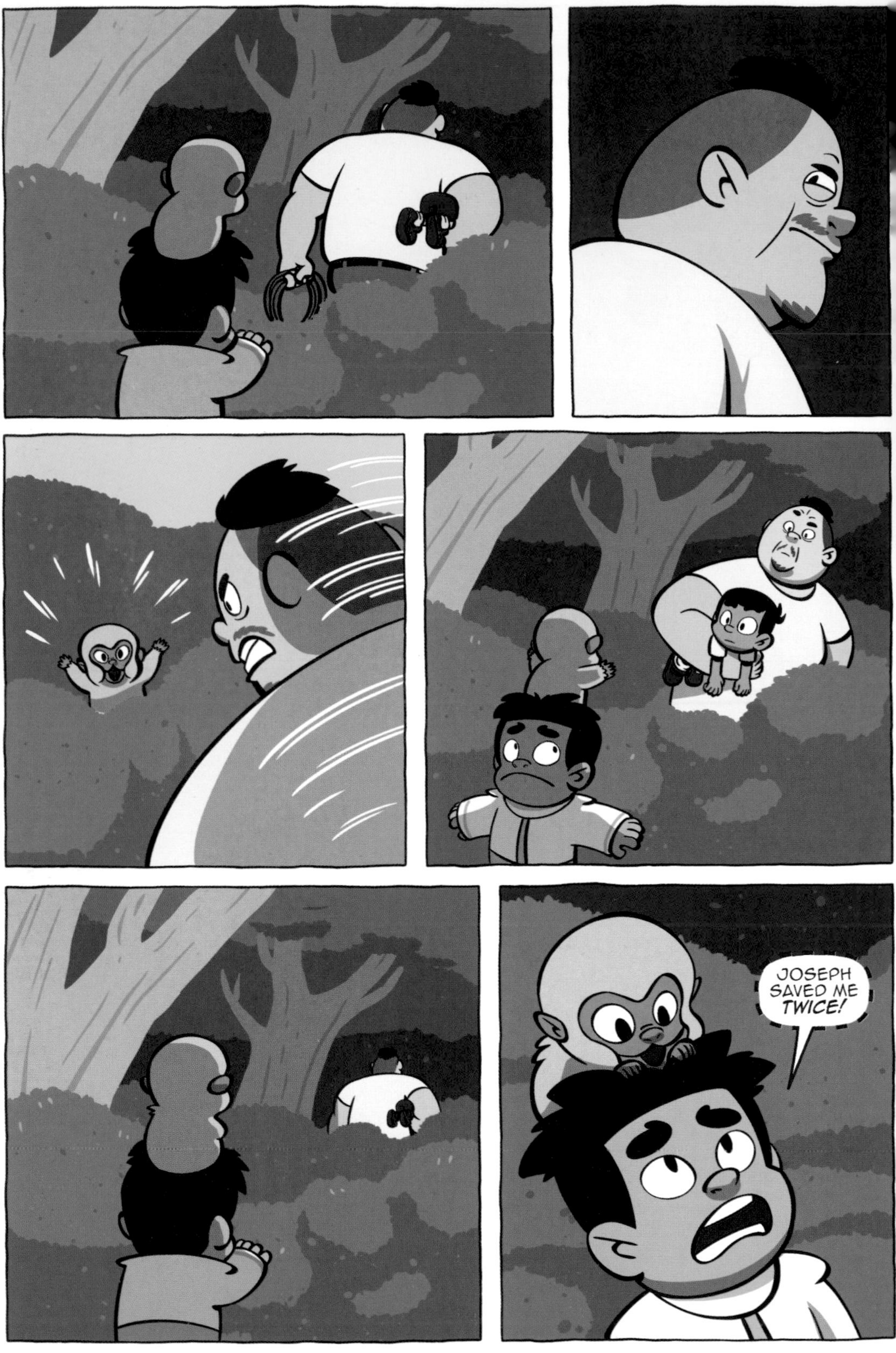
JOSEPH
SAVED ME
TWICE!

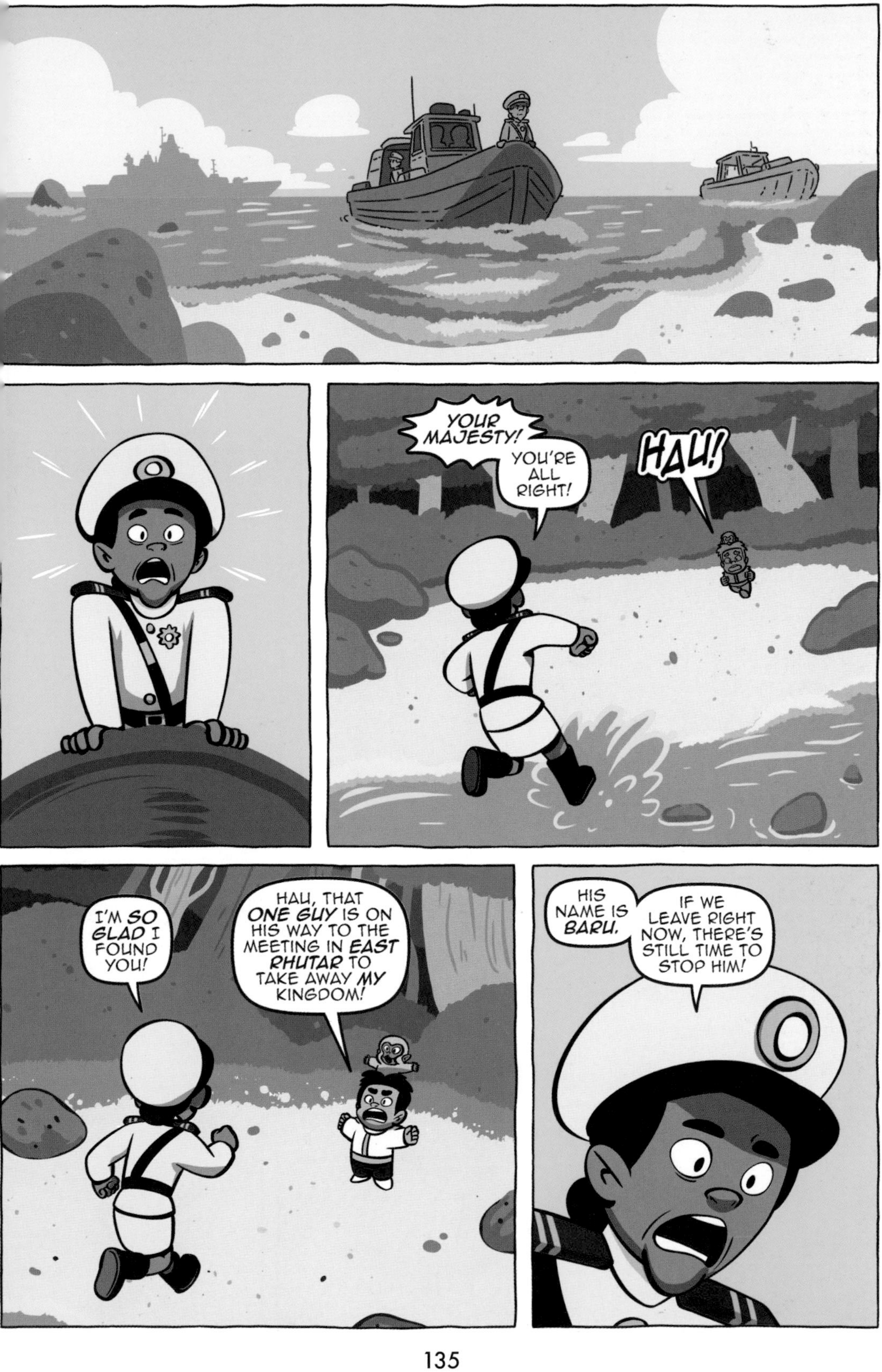
YOUR MAJESTY!
YOU'RE ALL RIGHT!
HAU!
I'M SO GLAD I FOUND YOU!
HAU, THAT ONE GUY IS ON HIS WAY TO THE MEETING IN EAST RHUTAR TO TAKE AWAY MY KINGDOM!
HIS NAME IS BARU.
IF WE LEAVE RIGHT NOW, THERE'S STILL TIME TO STOP HIM!

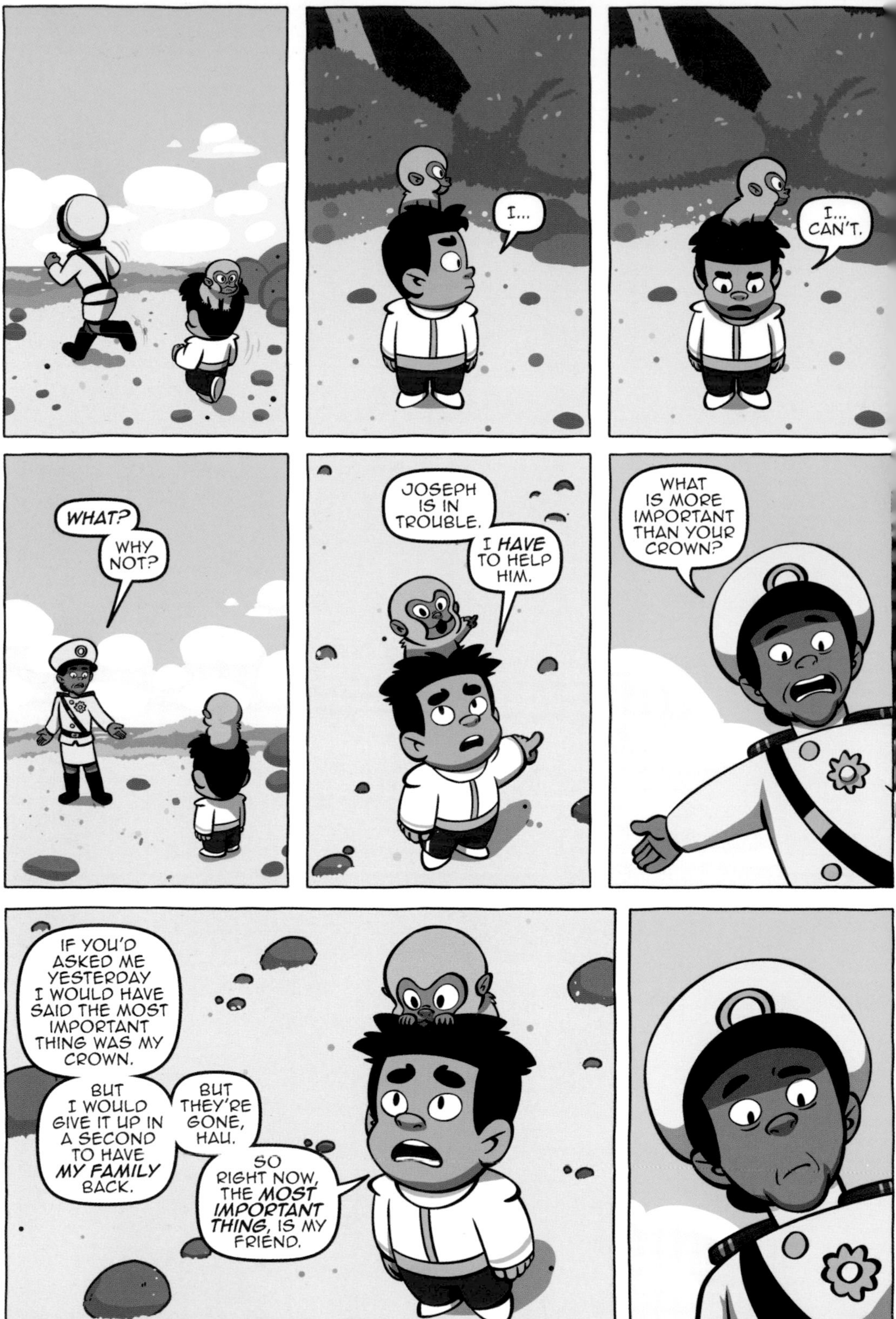

I...
I... CAN'T.
WHAT?
WHY NOT?
JOSEPH IS IN TROUBLE.
I *HAVE* TO HELP HIM.
WHAT IS MORE IMPORTANT THAN YOUR CROWN?
IF YOU'D ASKED ME YESTERDAY I WOULD HAVE SAID THE MOST IMPORTANT THING WAS MY CROWN.
BUT I WOULD GIVE IT UP IN A SECOND TO HAVE *MY FAMILY* BACK.
BUT THEY'RE GONE, HAU.
SO RIGHT NOW, THE *MOST IMPORTANT THING*, IS MY FRIEND.

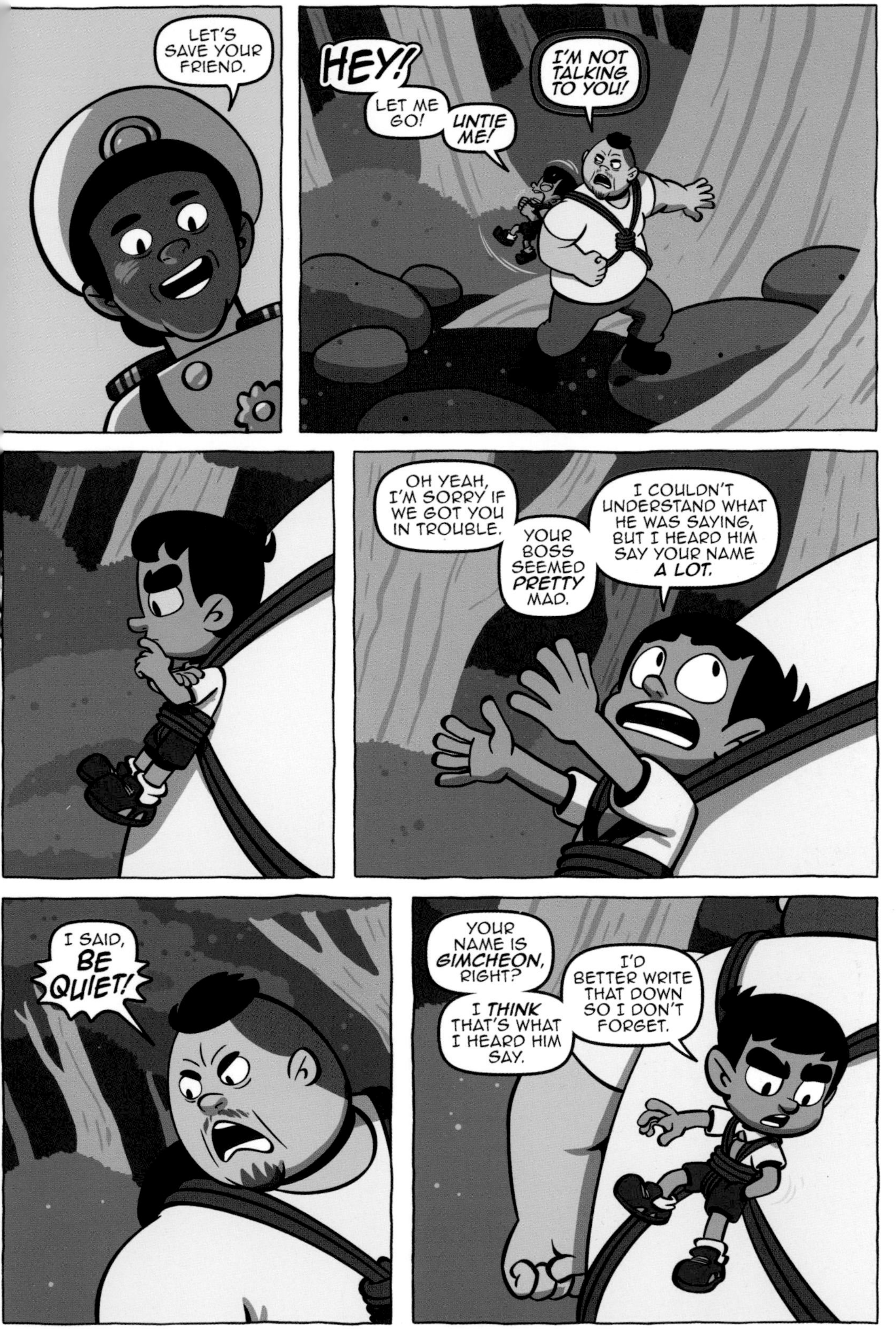
LET'S SAVE YOUR FRIEND.
HEY!
LET ME GO!
UNTIE ME!
I'M NOT TALKING TO YOU!
OH YEAH, I'M SORRY IF WE GOT YOU IN TROUBLE.
YOUR BOSS SEEMED PRETTY MAD.
I COULDN'T UNDERSTAND WHAT HE WAS SAYING, BUT I HEARD HIM SAY YOUR NAME A LOT.
I SAID, BE QUIET!
YOUR NAME IS GIMCHEON, RIGHT?
I THINK THAT'S WHAT I HEARD HIM SAY.
I'D BETTER WRITE THAT DOWN SO I DON'T FORGET.

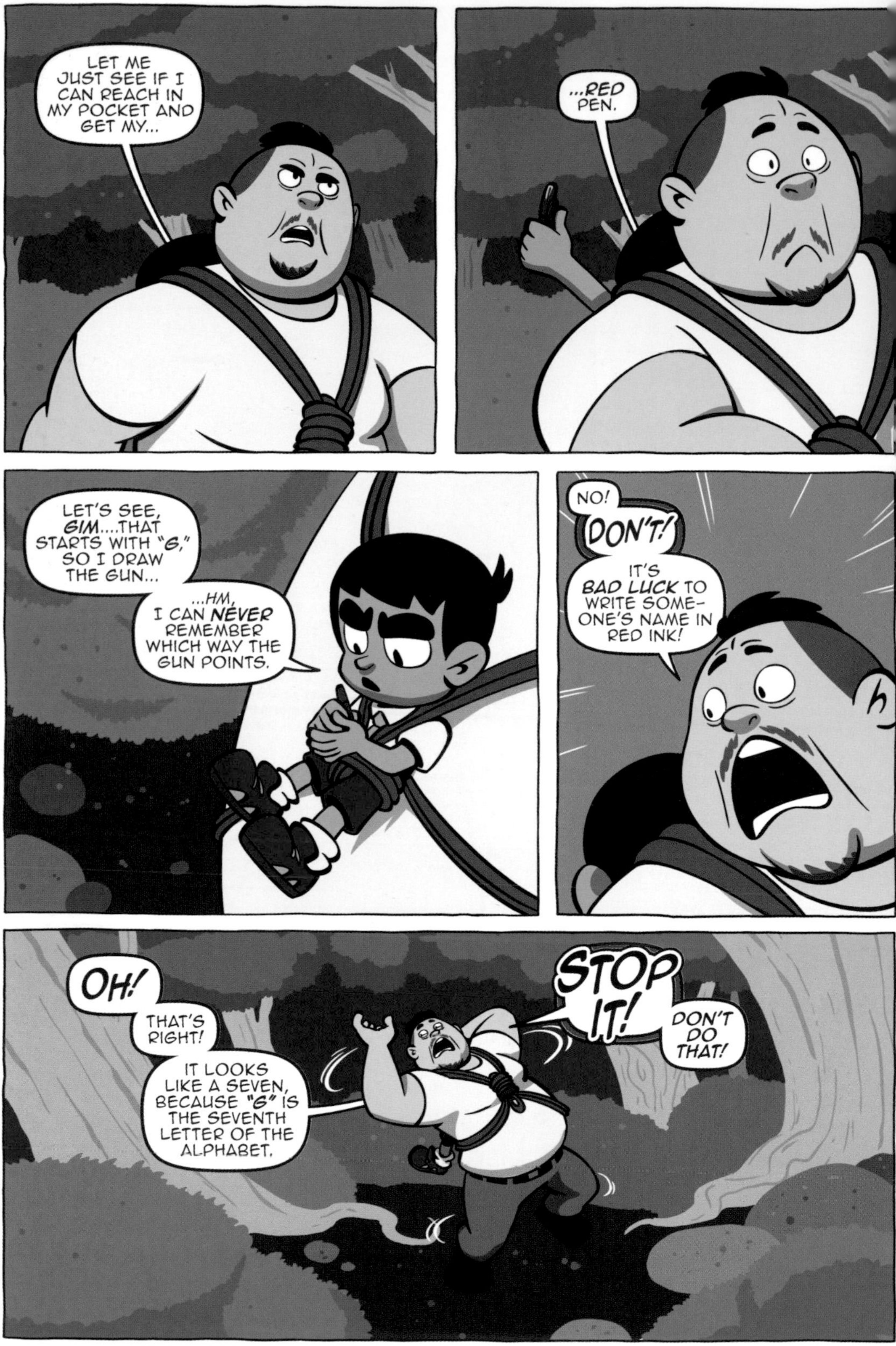

LET ME JUST SEE IF I CAN REACH IN MY POCKET AND GET MY...
...RED PEN.
LET'S SEE, GIM....THAT STARTS WITH "G," SO I DRAW THE GUN...
...HM, I CAN NEVER REMEMBER WHICH WAY THE GUN POINTS.
NO!
DON'T!
IT'S BAD LUCK TO WRITE SOME-ONE'S NAME IN RED INK!
OH!
THAT'S RIGHT!
IT LOOKS LIKE A SEVEN, BECAUSE "G" IS THE SEVENTH LETTER OF THE ALPHABET.
STOP IT!
DON'T DO THAT!

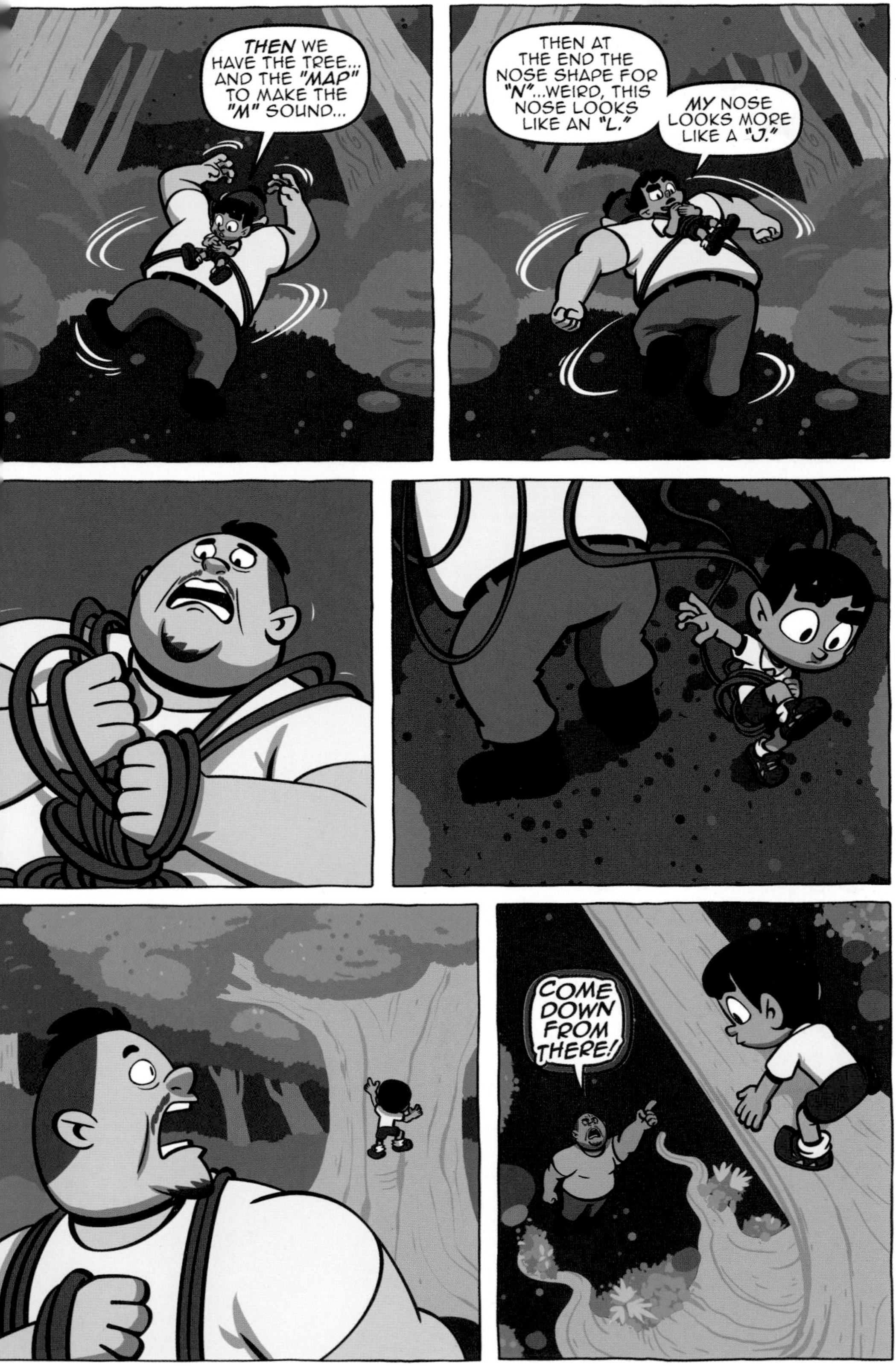
THEN WE HAVE THE TREE... AND THE "MAP" TO MAKE THE "M" SOUND...
THEN AT THE END THE NOSE SHAPE FOR "N"...WEIRD, THIS NOSE LOOKS LIKE AN "L."
MY NOSE LOOKS MORE LIKE A "J."
COME DOWN FROM THERE!

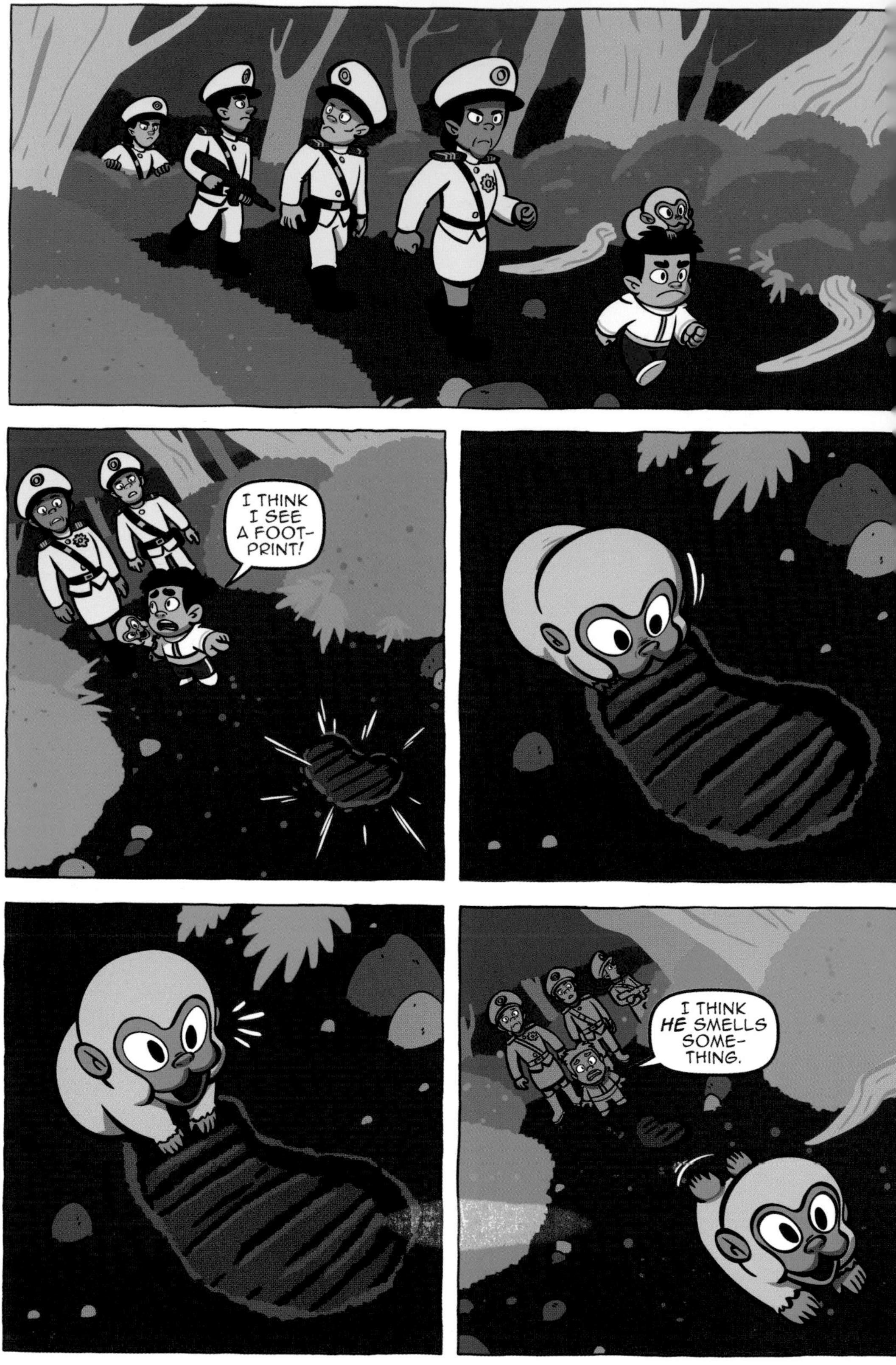
I THINK I SEE A FOOT-PRINT!
I THINK *HE* SMELLS SOME-THING.

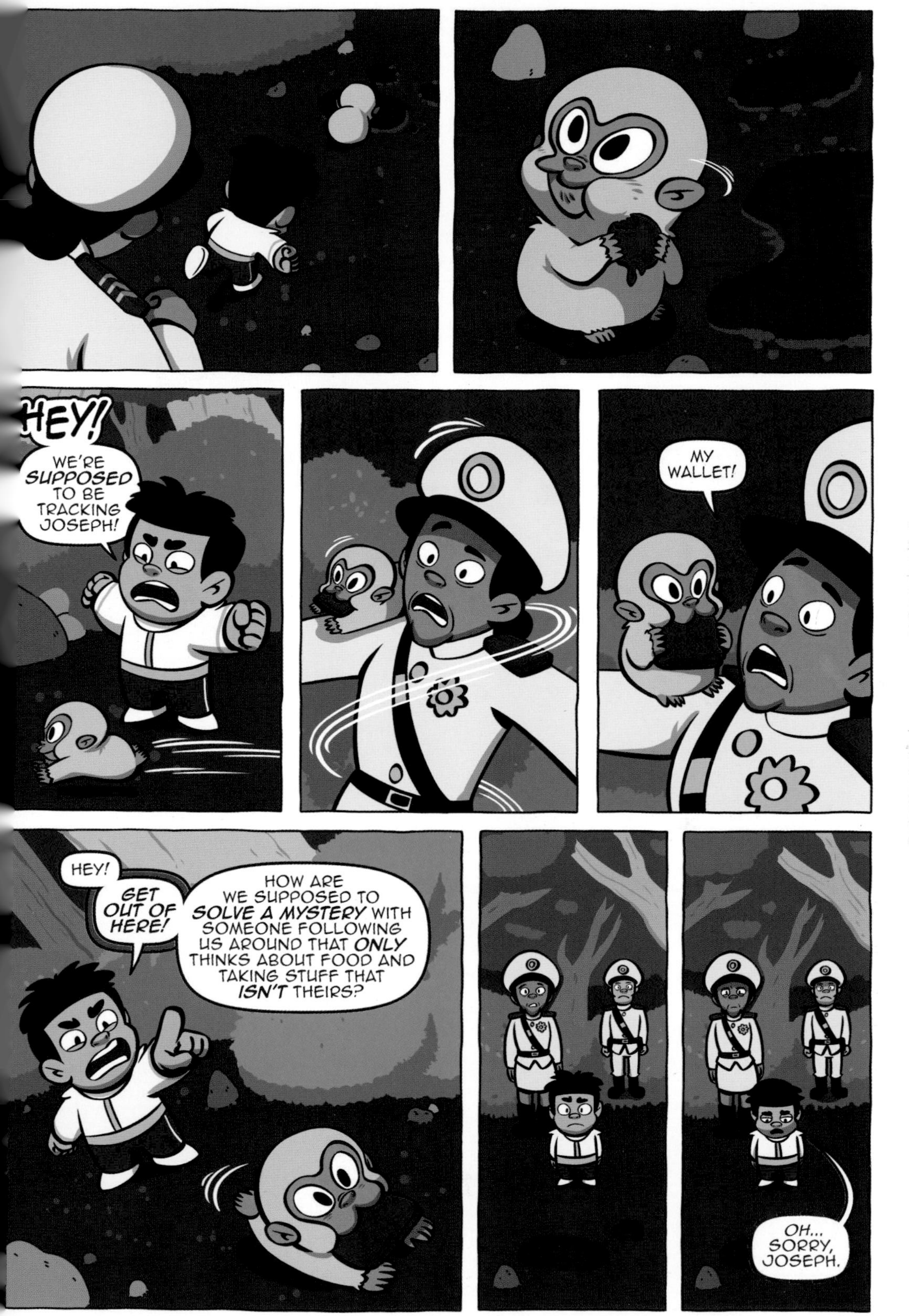

HEY!
WE'RE SUPPOSED TO BE TRACKING JOSEPH!
MY WALLET!
HEY!
GET OUT OF HERE!
HOW ARE WE SUPPOSED TO SOLVE A MYSTERY WITH SOMEONE FOLLOWING US AROUND THAT ONLY THINKS ABOUT FOOD AND TAKING STUFF THAT ISN'T THEIRS?
OH... SORRY, JOSEPH.

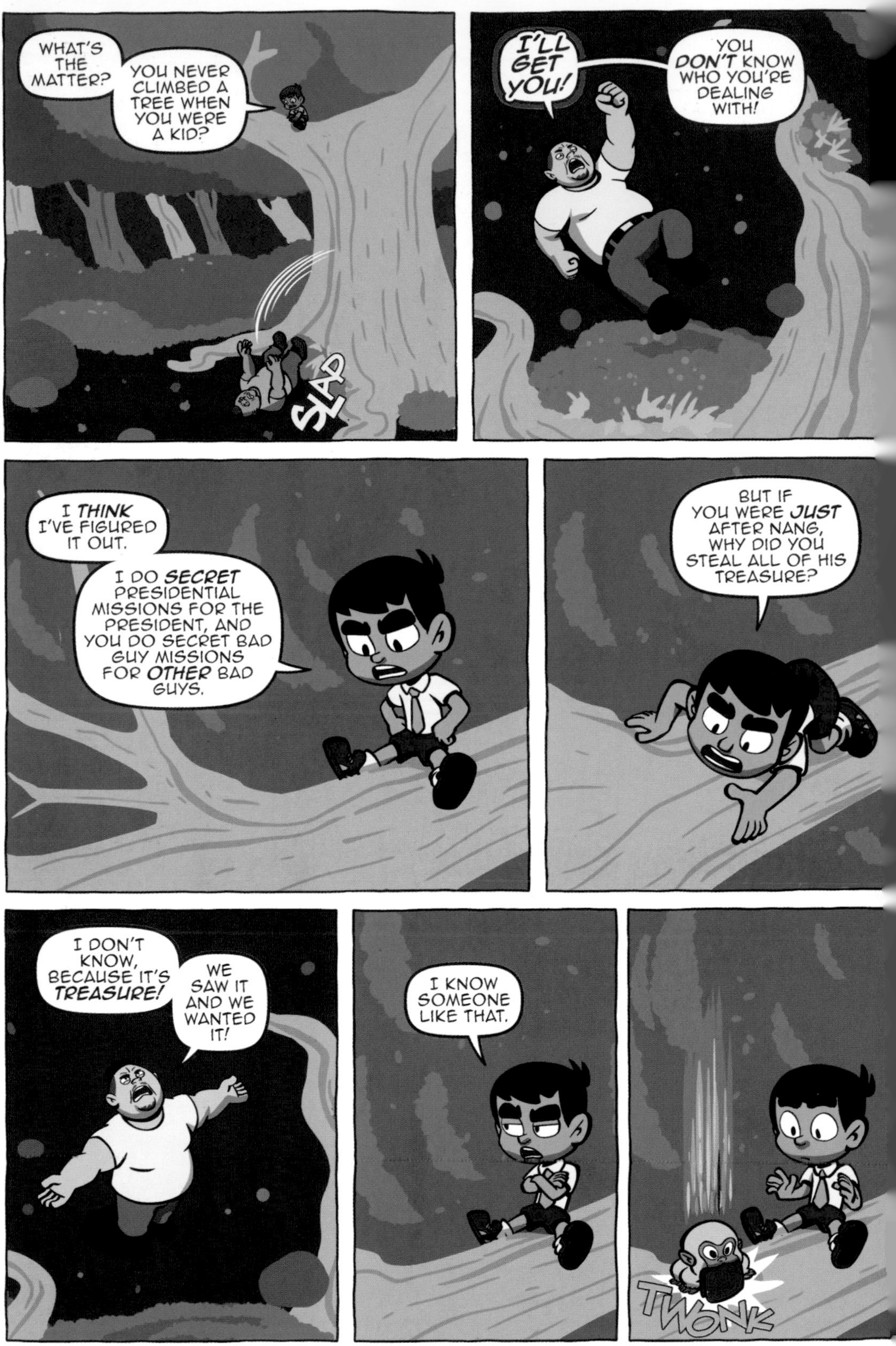
WHAT'S THE MATTER?
YOU NEVER CLIMBED A TREE WHEN YOU WERE A KID?
SLAP
I'LL GET YOU!
YOU DON'T KNOW WHO YOU'RE DEALING WITH!
I THINK I'VE FIGURED IT OUT.
I DO SECRET PRESIDENTIAL MISSIONS FOR THE PRESIDENT, AND YOU DO SECRET BAD GUY MISSIONS FOR OTHER BAD GUYS.
BUT IF YOU WERE JUST AFTER NANG, WHY DID YOU STEAL ALL OF HIS TREASURE?
I DON'T KNOW, BECAUSE IT'S TREASURE!
WE SAW IT AND WE WANTED IT!
I KNOW SOMEONE LIKE THAT.
TWONK

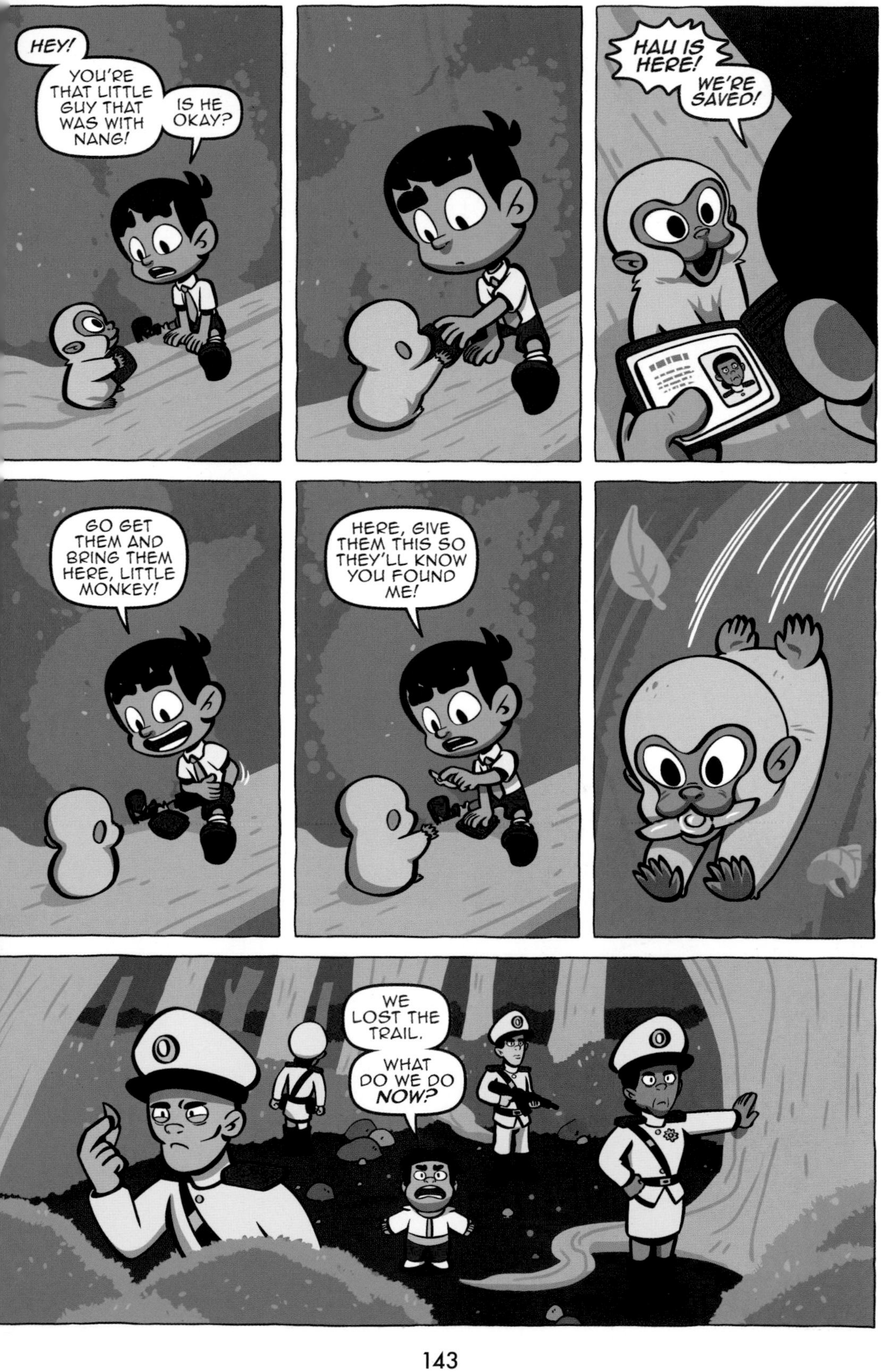
HEY!
YOU'RE THAT LITTLE GUY THAT WAS WITH NANG!
IS HE OKAY?
HAU IS HERE!
WE'RE SAVED!
GO GET THEM AND BRING THEM HERE, LITTLE MONKEY!
HERE, GIVE THEM THIS SO THEY'LL KNOW YOU FOUND ME!
WE LOST THE TRAIL.
WHAT DO WE DO *NOW?*

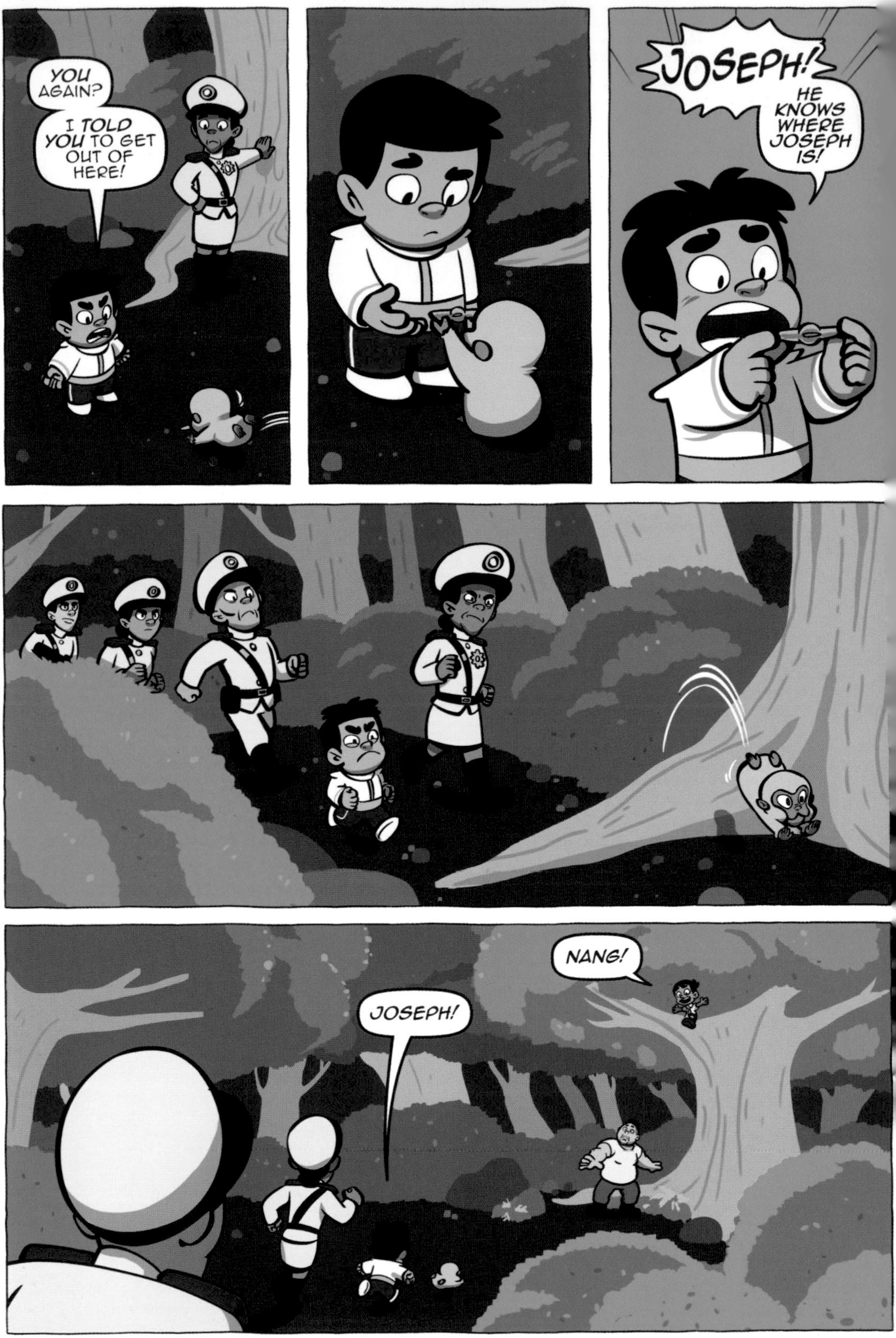
YOU AGAIN?
I TOLD YOU TO GET OUT OF HERE!
JOSEPH!
HE KNOWS WHERE JOSEPH IS!
NANG!
JOSEPH!

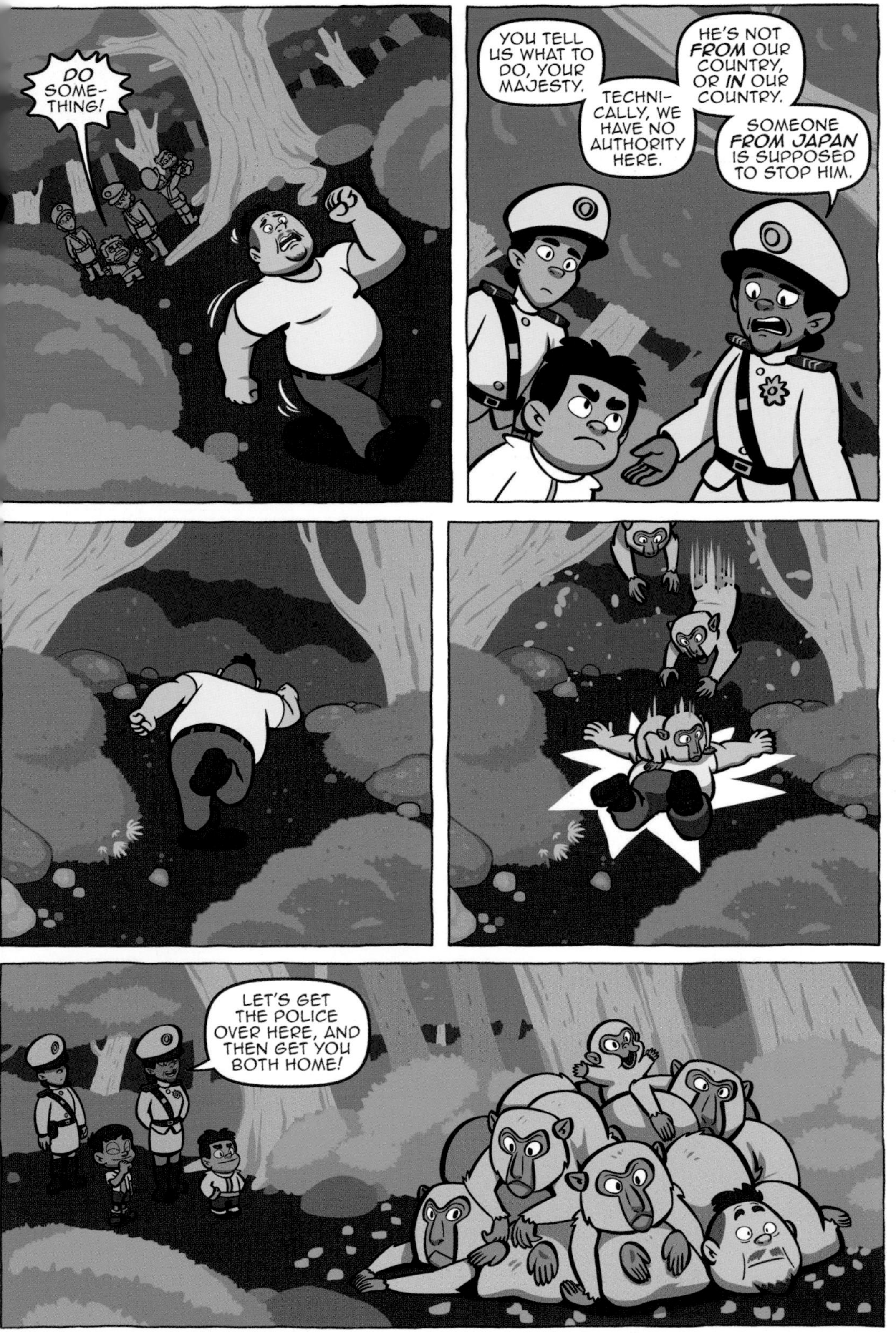
DO SOMETHING!
YOU TELL US WHAT TO DO, YOUR MAJESTY.
TECHNICALLY, WE HAVE NO AUTHORITY HERE.
HE'S NOT FROM OUR COUNTRY, OR IN OUR COUNTRY.
SOMEONE FROM JAPAN IS SUPPOSED TO STOP HIM.
LET'S GET THE POLICE OVER HERE, AND THEN GET YOU BOTH HOME!

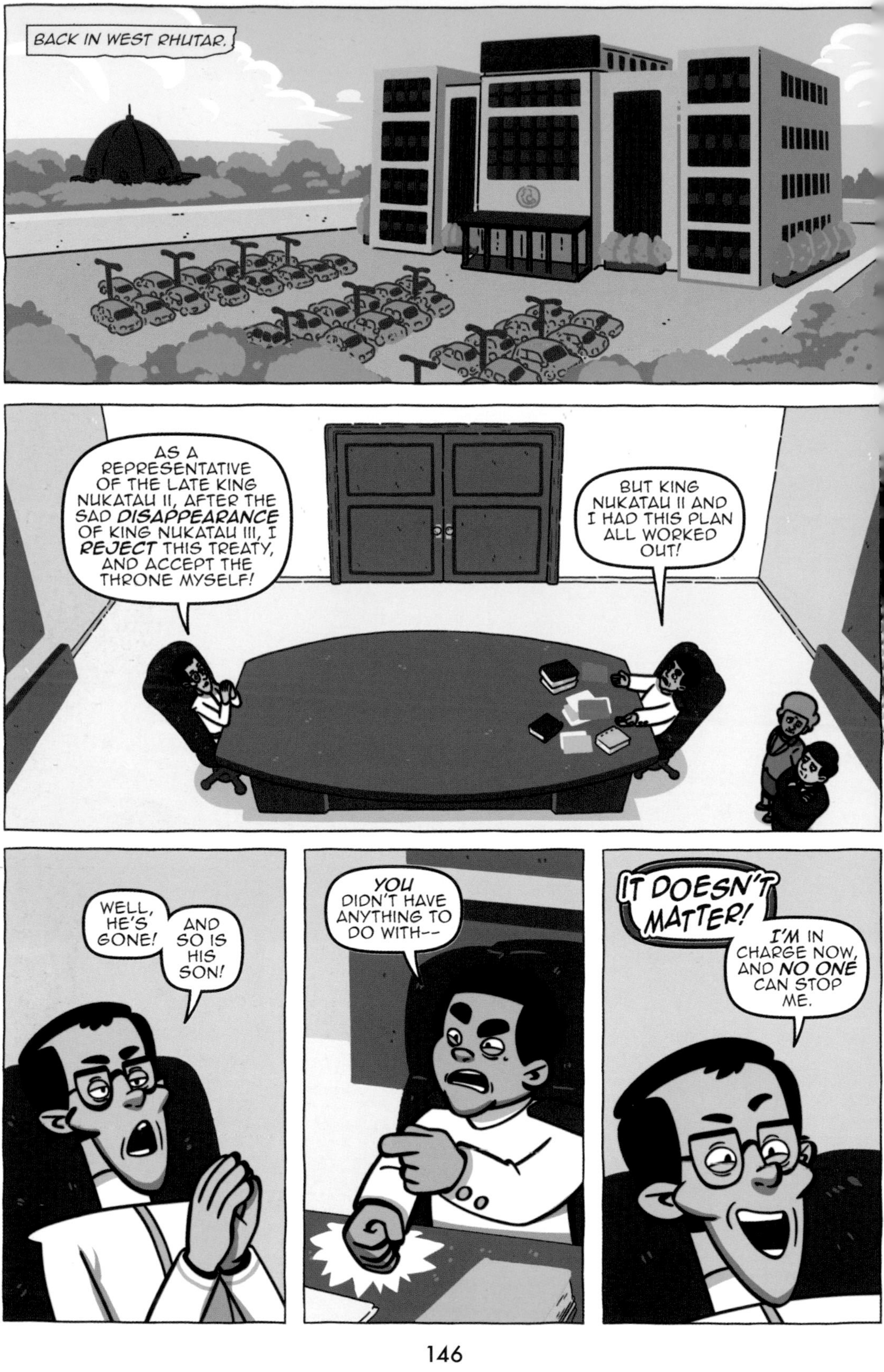
BACK IN WEST RHUTAR.
AS A REPRESENTATIVE OF THE LATE KING NUKATAU II, AFTER THE SAD DISAPPEARANCE OF KING NUKATAU III, I REJECT THIS TREATY, AND ACCEPT THE THRONE MYSELF!
BUT KING NUKATAU II AND I HAD THIS PLAN ALL WORKED OUT!
WELL, HE'S GONE!
AND SO IS HIS SON!
YOU DIDN'T HAVE ANYTHING TO DO WITH--
IT DOESN'T MATTER!
I'M IN CHARGE NOW, AND NO ONE CAN STOP ME.

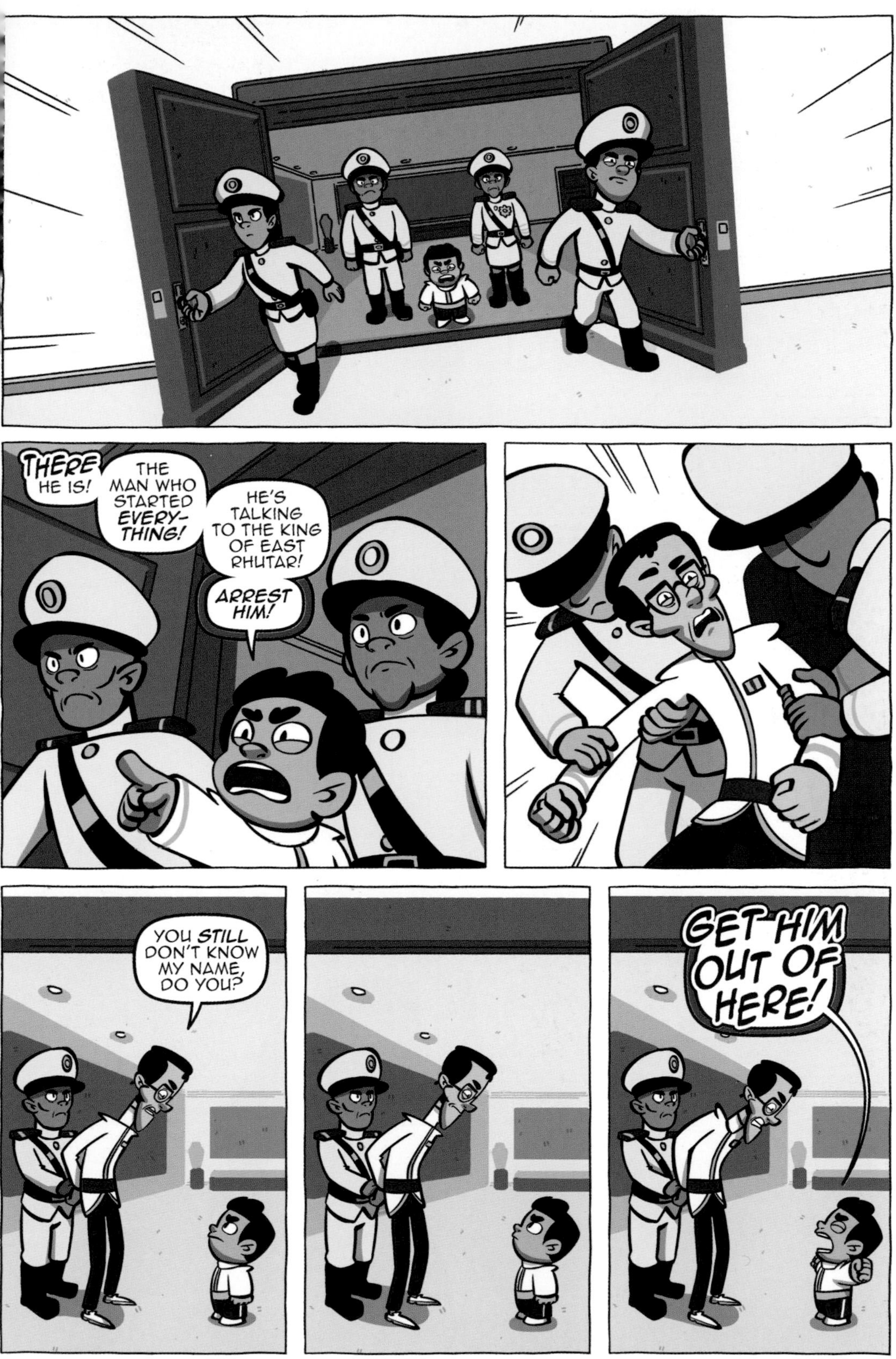
THERE HE IS!
THE MAN WHO STARTED EVERY-THING!
HE'S TALKING TO THE KING OF EAST RHUTAR!
ARREST HIM!
YOU STILL DON'T KNOW MY NAME, DO YOU?
GET HIM OUT OF HERE!

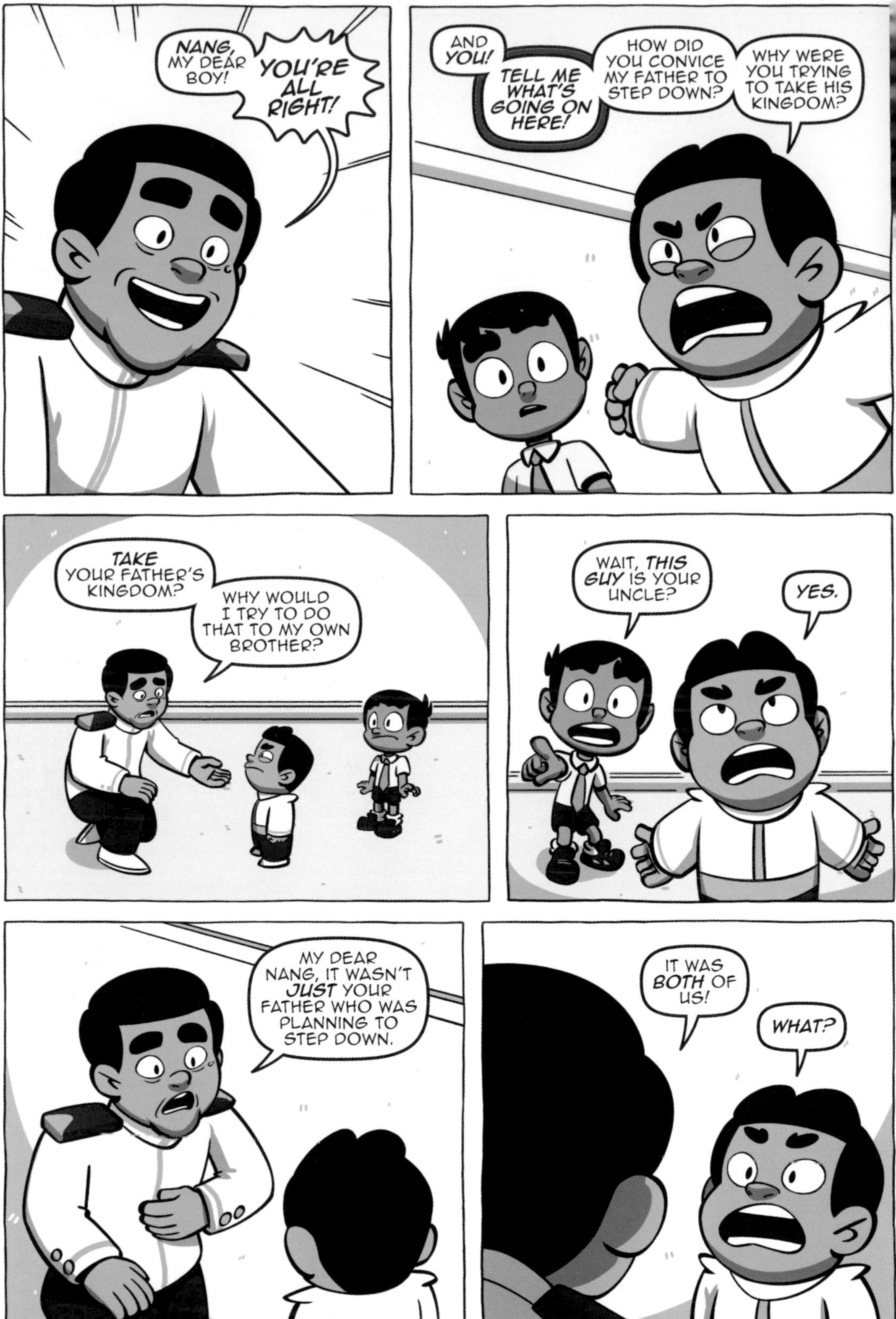
NANG, MY DEAR BOY!
YOU'RE ALL RIGHT!
AND YOU!
TELL ME WHAT'S GOING ON HERE!
HOW DID YOU CONVICE MY FATHER TO STEP DOWN?
WHY WERE YOU TRYING TO TAKE HIS KINGDOM?
TAKE YOUR FATHER'S KINGDOM?
WHY WOULD I TRY TO DO THAT TO MY OWN BROTHER?
WAIT, THIS GUY IS YOUR UNCLE?
YES.
MY DEAR NANG, IT WASN'T JUST YOUR FATHER WHO WAS PLANNING TO STEP DOWN.
IT WAS BOTH OF US!
WHAT?

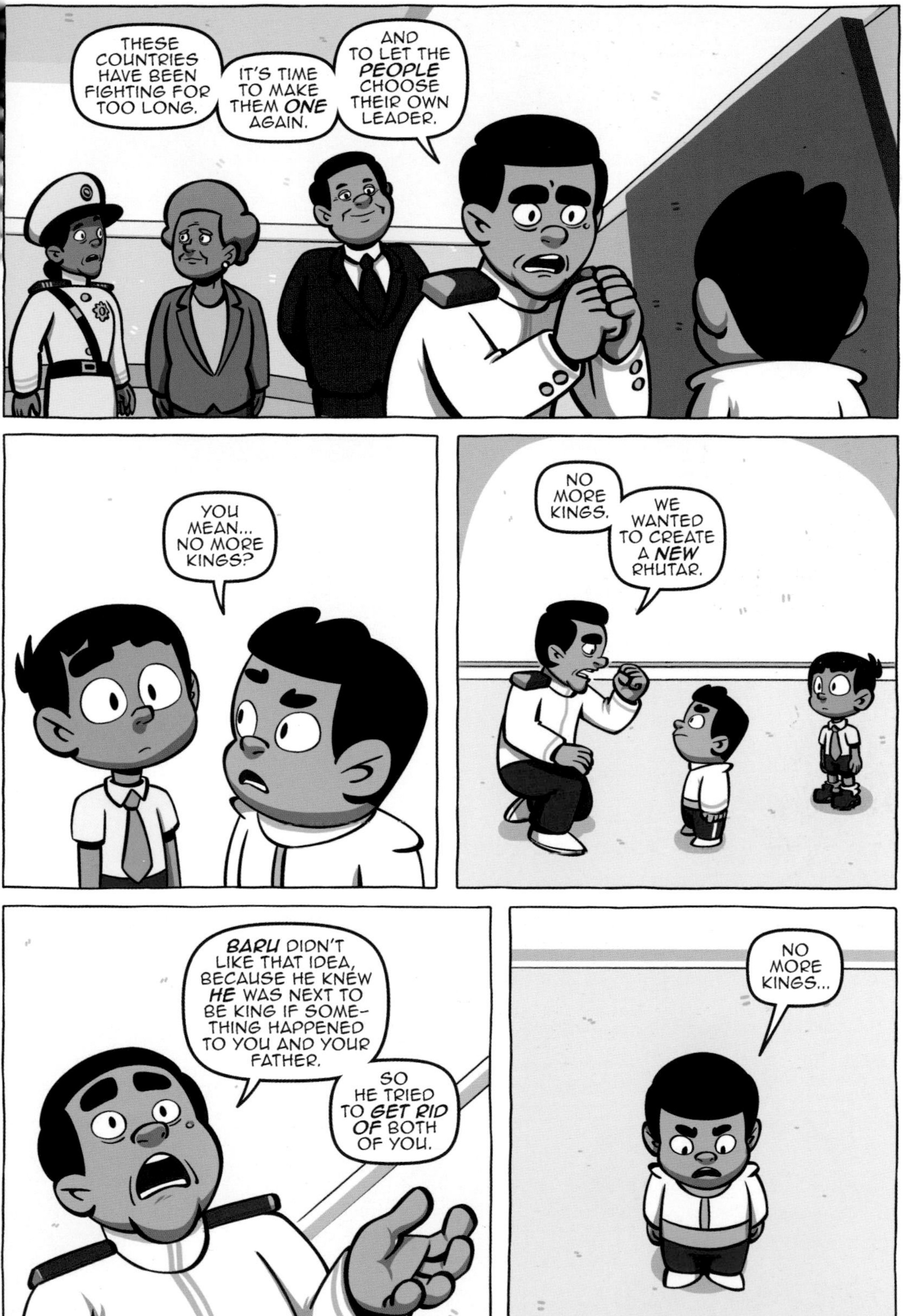
THESE COUNTRIES HAVE BEEN FIGHTING FOR TOO LONG.
IT'S TIME TO MAKE THEM *ONE* AGAIN.
AND TO LET THE *PEOPLE* CHOOSE THEIR OWN LEADER.
YOU MEAN... NO MORE KINGS?
NO MORE KINGS.
WE WANTED TO CREATE A *NEW* RHUTAR.
BARU DIDN'T LIKE THAT IDEA, BECAUSE HE KNEW *HE* WAS NEXT TO BE KING IF SOME-THING HAPPENED TO YOU AND YOUR FATHER.
SO HE TRIED TO *GET RID OF* BOTH OF YOU.
NO MORE KINGS...

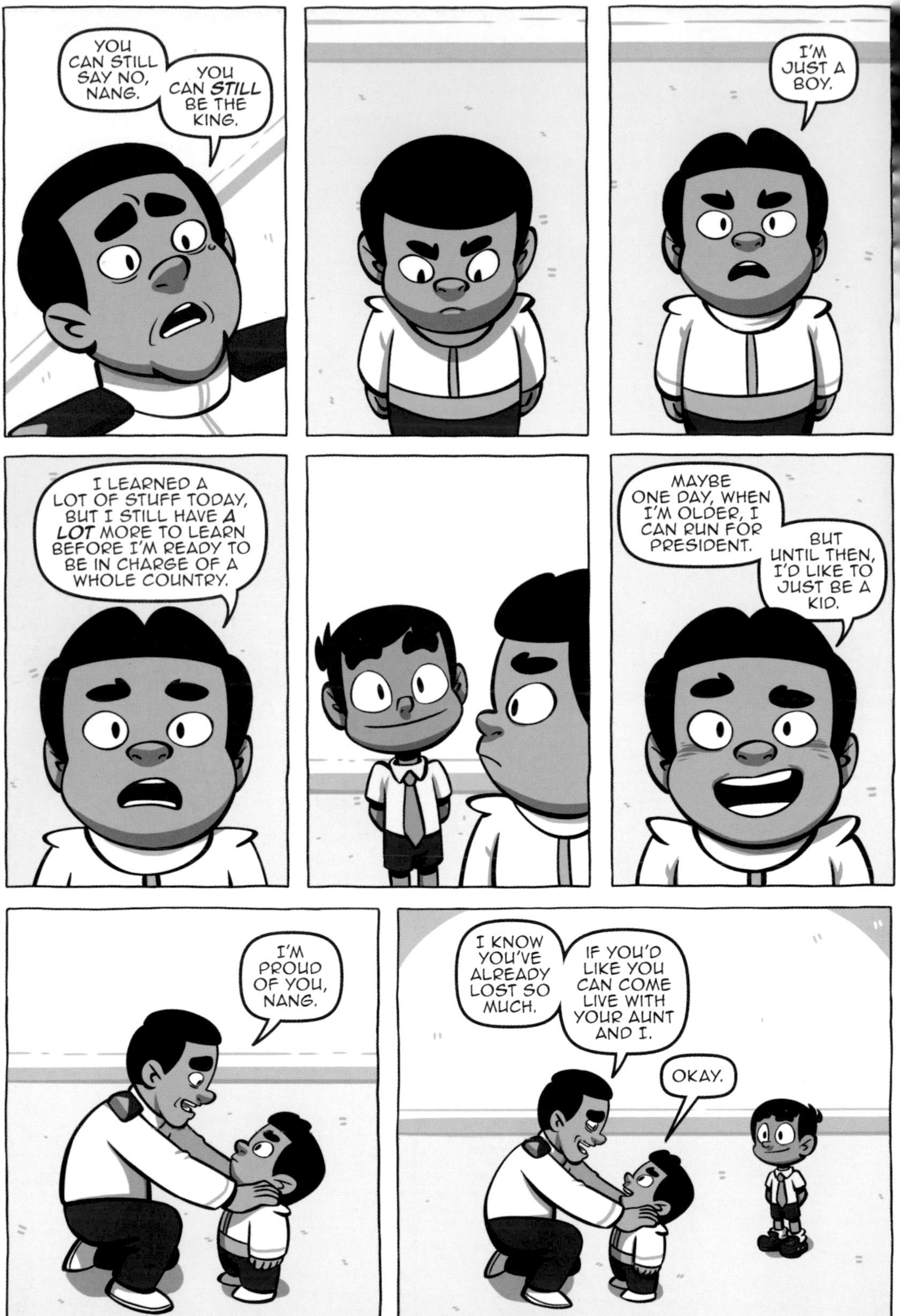
YOU CAN STILL SAY NO, NANG.
YOU CAN STILL BE THE KING.
I'M JUST A BOY.
I LEARNED A LOT OF STUFF TODAY, BUT I STILL HAVE A LOT MORE TO LEARN BEFORE I'M READY TO BE IN CHARGE OF A WHOLE COUNTRY.
MAYBE ONE DAY, WHEN I'M OLDER, I CAN RUN FOR PRESIDENT.
BUT UNTIL THEN, I'D LIKE TO JUST BE A KID.
I'M PROUD OF YOU, NANG.
I KNOW YOU'VE ALREADY LOST SO MUCH.
IF YOU'D LIKE YOU CAN COME LIVE WITH YOUR AUNT AND I.
OKAY.

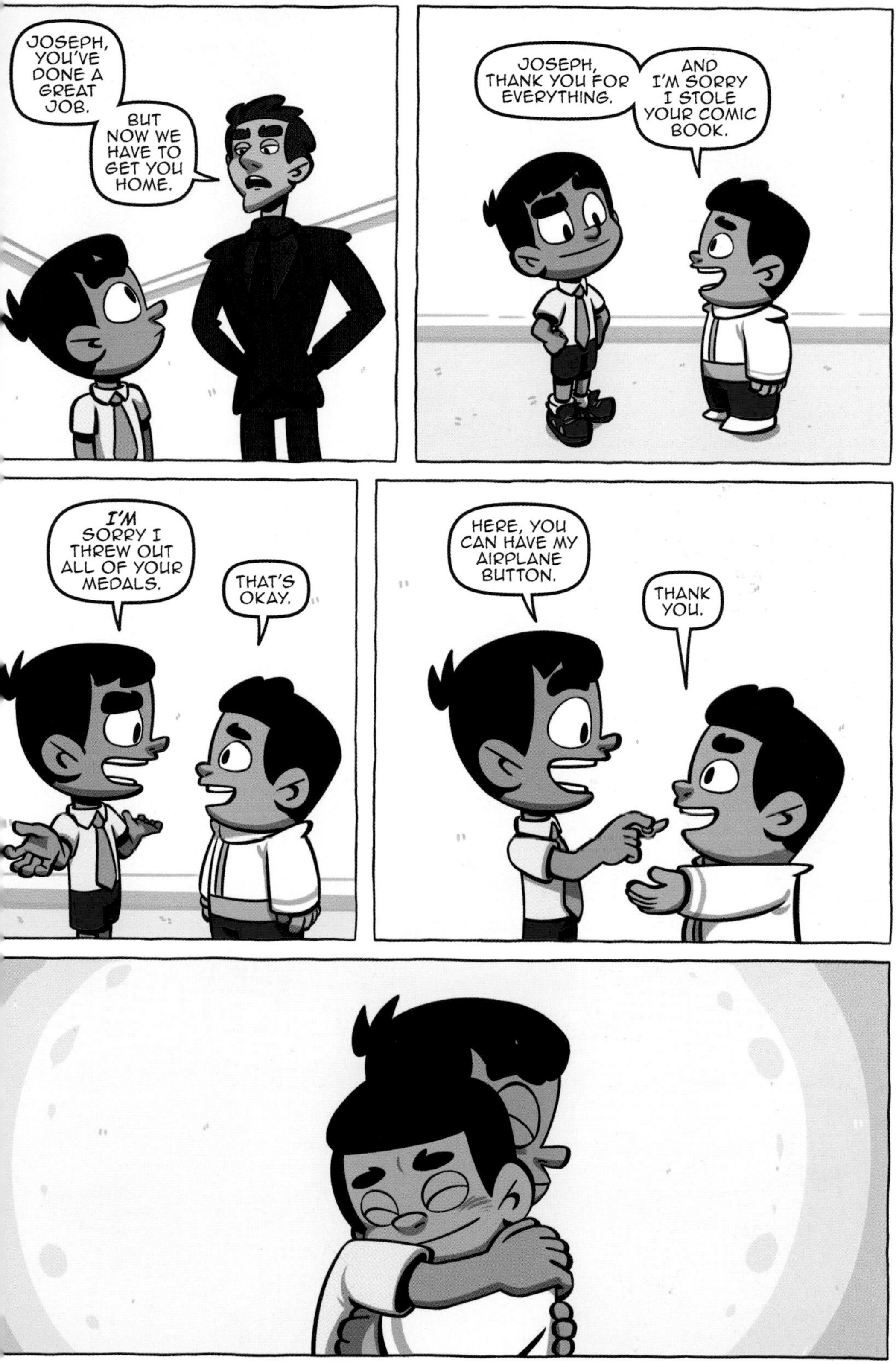
JOSEPH, YOU'VE DONE A GREAT JOB.
BUT NOW WE HAVE TO GET YOU HOME.
JOSEPH, THANK YOU FOR EVERYTHING.
AND I'M SORRY I STOLE YOUR COMIC BOOK.
I'M SORRY I THREW OUT ALL OF YOUR MEDALS.
THAT'S OKAY.
HERE, YOU CAN HAVE MY AIRPLANE BUTTON.
THANK YOU.

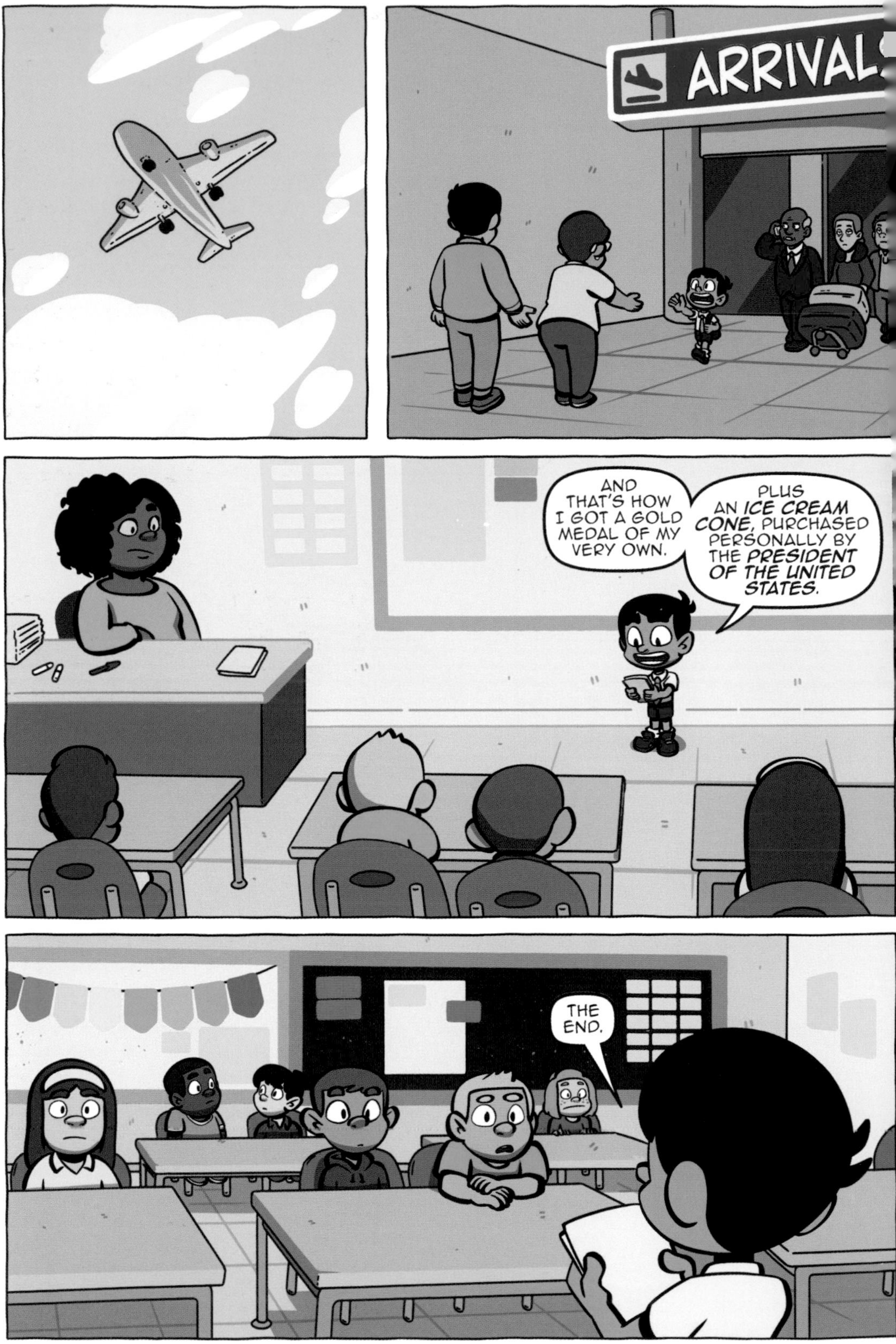
ARRIVALS
AND THAT'S HOW I GOT A GOLD MEDAL OF MY VERY OWN.
PLUS AN ICE CREAM CONE, PURCHASED PERSONALLY BY THE PRESIDENT OF THE UNITED STATES.
THE END.

About the Creators

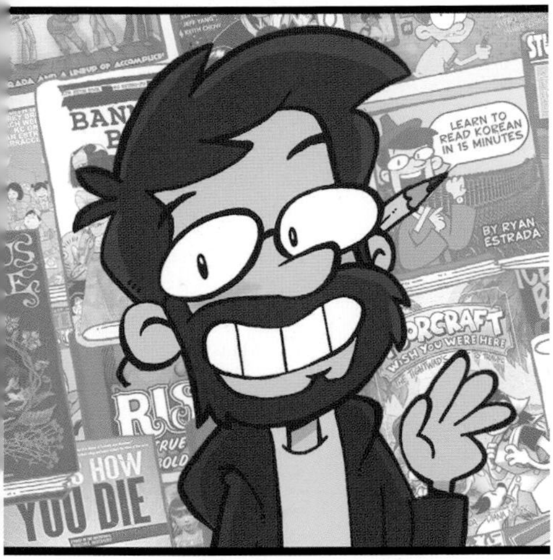
LEARN TO READ KOREAN IN 15 MINUTES
BY RYAN ESTRADA
WISH YOU WERE HERE
HOW YOU DIE

Ryan Estrada *(writer)* is an artist, author and adventurer. His work includes *Banned Book Club, Aki Alliance, Learn To Read Korean in 15 Minutes*, and *Poorcraft: Wish You Were Here*. He has worked on comics for Star Trek, Popeye and more. He is a Moth StorySLAM winner. He has dreamed of making this book since he was a student ambassador to Australia. His work can be found at ryanestrada.com

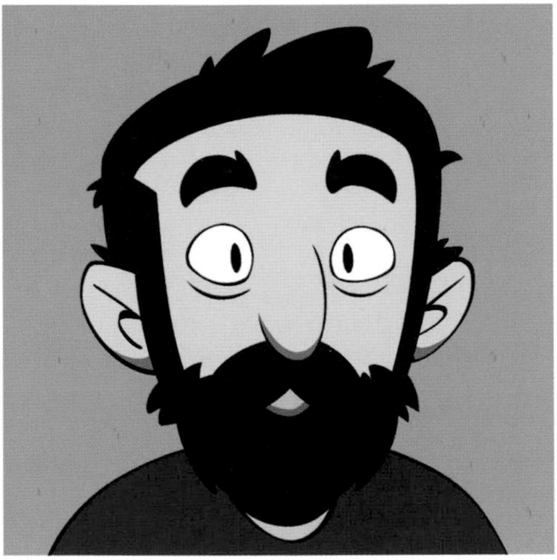

Axur Eneas *(artist)* is a comic book artist from Mexico City. He is the creator of *Toontorial*, a cartoon show for Cartoon Network Latinoamerica.

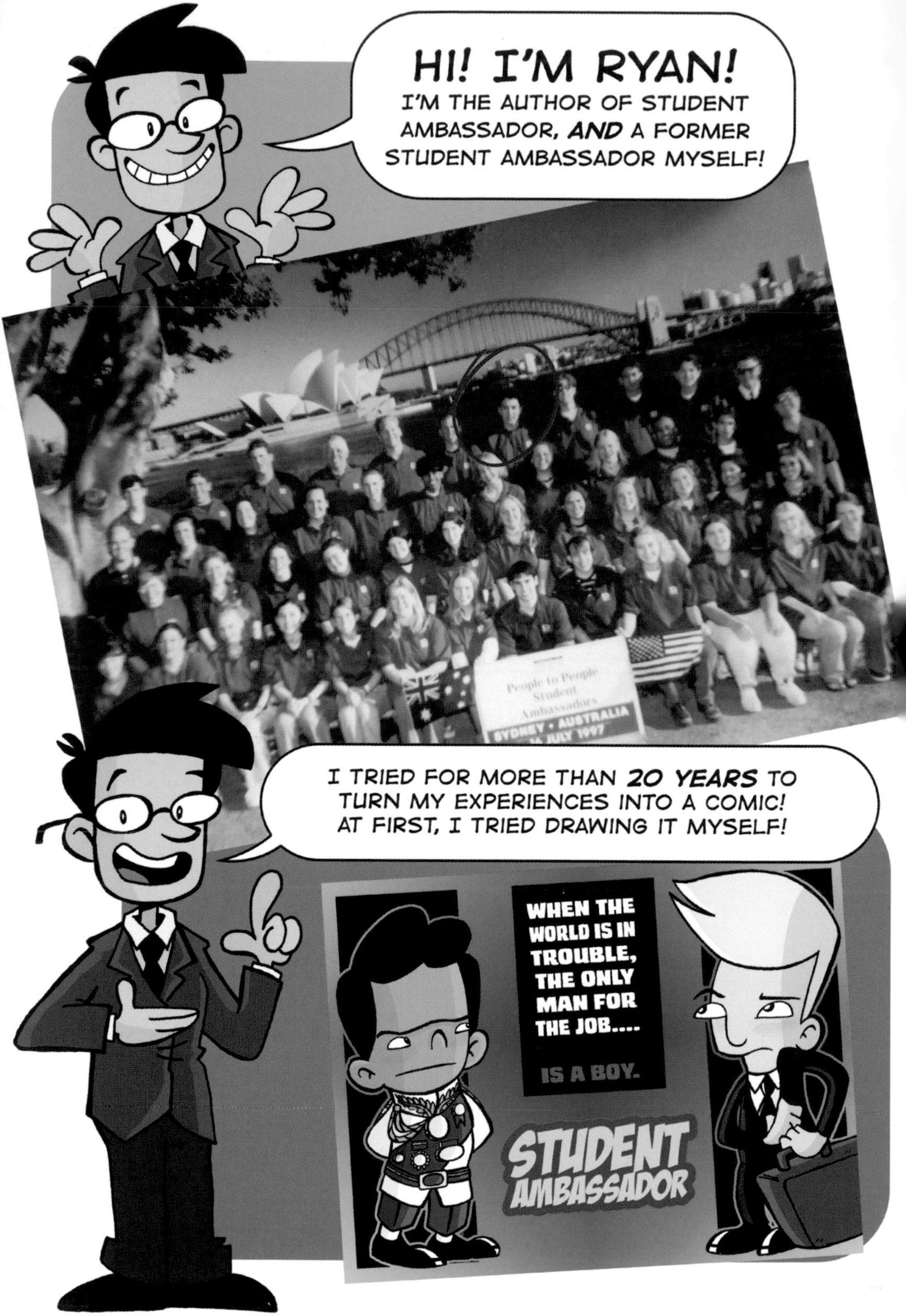
HI! I'M RYAN!
I'M THE AUTHOR OF STUDENT AMBASSADOR, ***AND*** A FORMER STUDENT AMBASSADOR MYSELF!
People to People
Student
Ambassadors
SYDNEY • AUSTRALIA
I TRIED FOR MORE THAN ***20 YEARS*** TO TURN MY EXPERIENCES INTO A COMIC! AT FIRST, I TRIED DRAWING IT MYSELF!
WHEN THE WORLD IS IN TROUBLE, THE ONLY MAN FOR THE JOB....
IS A BOY.
STUDENT AMBASSADOR

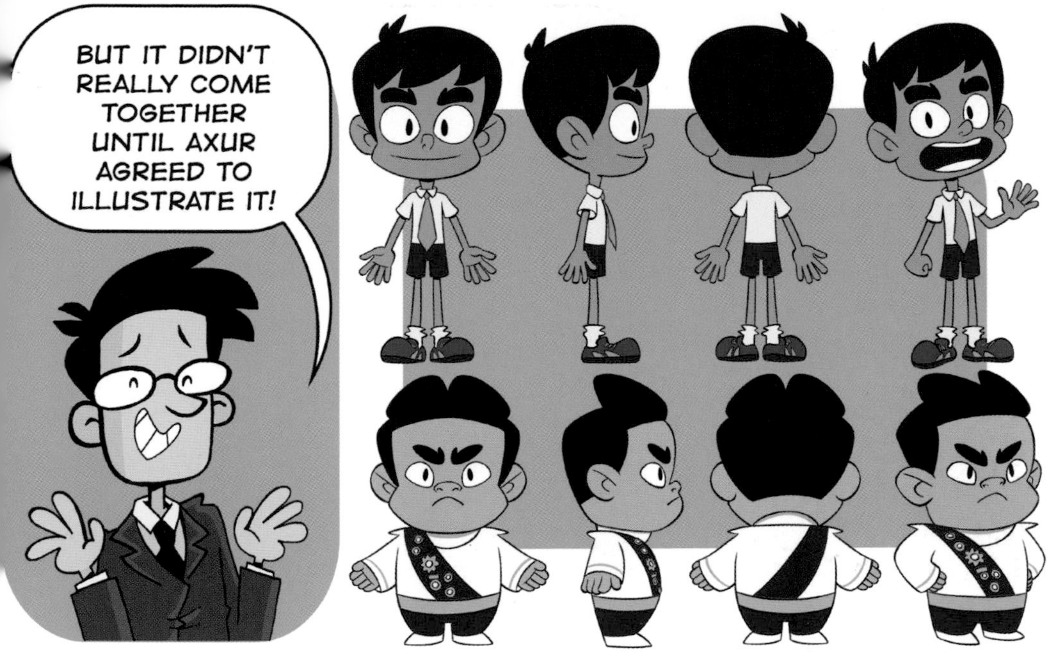
BUT IT DIDN'T REALLY COME TOGETHER UNTIL AXUR AGREED TO ILLUSTRATE IT!

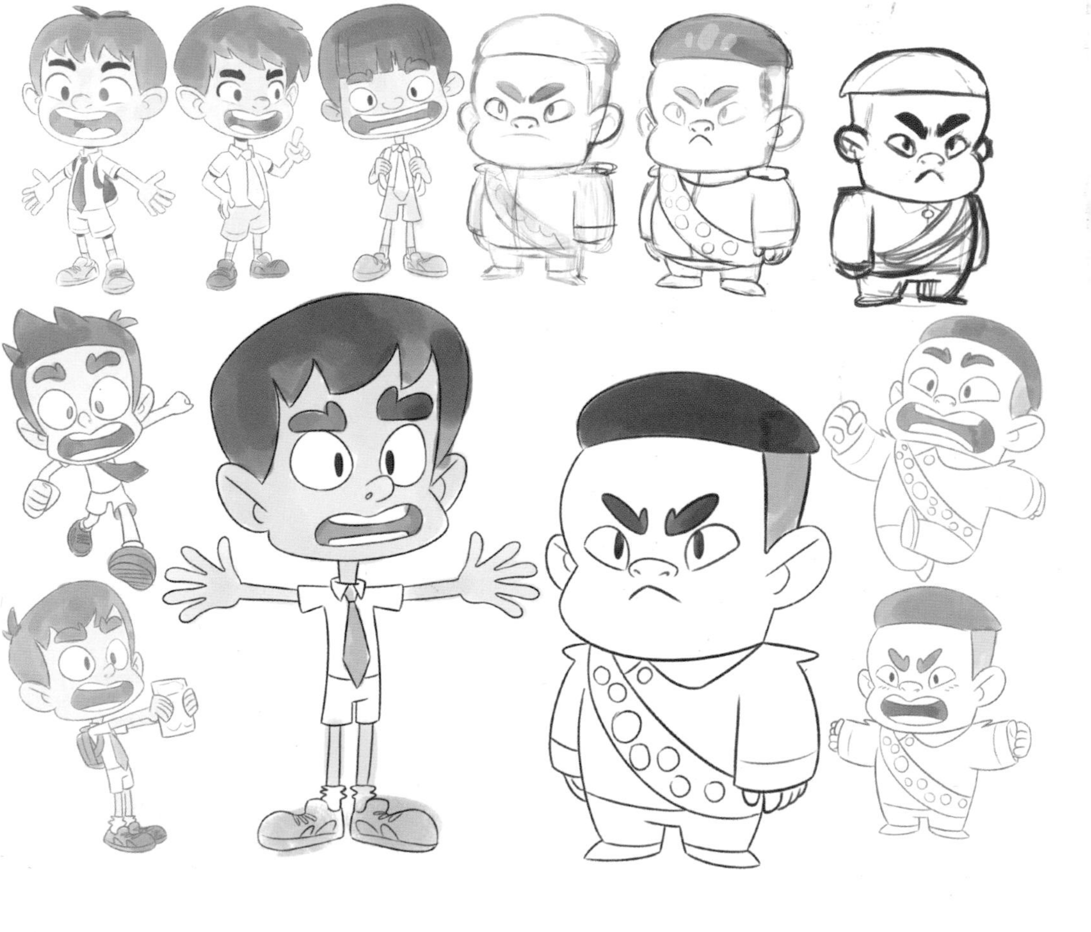

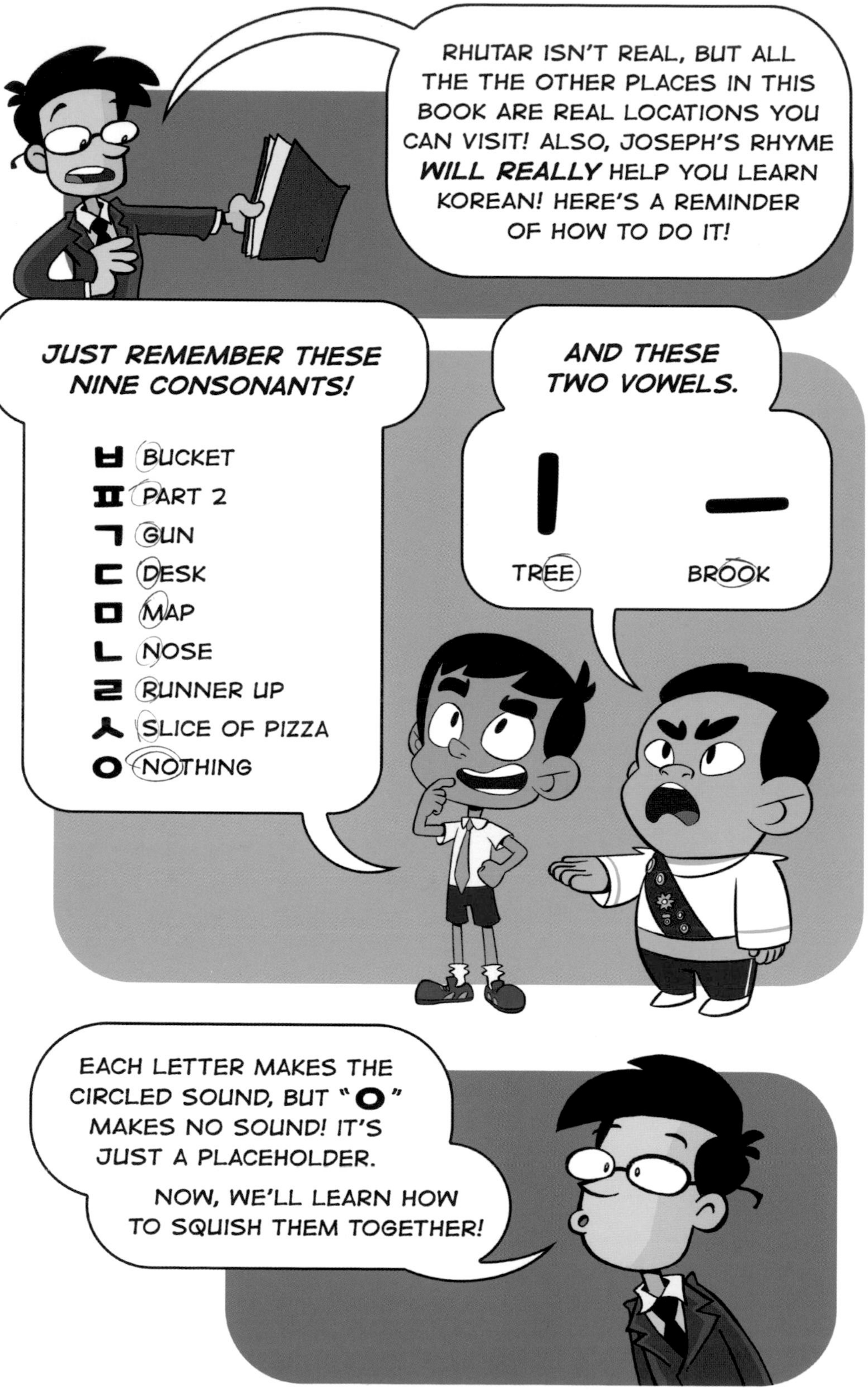
RHUTAR ISN'T REAL, BUT ALL THE THE OTHER PLACES IN THIS BOOK ARE REAL LOCATIONS YOU CAN VISIT! ALSO, JOSEPH'S RHYME WILL REALLY HELP YOU LEARN KOREAN! HERE'S A REMINDER OF HOW TO DO IT!
JUST REMEMBER THESE NINE CONSONANTS!
ㅂ BUCKET
ㅍ PART 2
ㄱ GUN
ㄷ DESK
ㅁ MAP
ㄴ NOSE
ㄹ RUNNER UP
ㅅ SLICE OF PIZZA
ㅇ NOTHING
AND THESE TWO VOWELS.
ㅣ TREE
ㅡ BROOK
EACH LETTER MAKES THE CIRCLED SOUND, BUT "ㅇ" MAKES NO SOUND! IT'S JUST A PLACEHOLDER.
NOW, WE'LL LEARN HOW TO SQUISH THEM TOGETHER!

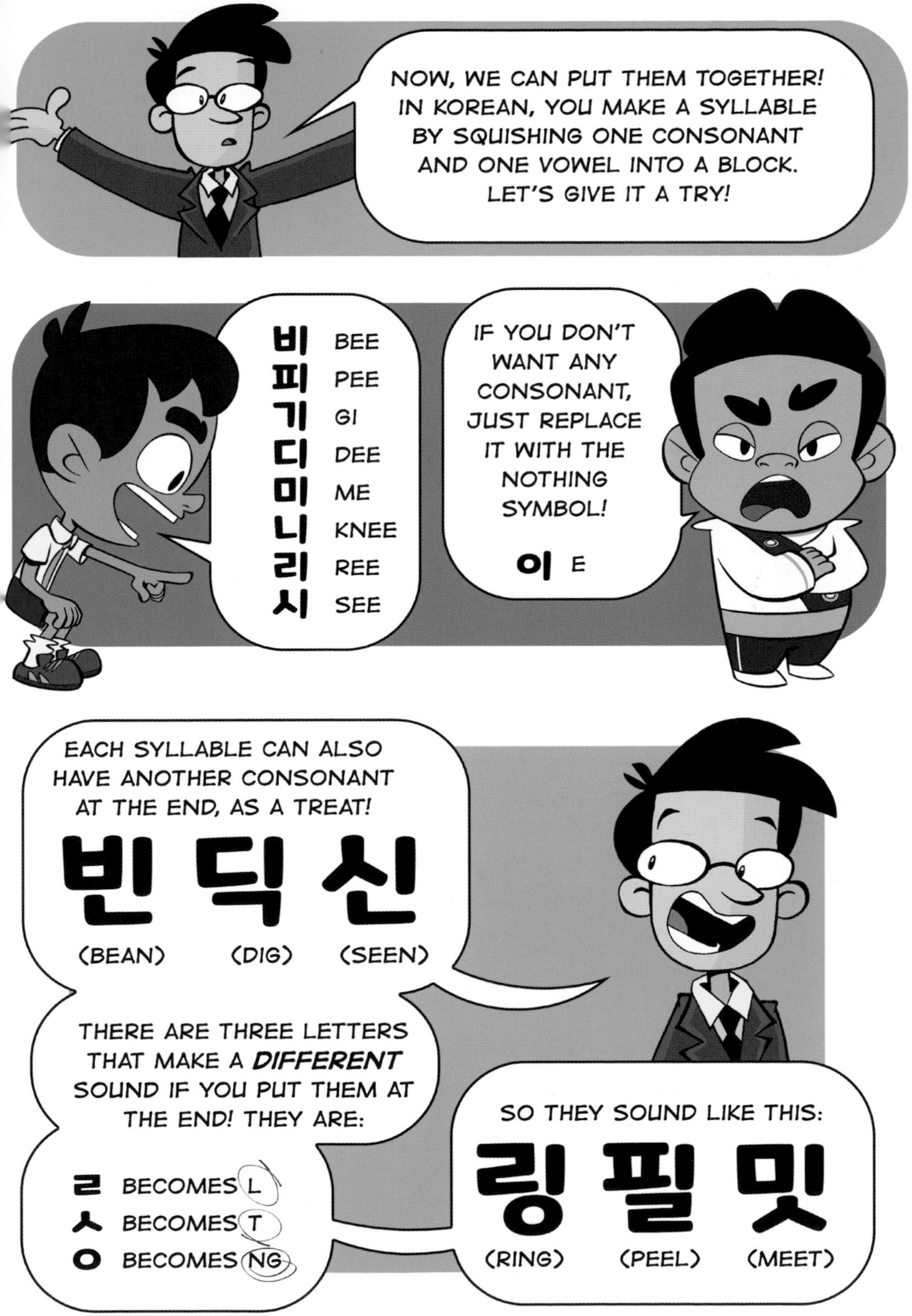
NOW, WE CAN PUT THEM TOGETHER! IN KOREAN, YOU MAKE A SYLLABLE BY SQUISHING ONE CONSONANT AND ONE VOWEL INTO A BLOCK. LET'S GIVE IT A TRY!
비 BEE
피 PEE
기 GI
디 DEE
미 ME
니 KNEE
리 REE
시 SEE
IF YOU DON'T WANT ANY CONSONANT, JUST REPLACE IT WITH THE NOTHING SYMBOL!
이 E
EACH SYLLABLE CAN ALSO HAVE ANOTHER CONSONANT AT THE END, AS A TREAT!
빈 딕 신
(BEAN) (DIG) (SEEN)
THERE ARE THREE LETTERS THAT MAKE A *DIFFERENT* SOUND IF YOU PUT THEM AT THE END! THEY ARE:
ㄹ BECOMES L
ㅅ BECOMES T
ㅇ BECOMES NG
SO THEY SOUND LIKE THIS:
링 필 밋
(RING) (PEEL) (MEET)

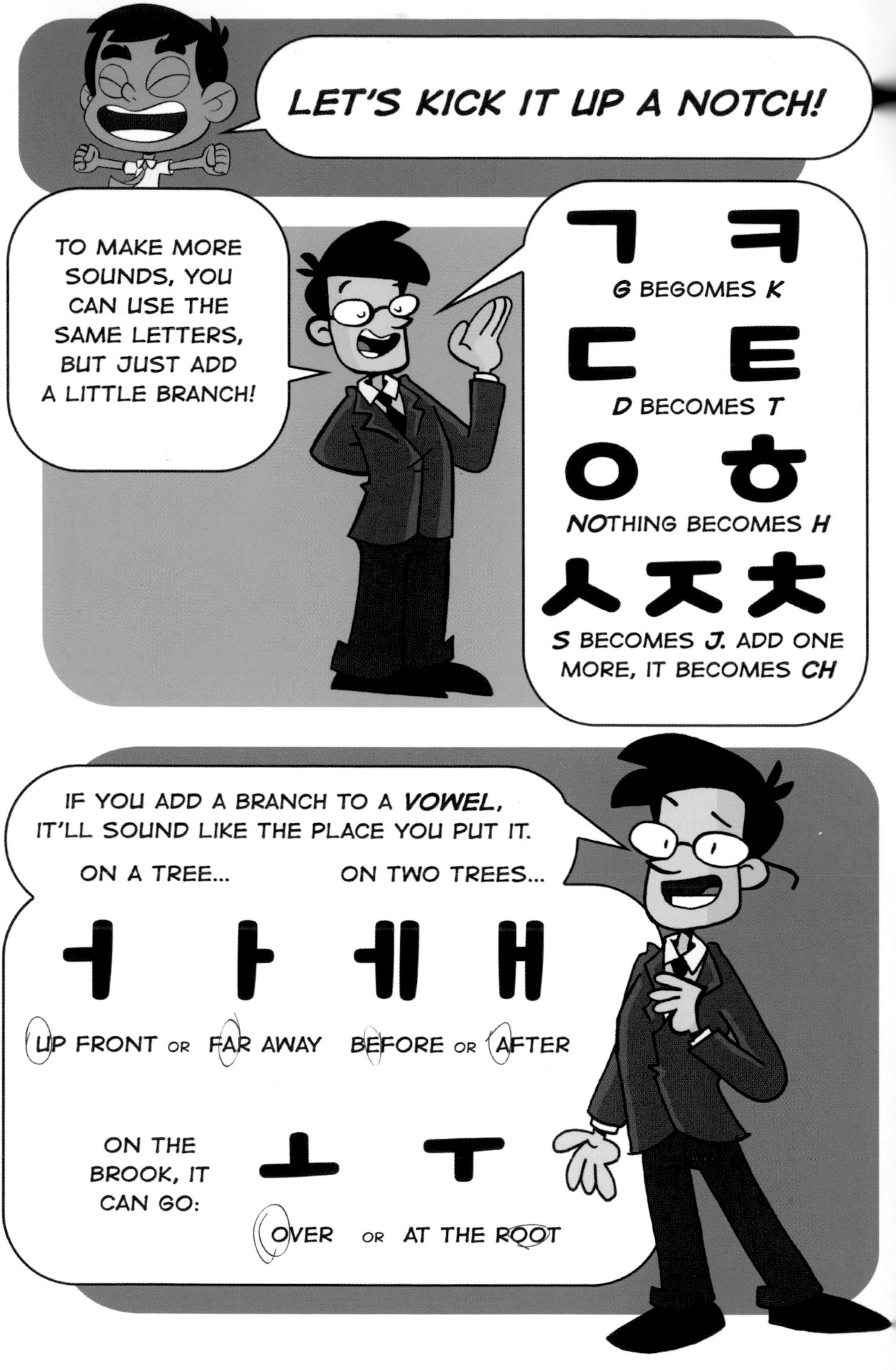
LET'S KICK IT UP A NOTCH!
TO MAKE MORE SOUNDS, YOU CAN USE THE SAME LETTERS, BUT JUST ADD A LITTLE BRANCH!
ㄱ ㅋ
G BECOMES K
ㄷ ㅌ
D BECOMES T
ㅇ ㅎ
NOTHING BECOMES H
ㅅ ㅈ ㅊ
S BECOMES J. ADD ONE MORE, IT BECOMES CH
IF YOU ADD A BRANCH TO A VOWEL, IT'LL SOUND LIKE THE PLACE YOU PUT IT.
ON A TREE...
ON TWO TREES...
ㅓ ㅏ ㅔ ㅐ
UP FRONT OR FAR AWAY
BEFORE OR AFTER
ON THE BROOK, IT CAN GO:
ㅗ ㅜ
OVER OR AT THE ROOT

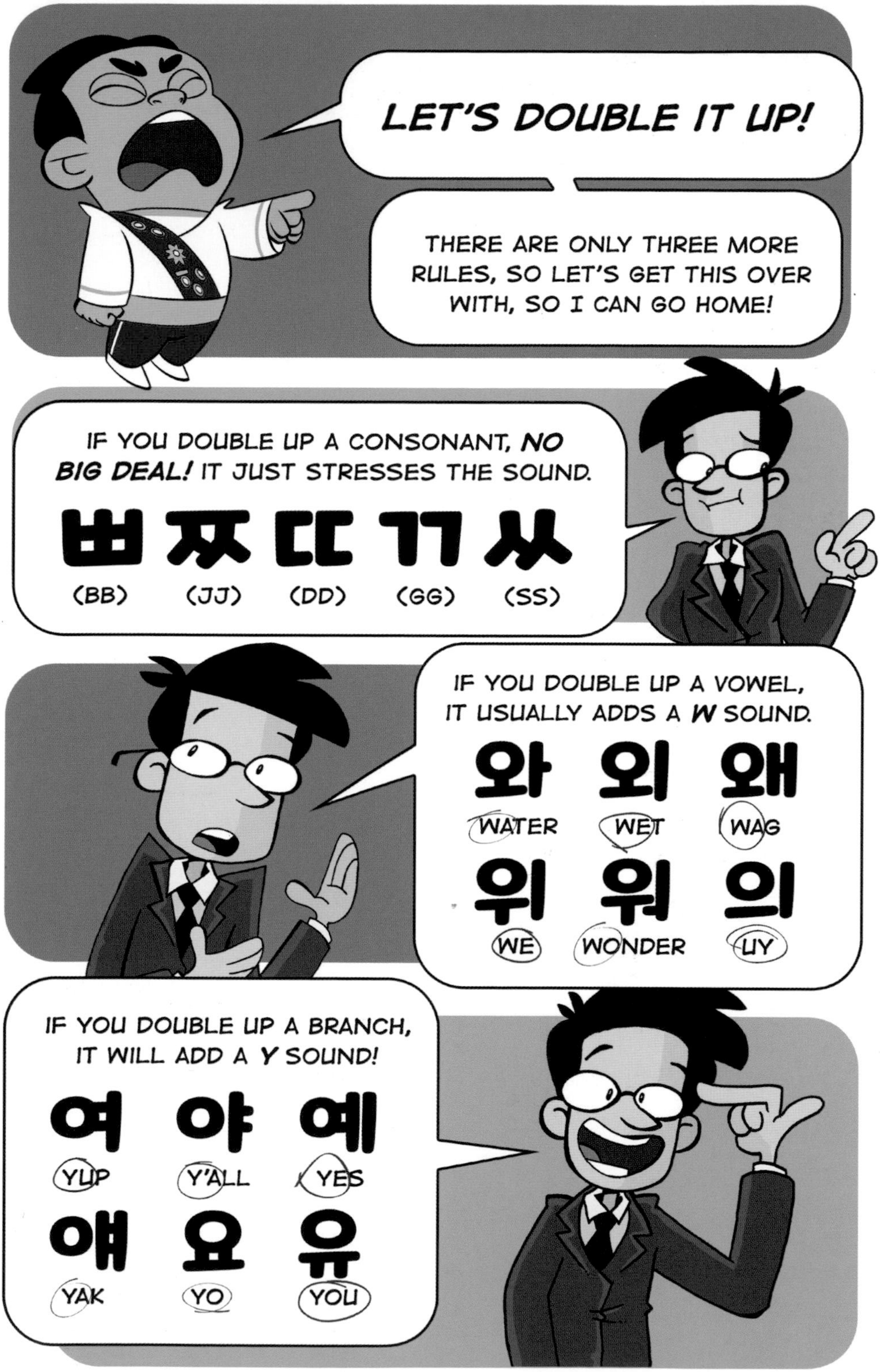
LET'S DOUBLE IT UP!
THERE ARE ONLY THREE MORE RULES, SO LET'S GET THIS OVER WITH, SO I CAN GO HOME!
IF YOU DOUBLE UP A CONSONANT, NO BIG DEAL! IT JUST STRESSES THE SOUND.
ㅃ ㅉ ㄸ ㄲ ㅆ
(BB) (JJ) (DD) (GG) (SS)
IF YOU DOUBLE UP A VOWEL, IT USUALLY ADDS A W SOUND.
와 외 왜
WATER WET WAG
위 워 의
WE WONDER UY
IF YOU DOUBLE UP A BRANCH, IT WILL ADD A Y SOUND!
여 야 예
YUP Y'ALL YES
얘 요 유
YAK YO YOU

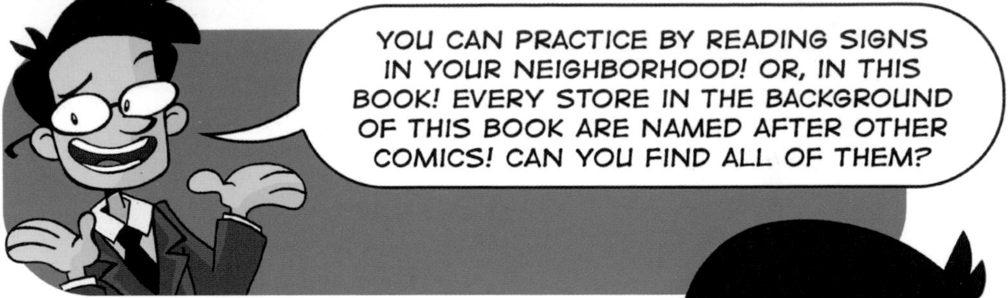
YOU CAN PRACTICE BY READING SIGNS IN YOUR NEIGHBORHOOD! OR, IN THIS BOOK! EVERY STORE IN THE BACKGROUND OF THIS BOOK ARE NAMED AFTER OTHER COMICS! CAN YOU FIND ALL OF THEM?

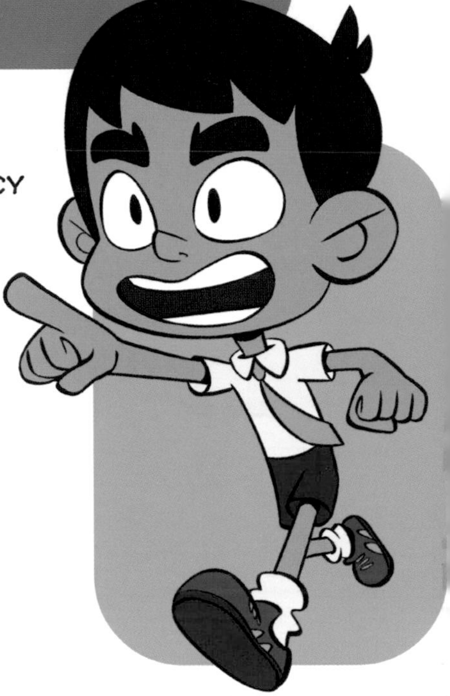

AKI ALLIANCE CREDIT UNION
AMULET JEWELRY
ARCHIE NIGHT CLUB
AS THE CROW FLIES TRAVEL AGENCY
BANNED BOOK CLUB BOOKSTORE
BONE BUTCHER SHOP
BOULDER & FLEET SHIPPING
CARDBOARD KINGDOM RECYCLING
DOG MAN VETERINARY CLINIC
DRAMA THEATRE
EL DEAFO GYM
GARFIELD CAT CAFE
GHOSTS ESCAPE ROOM
GUTS HEALTH CENTER
JELLABY ICE CREAMERY
JON SUPERMARKET
MEAL BONDAEGGI CART
MIDAS SINGING ROOM
MINUS MATH ACADEMY

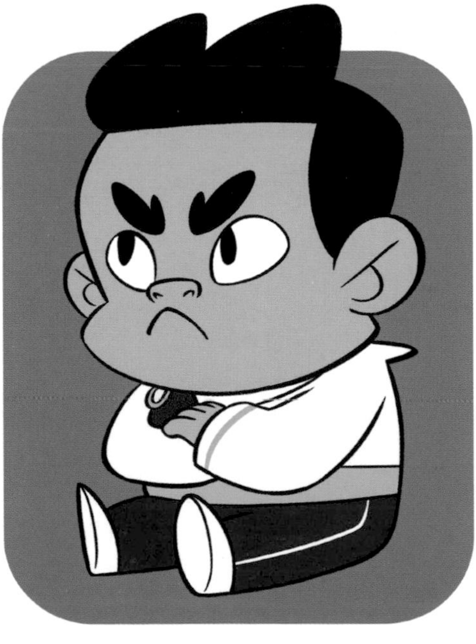

NANCY NAIL SALON
NEW KID KINDERGARTEN
OCCULTED DEPARTMENT STORE
RICEBOY GIMBAP
SISTERS CLOTHING STORE
SHADOWEYES OPTOMETRY
SMILE DENTAL CARE
SOFTIES TOY STORE
STARGAZING TAROT
TIM'ROUS BEASTIE PET STORE
ZITA THE SPACEGIRL PC ROOM

PLUS EVEN MORE HIDDEN COMICS-BASED BUSINESSES! CAN YOU FIND ANY OTHERS?